For Prof. Ba
the way to u
and in the p
friend
Na.

The Curse

The Curse of Ezekiel

NABIL SALEH

This is what the Sovereign Lord says: I am against you, O Tyre, and I will bring many nations against you . . . They will destroy the walls of Tyre and pull down her towers . . . Out in the sea she will become a place to spread fishing nets.

Ezekiel 26:3–5

QUARTET

First published in 2009 by
Quartet Books Limited
A member of the Namara Group
27 Goodge Street, London W1T 2LD

A catalogue record for this book
is available from the British Library

ISBN 978 0 7043 7167 5

Typeset by Antony Gray
Printed and bound in Great Britain by
T J International Ltd, Padstow, Cornwall

All of the characters in this book, except for a few historical figures, are fictitious. Some of the events actually took place.

ACKNOWLEDGEMENT

My deep gratitude goes to Jacqueline Jondot, *Professeur des Universités*, for the generous time and valuable advice she gave me during the inception of this book.

Contents

PART TWO

PART THREE

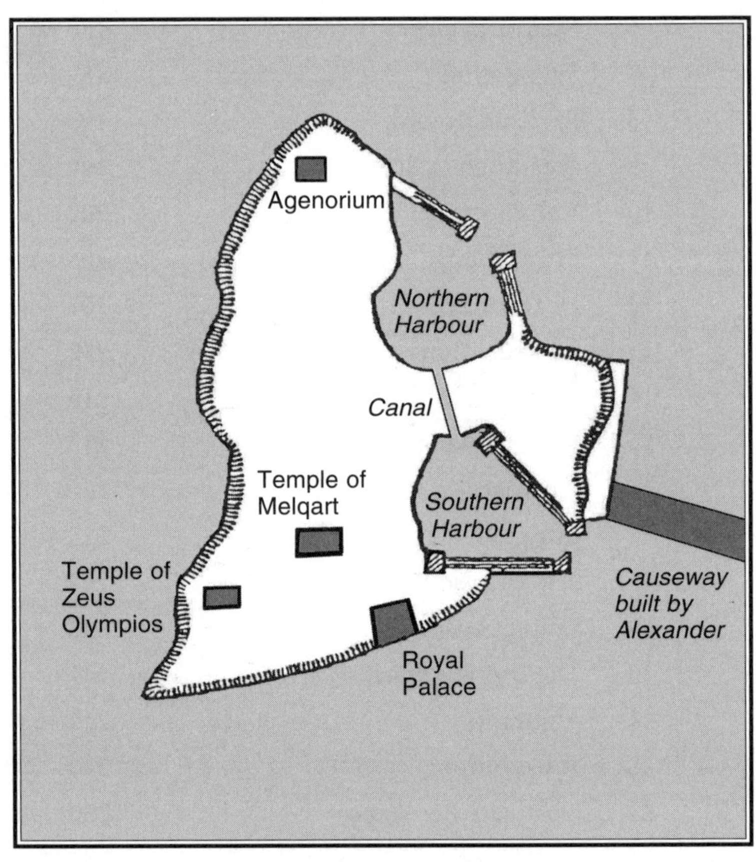

Tyre in Alexander's time

PROLOGUE

Trial in Macedonia (Winter of 334BC)

'You murdered Simmias in cold blood and you didn't deny your crime when the guards seized you. Lysinias, son of Nicanor, have you anything to say?'

The accused gazed scornfully at the vociferating public, which was demanding that he be put to death with no more ado. He was in his early thirties, stocky and muscular; his marked face and torn tunic indicated that he had taken a severe beating. Between two guards armed with long sarissas, his situation appeared desperate.

He challenged the crowd with another defiant glance before giving his judge the curt answer, 'All I did was to avenge my honour.'

The judge could not be satisfied with this simple assertion and made his dissatisfaction plain. 'I am waiting for an explanation and I am not prepared to be more patient. Explain yourself at once.'

His tone was stern and his face grim. Lysinias felt that he had to give the explanation; otherwise the order for his execution would come next. He hastened to say, 'I caught Simmias, this dog, with the mother of my son.'

The public roared angrily and the murdered man's relatives tried to push their way towards the accused. The two guards, who were there to prevent Lysinias's escape, had to protect him from the crowd's fury. Order was restored when the judge enjoined the accused to 'Tell everything from the beginning.'

Those present were hungry for the sordid details so they fell silent. The judge encouraged the accused, asking, 'Where did they meet? How did you catch them?'

Lysinias paused for a moment, torn between an understandable reluctance to display publicly the circumstances, which brought him dishonour, and his instinct to save his life. Eventually the latter won and he started the dramatic account of his misfortune: 'I fought Athens and Thebes under the command of Philip, our lamented king who is now the gods' companion in the Olympus. Then I fought with his son Alexander in Thessaly and the Greek cities. Back with our victorious army, I heard from Mena – that's the name of the woman who bore my child – that her brother had died and was buried while I was away. It was during his funeral that she and that Simmias met. She herself confessed to me.'

At this point Lysinias bowed his head, his chin resting on his chest, too ashamed to speak.

'What happened next?' asked the judge, losing patience.

'He bribed my slave and under the cover of darkness they started meeting in my house. I, in the meantime, was fighting for my King.'

He paused to give more weight to the contrast between his noble conduct and the despicable behaviour of those who had betrayed him. The public started to be impressed by the accused's account and remained quiet, except for the relatives of the murdered man who felt compelled to shout, from time to time, 'Liar, liar, finish him off.'

The judge ordered them to keep quiet, then addressed the accused in a more moderate tone, saying, 'These meetings, they ceased when you came back, didn't they? Don't tell me they kept seeing each other, with you in the house.'

'Yes, they did.' These words came with great difficulty from Lysinias's lips, so great was his shame.

'I don't believe it,' burst out the judge, who resumed his previous stern attitude. Lysinias gave a deep sigh then embarked on the explanation that his now skeptical judge was awaiting. 'The treachery of a woman has no limits and Mena's was no exception. She convinced me that it would be more convenient if she were to move from the first floor to the ground floor where I had my quarter.

She argued that from the ground floor she would have easy access to the well located in the courtyard, close to the altar dedicated to Zeus Phratrios. I believed her. How naive I was!'

He gave another deep sigh before he resumed his account. This time he needed no prompting, for he was motivated by the interest he had raised all round and the anger produced by his own words.

'Yesterday,' he said, 'I woke up in the middle of the night. I couldn't go back to sleep and my thoughts went to my son. I felt a compelling desire to take him in my arms and hold him tight against my heart. I left my bed, grasped an oil lamp and walked in the direction of his mother's room.'

Once more Lysinias paused, obviously finding it hard to describe events, which were too distressing to think of. Impervious to this feeling and impatient to know more, the judge pressed, 'Come on, come on. Finish your account. I have other things to do.'

'Once in the room I saw them with my own eyes lying down in the same bed, asleep but still intertwined. I went mad. I dropped the lamp I had in my hand, picked up a heavy bronze vase nearby, threw myself at the man who had dishonoured me and knocked him out with the vessel. Before he came round I strangled him with my hands.'

He was so intensely reliving the tragic event with his words, gestures and feelings that he became exhausted and had to break off to get his breath back. This time the judge let him be and did not press him to carry on. A few moments later he did so in a lower voice. 'I wanted to kill Mena too, and looked around for her; I saw her crouched in a corner with my son in her arms. I couldn't take him from her and carry out my design. I couldn't do it. I hit her hard and she told me all the details of her betrayal. Drawn by the commotion and her yells, guards seized me and took me to jail.'

Except for a few shouts of hatred emanating from Simmias's relatives, the public remained quiet, allowing the judge to proceed with his interrogation.

'Simmias's two brothers here present,' he said, 'claim that you wanted to settle an old score with the victim, so you laid a trap for him and brought him to your house to kill him. What do you have to say?'

'It's absolutely false!' shouted the prisoner, 'I barely knew Simmias. What's more, do you believe that a man worthy of that name would willingly dishonour himself to wreak vengeance? All I did was to wipe out the stain on my honour.'

The judge was listening and the change in his whole demeanour pointed out that lenience was what he had in mind. The judgment he then passed came as such confirmation, 'I am now convinced that you killed Simmias without premeditation, in a fit of anger triggered by an odious deed. Nevertheless, for the sake of peace I condemn you to two years of exile. You must leave Pella immediately; the guards will take you to the kingdom's borders.'

Part One

I

Tyre (Autumn of 333BC)

Rushing – nearly running – under heavy rain, he buried his head between his shoulders in a futile attempt to protect himself from the deluge of water. The distance between the house he had just left and the temple of Melqart, his intended destination, was insignificant, as indeed were all distances on the island of Tyre, which had a total circumference of no more than twenty-two stadia.

When he reached a grove of cypress trees much beloved by Astarte, he could see the facade of the temple built with stones and embellished with merlons and columns crowned with double voluted capitals. Having arrived, he climbed the few steps which led to a porch supported by two massive columns, the one on the right entirely covered with gold leaves and the one on the left set throughout with emeralds.

Once in the vestibule he undertook to smarten his appearance: he removed his soaked cloak and shook drips of water off; with a deft flick of each foot he got rid of his sandals, then smoothed out his costly robe of linen imported from Egypt. He was a young man in his early twenties, of medium height with a well-proportioned body. His hair was black and sleek and he did not grow a beard, unlike most of his fellow countrymen. A sparkle of impishness in his eyes signalled him to be a person inclined not to take matters seriously, although he had been convened to attend a council, which treated serious matters. It was not his choice to be a member of the City's Council of Elders. He had inherited the office after his father's death.

Barefoot, he felt the cold of the marbled floor. Instead of going into the central habitat of the city's god, he entered a large side room with thick windowless walls supporting a cedar roof. On the walls and ceiling danced shadowy contours projected by the flickering light of a dozen burning torches. Some twenty men were seated forming a half circle opened towards a ceremonial armchair raised on a platform. Its occupier was a middle-aged man, his face adorned with a well-kept beard and his slim body wrapped in a cape dyed purple, the colour worn by persons of authority. He made a point of acknowledging the newcomer who was trying to sneak in.

'Bomilcar,' he said, 'we appreciate your joining us despite the delay, which I ascribe to your numerous activities.'

Sarcasm was followed by a light reproach.

'Believe me,' he added, 'had your father Merbalos been alive, I would not have sent for you, but we are confronted with a very serious situation.' With a tired gesture of the hand he invited him to sit.

When Balator, the brother of Azemilk, King of Tyre, mentioned Bomilcar's 'numerous activities', a smile had appeared on many faces, for the reputation of the new-comer as a *bon vivant* was well established and accounts of his frolics were told everywhere in the city. After his father's death he had given free rein to a more carefree existence, for Merbalos was no more around to admonish him and, in addition, had left him a large fortune thanks to his flourishing maritime business. Their transport vessels left Tyre's two ports regularly between March and October, carrying in their large round hulls cedar wood logs from Mount Libanus; ivory objects finely engraved; cups, goblets and plates made of silver, bronze and glass; and linen and wool fabrics dyed purple through a jealously guarded formula which had made the name of the Phoenician cities.

On their return voyages from the borders of the Mediterranean Sea, the same vessels brought back iron bars from Crete, copper from Cyprus and Spain and tin from Anatolia by way of Rhodes. Elephant tusks and ostrich eggs were also imported from the African colonies.

Unruffled, Bomilcar took a seat after a bow in the direction of

Balator who, without further delay, disclosed the reason for the meeting he had called for. 'A messenger has just arrived from the north, bringing me the news that Alexander has defeated the Persian army at Issus. King Darius escaped to the east towards the two big rivers, leaving Phoenicia's coastal cities wide open.'

Stunned, the Council members received the information in shocked silence; then, like one man, they stood up and formed small groups to engage in over-excited discussion. A few gathered round the king's brother, trying to get from him any details he might have neglected to transmit to them. Unwilling to convey the impression that he did not care, Bomilcar also left his chair and drew close to the one group of people near him.

Four councillors were rallied round a tall and distinguished middle-aged man, who exuded authority and opulence. Chelbes was his name and he was the wealthy owner of a shipyard and a fleet of transport vessels.

He recommended remaining calm and advocated the need to find ways to make peace with Alexander. He had his own reasons for appeasement, in view of the fact that resistance to the conqueror would mean the end of his maritime commerce and the likelihood of seeing his fleet either destroyed or commandeered by one or other of the warring factions.

'We pay tribute to the Persians,' he said. 'Instead we will pay it to Alexander. What difference would that make? What do you think, Bomilcar?' Confirmation of his own view was what he expected from the young man, for both had the same financial interests. The non-committal reply he received satisfied him nonetheless.

'I would not be so presumptuous as to contradict the wise Chelbes,' said Bomilcar. Discussions were interrupted by the king's brother, who called the councillors to order. 'Take up your seats and let's discuss the situation calmly. The King's return is expected any day now. He monitors Alexander's movements while sailing with the Persian fleet and is most certainly aware of the latest battle between the Greeks and the Persians. This will prompt his homecoming. One matter, however, cannot wait and must be addressed immediately: Alexander may present himself at our gates at any moment and it's for us to decide how to receive him. In my brother's absence, I am asking for your views.'

The one person who hastened to speak was Chelbes; his aim was to prevent any view contrary to his being aired first and thereby winning over the audience. On his feet he pleaded for a policy of open doors and submission to the young conqueror from Macedonia. He concluded his speech with a passionate tirade against Persian oppression, which, he said, was being brought to an end by the Greeks' victory. Having concluded, he looked left and right to gauge the effect produced by his harangue; content with the result, he resumed his seat, a smile of satisfaction on his lips.

Not for long, for Abbarus, a hard-liner, stood up. Looking straight in front of him, as if reading the wall, he said, 'I heard a speech which takes no notice of the honour and dignity of our city. It's based on a misconceived perception of our interests. Unlike Sidon, our city is not occupied by a Persian garrison and governor, our temples are not desecrated, our island is impregnable and our fleet is invincible. Tell me, why should we open our gates to an adventurer? He may have defeated a Persian army at Issus but remember, Darius is still alive and able to raise another army, ten times, a hundred times, more numerous than the Macedonian troops who have foolishly strayed away from their base. I oppose surrendering to Alexander. If he chooses to use force we should resist.' Abbarus seated himself, his back erect, his face unremitting and his look fixed as if he was intent on shutting out any discussion.

Chelbes realised that unless he attempted something the faction advocating resistance would win. He jumped promptly to his feet with a delaying tactic in mind. 'I want you to be absolutely clear about the reasons that make me hold tight to my position. It's our survival and that of our people I have at heart; if we resist Alexander we will put everyone in deadly danger. This young tyrant suffers no opposition to his will and will have no mercy if ever resisted.

Would you listen to an eyewitness? . . . ' He paused for a moment to raise the interest of his audience, then carried on: 'Would you listen to a man from Macedonia? He is in Old Tyre. I invite the Council to hear him.'

'What can he tell us that is more than what duty dictates?' burst out Abbarus.

Trying to keep calm, Chelbes explained. 'This man, Lysinias, has fought under Philip and under his son. Unjustly banished from Macedonia, he became a mercenary and was hired by the Persian king. He has a first-hand knowledge of Macedonian tactics and of the hoplites' and cavalry's strengths and weaknesses. Above all, he has seen what Alexander is capable of doing whenever there is opposition to his will. This man is prepared to give us an account of all he knows.'

Balator did not leave time for more discussion, but stepped in. 'We will hear this Lysinias no later than when the sun starts declining today. Councillor Chelbes, send a boat to Old Tyre to bring this man to us. We will then hear the Carthaginian delegation. We must know from our brothers what kind of assistance the colony is prepared to provide us, in case we are attacked.' Balator stood up to indicate that the meeting was over.

King Azemilk and his son being at sea with the Persian fleet, it would have been most improper to hold the Council meeting in the palace in their absence. The choice of the temple as a meeting place had been made by Balator, who was the Great Priest of Melqart, the god of the city, light and fire. Twice a year he was celebrated: in winter when his effigy was burnt; and in summer when his resurrection took place. Year after year, Carthage, Tyre's North African colony, sent an offering, which amounted to a tithe of its public treasury. The offering was brought by a delegation that remained in Tyre to partake in both ceremonies. The members of that year's delegation were already on the island and would be able to answer the Council's queries.

Relieved to see the morning session over, Bomilcar hurried out.

2

Mother and Son

Speed was Bomilcar's technique for avoiding old Councillor Himilk, who hung on him whenever he had the opportunity, hoping for an invitation to one of the young man's evenings during which wine was served generously by pretty young slaves. The most dangerous point in time was at the close of any Council session. Bomilcar's speed was usually sufficient to elude the old scrounger; not that time though. A funeral procession blocked the way in front of the temple and he had to wait for the cortege to move past. Held back, he saw pass by a body wrapped in bandages and laid on a stretcher carried by four men, who wore sackcloth as a mark of mourning. On each side of the stretcher walked professional female mourners, tearing their hair, beating their breasts, weeping and lamenting aloud, their gestures performed exaggeratedly. Behind came family and friends of the deceased, followed by a few onlookers. The cortege was on the way to the south port to cross 2,400 feet of water, which separated the island from Old Tyre where the dead were buried.

When the cortege was about to reach an end, an impatient Bomilcar looked left and right to secure a passage. To his surprise he realised that Himilk was standing beside him, silent and reflective. Instead of running out of sight, the young man was goaded by his curiosity and concern to ask, 'Anything the matter?'

'No! Why?' replied Himilk.

'Because you're not your normal cheerful self.'

'How can I be under the circumstances? I'm very worried neither Chelbes' appeasing discourse nor Abbarus's harangue bodes well.'

Having said that, Himilk departed hurriedly, leaving the young man puzzled. Until that moment it had not crossed his mind to wonder in which camp he would place himself. A choice would be meddling in politics and his father had taught him to avoid that at any cost, for the sake of the business. That was the line of conduct followed by Merbalos during his lifetime and it had served him well. He did business with the Greeks and the Persians in addition to dealing with the Egyptians, the Israelites and any other person who came to him with a promising commercial transaction.

Habitually, Bomilcar was able to shake out irritating thoughts easily this time he could not. An inner voice kept telling him that the discussion at the Council meeting was not a simple matter of politics but a question of survival.

The rain had stopped and a light wind forced the clouds off; slowly, reluctantly, they moved away, allowing sparse rays of sunshine to filter through. He crossed the open space surrounding the temple, then went through a maze of narrow streets bordered by houses built on several storeys and in close proximity to make the best use of land.

He headed towards the house that his father had constructed on one level amidst a garden, in sharp contrast to most houses on the island. The house stood by the artificial water canal, which connected the northern port to the southern one. The canal gave vessels a secure passage from one point to the other, in all seasons or should one of the ports come under attack.

He soon reached the property and entered the garden where, not long ago, he used to play under the olive, almond and fig trees, inventing games to ease the loneliness and boredom of the existence of a lonely child. He was greeted by his dog's joyous barking, which alerted Inat, his mother, to his arrival and brought her out to welcome him. She was a small, plump person who looked even smaller and rounder standing besides the two graceful columns that flanked the door of the house. If at first glance she appeared to be an insignificant middle-aged woman, another look would make one notice her alert and sparkling eyes and her air of authority, accentuated by an aggressive aquiline nose.

Followed by two female slaves who attended her permanently, mother and son entered the house. It formed a long rectangle with a courtyard in its middle; at the right side of the vestibule was a dining room reserved for the men of the house and their friends, a custom imported from Greece and adopted by wealthy Phoenicians; at the rear were several rooms, including a suite of rooms for Bomilcar and another one for his mother.

It was there that they were served lunch, a light meal consisting of roast quail, salad and cheese. When they had finished and were nibbling a few dried fruits, Inat said, 'Little Agbalos is not well; my young sister is very, very concerned about her son. She wants to take him to the temple of Eshmun, bathe him in the holy water and give sacrifice to the god. You know how much I love Amatbaal, having raised her as a daughter after the death of our poor parents; I'll never forgive myself should she lose her son.'

Knowing his mother well and her circuitous way when she wanted something from him, Bomilcar sighed and asked, 'Do we know when her husband is coming back?'

'No, we don't. He is at sea and the baby might die before he returns.'

He sighed more deeply this time and posed the question, which answer he already knew. 'What do you expect from me?'

'I'd be very happy if you were to take her and her son to Sidon. It's only one night away.'

'But mother, I'm very busy right now. Then, remembering the potential threat posed by Alexander, he added, 'you know the situation is critical and I'm needed here to attend the Council's sessions which could be convened unexpectedly. See now, I must return to the temple straight away for further consultations.'

Inat was not impressed and made her feelings known. 'Now and then we hear that Tyre is in danger. The prophets of doom are always those politicians who spread a climate of fear for reasons of their own. Tell me, what could ever happen to us in our island? No harm, believe me; on the other hand, Agbalos will certainly die if we do nothing for him.'

He realised that he was trapped, for if the baby were to die his mother's reproaching eyes would be ever present, not counting the guilt he would necessarily feel. Once more he sighed and voiced the words Inat expected: 'Tell my aunt to he here with the baby tomorrow morning. We will leave at daybreak. Send also for a boat. Now I must rush to the temple.'

3
Testimony

Bomilcar took a seat among his fellow Councillors. From where he was he could see Himilk a few paces away, dozing off and risking falling from his seat. A generous lunch and copious amounts of wine were the likely explanation for his wobbling. The image projected by Abbarus could not be more distinct: motionless and upright on his chair, he was gazing fixedly in front of him, to emphasise his unshaken determination. Surrounding him were a few members who had adopted the same bearing to emphasise their belonging to the same clan. By contrast, Chelbes was on his feet, moving from one Councillor to the other, joking with one, patting the shoulders of a second and conversing with a third. It was clear that the advocate of appeasement was trying to win over the greatest number of supporters.

For the first time since he had joined the Council, Bomilcar was prepared to follow with interest the debates between the opposing factions and was curious to know the result of their conflicting positions. It did not cross his mind to join one clan or the other; nevertheless, his interest was aroused and he had not experienced such awareness before in matters of politics. Strangely, he felt uneasy about the alien feeling and tried to shake it off by directing his attention towards trifling details.

He concentrated his attention on the two doors behind the ceremonial chair; the King's brother could make an entrance through either and Bomilcar bet with himself that he would come from the one on his right. If that was the case then the auguries would be favourable and no sinister event was to be expected. In fact, Balator did come through the door on the right which comforted Bomilcar's optimism.

'Is the Macedonian here?' asked the King's brother, passing over ceremonial formalities. Chelbes knew that the question was addressed to him so he stood up and replied, 'Yes my Lord, he is outside and ready to testify.'

'Bring him in.'

Chelbes made a sign to one of his slaves. He understood the message, went out and came back with Lysinias. Both waited at the end of the room. Balator signalled to the Macedonian to come closer. He obeyed and bowed out of respect but showed no signs of fear or servility.

'Where are you from?' asked Balator.

'From Pella, my Lord.'

'Why did you betray your people and lend yourself to the Persians?'

Lysinias controlled a quiver of anger and replied, 'My Lord, I did not betray my people, they betrayed me. I was unjustly sentenced to a two year banishment and deprived of my son.'

'What happened to you after that?' pressed the King's brother.

'I was hired by the Persians as a mercenary. I took part in the battle of the Granicus river, on their side, and I was there when Alexander won the day. When the Persian soldiers fled for their lives, I did the same for I knew what would be the fate of anyone who dared oppose Alexander, It's either submission to his will or death.'

The Macedonian's words put the audience ill at ease; silence followed and was interrupted by Chelbes, 'If it pleases, my Lord, ask the man what was Thebes's fate when that city rose in rebellion against Alexander following his father's death.'

Balator turned towards Lysinias and with an economical movement of the hand in Chelbes's direction indicated that his answer was awaited. He complied: 'My Lord, that was a most terrible and terrifying day. Thebes was attacked, taken, sacked and utterly destroyed. Thirty thousand Thebans were enslaved, women and children included. Many lost their lives during and after the fighting. I was there and saw it all.'

That said, Lysinias was dismissed by the King's brother after he was ordered to remain in the island at the disposal of the army's commanders, who were eager to learn all that he knew about Alexander's tactics, particularly when besieging cities and fortresses. The number and sort of siege engines he may have at his disposition also interested them in the extreme.

No sooner had the man left the room than Chelbes drew what he believed to be the only sound conclusion, 'We have no quarrel with that young conqueror who seems to be favoured by the gods. He is set not against us but against Darius. I urge my fellow Councillors to take the decision to receive him with the honours due to his rank and good fortune. I urge you . . . '

Abbarus interrupted the speaker's appeasing words with words which played upon the assembly's religious feelings. 'Do you mean,' he said, turning towards Chelbes, 'that Melqart and Astarte have forsaken us to bestow their favours on a foreigner who came from a country which barely has access to the sea? What would be your response if this foreigner and his armed hordes were to demand entry to our most sacred temples to sacrifice to their gods?'

A horrified roar emanated from all lips, which Chelbes tried to silence with his extended hands moving to and fro. It took him some time before he succeeded and was allowed to regain some initiative.

'The foreigner, as you call him, is much closer to us than the Persians ever were. Many among us speak his language, have adopted Greek customs and have business ties with the Greek cities. Moreover, we don't know whether he intends to occupy our island or be satisfied with a ceremony of submission. Don't take any rushed decision before we know his real intention.'

Most Councillors showed signs of indecision and the discussions might have dragged on forever, had the King's brother not intervened. 'Before we take a decision, let us hear what assistance our African colony is prepared to provide us if we are attacked.' Then, turning to one of his attendants, he ordered, 'Bring in the Carthaginian delegation.'

The members of that delegation were waiting in an adjacent room and were led in quickly. First came the priests of Baal Hammon wearing purple cloaks belted with gold chains. Then came the priests of Tanit in turquoise garb, each holding a gold staff surmounted with an emerald stone carved in the figure of a snake. They were followed by the other members, who were mostly elderly people.

When Magon, the head of the delegation, was asked what help could be expected from Carthage, he replied: 'The colony would not tolerate Tyre's occupation and would race to rescue her mother island city.'

He then added, weighing each of his words, 'Carthage does not forget that Tyre resolutely resisted the Persian Cambyse when he gave the order that your war vessels should attack us.'

Pleased to be reminded of the stand Tyre had taken, even if it was some two hundred years ago, Balator thanked the members of the delegation before dismissing them. He then addressed the Council. 'After winning the battle of Issus, Alexander has two options: either to pursue Darius in the direction of the Euphrates, or to capture the Mediterranean ports. Should he choose the latter we will receive him on the mainland and present him with the gold crown in sign of submission. Satisfied, he will have no cause to set foot on the island, or so I expect. Do we agree on that?'

Abbarus gave his agreement, on condition that should Alexander take the direction of the Mediterranean sea instead of the Euphrates, the island would immediately adopt measures to withstand a siege:

foods would be stored, weapons stocked up, water tanks filled and new reservoirs dug down.

Chelbes was triumphant. In his mind he dismissed Abbarus's condition as a mere face-saver. Bomilcar and the rest of the members were satisfied because the two leaders of the opposing factions were finally in agreement; as a consequence Balator's proposed resolution and Abbarus's requirement were passed by a unanimous vote.

4
Pilgrimage

Bomilcar spent a good part of the night drinking with friends and when he finally went to his rooms he was not alone: a female singer who had enlivened the evening went with him. Finding her in his master's bed early in the morning did not surprise Tansu, the Iberian slave sent by Inat to remind her son of the promise he had made the day before. The old man was accustomed to the familiar sight, which kindled the pride he had for his master. His good nature made him satisfied with his station and devoid of any envy or resentment even though he had been kidnapped by the crew of one of Merbalos's ships when he was in his teens and brought from Gadir to Tyre. Tansu's life in the household of his abductors turned out to be much more pleasant than it had been among his backward people; after weeks of crying and longing for his mother he came to appreciate the relative comfort of his new situation and ended up being attached to his masters, who treated him benevolently. Although he had lost his freedom he did not bear any grudge against them. In time they treated him as a member of the family and his attachment to them grew to complete devotion, particularly with regard to Bomilcar, whom he came to see as the son he never had.

He ignored the sleeping woman and gently poked Bomilcar's shoulder which emerged from beneath the covers. He opened his eyes, saw the slave and mumbled hazily, 'What do you want?'`

'The boat is waiting, master.'

Bomilcar frowned, trying to remember why that information should make any difference to him. Tansu explained, 'The boat that will take you to Sidon is here.'

Memory came back in a flash. He cursed under his breath against his family's exigencies and against himself for the commitment foolishly given the day before.

The motion awoke the young girl; she opened her tired eyes, saw the two men, turned her back on them and tried to resume sleeping. Bomilcar did not give her a chance, sending her away without ceremony.

Hot water in a large earthenware jug had been brought by Tansu for Bomilcar to wash and shave. When that was completed the young man looked at his face in the polished silver sheet which served him as a mirror and did not like what he saw: his eyes were red and swollen from lack of sleep and excesses and the colour of his skin was unnaturally pallid.

Unhappy with himself, he decided to have an early night every now and then, with no one to keep him company. That reminded him of the young singer he had just dismissed and he tried to remember her name but could not. What he vividly recalled, however, was the pleasure he had had from their lovemaking. He smiled and instantly forgot his earlier resolution. The girl's name and where to find her, he could always obtain from Matten, his childhood friend, who had brought her to entertain them and forsaken her once she caught Bomilcar's eyes.

Warmly dressed for a sea crossing, the young man left his rooms followed by Tansu, who was carrying a change of clothes packed in a bundle. He found his mother and his aunt waiting in the reception hall. Amatbaal was also holding with her two hands a bundle, which wrapped a moaning Agbalos.

She apologised for having to inconvenience her nephew. Bomilcar put an end to the flood of words with a dismissive gesture, while he broke his fast with the collation of bread and cheese ordered for him by his mother. Sea travel on an empty stomach was not advisable.

Then the would-be-travellers, accompanied by Inat, crossed the rear garden, which led to the canal where four oarsmen were waiting for them in a small boat. Bomilcar was familiar with the crew who ordinarily manned much more important vessels than the modest craft which was needed to cross the hundred and seventy stadia separating Tyre from Sidon.

Amatbaal handed her infant to one of the oarsmen before she was helped into the boat. Then it was Bomilcar's turn to embark as the first rays of the sun were dawning. The rhythmical propulsion of the oars moved the boat towards the northern port. When they were there the crew had to manoeuvre carefully between numerous small craft and large transport vessels, with rounded sterns culminating in a fishtail and bows terminated with the representation of a horse's head. Once they had passed the port's boundary, the men ceased rowing and hoisted a sail. Propelled by a favourable wind, the boat headed for Sidon, keeping close to the coast. Wrapped in their cloaks, the travellers contemplated from afar the coastal city of their fathers, which had been destroyed by the Persians and never completely rebuilt, most of the Tyrians having chosen to move to the safety of their island.

The boat sailed along the rocky coast, past the village of Sarepta and the city of Sidon. Some twenty stadia further on, at the mouth of the river Bostrenus, the sail was folded and the boat drew alongside a makeshift landing stage, where the passengers left the crew with instructions to collect them the following day, when the sun would be at its highest point.

Bomilcar, holding two small bundles of spare clothes, and Amatbaal, her son clasped to her breast, walked uphill along the river's bank. After a short while the narrow path branched off inland and, by now out of breath, they suddenly came in sight of the temple of

Eshmun, the god of healing. The temple was erected in large grounds and rested against a hillside; it was a monumental structure made from large blocks of limestone, comprising a huge podium supporting a terraced pyramidal construction that rose to the height of twenty men.

Greatly impressed, the travellers paused in silent awe; to the right of the podium stood the empty throne of Astarte and everywhere were pools for ablutions, some in open air and others roofed over to be used when the temperature dropped. Water from Ydlal spring was conducted through an elaborate network of conduits.

Opposite the temple was an awning which sheltered two men, one busy cutting stones and the other working with clay. The two travellers, in need of information, went to the stonecutter. They found him working on a piece of marble in the indistinct shape of an infant. Behind him was a whole range of finished statuettes. The man ceased working and asked, 'What's the name of the child?'

'Agbalos,' replied Amatbaal.

'I'll engrave that lovely name on one of my best offerings to Eshmun. May he bless you and your infant.'

'We've just arrived,' interrupted Bomilcar, 'the baby is not yet cured. When he is, I promise you, we'll not leave without buying one of your statuettes.'

The sculptor raised his two hands up and uttered, 'Eshmun, the powerful, will cure him. Come back to me then or, if you so choose, to my brother who is making cheaper clay statuettes. That's if you don't want to spend much money for a saintly cause . . . '

Bomilcar started being exasperated by the man, so he cut him short, 'All I want, my good man, is a piece of information. As I told you, we've just arrived and we don't know where to go.'

'Ah! Now I understand. You see this row of rooms?'

Bomilcar followed the man's index finger pointing at a low built area by the temple that he had failed to notice until then. He nodded in confirmation. 'In the first room you'll find the priest Tubal who will take care of everything. Tell him I sent you. My name is Hanon.'

5

Love at First Sight

They found Tubal at the place which had been indicated to them; the door of his room was open and he could be seen seated on a low chair, his clean-shaven head leaning over a papyrus and a sharpened piece of reed between his fingers. The sound of footsteps made him lift his head and two inquisitive eyes darted at them.

'Respects to the servant of the god. We have just arrived from Tyre and we know no one here. Hanon, the stonecutter, told us to come to you,' said Bomilcar. He added, 'my aunt brings you her son; he is suffering from an illness and wastes away. We came to bathe him in the holy waters, to appease the gods and please Eshmun.'

Tubal left his seat, stretching out a tall and slender frame; he took Agbalos from his mother, laid him on his back on the ground, unwrapped his clothing and examined him briefly. Then he gave him back to Amatbaal, recommending, 'He must be immersed in the holy waters twice daily for at least three days. For your good luck you can be accommodated in here, one room has just been vacated by its occupants. But first you ought to offer a sacrifice to Eshmun, the benevolent, the omnipotent. Without his blessing the treatment will not work. Follow me.'

He covered his head with a truncated conic hat and left the room expecting them to be on his heels. It took Amatbaal a moment to wrap up her son, so when she and her nephew stepped out and looked for Tubal he was nowhere to be seen. They waited for him, Bomilcar silent but furious, because he would have to stay away from Tyre longer than anticipated. He felt trapped, unable to escape, for he could not leave his aunt and cousin without the protection of a male member of the family. Amatbaal, who had an inkling of what his mood might be, pretended to be busy with Agbalos and did not look at him.

After a short while Tubal came out of a room next to his, followed by a young woman holding an infant against her bosom. The woman's head was covered with a blue veil and a cloak of the same colour concealed her body.

At first Bomilcar did not take much notice of her, but when she came closer he realised how beautiful were her black eyes, how well defined her red lips and how delicate her features. His interest mounted and he tried to imagine her body beneath the cloak. From what he could reckon she appeared to be slender with a well-proportioned frame. When she stood next to Amatbaal, she was much taller, but then Amatbaal was petite like his mother.

The beautiful stranger's son was asleep and his face was red from fever; obviously she was there for the same reason that had brought them. Instinctively, the two women felt drawn to each other owing to the condition of their respective offspring; they walked side-by-side behind the two men, and engaged in conversation about the health of their little ones.

From time to time Bomilcar looked back to admire their new companion and her graceful gait. She, as Tubal had explained, was also about to offer a sacrifice to Eshmun. Never had Bomilcar been so fascinated by a woman he had just met. Strangely enough, it was not love-making that was his immediate objective, but a yearning to be singled out by her and win her attention. All the inconvenience of the pilgrimage faded away; what he wished now was for the beautiful stranger not to leave the temple before the end of Agbalos's recommended treatment. He was confident that with his aunt's help he would be able to get to know more about her, maybe even speak to her.

'This is the butcher; tell him which animal you wish to sacrifice.'

Bomilcar started at the priest's voice; he looked around and found that he was behind the temple in an enclosed area with several partitions, one for each species. The animals ranged from bulls to small birds in cages.

'I don't know,' said the young man who had been caught off guard. 'Why don't you help me choose,' he added.

From Bomilcar's clothes, the priest had already guessed that he could afford a sheep. He did not mention that the young woman accompanying them had chosen a chicken, so he went for the animal which he had thought appropriate, 'I recommend a sheep,' he said, 'unless you don't want to pay for a large animal.'

The reaction did not disappoint the priest.

'Take this double stater,' said a vexed Bomilcar, 'if it isn't enough to pay for a sheep, the butcher, the incense and our accommodation, all you have to do is to tell me.'

'It is enough. Now follow me; I will bathe the two infants in the sacred waters while the animals are prepared for the sacrifice.'

Tubal led them to a low structure, unlocked the door with one of the keys hanging down from a cord attached round his waist and invited them to enter. They found themselves in a windowless area, which comprised an indoor pool, lit through a number of tiny glassed apertures scattered in the ceiling. Tubal explained, 'This pool is for the children of important people and its waters are known to be particularly blessed by the god. If you ask yourselves why you are here and why I am doing you this favour it's because Chiboulet is with you; she is a cousin of mine.'

Bomilcar and Amatbaal looked in the direction of the young woman who blushed but did not seem particularly pleased. She turned her head away and made no comments. The young man was at an emotional juncture which made him admire the becoming effect of the colour red on Chiboulet's cheeks rather than wondering why she had reacted the way she had.

Several times Tubal plunged the two infants into the pool while he intoned a prayer. The contact with cold water made them scream throughout, which made the two mothers very nervous. When it ended each woman was given a piece of cloth, with the recommendation to dry her baby but not to cover him with heavy clothes, and that worried them too. They nevertheless complied with the instructions.

Bomilcar was following with great interest Chiboulet's activity, which, in normal circumstances, would have sent him running away. Realising that she was the focus of his attention; she made a great effort to carry on her task as normally as she could. That was too much to ask in these unusual conditions. She finally acknowledged his interest by sending him a quick smile that made him wish the pilgrimage would never end.

'Follow me,' said Tubal, leading the way up a steep flight of steps in the open. They climbed behind him until they reached the summit of the temple. The priest stood before the betyl, the divine marker that indicated the god's presence. It was made of stone in the shape of a cone, and set before the altar, which supported a three-branched candelabra.

Putting his right hand before his mouth, Tubal prayed three times: 'May god bless you and hear your voice.'

A young priest burned incense on the altar and accompanied Tubal in reciting prayers in the names of the offerers. The incantations ceased when the butcher and one of his aides appeared carrying a big tray which held the sheep and the chicken cut into pieces.

The offal was offered to the god and the meat distributed between the offerers and the officiants. Thereafter Bomilcar asked the butcher to prepare their share of meat for supper and turning to his aunt said in a whisper, 'If it pleases you, invite our new friend here to join us for supper.'

She looked at him and smiled approvingly.

6

A Woman in Distress

'She's too shy to come and share our meal; it's because she knows you'll be present. However, she has accepted the cooked meat I gave her.'

Bomilcar and Amatbaal were resting in the room rented for their temporary accommodation while a much better Agbalos was asleep. The young man was very disappointed by Chiboulet's decision, for he had expected to spend the evening in her company and get to know more about her. What might be possible in a foreign environment, with no one to watch over their reactions and to listen to the words they would exchange, could hardly take place among his people or hers. He resigned himself to the circumstances and attempted to pry from his aunt whatever she had learnt about the young woman from their conversation.

'What's the infant to her? A young brother? A nephew? he asked.

'He's her son.'

Finding out that she already belonged to a man filled him with consternation and all he could to let out was an 'Ah!'

For a short while she remained silent, finding a perverse enjoyment in making him wait. This was an unexpected pleasure presented to a person who was told what to do most of the time, forced to beg favours for nearly everything. Eventually she relented. 'She's a widow.'

This 'Ah!' conveyed a different connotation, one of relief, and the word 'widow' lit up his face. 'Tell me everything you know,' he urged her.

'A few days after being wed to a cousin, a sailor, he took to the sea and his boat was lost off the city of Kition. All the hands went with her. Their little one will never know his father. What a tragedy and it could well happen to me, having a husband always at sea. Woe is me!'

Bomilcar did not let her go on with her laments, but interrupted, asking, 'Where is she from? How long will she stay here? Speak to me about her.'

Amatbaal's answer was an indirect one but it delighted him. 'She asked me whether you were my husband, and when I told her that you did not have a woman, she blushed.'

'You didn't answer my questions,' he insisted.

'She's from Sidon where she lives with her parents; her father cultivates a farm just outside the city's walls. When her child fell ill and didn't show signs of improvement, Tubal, her first cousin, recommended a seven-day treatment and prayers at the temple. You see, you won't be deprived of her company throughout our stay here.'

'I believe I'm already in love with her.'

'We know very little about her and then there's the child.' Amatbaal's objections were expressed much more on behalf of Inat than herself.

'What does it matter,' he replied, 'she's the first woman for whom I've had this feeling. Now let's have some rest.'

They each chose a litter in a corner, wrapped themselves in their cloaks and tried to sleep. Bomilcar tossed and turned but could not get Chiboulet's image out of his mind. After a while, feeling a presence in the room, he lifted himself up on his elbow and opened his eyes wide to find out who the intruder was. The flickering light supplied by an oil lamp uncovered Chiboulet's face. She was holding her son. She also recognised him and went to the other form, which could only be Amatbaal. She gently shook her to wake her up.

He stood up, came closer to the two women with the lamp in his hand and heard Chiboulet's plea, 'Let me stay with you until tomorrow.'

'You're welcome to stay, but do tell me, what's going on?'

Chiboulet turned to look at Bomilcar. He felt a shock because of the beauty of her face. She had forgotten, or probably not had time, to cover her head; so he could admire her long black hair, sleek and shiny, her beautiful eyes, which were filled with fear and distress, and her chiselled mouth and bright teeth. He got a grip on himself and repeated his question. 'What's going on?'

'He came to my room.'

'Who?' asked the young man.

'Tubal.'

She started to shiver from cold and retrospective fear. Amatbaal covered her shoulders, took the child from her arms and when she had calmed down asked her, 'What did he want?'

Chiboulet's eyes expressed what she was unable to voice; anyway words were unnecessary, for her companions had well understood what Tubal expected from her, and the superfluous question was not repeated. Just the same, the young woman vented her fear: 'I'm frightened, very frightened. He has threatened to lock me up in the sanctuary dedicated to Astarte to make a sacred prostitute of me. He told me I'll have to sell my body to any traveller who wishes for one shekel or two remitted to the temple. He pledged that this will be my fate unless I'm his.'

It was absolutely not the time to blame her for anything, yet Bomilcar could not prevent himself blurting out, 'How did it happen that you left home without the protection of a male member of your family?'

'But Tubal is my first cousin,' she replied indignantly, 'he even wanted me for his wife; my father left me free to accept or reject him. I chose to be the woman of another cousin of mine whom I had loved since childhood. Now he's dead but he gave me a beautiful child who does not enjoy the best of health. Tubal asked my father's permission to bring us to the temple to pray for his recovery. My father trusted him, I should have known better. Now it's too late'

She started crying silently while Bomilcar paced the room. She misunderstood the reason for his apparent concern, picked up her son and stepped in the direction of the door.

'I'm leaving; I don't want you to have any trouble on my account,' she said.

Bomilcar ceased his toing and froing and solemnly declared: 'From now on you are both my responsibility. You came to this place for protection and I gave it to you. Tonight you won't budge from here. Tomorrow we'll consider it. Now try to get some sleep.'

7

Showdown

Bomilcar's words came from his heart, yet worry weighed on his mind. Tubal seemed to be an influential person and to defy him would not be without risk, the more so because he was in an alien environment and not at Tyre, where local support would have been on hand.

Although he was fully conscious of the danger he was putting himself into, it did not cross his mind to let down the woman who had put herself under his protection and captured his heart. His natural optimism made him assume that the unpleasant situation would resolve itself the following day and all he and his companions would have to do when seeing Tubal was behave as normally as possible; yet being no fool, he had also to anticipate a possible showdown with the priest.

All these conflicting thoughts kept him awake for most of what remained of the night. He dozed off a couple of hours before sunrise, waking up when the sun's rays forced their way inside the room.

From his corner he was able to see that Chiboulet was still asleep, her son nestled against her chest. He took his time admiring her features, beautifully serene because of her temporary unconsciousness. He did not move, so as to give her a chance to rest a little longer and recover from the emotion of the night's events.

His emotional response to the situation he was in baffled him; never before had he desired a woman more than he longed for Chiboulet, yet he had denied himself any physical contact with her because of her vulnerability.

A sense of responsibility was not the only factor ; he was afraid of disappointing her. Any hasty moves might make her believe that the protection he had offered was, after all, less than candid and generous. It was this proclivity to take her feelings into account which was novel and unexpectedly gratifying.

All of a sudden her face tensed, as if emerging from a merciful sleep, the memory of the ordeal she had gone through was coming back to her. She opened her eyes and saw him; he smiled to reassure her and was repaid with a poor smile. He did not move lest he frightened her and she, realising the ambiguity of the situation they were in, tried to summon a sense of dignity by clasping her son to her breast in an attempt to underline her motherhood.

Amatbaal woke up, putting an end to the silent interplay. Bomilcar broached the subject which was worrying them all. He did so with a confidence he was far from possessing. 'We will go to the pool as if nothing has taken place. There, the priest's behaviour will dictate ours.'

Having said that, he saw terror in Chiboulet's eyes, so he hastily added, 'Don't be afraid, I'll never let you down. I have already told you that; I'll allow no one to harm you, least of all this Tubal.' A glance filled with gratitude rewarded the young man and strengthened his determination.

It did not surprise Tubal to see them arriving all together. He already knew that Chiboulet had taken refuge with them the evening before and he had to assume that she had told them of his unwelcome proposals. Forsaking none of his arrogance, he took control of the situation as if nothing had occurred between him and the young woman.

'I want to examine the child one more time.' he said to Amatbaal. When he did that and gave him back to his mother, the look on his face was mournful and the words he uttered worrying, 'Go to the top of the temple, present another offering to the god and pray. This child needs both the sacrifice and your prayer. Don't come back before sunset.'

Amatbaal stood motionless looking stunned until the priest's words sank into her mind. Then she started lamenting, 'My Agbalos is about to die; god have pity on me, he is my only child and I cannot have another at my age. Have pity on us, Eshmun!'

With a firm hand Tubal pushed her outside the building. Bomilcar, with one arm around her shoulders, moved her away from the pool's door. A few paces away he stopped and whispered in her ear, 'Stay here, don't move. Agbalos is fine. I give you my word. He is fine. The whole matter is invented by Tubal to get rid of us and remain alone with Chiboulet. Stop crying and wait for me here; I won't be long.'

Before she could object, he went back into the vestibule, making sure not to produce any noise. Hugging the walls, he made his way to the opening that led to the pool and listened, without being seen, to the exchange of words between the priest and the young woman.

'Why do you deny me your confidence, Chiboulet, when you give it to a perfect stranger? Who are these people you associate with? I love you and I wanted you for a wife but you chose someone else and now he's dead. Don't you see that the gods took exception to your choice and punished you? And what about your son, he's not in the best of health. What are you going to do about that? You ought to accept that you belong to me.'

'What you say is despicable. My father trusted you, believing I would be safe with you.'

Tubal took two paces closer to her and nearly shouted, 'Give yourself to me and I'll protect you and your son.'

Disgusted, the young woman moved back to keep a safe distance from him.

'Never,' she yelled.

Humiliated and goaded, he resorted to disparaging her. 'It's clear that you've chosen the protection of this young Tyrian, a foreigner, instead of mine. He is unable to take his eyes off you. What can he do for you here? Nothing at all.'

The priest's tone rose when he mentioned Bomilcar's name and he started shaking with anger. Chiboulet's riposte did nothing to calm him down, 'This foreigner, as you said, had nothing but kindness for me; I shared his room and he didn't even try to lay a finger on me.'

This was too much for Tubal, furious, he threatened, 'Since you appreciate foreigners so much, it means that you're perfectly suited for Astarte's sanctuary. There you'll wait for those pilgrims who desire the company of a woman. Come with me to your new lodging. The child stays with me; I'll send him to your parents later.'

These words gave Chiboulet wings; she grabbed her son and ran towards the door, followed by the priest. In the vestibule Bomilcar stood firmly between the two; the young woman took refuge behind him while her pursuer barked at him, 'Move away, this matter is of no concern to you, move away, or else.'

The result of the menacing words was not what the priest expected as the young man answered back, 'She and her son are in my charge. I'll take them back to her parents.'

'She will not move from here. Go!'

Tubal tried to push Bomilcar aside with a forceful movement of the hand. The Tyrian retaliated with a punch, which landed on Tubal's chest, sending him into a paroxysm of rage. He pulled a dagger from beneath his robe and tried to strike the young man. Instinctively the latter lifted his left arm for protection and received a slash on his forearm.

Unwilling to wait for another charge he hurled himself against his assailant and grabbed the hand holding the dagger. Thrown off balance the priest fell on his back, Bomilcar on top of him. The weapon dropped from his hand and was immediately seized by the young man.

No sign of life came from Tubal who lay underneath Bomilcar. Slowly, carefully, Bomilcar stood up without dropping his guard, the weapon in his hand ready. The priest's eyes fixed and a small pool of blood seeped under his head. Most probably his fall had caused his death.

Bomilcar did not lose any time checking; he looked for Chiboulet and found her and her son in a corner, frozen with fear. She had followed the struggle from her place of refuge when both men fell her heart had nearly stopped in her chest. She had calmed a little when Bomilcar got up, disclosing the inanimate body.

Blood trickling down his forearm threw her into a panic but she pulled herself together, put her child on the ground and made a dressing for the wound with her head covering.

The bleeding had to be stopped so Bomilcar let her, hurrying her just the same. 'That's fine. Let's go.'

When she had finished he hid the dagger beneath his tunic, knelt before the lifeless body and untied the cord that held the bunch of keys which he took. Outside, he locked the door and they rejoined Amatbaal who was dying of impatience and worry.

'What's going on? she kept asking.

A few pilgrims and temple personnel were attending to their own business and no one paid any attention to them. The first danger over, the young man looked at Chiboulet and saw that she was in an awful state. Impulsively he pledged, 'You're coming with me, I'll never desert you.'

These words, intended to be reassuring, were said with such warmth and affection that Chiboulet was deeply touched; abandoning all restraint, she seized his hand surreptitiously and pressed it to show him her appreciation.

8

Escape

'By Baal Shamem, tell me what's going on?' asked a breathless Amatbaal, moving as quickly as she could with Agbalos in her arms and struggling not to be outdistanced by Bomilcar and Chiboulet, who had her own load.

'Later, I'll tell you everything. Now we must leave this place immediately,' replied the young man.

'We can't leave our belongings behind.'

'We have no time; follow me.'

Not convinced in the least, she did not insist, detecting a hint of irritation in her nephew's voice. They all rushed in the direction of the landing stage. On their way Bomilcar promised to sacrifice a bull to Melqart if they found the boat there.

If the boat was not to be found, they would have to walk to the port of Sidon and from there hire a boat to take them to Tyre. Walking all the way would put them in danger of being caught, if, in the meantime, Tubal's body were found and a search party sent after them.

Following the narrow path to the river's mouth, they reached the point from which they could see their moored boat and the four-man crew who had settled on the riverbank. Luckily for them, the sailors must have found it more practical not to leave the meeting place.

The runaways went straight aboard while Bomilcar shouted to the crew to cast off; the sailors complied with the order. In no time they were on their way, gradually putting more distance between them and the temple, propelled by powerful winds.

A little reassured, Chiboulet took stock of her own emotions.

Finding herself on the way to a foreign place in the company of a stranger made her feel uneasy, the more so because he seemed to have fallen in love with her. True, she was most grateful because he had put himself in deadly danger to save her from Tubal, but she was not in love with him. She decided to speak her mind while trying not to hurt his feelings.

'I wish to go to my parents. Please take me to them,' she said.

He decided to make her see reason, even frighten her a little to make her change her mind. 'The first step the temple authorities will take is to go to your parents' house. Finding you there, they will take you back to the temple for questioning. Is that what you want?'

She looked very afraid and he felt that he was making headway. He, however, did not pursue that argument, having taken pity on her; instead he wished to comfort her. Before he could do that Amatbaal intervened: 'Why are we running away? From whom? In the name of the gods I beg of you to tell me.'

Her nephew realised that she had been unfairly left in the dark and with a few words explained the reason for their hasty departure. While he did so he unfolded the improvised dressing made by Chiboulet and examined the wound. It was in the process of healing with dried blood all around. In Bomilcar's account no mention had been made of the wound, which appeared horrendous to a panicking Amatbaal.

'I'm responsible. I brought you to the temple. You could have been killed,' she said and sobbed, the more so because she dreaded the reaction of her sister when she found out that her son had been wounded. Bomilcar reassured her that it was a mere scratch which did not deserve to be fussed about.

'Without the pilgrimage I would have never met Chiboulet. I love her and I'm going to take her for a wife.'

The emotionally charged events through which she had been, and the real danger of being separated from her son and confined in Astarte's sanctuary had not given Chiboulet either the opportunity or the inclination to become emotionally involved. Nonetheless, Bomilcar's unexpected declaration caused her to search her own heart: he was good-looking, appealed to her, most courageous and she needed no reminder that without his gallantry she would have been left at Tubal's mercy. Yet barely a year had passed since her husband's death; she considered herself to be in mourning still and intended to so remain for a long time, maybe forever. On the other hand, she was not indifferent to Bomilcar's charm and the protection he could afford to her and her son was not a negligible factor. Circumstances and emotion had moved too fast for comfort. She needed more time and space and decided to try to get them.

'You know nothing about me,' she objected.

'What I've witnessed has convinced me of your virtues. For the rest, the time we'll spend together in Tyre will tell me what I don't know yet. You want to see your parents; you'll see them soon, rest assured. The moment the danger recedes, we'll go to your father and I'll ask his permission to take you for a wife.'

His words sounded so forthright that her misgivings were shaken, not to the point of making her endorse his unilateral arrangement, but at least to consider it in a more favourable light. Her fear that she might be forced to do something she was unprepared for was alleviated. Because Bomilcar had pledged to take her back to her parents and not to consider her his instant property, she relaxed.

Their boat was in full sail under favourable wind and in calm water, as was usual during the autumn season; she let her body sway, following the gentle movements of the boat while a mild breeze caressed her face. Even Amatbaal could not take her eyes off the young woman's beautiful features, while she developed a new worry about how Inat was going to react to her son's choice of a wife, a choice for which she might be blamed on account of the pilgrimage. Even so, she made a move which could be another cause for rebuke if her sister was to learn about it; she took Chiboulet's son from her arms and gently placed him beside hers; the aim was to free her mind of any concern about the child and give the two youngsters an opportunity not to have their attention distracted. Instinctively they moved closer to each other, remaining most of the time silent but obviously happy to be together.

When they reached Tyre's northern harbour they witnessed an unusual activity. Cargoes were being unloaded from a great number of moored vessels by an army of toiling porters, watched over by exacting port officials. Other ships with empty hulls were about to put out to sea. All these operations were conducted amidst a great confusion, and a lot of shouting and swearing.

It was clear to Bomilcar that since his departure from Tyre, important events must have taken place, which would account for the frantic activity. He was slightly worried, but unwilling to spoil his joy, he quickly put any disquiet out of mind.

9

Concern

'Mother, this is Chiboulet and her son; they will stay with us for the time being.'

Taken aback but disclosing none of it, Inat nodded politely at the young stranger who, she noticed, had her head uncovered and wore a dirty and torn robe. Bomilcar's attire was not in a much better condition, as she noticed when she was about to press him to her bosom. Greatly concerned she asked, 'What happened?'

'I must leave; my aunt will explain everything. Just tell me the reason for the port's frenzied activity. What happened during my absence?'

'What counts is that you've all returned safely. I must thank Melqart with an offering.'

Inat left her son's question unanswered on purpose, to make him understand that she could not be dismissed in an offhand manner; and that she deserved an explanation from him, not from her sister, whose expected contribution was to elaborate all the small details. He understood and apologised: 'Forgive me, Mother, but I have to show our guest her quarters. Will you please tell me what's going on?'

She smiled, pretending to have forgiven him but in fact was more angry with him for the precedence he was prepared to give to a stranger. She hid her feelings, however, and gave him the information he expected. 'Balator's orders are to bring to the island all available foodstuffs, especially the durable ones. The orders apply to all kinds of weapons as well. Vessels were sent to Old Tyre and nearby hamlets and farms to seize pickings and harvests and whatever else the soldiers may lay their hands on. Very soon the news of the danger will spread and this place will be swarming with thousands of refugees from the mainland. The southern port is as congested as the northern one.'

'Do you have any idea why these orders were given?'

Bomilcar already knew the answer; nevertheless, he had asked hoping to receive a somehow reassuring reply. That was not to be for Inat confirmed his doubts. 'I can't see any reason other than the prospect of a siege. Ah! I nearly forgot, a messenger came this morning to let you know that the Council is in permanent session and your presence is required.'

There was no room for doubt. Tyre was being readied to withstand a siege. What could have happened in twenty-four hours to make these measures necessary? he wondered.

Suddenly apprehensive, he made sure not to show his feelings lest he frighten Chiboulet. He decided to remain with her for a few moments before he joined the Council, to give her time to become accustomed to her new surroundings.

The two sisters retired to the intimacy of Inat's rooms and Bomilcar made Chiboulet comfortable while they waited for her quarters to be made ready.

He noticed that tears, which she had been able to hold back until then, started running down her cheeks while she rocked her son. Despite their distance from the temple of Eshmun, despite the care shown by her host and the soothing atmosphere of the new place, she was in the grasp of a retrospective fear and longed for her parents. Bomilcar tried to take her mind off these dejected thoughts, asking, 'With all that has taken place, I still don't know the name of the little one. Is he better?'

'His name is Jason and he is better,' she answered back, her face brightening with a feeble smile.

He gave the baby's head a friendly tap and was rewarded with a broad smile and a happy gurgle.

'Jason needs to rest and you too. You probably want to retire to your room until dinner time. Lula! Lula!'

Lula was the fifteen-year-old black Nubian slave chosen to serve Chiboulet during her stay. For once, she appeared as if by magic and had most probably been listening behind the door.

'Lula,' he said, 'take your mistress and her son to their room. You will do whatever she orders.'

Then turning to Chiboulet he said, 'Mother will send you a change of clothing. I must leave for now, but I'll not be long.'

Although she had calmed down a little she had not given up her wish to go back to her parents. She told him that, adding, 'Don't think for a moment that I'm ungrateful; how could I be after all you've done for my sake. However, Father and Mother will be worried about me. In no time Tubal's death and my disappearance will come to their ears. Imagine their anguish and their pain. No, I can't let them go through that. Give me the means to go back to them, I beg of you.'

Her imploring eyes made him feel sorry for her, but he stood firm for her own good. 'Sidon is a dangerous place at the moment. Tubal belonged to a powerful fraternity of priests. They will want to avenge the death of one of their own and will have no hesitation in blaming us. No explanation will be listened to, certainly not that his death was an accident. Our flight will be deemed an admission of guilt. I understand your concern about your parents: tomorrow morning I'll send them a messenger who will explain what happened and put their minds at rest concerning your safety. Then it will be up to your father to tell us when you can go back without putting yourself in danger. Until then, you'll stay in this house which one day will be yours forever, if you accept. Are you satisfied?'

She felt she had to give him an answer to his renewed proposal, but she decided on a non-committal one. 'Wait until you know me better. You might change your mind, besides . . . '

He had no wish to listen to any objection, even one given in a self-derogatory guise. 'Don't count on that,' he said, 'I loved you the first time I laid my eyes on you. Fate brought us closer to each other. Who am I to stand against its decrees? Follow Lula, she'll take you to your room and will remain at your service. Command and she will obey. Do you understand, Lula? As for me, I'll see Mother, change my dressing and find out why the Council is still in session this late.'

10

Amorous Determination

'Why has no one told me? How did you get wounded? Let me see.' Very concerned, Inat unwrapped the soiled veil from Bomilcar's forearm while she cried out her worry. Her sister had not dared tell her that her son had been knifed, and when he had first arrived she had not seen the dressing, involved in welcoming him and trying to understand why he was bringing a perfect stranger and her infant to stay.

At first sight she had distrusted the scruffy foreigner with unkempt hair; when she was told that her son could have been killed because of her, she became hostile. She, however, hid her feeling lest her son reacted badly. She knew he was in love for it was the first detail Amatbaal had told her.

'See, mother, it is nothing, a mere scratch; what I need is a clean dressing.'

Bomilcar's protest went unheeded. Inat ordered a mixture of vine, vinegar and honey. With that mixture she washed the wound and dressed it with a clean piece of linen.

Once that was done she tried to learn more about her son's feelings towards the young woman. She wanted to know whether he was seriously in love or was feeling a passing infatuation. She had never seen him prepared to neglect his own mother for the company of a woman. Finding an answer was not easy at that moment for he was in a hurry to join the Council; moreover, she had to take great care not to let out any unwelcome words which might make him baulk and refuse to talk. Summoning all her cunning, she took a roundabout approach. 'She's really pretty, this young woman, despite her shabby appearance. I immediately liked her but after what Amatbaal told me I keep wondering why misfortune is her lot. There must be a reason that she is dogged by hard luck. Poor woman.'

The game she was playing did not escape Bomilcar; his mother was trying to warn him against associating with a person who was clearly without the gods' protection. He accepted the challenge despite being pressed for time and decided to make his mother understand that his determination to take Chiboulet for a wife was unshakeable. Because superstitious fear was the weapon she made use of, he had to show his readiness to go along that line.

'I'm sure, mother,' he said, 'that your favourite amulets, talismans and scarabs will protect her. If need be I'll buy more powerful ones from Tharros. Your offerings to Ashtart asking for protection will also help. One way or the other you have to make sure that your prayers are answered and your offerings accepted, for she is the one I'll marry as soon as I have met her father.'

Inat had already heard from her sister that her son had such a project in mind, but hearing it from his own mouth shocked her. She controlled herself and discarding superstition as a weapon, gave him the advice that any mother would give to her son in such circumstances, particularly when she had not chosen the future bride.

'Nothing will please me more than seeing you married and this house full of children. All I'm asking is for you to be absolutely sure of the choice you've made. For that, you have to be better acquainted with Chiboulet and her family. A brief association is not enough. Give yourself time to know all you need to know.'

She paused lest she might have already said too much. Unexpectedly, Bomilcar did not lose his temper, but countered her argument, 'Our acquaintance is recent, I admit, but in this short time I have come a complete understanding of her worth. My aunt can vouch for her virtue and her noble nature. Ask her.'

Inat did what he suggested, looking at Amatbaal with questioning eyes. Having always had an ascendancy over her younger sister, she naturally expected full support for her cautious advice. Not this time; willing to win favour with her nephew, whom she had started seeing in a new light, she carefully chose words which could please him without upsetting her sister much.

'I have not known Chiboulet for long,' she said, 'but we have met under difficult circumstances which allowed me to witness her courage and virtue. I know no more about her. Why don't you give yourself time for the confirmation of this first impression?'

The last words were intended for Bomilcar, who pretended not to have heard them. Before leaving the room, he gave instructions aimed at his mother. 'She and her son need a clean change of clothing. Please send them what they need.'

11

Frank Explanation

'Tansu, I want a singer and a flautist with the evening meal. Where is the young woman, my guest? Where's mother?'

Back home after the Council's session, Bomilcar was in need of relaxation after the dramatic events of the last two days; he also wished to honour his guest.

The old man knew perfectly well in which tavern the musicians could be found, so he nodded to indicate that the instructions were understood and would be obeyed. At the same time, not being talkative by nature, he answered his master's questions by a movement of the arm indicating the rear of the house. Dissatisfied with the vague indication, the young man insisted, 'Where are they?'

This time Tansu had to provide a verbal answer, which he did economically: 'In their rooms.'

'Go and ask if I may visit her.'

'Who?'

'The young lady.'

Moments later and Bomilcar found Chiboulet in tears, Jason moaning in her arms. It was not easy to make her talk and tell him the reason for their unhappiness, impervious as she seemed to his persistent questioning. Eventually she lashed out, 'I'm unwelcome here, I want to go home.'

'Why do you say that? What happened?'

He looked very annoyed and she felt she had to provide the explanation he was entitled to, 'See for yourself, I'm still wearing the same dirty and torn clothes I arrived with and I could not clean Jason. He's been in that state since I came in here.'

'Did you call out for Lula?' he asked.

'She brought us milk then disappeared. I needed to change Jason so I shouted her name several times but received no answer from her or from anyone else.'

His anger mounted against his mother, for he had guessed from the first words that his young guest's misfortune was Inat's doing. He controlled himself for his first duty was to calm an infuriated Chiboulet.

'No doubt there is a misunderstanding, which I'll dispel, be sure of that. I can't bear to see you unhappy. You will return to Sidon in a matter of days, but not for long; as my wife, you will be the mistress of this household and no slave will dare pretend not to hear your commands.'

She was in such a state that she gave up the light equivocation that she had used until then when she needed to disengage herself from an embarrassing situation. This time she let her heart speak.

'After the disappearance of my husband I was interested in no man; you, Bomilcar, are the first towards whom I have felt inclined and it's not only due to a sense of obligation. Even before you saved me from Tubal I was pleased to be in your company.'

The recollection of her feeling mollified her attitude. She gave a fleeting smile and continued as if talking to herself. 'When we went to the pool – I mean the first time we were there – you kept looking at me so persistently that I let a smile escape me. I couldn't prevent it and for once I was relieved of the sorrow that weighs me down.'

He saw an opportunity to further his case and seized it. 'Since we share the same feelings I don't see what we are waiting for.'

'I need time to accustom myself to the idea of the new life that you generously offer me. I'm used to presuming that I would end my days in my parents' house, devoting all my time to Jason and also . . .' She hesitated for a moment, then proceeded: 'I'll not hide from you that when I'm on my own in our house I often watch the door for hours, hoping, even believing, that it will open and my poor husband will step in, making me realise that I was just having a nightmare. That's not all, there's also the situation.'

'Which situation?' he interrupted, genuinely surprised.

'The port's activity, the commotion . . . all that has a meaning, has it not?'

She was bewildered by his lack of concern and her face showed her perplexity; he misunderstood it, thought she was afraid and endeavoured to reassure her. 'Ah! That was merely a precaution. Some of the Councillors have insisted that Tyre must be prepared for a siege. When I saw the port bursting with activity and I heard their demand, I became worried. Not any more. The majority of the Council, in particular, Councillor Chelbes, convinced me that Alexander does not destroy when he obtains what he wants. He's not after laying waste and will be satisfied with the tribute he receives from those who yield to him without a fight.'

'How can you be sure of that?' she asked.

'Oh! I'm sure. First of all, a witness brought by Chelbes confirmed all that I've said. The man, a Macedonian by the name of Lysinias, went to great lengths to describe Alexander's benevolent attitude when pleased and his terrible reaction when provoked. Then there's the precedent at Aradus.'

'Isn't Aradus the island north of Byblos?' she asked.

'Exactly. When Alexander vanquished Darius at Issus he didn't pursue the defeated army but chose to receive the tribute of the coastal cities. Aradus was the first maritime city which offered the victor the golden crown and yielded of its territory. He accepted both without even trying to occupy their island. For the time being he is heading for Byblos. I'm sure that what took place at Aradus will be repeated. After that it will be Sidon's turn, then Tyre. He will not attempt to set foot on our island, I promise you.'

Bomilcar's explanation, which was meant to have an appeasing effect, had exactly the opposite. Having learned that Alexander's next objective was to be Sidon, she stated adamantly: 'I must go back to my parents. Don't you see I must be by their side? Right now the priests must have other worries than going after us. I implore you, Bomilcar, help me once more and send me back right away.'

She was peering at him with tears in her eyes which broke his heart. Of course he wanted to keep her beside him, but not against her will. He bitterly regretted having expounded what he believed to be Alexander's plan of campaign; too late now, she was standing there looking miserable and waiting for his reaction to her emotional appeal. He knew he was going to do exactly what she wished, for he was not prepared to disappoint her and run the risk of killing the feelings that, by her own admission, she had for him.

'Tomorrow,' he said, 'a boat will take you to your parents. A few days later I'll join you and ask your father's permission to bring you back as my wife. After that I'll allow nothing and no one to separate us.'

His words had a double effect on her: she felt relief that he had responded positively to her urgent wish, as well as a sense of elation, which had a greater implication for their future relationship. Tender words let him know her appreciation. 'I'll look forward impatiently to the moment you'll come.'

That was the first time she had responded unambiguously to his advances. He was exhilarated and could not resist taking her in his arms and kissing her lips. She let him but gently disentangled herself when he became more pressing; he did not insist. Leaving the room, he said, 'In a short while we'll have dinner with music. Mother will attend.'

12

Prompt Recovery

'Why isn't there more light? Are you unwell?' Immediately after leaving Chiboulet, Bomilcar had rushed into his mother's bedroom, prepared to remonstrate with her for having neglected their guests. In the half-light he could see, or rather guess, that the figure lying down on the bed was Inat.

'Is it you, my son?' The voice was faint and quivering and made him instantly forget his reason for feeling angry. He picked an oil lamp from a recess in the wall and held it above the bed, trying to detect on his mother's face signs that would indicate the degree of her languor. At the same time he asked, 'What's the matter, Mother?'

'After you left me I felt a splitting headache. I lay in bed and placed compresses soaked with vinegar on my forehead. Lula rubbed my body with oil and I tried to sleep. Now that you are here I feel better.'

'Ah! I understand,' mumbled Bomilcar.

'You understand what?' she asked, prompting a reply which intended to cut short more questioning. 'Nothing. A silly idea which went through my mind.'

They both remained silent for a moment, which was interrupted by the young man. 'I'm glad to hear that you've recovered. I expect you to dine with me and Chiboulet. She's leaving us tomorrow.'

'Where's she going? Wasn't she supposed to stay with us for some time? What happened?'

Inat was trying her best not to let her voice expose her joy at hearing the news that the young woman was about to leave. It was only just that the choice he had made without any assistance from her had been quickly recognised as a mistake. She pledged to herself to introduce him promptly to a suitable girl unburdened with a child.

'She's going back to her parents. That's her wish. She dreads that the Macedonian advance might cut her off from them,' replied Bomilcar.

He was about to add that he was determined to follow her in a matter of days and bring her back. His instinct told him that his mother needed time to familiarise herself with the idea that his future wife would not be chosen by her, and that her opinion was not even to be sought.

Inat concealed the hurt she felt at being deprived of the duties afforded to mothers and readily accepted by sons; instead she turned to politics to stress that Chiboulet's departure was the most sensible option under the circumstances, 'It seems that Alexander's plan is to occupy one city after the other. Soon it will be our turn.'

'What happened to your good sense, all of you?' he said, incensed, for what he had just heard did not square with his projects. He addressed his mother as if Chiboulet was also present: 'Alexander is not after occupation but snatched victories and recognition. Instead of paying tribute to the Persians, we'll pay it to the Macedonian and he will not consider setting foot on our island. He didn't do it in Aradus's case and he will not do it in ours.'

'I don't understand. If the Council is sure of that, why all the preparations for sustaining a siege? You've seen that our ships bringing home all the foodstuffs and weapons that their crews were able to grab? Why are they under such orders if there is no danger?'

'That's a different story; it's a political game. You know Abbarus, the leader of the fiercely nationalistic Councillors? Well, he called for the measures you just mentioned. Seeing no harm in complying with his demands we have agreed. You will see nothing will happen to justify these measures.'

Being superstitious, Inat touched wood and as an additional

precaution, appealed for Melqart's and Astarte's protection over the city.

Taking for granted that his mother would join him and their guest for dinner, he said, 'Mother, I rely on you to send Chiboulet decent clothes so she won't be ashamed to appear in your company.'

The last words were intended to appease her and give her back the first place she believed was hers. They made her beam with pleasure.

13

An Intimate Dinner

When she appeared in the doorway of the family dining room, Inat could not suppress an admiring look.

Chiboulet was indeed dazzling in a white gown held together by a golden brooch pinned at the level of her left shoulder. Coiled black hair highlighted her prominent cheekbones and enhanced her fine features and the beauty of her eyes, heavily made up in the Sidonian style.

Her radiant beauty made a strong impression on mother and son with distinct results. Inat realised instantly the insurmountable difficulties awaiting her if she wanted to interest her son in any prospective wife of her choice; no one she knew could compete in terms of beauty with this woman. As for Bomilcar, he became more determined than ever to marry that same woman who had been a perfect stranger only two days ago.

He invited Chiboulet to take one of the unoccupied couches; she complied and assumed the same posture as her hosts, lying on one side with her upper body propped up on cushions. Her right hand remained free to pick at the food which was placed on a table within reach of the three diners.

The meal consisted of fishes fried in olive oil, a small lamb baked in the milk of an ewe which had recently given birth and a green salad dressed with olive oil and a fish condiment called garum.

Bomilcar ordered Tansu to serve the wine. The slave picked up an amphora and poured some into a large bowl where he mixed it with an equal quantity of water. When the operation was completed he served the watered wine in glass cups produced in Sidon, using a secret manufacturing process.

In one corner of the room the two musicians hired for the evening delivered melodious tunes that did not interfere with the conversation.

Inat waited for the honeyed dessert to be served and for the wine to produce its effects before she tried to get information out of Chiboulet. Her aim was to extract from her facts which could be turned against her, if used in an intelligent way.

'What does your father do?'

'He has a farm,' came the reply, which delighted the older woman who concluded that a man who was not in trade must have meagre resources and no standing in his community.

'I see.' Encouraged, she asked, 'Your late husband, was he a simple sailor?'

That was too much for Chiboulet who did not need more proof that her hostess was trying to demean her in the eyes of Bomilcar. With no fear of the consequences, she retorted, 'The father of my son was the best of men. Had fate been less cruel, you wouldn't have to bear my presence. Rest assured, I'll never forget what Bomilcar did for me, but . . . '

The young man felt enraged by his mother, but he controlled himself and cut Chiboulet off in case she said something which could ruin the hope he had cultivated.

'Mother was not trying to hurt you,' he said, 'she was simply interested in knowing more about you. Am I right, Mother?' Lashing out his question, he stared at Inat fixedly so that she could see his unbending determination to force her to apologise. She knew that she had lost a round; Chiboulet, far from having been intimidated, had made her besotted son take her side. The only option left to her was a quick volte-face, which she made without hesitation, not ashamed in the least. 'It never crossed my mind to make you unhappy. All I wanted was to make better acquaintance with the woman who has charmed my son. What I've realised is that in addition to her great beauty, she is also a very capable person. Please have more of this cake and let's drink to the future.'

The matter was closed for the time being but the lines had been firmly defined.

14

A Tormented Man

Matten, absorbed in his thoughts, went to Bomilcar's house expecting him to have completed his pilgrimage to the temple of Eshmun. He needed to confide in the person he considered as a brother, who looked upon him in the same way.

Their friendship had started when they went to the school attached to Agenor's sanctuary, aged seven. They were from two very different parts of the island; while young Bomilcar came from the primary residential quarters in the centre of the city and was escorted by the faithful Tansu, Matten arrived on his own, from the eastern industrial district. Their social difference went unnoticed by the two boys who immediately became inseparable. That did not please Inat who tried to cut short the burgeoning friendship between her son and the boy from the poor area. All her efforts failed. Finally, she had to resign herself to the whim of her only child, who regularly brought the son of Meges the dyer, to play in their garden

Meges's skill was purple-dyeing. The dye was produced from

murex, a marine snail found in large numbers in Tyre's coastal waters. The dyeing process was said to have been discovered by mere chance and was kept secret for a long time. It had contributed to the wealth of the city but also to a permanent foul smell hanging over the areas where the work was done.

Business was conducted in an orderly manner; only in exceptional circumstances did anyone try to overstep the boundaries of his regular activity. Fleeces were brought to Tyre by caravan from the east and flax from Egypt by boat; local merchants bought them, gave them to private individuals to be spun and then allotted some to dyers. The treated fleeces and flax were delivered to households scattered all over the city, to be woven. The merchants who eventually sold the purple material to the rich and powerful, either in the local market or abroad, made good money for virtually no risk.

Bomilcar's father had his shortcomings but he did not have high regard for his social position and wealth, nor indeed any disdain for people considered socially inferior. His son's association with Matten left him indifferent until he realised the advantages he could gain from their friendship.

One afternoon the dyer come to collect his son and was invited by the master of the house to have a cup of wine. He was delighted by the honour while Inat was utterly disgusted at the sight of her husband mixing with a person below his status.

Merbalos had a business proposal in mind: he would buy most of the wool and flax brought by caravans and boats during a single year and Meges would hire workers to assist him with dyeing these unusually large quantities. With most of the purple material hoarded and controlled by Merbalos he would be in a position to ask for any price he wanted with no fear of being challenged by any competitors.

The merchant's fortune increased, as did the friendship between Bomilcar and Matten through childhood and adulthood. The former admired his friend's physical strength and courage. He had developed a gigantic muscular frame, crowned with ginger hair that did not allow him to go unnoticed. As for Matten, he was dazzled by his old playmate's astuteness and his open and sharp mind.

Nevertheless, he had resisted Bomilcar's attempts to employ him at his father's shipping enterprise, nor would he work for him after Merbalos had died. Nothing could convince Matten to relinquish his independence, even with regard to his own father; he had spurned the dyer's craft, choosing instead to be a blacksmith.

As an apprentice he quickly mastered how to ply the white-hot metal, helped by his great strength. Before long he had his own forge established, as the regulations dictated, a little apart from the built-up area to avoid an accidental fire spreading to houses, but not far from the temple of Melqart. An extremely devoted man, he was waiting for the moment when the saintly task of keeping alive the fire burning under the altar dedicated to the god of the City would become vacant. When that moment arrived, Matten was put in charge of the coveted duty, with no other candidates in sight.

The news that Aradus had surrendered to Alexander without a fight and the conqueror was on his way to Byblos filled the blacksmith with worry. He wondered how much time was left before Tyre had to choose between resistance or shameful capitulation.

It was not that he would have any regret seeing Persian domination crumble; nothing of the sort. What excruciated him had to do with the Persian king's belief in one God whom he did not try to foist on his Phoenician subjects. With Alexander it would not be the same; accompanied as he was by a cortege of foreign gods it would not take long for Matten's fellow citizens to desert their own gods and adopt those of the new master. Already everything Greek was fashionable, at least for well-to-do Tyrians, and much more for Sidonians, who execrated the Persians, remembering still the destruction of their city some fifteen years ago. It was to be expected that Sidon would receive the conqueror with open arms. That would leave Tyre on its own, albeit under the protection of Melqart and Astarte, the sea and its bulky walls.

It was unthinkable that its gates were to be voluntarily opened and its walls torn down to allow foreign gods to supplant the gods of the City. The idea was abominable and should be resisted at any cost. But he did not know how or where to start.

Guidance must be sought from the one person who had his full confidence and who had brains. He was dying to share his concern with him and listen to his advice, so he speeded up while making a silent prayer to his favourite god that he would find Bomilcar at home.

15

Dialogue of Deaf

'Take me to your master.'

Tansu led Matten to the garden, where Bomilcar was pacing the grounds, enjoying a sunny day. Seeing his friend, he made a few steps to meet him and welcomed him with a large smile.

'You couldn't have come at a more appropriate time,' he said. 'I have so much to tell you.'

'Me, too. Maybe it's about the same subject.'

Matten naively believed that his worry was shared by all the inhabitants of the island. The reply he received proved otherwise.

'I don't think so,' said Bomilcar. 'What I'm going to tell you has just happened. At the temple I met the woman who's going to be my wife. Her name is Chiboulet and she's from Sidon. It's about her that I want to talk.'

'Ah!' That was Matten's only reaction; although he was curious to know more about the person who had cast such a spell over his friend, he was disappointed by Bomilcar's indifference to a critical situation.

'Listen,' said Bomilcar, and he told him all about the events of the pilgrimage. He concluded saying, 'Chiboulet left this morning to go back to her parents. I'll join her in a couple of days and I want you to come with me.'

'I'll do that but we can't stay away more than one night because of the situation.'

'What's the matter with you all? Chiboulet implored me to send her home because of the situation; my mother is worried for the same reason and now it's you. I accept that the situation requires careful consideration, but it doesn't mean we have to change the course of our lives. We must pursue a normal existence and deal with a conqueror who has no quarrel with us, only with the Persians. With neither means nor desire to fight him, we must submit to his rule, recognise his authority and pay him tribute. The likelihood is that he will not linger long in the region but will be lured by the prospect of other conquests. That's what's to be expected. Now, if you tell me that arms and food should be stored as a precautionary measure, I see no objection, but I refuse to be worried for no good reason.'

Bomilcar's speech infuriated Matten, who could not comprehend how a person usually bestowed with great insight could remain blind to the imminent danger. He nevertheless endeavoured to remain calm and challenged his friend's optimistic anticipation. 'Imagine for a moment that for one reason or the other, Alexander chooses to set foot on our island. If we let him do that, we will end up with a garrison of Greeks, Macedonians and other adventurers among us. Where do you expect these soldiers to worship and offer sacrifices to their gods? In our temples and sanctuaries, of course. In no time Melqart will be supplanted by Heracles and Astarte by Aphrodite. Better to be dead than this!'

Matten's passion surprised his friend whilst giving him ground for serious thought. He refused to show that his earlier assurance had been shaken, objecting, 'We are a long way off the situation you have just described. I'll remind you that the Persians keep a garrison in Sidon and yet the gods of that City are still honoured.'

Matten countered: 'But it's not the same, far from it. The Persians worship one god who can't compete with the numerous ones we have. They know that and never tried to force their god on us.'

'Relax, my friend. Believe me, there is no real cause for concern; we at the Council have reviewed the situation and found that there is a good prospect of reaching an agreement with the Macedonian. Now, I want to hear that you will be with me when I ask Chiboulet's father to give me his daughter for a wife. I don't want to be on my own then, and I've no friend dearer than you for such a mission.'

Bomilcar's statement of friendship moved the blacksmith more than he wished to admit. To hide his emotion, he gave a conditional consent.

'Accepted,' he said, 'but on one condition; I want your promise that we'll come back the following day. There are so many things to deal with.'

'Promised. I see that you're still convinced that no arrangement can be made with him. I believe just the opposite but I see no harm in taking a few safety measures. We'll not stay in Sidon more than one night, you have my word. Now let me tell you about Chiboulet, her beauty, her courage, her other virtues.'

'I'll be glad to listen, but first tell me who are the Council members who hold the same view as mine.' It was obvious that Matten was not prepared to relinquish this fixed idea. Bomilcar obliged him.

'Abbarus is their leader,' he said with a hint of impatience in his voice.

'When we come back, will you take me to Abbarus?'

'Together we'll visit him. Satisfied?'

'Yes.'

16

Visit to the Country

The boat, deftly manoeuvred, drew smoothly alongside the quay. One of the crew members disembarked holding a rope which he fastened around a stone stuck firmly in the ground. Once the boat had been secured, he extended a hand to Bomilcar, then to Matten to help them go ashore. He neglected to do the same for Tansu, although he was unsteady, each hand being encumbered with a bundle. The slave shouted abuse at no one in particular but the unhelpful sailor countered with a string of insults concerning Tansu's mother and sister. The two protagonists being even, the exchange came to an end.

Having visited Sidon several times before, the travellers knew their way about, except that this time they were not looking for an established town merchant or craftsman, but a simple farmer who lived outside the walls. Bomilcar had tried to obtain indications from Chiboulet of how to find her father's farm, but her information lacked precision. What he could remember from her directions was to cross town, leave from the eastern gate and . . . At that juncture the explanation became confused. The two friends were not unduly concerned for they were confident that sooner or later, someone would tell them how to reach Abdalonymus's farm.

Leaving the port area, they entered the town and took an uphill street to the foot of the Acropolis. They also passed the Persian governor's mansion, the king's palace and the temple of Astarte. Eventually they came out of the city walls through the eastern gate. The first person they encountered, a peasant working his field, was able to give them the directions they needed.

From afar the farm seemed uninhabited but when they arrived, a dog ran up from the backyard and barked a couple of times, more to announce the newcomers than to intimidate them. The door was half opened by a middle-aged woman, of medium height with good-looking features. She examined the intruders with inquisitive and watchful eyes, which was to be expected from people living in the middle of nowhere.

'What do you want?' she asked.

Bomilcar knew that they had reached their destination; the woman bore a striking resemblance to Chiboulet. 'She must be her mother or her aunt,' he thought.

'We're looking for Abdalonymus's farm. Is this the place?'

Barely had he finished his question than a brief joyful cry was heard from the interior. Then the door opened completely and Chiboulet stood beside the other woman.

'I recognised your voice immediately,' she said. 'I'm overjoyed to see you here.'

She hastened to explain the reason for her friendly reception. 'Mother this is Bomilcar, my saviour and Jason's.'

The mother's face relaxed and she stepped aside to allow them to come in. 'Abdalonymus will return any moment now. You're welcome to wait for him inside.'

The room they went into was small but spotless. It was furnished with three stools and a beautiful woollen carpet, which appeared incongruous in the simple environment. Bomilcar and Matten took a seat each, while Tansu sat on the floor in one corner. The two women left.

Soon Chiboulet came back with a wine jug in one hand and two cups between the fingers of the other. She directed Tansu to go to the kitchen to join the household slave.

While she poured the wine, she and Bomilcar exchanged looks as tender as caresses and as eloquent as any love pledge. When it was Matten's turn to be served with wine, Bomilcar presented his dearest friend, and Chiboulet gave him an exquisite smile which conquered him instantly.

Unable to stay longer with the two men she stepped outside the house, most probably to intercept her father before he got in and to tell him who his visitors were.

Chiboulet's warm welcome and behaviour rejoiced Bomilcar and left him with no doubt that his love was reciprocated. Their four day separation had given the young woman an opportunity to order her confused thoughts after the dramatic events she had suffered and interrogate her heart about the true nature of her feelings towards the young man.

Alone with Matten, Bomilcar was anxious to sound out his friend. 'Isn't she how I'd described to you?' he asked.

'And better,' came the answer, which filled him with joy.

At this juncture a man in his fifties entered the room. He was slim and tall, with a white beard that made his tanned face stand out revealing that he was an outdoor person. He was followed by Chiboulet and her mother, whose name was Artas.

'This humble house is yours,' he said to Bomilcar. 'You've saved my daughter and my grandson from a terrible ordeal and a despicable person. I'll be indebted to you for the rest of my life.'

'I did what any man would have done. My friend Matten here would have fared much better than I did; on the other hand it's highly improbable that Tubal would have confronted him.'

'You'll have dinner with us and stay with us as long as you wish.' Abdalonymus's invitation was made in a tone which did not allow any argument; it also suited Bomilcar admirably so he accepted it straightaway. He then called Tansu and ordered him to fetch one of the two bundles which nearly had caused the slave to fall in the water.

From that bundle, the young man removed a piece of linen, a small box inlaid with carved ivory plates and a golden chain with a coralline pendant. He spread the precious objects on the floor, drank a sip of wine for courage, and said: 'I wish to wed Chiboulet. I have come to ask your permission; if you consent I would like to take her with me. Please accept these modest presents.' He indicated the material and the box. 'The chain,' he specified, 'is for Chiboulet. I beg of you to allow our two families to unite . . . '

With a smile in lieu of an apology, Abdalonymus raised his hand to interrupt him. 'I already know Chiboulet's feelings towards you and I'm glad to give you my permission, but she cannot leave straightaway.' With another gesture, he frustrated Bomilcar's attempt to interrupt. 'You must be tired. Follow my slave, he will show you to your room. Have some rest and then come back for dinner; we'll continue our conversation then.'

Bomilcar had no chance to object; he and his friend followed the slave. The young man was bewildered; the old man's words and his reception had been extremely amicable; but why could Chiboulet not leave immediately? Why the delay? What obstacle prevented their immediate marriage? He threw all these questions at his friend, who tried to find an answer that would assuage the impatient lover. Out of arguments, he finally told Bomilcar, 'If we spend less time wondering about Abdalonymus's reasons, we'll be informed much, much sooner.'

17

Unwelcome Delay

The three men sat on the carpet cross-legged, and waited for the food prepared by Chiboulet and Artas to be brought to them. From the kitchen came Tansu and the household slave carrying a large copper tray laden with food on earthenware plates.

They placed the tray on the carpet and stepped back, ready to satisfy the diners' demands. The food was simple: bread, olives, cheese, an omelette and a green salad. Local wine was also served.

As a mark of confidence in his guests, Abdalonymus invited his wife and daughter to eat with them. Although Bomilcar was anxious to resume the discussion, the conversation revolved around the events which had taken place at the temple. Genuinely worried about Chiboulet's safety, and seeking an excuse for her to leave Sidon with him, the young man said: 'I apologise if I appear indiscreet but there is one question which is burning my lips. I'm going to voice it because I care for you and Chiboulet. Have you been troubled by the priests or the authorities since her return home?'

Abdalonymus reassured him, 'Not in the least. I presume that current events are of more concern to everyone here than Tubal's accidental death'

Matten gave his friend a triumphant look as if to tell him, 'You see, Alexander's progress is a cause of worry.'

Bomilcar pretended not to have understood the mute message, while Abdalonymus expounded his view. 'You mentioned the authorities, but which do you mean? The Persian governor and his garrison left Sidon when they heard of Byblos's surrender. Strato, the King they chose, is not listened to, the population hate him because of his servility.'

This time it was Bomilcar who turned towards Matten with a satisfied look as if to say, 'What did I tell you? Alexander will not meet opposition and therefore no reprisals and no siege are to be expected.'

The silent dialogue went unnoticed and Abdalonymus pursued his assessment of the situation. 'No one can predict exactly what's going to happen. That's why I've decided to keep Chiboulet and her son by my side until we have a clearer view. When the uncertainty is dispelled I'll be more than happy to give you my daughter. In a while we'll know more.'

Bomilcar could not accept a delay of even one day. 'Because the situation here is uncertain, please allow me to take your daughter and grandson to a safer place. The sooner they leave the better. In Tyre they will have nothing to fear if you so desire, all of you can come as well.'

The old man shook his head. 'I don't believe Chiboulet and

Jason will be sheltered from danger in Tyre; in fact I believe the opposite. The sea and the mighty walls count for little to Alexander.'

Carried away by his youthful ardour, Bomilcar broke all rules of good manners and interrupted. 'He didn't set foot in Aradus, why should it be otherwise when it comes to Tyre?'

'It's not the same.'

'I don't understand why.'

'Alexander would never turn his back on a fortified island which declares itself to be neutral but remains in possession of a powerful war fleet. He did not leave his pursuit of Darius for a later day, electing instead to subdue the Phoenician cities and control their ports, to discard the most powerful of those cities, the one which would constitute a grave danger at the first military setback he might suffer. No, my young friend, you'd do better to stay here until things are clearer.'

The old man's words stunned his guests who asked themselves: 'How could a simple farmer know that much?'

For the time being Matten was afraid that Bomilcar might be tempted to accept Abdalonymus's invitation, not out of fear but to stay with the woman he loved. He did not need to concern himself; Bomilcar's thoughts were in turmoil. 'What if Chiboulet's father is right? What if Tyre is in danger?' Aloud, he said, 'If you believe that Chiboulet's safety is more guaranteed here, I'm prepared to wait. As for your kind invitation, I must decline it. Believe me, this decision is very hard for me to take. However, duty dictates that I should be with my compatriots at a time like this.'

Having said these words, Bomilcar looked towards his friend, expecting to see a triumphant glimmer in his eyes. To his amazement, all he could see was a tough man very much moved.

18

Perfect Harmony

Back in the room they shared, the Tyrians were not in the mood to engage in any kind of conversation. Matten had been made aware that, added to his fear of seeing his gods upstaged by foreign ones, he also must expect the disarmament of Tyrian ports and the commandeering of the Tyrian fleet by the Macedonian. Bomilcar's fanciful world had disintegrated under the Sidonian's striking words, which had crushed the illusory walls he had erected around his person. He felt ashamed by his earlier refusal to see the obvious.

They lay in their beds and tried to sleep. Merciful torpor came to Matten after a while, confirmed by vigorous snoring, but Bomilcar was unable to rest. He focused his thoughts on Chiboulet, with whom he had not spoken throughout the evening; he had to remain worthy of his host's confidence, give him all his attention and display no interest in Chiboulet or her mother. Although they had not exchanged words, their eyes were eloquent enough and her mere presence had increased his desire to possess her. He could imagine her magnificent body which would be his very soon, if the gods were in their favour.

He left his bed, making sure not to wake his companion or any member of the household, covered himself with his cloak and went out to get fresh air. Two lit torches were placed on each side of the farm to keep wild animals at bay. The dog who had announced his and Matten's arrival was asleep next to the entrance; he opened an eye to make sure that there was no intruder and then went back to sleep. Without the flickering light dispensed by the torches, the young man would have been unable to find his way, for thick clouds concealed the moon and the stars. He paced up and down the yard and from time to time he heard the howling of wolves and the screeching of hyenas. He was not completely at ease, for he had spent all his life in a city located on an island and was not accustomed to hearing these sinister voices. He shivered and turned to go back inside.

He saw a figure standing on the doorstep and recognised Chiboulet. He went to her and took her by the hand to lead her somewhere they could not be heard or seen. She followed him to a place where the branches of an old fig tree provided shelter. He kissed her face; when their lips touched, she put her arms round him, which made him more daring. Without relinquishing his embrace he started fondling her, exploring intimate parts of her body. Her passionate response to his caresses exacerbated his desire. Spreading his cloak on the ground, he made her lie down on her back. She did not offer any resistance or affect a prudish demeanour but extended her arms towards him, uncovering her white skin, which glimmered in the dark. He crushed her and kissed her face, lips and breasts, caressing her thighs.

Afterwards they lay side by side wrapped in their cloaks, relishing their pleasure in silence. Eventually, Chiboulet said, 'I couldn't sleep.'

'Do you have any regrets?' he asked.

She gave a brief loveable laugh before answering, 'What do you think? I knew what to expect, that's why I followed you.'

She had no reason to be constrained, and nor did he. Their gods lived as couples and engaged in carnal relationships; following this example, their religion did not consider sex to be taboo, but as a most natural act.

He leaned over her and caressed her face, 'Leave with me,' he pleaded.

She sighed which was as good as a reply. Nevertheless she gave him an answer: 'I cannot disobey my father and my mother would be terribly upset. I can't do that to them, not after the protection and the shelter they gave me when I found myself alone with an infant. I'm convinced that everything will be sorted out in a matter of days, then I'll join you, never to leave you.'

The tender words moved Bomilcar. Deep down, he was convinced of their relevance, so he did not insist.

Part Two

I

Sidon's Surrender

Halfway between Berytus and Sidon, Alexander's army had set up camp by the banks of the river Tamyras on the piece of land that extended between the green slopes of Mount Libanus and the blue Mediterranean sea. Fresh drinking water was plentiful, as were the produce of the sea and the land. Fish, game, vegetables and fruit were a welcome substitute for the poor rations of the ordinary soldier, which usually consisted of bread, cheese, olives and anything edible he could lay his hands on. Hundreds of tents made of hides were pitched in rows forming a circle; in the centre, the king's tents were connected to a huge pavilion which could accommodate up to one hundred people.

Moored by the mouth of the river were transport ships used to carry supplies: siege equipment and long-range catapults; stone-throwers; and other war machines designed by the Greek engineer Polyeidus of Thessaly. The engineer's pupils had produced a siege train that was much more advanced than anything available at the time; the newly invented springs and torsions doubled the range and power of their war machines.

For the time being these machines were stored, unassembled, in the ships, while on land soldiers went about their menial tasks peacefully, as did their women and slaves. It was obvious that no action was contemplated.

The army's splendid victory at Issus opened the Mediterranean coast wide before the young conqueror. With the peaceful surrender of Aradus and Byblos, Sidon and Tyre would necessarily follow. There was little doubt about it. Had not the Persian governor and garrison fled from Sidon? Was there not a Sidonian delegation in the tent of General Hephaestion at that very moment, to make the city capitulate officially? Had not Alexander and a small group of his Royal Bodyguards gone hunting wild boar in the dense woods of Mount Libanus?

Macedonian hoplites and cavalrymen, who had fought with their king in the north of the kingdom, then in the Greek cities that rebelled after his father's death, could not be wrong: if their king was having a good time hunting, it could only mean that there was no battle in sight and a well deserved rest could be enjoyed.

In short, the camp's mood was relaxed, and what was taking place inside Hephaestion's tent would have reinforced that mood if only the ordinary soldiers were able to witness the ceremony of Sidon's surrender, a victory without bloodshed.

The Sidonian delegation comprised six dignitaries who had arrived with a train of mules laden with gifts to offer the city's surrender to Alexander as well as the golden crown, in acknowledgement of his authority. They were received by Hephaestion, Alexander's most trusted general. The king's absence would make them realise how of little importance they were.

'Noble lord!' said Ennion, the man who seemed to be heading the delegation, 'we came to offer the great King Sidon's total and unconditional submission. We implore you to regard us as the most humble and obedient subjects of the great King, our liberator.' He continued: 'Please allow me, my lord, to speak my mind and bring to your attention a matter of the greatest importance.'

Towering above the delegation, Hephaestion listened to the man, curious to know what he had to say

'Victorious general!' said the Sidonian, 'you should know that Strato, the king of our city, is not worthy of your trust. We implore you to remove him and appoint a person who will be entirely devoted to our liberators.'

Although much more informed than the members of the delegation suspected, the general affected complete unawareness and posed a question, the answer to which he already knew. 'What do you have against your king?'

'He's the Persians' man. They imposed him on us and it's only fair that he goes with them. Most importantly, his dependency on his masters will manifest itself on the first occasion and that makes him a dangerous liability; he cannot be trusted.'

Hephaestion listened without saying a word; now his long nose quivered, a sign that anger was mounting in him. He was appalled by the delegates' treachery, having been informed by his chief spy of the background of each one of them. He knew that Ennion had been the closest adviser to the king up until a day or two ago; he also knew that two other delegates still held high office at Strato's court and that all the members of the delegation had agreed on who was going to be the next king. Hephaestion was certain that if he pursued his questioning, Ennion's name would eventually be put forward.

The army man had neither the time nor the propensity to beat about the bush; a victor is rarely magnanimous when the loser is visibly about to deceive him, trying to turn a defeat to his advantage. He decided to teach the delegates a lesson, at the same time making them realise that their new masters had a perfect knowledge of the situation within their city.

He made a few steps forward. The Sidonians, who were standing before him, heads bent in submission, could not refrain from shivering.

'Were you not the first counsellor to Strato?' he said to Ennion, 'and you, were you not responsible for his food and, you, for his horses? Have you no shame in betraying the man who showered you with favours?'

The delegates were terrified by Hephaestion's angry words and contemptuous demeanour and became convinced that their time was near. Instinctively, those delegates who had not been mentioned moved away from their three unhappy colleagues.

Their terror was justified for Hephaestion's impulsive reaction would have been to cut off their tongues and noses; nevertheless he restrained himself because of the strict orders issued by Alexander following the fall of the City of Ephesus.

When that city had fallen to the Macedonian, the mob unleashed its anger against the ruling class, which had been appointed by the Persians, and stoned a great number of them to death. More massacres were frustrated by Alexander, who ordered that from then on no one belonging to the local administration appointed by the Persians would be subjected to any sort of harassment, provided that the seat of that administration had surrendered without combat.

Reluctantly, Alexander's companion dismissed the delegation with words which left no doubt about his intentions.

'Sidon's surrender is accepted,' he said, 'go back to whence you came. I will choose your next king and none of you is among my candidates.'

The delegation rushed out, unbelieving that they had got off so lightly. Without wasting a moment, they jumped on their mules and left, before the general could change his mind. It took some time for their stunned servants and slaves to realise that the initiative was left to them; when they did, they gathered together the train and followed suit.

2

A Master Spy

'Come out,' ordered Hephaestion. The cloth which divided the tent was lifted and Lysinias stepped from his hiding place.

'Did you hear these vile hypocrites?' said the general, more a comment than a question. His interlocutor took it as such and remained silent, his deportment respectful. Although he had been the source of valuable information, much needed by Alexander's army advancing through unknown and often hostile territory, he was careful not to overstep his station. He had been a spy for the Macedonians since the day he was about to be thrown out of the Kingdom to start his exile. The army officer who had approached him after his sentence had pledged that he would be able to see his son earlier, if he agreed to spy on the Persians in anticipation of the planned invasion of Asia.

He had enlisted in Darius's army as a mercenary, communicating whenever possible with the emissaries sent by his recruiting officer. He had participated in the battle at Granicus, seemingly on the Persian side; when they had been defeated, the ensuing rout had enabled his return to his real camp. Fortunately his recruiting officer was still around, so he reminded him of his promise to allow his return to Pella before serving his sentence in full.

The officer showed signs of uneasiness, an indication that he was prepared to renege on his promise. This is what he did, claiming that Lysinias's activities had been invaluable and were still much needed. He promised him a handsome reward if he carried on with his mission for a little longer.

It was obvious to Lysinias that he was left with no real choice, so he had accepted the offer, but his state of mind troubled him: although he missed his son and longed to hold him in his arms, the decision he had been forced to take had affected him much less than he had expected. Eventually he came to realise that he had become fond of his covert work, more particularly of his power over the people he had deceived. On no account would he acknowledge that feeling to anyone, lest he lose the moral edge he had gained in sacrificing an early return home to continue his dangerous task.

After Alexander decided to take his army towards the Mediterranean coast, Lysinias's mission had consisted of stays in Sidon and Tyre using his cover as a travelling trinket merchant who had also fought with the Persians. As expected, his trips had allowed him to gather intelligence and spread disinformation.

This success so far had brought him to the attention of Hephaestion, who considered him his master spy. That was why he had been listening behind the curtain and why he had been privy to the general's outraged reflection after they left.

'What hypocrisy!' repeated the general, who added, 'You were right about them and about Strato; at least we know the colour of the latter. I wonder whether he would serve Alexander as well as he has served Darius. What is your view?'

'With my lord's permission, I'd advise against that, for the people of Sidon hate the Persians. For them, the king personifies Persian occupation. What the Sidonians need is a new king.'

'Do you know of such a man?' asked Hephaestion.

'Unfortunately I didn't have the opportunity to find out whether such a candidate exists. It was not a subject I could easily explore before Sidon's surrender. What I can say is that no name was mentioned in my presence. Of course, now that the circumstances have changed I can go back to Sidon and start enquiring.'

'No, said the general, 'I'll do that myself. You're needed in Tyre.'

'It will be as you order, my lord.'

'I'll spend some time in Sidon, so find me a lodging place. You can do that on your way to Tyre. Now tell me about that city. What is the situation there and what did you do for us?'

The spy reflected on how his report could remain cautious in its assessment whilst inflating his own role. The army man grew impatient. 'What's the matter, Lysinias, have you lost your tongue?'

'On the whole, my lord, the Tyrian population feel safe on their island, behind solid walls and protected by a powerful navy. What I did was to encourage a group of influential Council members, headed by a certain Chelbes, to yield to the might of our king. I believe that this group seeks peace at any cost.'

The general did not seem completely satisfied; he said, 'Our scouts at sea have noticed a very dense traffic of vessels entering and leaving the northern port. Do you know what's going on?'

The secret agent realised that he had made a mistake in not

mentioning the Council's decision to store food and weapons; that omission could be damaging to his reputation and credibility, so he endeavoured to recover the ground he might have lost.

'Ah! That is a cautionary measure demanded by a handful of Councillors . . . '

The general interrupted him, asking, 'How many are they? Does the population listen to them?'

'They aren't many, my lord, maybe five or six. Their leader is an extremist, Abbarus is his name. The population is on the whole, as I said, rather unconcerned.'

'One man by himself could be very threatening if, during times of danger, he had the skill to arouse the indifferent masses. Is this Abbarus capable of doing that?'

The question required a straight answer, which Lysinias knew would be used against him if subsequent events were to prove him wrong. To keep on the safe side he chose not to play down Abbarus's influence and authority. 'The man is a fanatic and a good speaker. If he were to address the People's Assembly, he might well incite them to rise against those who advocate accommodation . . . '

'This man cannot be allowed to live. Kill him before he does more harm. Go now. You know what to do.'

3

Alexander

A commotion brought Hephaestion outside his tent. Alexander and his party were returning from the hunt at a gallop, amidst a cloud of dust. The young conqueror reigned in his black horse by the entrance of his tents and leapt off the magnificent beast. His party dismounted as well and gathered round their leader, waiting to hear what he was inclined to do next. The attendants began collecting the game the hunters had killed and the weapons they had used to kill them.

Alexander's well-proportioned body made him look taller than he was and his clean-shaven face was strikingly beautiful. Under a crown of curled blond hair cropped round his forehead, his eyes, one blue and the other black, had unsettled more than one interlocutor.

He ignored his companions, took Hephaestion by the arm, moved aside with him and enquired, 'Well?'

'As you ordered. I received the Sidonian delegates and accepted the surrender of their city. They . . . '

Satisfied, Alexander interrupted. 'We'll talk about serious matters after I have bathed.' Turning towards his companions, he asked, but did not wait for a reply; 'A run to the river?'

Following the king's example, Craterus, Perdiccas, Ptolemy and Seleucus, Alexander's devoted comrades in arms, started taking off their garments, soiled by sweat and dust, throwing them left and right as they ran behind him towards the river. They all arrived completely naked. Whether in sporting events or in battle, Alexander was always in the vanguard and usually the victor.

Hephaestion was not keen to swim, but his hesitation lasted only a few seconds. He was unwilling to stay away from his king, particularly when he was surrounded by the other courtiers, some of whom Hephaestion hated simply for being as close to Alexander as he was. He was not alone; nearly all the king's familiars were jealous of his other intimates.

Hephaestion joined the party, which stayed frolicking in the cold waters until enjoined by the king to return to their tents and wait to be summoned to a working session.

As Alexander emerged from the water, his athletic white body was wrapped by his servants in a large piece of linen. Inside his sleeping quarters, he surrendered to their hands. His body was rubbed with olive oil and scraped with a pumice stone and a silver scraper. Perfume was doused on him while he crunched an apple, a fruit he was very fond of.

His toilet finished, he ordered that Barsine be brought in. His newly acquired mistress had been found in Damascus, one of the spoils of war taken from Darius after his defeat at Issus. Barsine was already known to Alexander who had seen the beautiful girl, ten years older than him, as a little boy when her exiled Persian father brought his family to Pella. Now in her early thirties, she was a beautiful widow, having been married to a Greek who had chosen to serve the Persian King. When he died, she married his brother, who was also in the service of the Persian camp. Because she was of royal blood on her mother's side, she had remained with the Persian court after his death.

Parmenion, the second in command, had been sent to Damascus to seize Darius's treasures. That was when the well-mannered Barsine had made herself known to him and had informed him of her old acquaintance with the young conqueror. Sent to Alexander, she had instantly enchanted the young man just as she had enthralled the small boy.

She came to him in no time, beautifully radiant. Her light blue dress seemed to be covering thin air and not her tall slender body; her well-marked nose was not an imperfection, but gave her nacreous face an intelligent dimension, often denied to excessive perfection. Alexander opened his arms to her and they made love. Homosexuality, experienced during his youth and still practised occasionally, did not exclude carnal relations with the opposite sex.

Gratified, he played the lyre, inviting her with a motion of his head to sing. She sang an excerpt from The Iliad, a copy of which, annotated by Aristotle, he kept permanently in his living quarter.

After a short while his mood suddenly changed, an occurrence which often took his interlocutors by surprise. He slipped on a purple tunic and ordered that Aristander, his favourite seer be brought to him. Barsine was completely ignored and left on the tips of her toes.

The old white-bearded seer from Telmessos entered Alexander's tent and stood motionless, leaning on his long staff, from which hung a small leather satchel. The satchel contained knucklebones to be thrown on the ground with a single movement of the hand. He made predictions based on the way they had landed.

Alexander did not like this particular method of prophecy and the seer knew it, so he resorted to the knucklebones only when he had no other sign to guide him.

The Macedonian had made up his mind about the military strategy he had to follow after Issus; he was convinced of the necessity of controlling all Phoenician ports before setting off into the hinterland in pursuit of Darius. Nevertheless, he needed reassurance about the issue of his coastal campaign, so Aristander had been asked to look at any sign which boded well.

'Anything to tell me?'

'Yes, my lord King; on my way to you I saw a flight of birds high in the sky.'

'What does this tell you?' asked Alexander.

'The birds were flying high in the sky in the direction of the south. It means that you will be successful in capturing all the southern ports and your fame will continue rising to the limit of the sky.'

'Take this phial of perfume and pour it on your hairless scalp.' Mentioning the seer's bald head in a playful manner was a clear indication that Alexander was pleased with the old man's interpretation of the omen.

4

Strategy

Standing round a table covered with maps, Alexander, his four companions of their earlier hunting party and Hephaestion were discussing military matters. Also present was Callisthene, Aristotle's cousin, not there in any martial capacity but as an historian following the king on his Asian venture to chronicle his deeds.

'My priority now is to make sure that the fifty or so warships manned by Sidonians and still on the high seas return to Sidon. They shouldn't be given any other choice they must certainly not be allowed to remain under Persian command or to take refuge in a Tyrian port.'

Alexander paused and his military staff waited for him to disclose how he intended to achieve that objective without a war fleet.

'The families of the sailors,' he carried on, 'should not be allowed to leave Sidon. This does not mean that they are to be held prisoners; we do not know who they are nor do I wish to antagonise the population which has declared its allegiance to me. So Sidon and the immediate countryside must be garrisoned and a strong military presence left there, even after I march on Tyre. Henceforth the sailors will find out that the only way for them to be reunited with their families is to come back to Sidon with their ships.'

His plan disclosed, Alexander turned to specific issues. He asked Perdiccas, the infantry commander, 'What's the distance between here and Sidon?'

'The Greek surveyors I sent yesterday reported that on foot it could be covered in three hours.'

'Good. Take one thousand shield bearers and secure the city. You, Hephaestion, will follow him after two days with a contingent of five hundred men and enter Sidon. You have two objectives there: control the town and choose a new king. Any name so far?'

'The delegation I saw this morning had in mind one of its members as a candidate. I refused to listen because nearly all of them are Strato's courtiers and were prepared to betray him.'

Indignantly, the king cried out, 'That's a horrible crime, they should be put to death!'

'I was tempted to do just that, then I remembered your orders,' said Hephaestion.

'Yes, of course,' said Alexander, recalling the policy he had decreed after the fall of Ephesus. 'What you have to do,' he instructed, 'is to find a king who will not betray me the moment I turn my back. Now, do we have any latest information regarding Tyre?'

'We have,' replied Hephaestion. 'The population seems rather unconcerned with our progress. However, there is one member of the Council of the Elders who could represent trouble. He has convinced the Council to ready the island to sustain a siege. For the time being he has a limited number of followers but his influence could increase rapidly. I've ordered that he be killed before he becomes a real threat.'

'You did the right thing,' approved Alexander, who then turned towards the other commanders who had been silently listening, and proceeded with his instructions. 'Craterus, take a small party, survey the mountain above the camp and see if you can find wood suitable for the construction of siege engines and battlefield machines. If Tyre resists, we will need plenty of planks and beams.'

'Unless you order otherwise I'll choose one or two Phoenician carpenters who speak our language from among the auxiliaries who followed us after Byblos's surrender. Their mastery will be useful and they will assist our communications with the inhabitants of the mountain villages. I do not expect those people to speak anything but their own language.'

'Do that but don't antagonise the villagers. Buy their wood and their services. I've taken enough gold and silver from Darius to afford that.'

All of a sudden a matter of vital importance, neglected so far, rushed into Alexander's mind. He exclaimed, looking at Hephaestion, 'The Carthaginians! No one told me about them. Would they come to the assistance of their Mother City, if attacked? Do you have any information in this regard?'

Taken by surprise, Hephaestion was utterly embarrassed; he had neglected to question Lysinias about that important issue. He tried to cover his blunder by putting the blame on the latter.

'My spy told me nothing about the Carthaginian delegation. I'll reprimand him and send him strict instructions to discover the extent of the assistance that the African colony is prepared to give to an embattled Tyre.'

Craterus, who hated Hephaestion, smiled sneeringly in an attempt to attract Alexander's attention to the mistake, but the latter pretended not to notice. He went to Callisthene and leaned over his shoulder, trying to read the notes he had been taking. Restless as he was, he did not dwell on them, choosing instead to question the historian. 'Did you write down everything I said?'

'Yes sire, how could I miss a word uttered by the new Achilles.'

None of those present dared smile, and the sycophantic answer went down well with Alexander and put him in a good mood. He gave orders to the attendants to prepare a banquet for the evening to celebrate the surrender. Visibly, Ptolemy was not in the same cheerful spirit as his companions and he told Alexander the reason. 'You didn't assign me any mission.'

Ptolemy was the king's childhood friend and because of that he could speak his mind; Seleucos, a junior member of Alexander's staff, did not have that privilege and remained quiet although he too had no specific orders.

'All that's left for the time being,' said Alexander, 'is to hire women dancers for the evening. I didn't want to burden you with that task.' Ptolemy was known for his great reserve, which was often the gentle butt of the king's jokes. Everyone, including Ptolemy laughed.

5
Conundrum

As Lysinias was leaving the Macedonian camp, he was given a large purse full of gold Daric staters. He was also provided with two armed men wearing no distinctive uniform; their task was to protect him against the bandits who were roaming the countryside following the collapse of the Persian administration.

On the way south, he was engulfed by his thoughts, trying to find a safe way to perform his seemingly conflicting missions. To disclose his true allegiance could jeopardise his other mission should his sudden metamorphosis be noted by a Tyrian spy and reported to home.

His second assignment was the most important and the most dangerous, so he decided not to increase the risk. What he finally resolved to do was to set up camp outside Sidon's walls and remain out of sight, using his two guards as emissaries to establish contact with an innkeeper who gave him shelter whenever he came to Sidon. The man hid neither his hatred of the Persians nor his Greek inclinations; without knowing, he had been a source of valuable information. That sort of person would be useful and would not betray him.

Having found a solution to what at first had seemed an impossible situation, he relaxed and let himself be gently moved back and forth at the rate of his horse's hoofbeats. Only now did he notice the scenery rolling past him; on one side was the sea, heavy, as was usually the case when winter drew near; on the other were high hills, densely wooded and sparsely populated. He was not a contemplative person by nature and the beauty of the view left him indifferent. He speeded up and his two companions followed suit;

after a while they reached the river Bostrenus, which they crossed. When Sidon's walls came within sight, they pitched their tent in a orchard of pomegranate, almond and fig trees.

Lysinias sent for the innkeeper, who arrived a couple of hours later, visibly worried, not knowing what to expect. When he was brought inside the tent and realised that the person who had summoned him was the same one he had always seen as a Macedonian renegade, he became terrified. He believed he was the intended victim of a Persian bid for revenge because of his well-known political ideas.

Fear was written all over his face and the words which came out of his mouth expressed his sudden deep regret for the departure of the Persian governor. Lysinias interrupted him before he could embark too far in that direction and embarrass himself. He reassured him, 'Don't worry, you're among friends who share your ideas, at least those you had before setting foot in this tent. I brought you here because I need your services.'

No explanation was given by the spy about what seemed to be his new allegiance and the innkeeper was too frightened to ask for one. He hardly believed that he was out of danger and his instinct of self-preservation warned him to keep quiet lest curiosity brought back the state of terror he had experienced a moment ago. He bowed obsequiously and responded, 'Just tell me how I can be of service.'

'In a matter of days Alexander's envoy will visit Sidon. I need to find him proper and safe lodgings for the length of his stay. Knowing your feelings, I thought you might be able to help.'

The explanation left the innkeeper bewildered. He could not understand why the royal palace would not be used to accommodate the envoy. All the latter would have to do was depose or execute the king and take over his residence. He did not dare express what was going through his mind and tried to be helpful, 'In my view, the place that is worthy of Alexander's envoy is the mansion which belongs to two local gentlemen, Theron and Tryphon.'

'What do they do?'

'They are from very good families and one of them, Theron, inherited a vast fortune from his father. I don't know if he has ever needed to work.'

'Are they not brothers?' asked Lysinias.

'No, lovers.'

'So much the better!' The interjection baffled the innkeeper more than ever; he could not possibly know that the envoy in question would be more comfortable in the company of men. The spy did not pay attention to the effect of his curt remark on the innkeeper and resumed his questioning. 'Are you sure that they have always opted for the Greek camp?'

'I'm positive about it that is why King Strato never gave either of them an office or allowed them at his court.'

'That‘s convincing. Now, tell me about their mansion. Where is it located? Is it worthy of the envoy's rank?'

The probing vexed the innkeeper, who had not expected his choice of accommodation to be doubted. He gave the required indication nevertheless. It seemed to be to Lysinias's satisfaction, for he eventually issued his instructions: 'Tell Theron and Tryphon to make the necessary preparations for the envoy's stay. Above all, tell them that they should keep their lips sealed until his arrival. That goes for you too. If a word about the envoy's planned sojourn slips out, I would know who is responsible and the culprit would have to expect a terrible retribution.'

To tone down his threatening words, Lysinias drew a gold Daric from his purse and gave it to the innkeeper with encouraging words. 'This is from the great king, take it. He's aware of your loyalty and wished to reward you.'

The man could not believe his ears; he was elated with joy and blared his feelings. 'I'm ready to die for the great king. Just tell me what to do.'

Lysinias calmed him and sent him back to the city.

The following day he was about to strike camp when Hephaestion's emissary arrived on horseback. The general wanted information about Carthage's likely disposition in case of war with Tyre. Lysinias had no information but promised to find out.

6

Carried Away

'Chiboulet should have left with me. I should have insisted. I'm worried and I miss her.'

On their way to visit Abbarus, Bomilcar was pouring out his feelings to Matten who, although sorry for his friend, was unable to comprehend his obsession with matters of the heart at a time when deadly danger was looming over their city. Nevertheless, their friendship prompted him to show him sympathy.

'What I've heard,' he said, 'is that no one is allowed to leave Sidon. I don't understand why but those are the orders of the new Greek governor.'

'I don't understand it either but the result is the same; Chiboulet cannot come to me. Maybe I should go to her.'

'Are you mad? Do you want to be held by the Greeks while the fate of our city is in the balance?' The blacksmith became agitated; the last thing he wanted was to be parted from Bomilcar, and lose a potential supporter for the cause.

Bomilcar did not give him a direct answer but said reflectively, as if talking to himself, 'There must be a way to get to Sidon and come back without being noticed.'

'If there is such a way I don't know about it,' responded the blacksmith curtly.

Eventually they reached their destination, which was Abbarus's house, a tall, narrow building in a densely populated sector of the island. A young man let them in and they found themselves in a hall which received sparse sunrays from one small opening high in the wall. When their eyes became accustomed to the dim light they noticed six or seven young men seated on benches placed against the walls. The young men remained motionless, staring at the newcomers without uttering a word. That made Bomilcar feel uneasy.

Fortunately, he and Matten were promptly taken to the first floor and left on their own. The room had two windows, which made it bright but not welcoming, for all it had for furniture were a dozen small, inexpensive chairs on a bare floor. Obviously that was the place where Abbarus held his political meetings.

He was not in there but arrived soon after in the company of two young men, one of whom was the person who had received them. The hard-line councillor was a middle-aged man who gave the impression of being older, for he never smiled and his lean body was bent under the weight of heavy responsibility. His black beard was well trimmed and his clothes were simple but neat.

His welcome was courteous but not particularly warm. It was clear that Bomilcar, the one person he already knew well, had no high place in his esteem; the young man's established reputation as a pleasure-seeker did not accord with his ascetic standards.

After the usual exchange of polite formulas, Bomilcar introduced the blacksmith. 'Matten, son of Meges, is my childhood friend. I don't know if you ever saw him in Melqart's temple; he's the one responsible for keeping the sacred fire going.'

Abbarus nodded to convey that Matten was no stranger to him and Bomilcar explained the reason for their visit. 'Matten has a bleak view of the future. He believes that a golden crown and sumptuous gifts will not satisfy Alexander who will seek anyway to occupy our island. He's heard from me that you are convinced of the same and that prompted you to take action. At his request I brought him here.'

Bomilcar turned towards his friend as if to tell him, 'Now it's for you to explain what you expect from this meeting?'

Matten read the wordless message. 'I can't stand the idea of Greek soldiers being allowed to set foot on our island and to worship in our temples. I'm prepared to die rather than let these outrages take place. I came to you for guidance.'

Having said that much, the otherwise reserved Matten waited for Abbarus's reaction. The expression on their host's face remained unchanged, but he whispered in the ear of one of the two young men present, who left the room. A few moments later he came back followed by a young male slave carrying a wine jug and cups.

'Put it here, Laïs,' ordered Abbarus indicating one empty chair, 'and serve us the wine.'

The lad's demeanour while he carried out the order indicated that he was most unhappy. Having reluctantly served the wine he left. After a few sips, the mood in the room became more relaxed.

'The people you see in this house,' said Abbarus, 'are all of the same disposition of mind. When they came to me I started preparing them for the difficult time ahead. Idbal, on my right, proved to be a born organiser, so I put him in charge of mobilising people for our cause. Anysos, on my left, is a good soldier, a leader of men; he is in charge of the drills. And you, Matten, what do you do?'

'I'm a blacksmith.'

'That's exactly what we need. Persuade craftsmen with your own skill to manufacture and stockpile arrows, harpoons, swords and mechanisms for catapults and other weapons.'

Matten's face became as red as his hair with excitement.

'When do I start?' he asked.

'You've started now. And you, brother Bomilcar, can we expect any helping hand from you?'

The direct question caught the young man off guard. As promised, he had taken Matten to the hard-liner's den, but he had never envisaged getting involved himself in what was going on here. Now he was less sure, perhaps he had been contaminated by the nationalistic ambience and he heard himself saying, 'I'll be happy to help financially.'

He also felt the urge to explain why he could not give more than his gold. 'You see,' he said apologetically, 'I have an urgent matter in hand. Maybe later I will be able to do more.'

By then he was angry with himself; not only had he been carried away; he was left with an annoying guilt that he had not done enough.

Having taken leave of their host, he made a point of resuming the discussion he and Matten had been having on their way to the meeting, as if to prove to himself and his friend that his priorities had remained unchanged. They were standing in the street outside Abbarus's door before they separated into different directions.

'I want to see Chiboulet. I need to know she is safe. Most of all I miss her. I beg of you,' said Bomilcar, 'help me go back to Sidon.'

'If I knew of a way for you to go there and come back safely, believe me I would tell you, but I don't. What I can do for you is to think it over and to ask around; maybe there's such a way after all,' replied Matten.

The two friends parted without paying any attention to the man who was hidden behind a heap of refuse in an alley with a direct view of Abbarus's house. From his post he was keeping close watch.

7

Gullible Recruit

The man keeping watch was Lysinias, back in Tyre with two missions in hand. There was Hephaestion's order to kill Abbarus, a more difficult assignment to carry out than he had first believed, for the intended victim was surrounded by his partisans whenever he left home. The other task was equally daunting: it required one of the councillors to tell a stranger what sort of assistance the African colony was prepared to provide if its mother city were attacked by Alexander.

In addition to being difficult, both assignments were equally important; for that reason Lysinias decided to plan them simultaneously and to execute either whenever a favourable occasion presented itself. Abbarus being both the intended victim and a councillor, a good start was to mount guard over his house, gather information and then take action.

Having acquired a great deal of experience during a year of spying, he was convinced that the lowest level of people were the best source of information and the cheapest. Lying in wait opposite Abbarus's house was not aimed at watching the movements of any high ranking visitor, nor of any of the young men he had witnessed coming in and out, for he had quickly realised that they were too indoctrinated, too fanatical, to be of any use to him. What he had concluded from his lookout post was that Laïs was his best chance. He had not failed to notice that the young slave was a very unhappy person indeed. Maybe he was mistreated by his master or simply not yet accustomed to his degrading condition.

What had drawn his attention to Laïs's discontent was his strange behaviour at the food market, where he had followed him on several occasions. Not only did he waste time, a characteristic of most slaves on errands; he made it a point to choose the least appealing fruits and the most withered vegetables for his master's table, as if he was settling a score with the modest means at his disposal. In addition, his general off-handedness was a clear indication of his rebellion.

It so happened that that was the day the spy had decided to approach the slave, talk to him and sound him out to ascertain whether he could be manipulated.

He followed him to the food market where peasants from the mainland gathered every other day to sell their produce. While Laïs was talking with a vendor of olives, Lysinias interfered. Having made preliminary enquiries, he already knew that Crete was the slave's country of origin, so he seized the occasion to ingratiate himself with him.

'Your olives are very poor, my good man, nothing compared to the ones you get from Crete,' he said to the vendor.

Laïs's face brightened and he turned towards the intruder asking, 'Have you been to Crete?'

'Of course I have. Why do you ask?'

'That's where I came from.' The slave's voice broke with sadness.

'Really? We must celebrate our chance encounter, come.'

The older man led Laïs to a nearby tavern where he ordered a jug of decent wine. The innkeeper disappeared behind a curtain, to reappear almost instantly with a jug in one hand, a pitcher in the other and a triumphant smile on his face.

'Taste this and tell me what you think,' he said while he mixed wine and water in two cups which were already on the table and which must have been used by successive drinkers. Lysinias got rid of the innkeeper as quickly as he could and made his new friend gulp down one cup after the other while he pretended to keep him company.

When Laïs had had more than enough, Lysinias pushed aside the jug and started a careful approach. 'I cannot believe that you have always been a slave. You must have been the son of a prince in your country. Am I wrong?'

That was the kind of overture that could make any slave tell a fairy tale and produce for himself a noble pedigree. Laïs did exactly that.

'I was with my attendants strolling on the beach at Knossos, when a Tyrian ship dropped anchor in a nearby cove and a party of sailors disembarked. When they saw me they singled me out and decided to lure me on board on the pretext of having precious merchandise that only I was entitled to see and buy. Once I was on the ship they sailed away and brought me to Tyre where I was sold to Abbarus. I hate him, I hate this place.' He buried his head between his arms and sobbed.

'Poor you,' commiserated Lysinias, 'don't lose courage. You might regain your freedom much earlier than you think.'

Laboriously, Laïs lifted his head to stare with hazy and interrogating eyes at the man who had made such an extravagant statement.

'Yes,' re-affirmed the spy, 'you will soon be free. The Greek army is very close. Tyre has no option except to surrender to Alexander, who will liberate all Greeks from slavery. The obstacle between you and liberty are men such as Abbarus.'

'How could it be?' asked a disconcerted Laïs.

'Isn't he preaching resistance to Alexander? And those young men coming in and out of his house, aren't they being trained for combat?'

'Of course! You're right,' exclaimed the slave, 'my master and his friends prepare for war. They don't want me to be free.'

'No doubt they don't want it, but we can outwit them,' Lysinias reassured him.

'Tell me how.'

'Listen very carefully to their conversations, remember everything you hear and report it to me. We will meet every afternoon in this tavern. By the way, your master – not a master to be for long – received two visitors this morning. What did they want?'

'Ah! you mean the big man with red hair and his companion. I didn't pay attention to their discussion. I didn't know it could be important.'

'Try to think back,' insisted the older man.

'The one thing I can recall is that after they had left, Abbarus told Idbal, "The blacksmith is a useful recruit, he will incite others to forge the arms we are so much in need of."'

'That's a good start,' Lysinias encouraged him. 'Do what I told you, listen carefully to what's said, whether by or to Abbarus or between his partisans, and try to remember what you hear. I'll see you tomorrow at this place.'

8

One Mission Achieved

'Go tell your master I will take the early meal in his company.'

Tansu left the room where Inat and her sister were having their usual small-talk only to come back straight away to report that Bomilcar was not hungry and did not want to be disturbed. Inat dismissed him, complaining to Amatbaal, 'What did I tell you? He's madly in love and he is letting himself waste away. This Chiboulet has cast a spell on him. I've never seen him like this. Tell me, what does she have over the others?'

Amatbaal sighed, for she had already had this discussion with her sister a dozen times. Knowing how unbearably persistent she could be, she gave her the reply she already knew. 'You've seen for yourself how beautiful she is.'

'Yes, but there are other beautiful girls and my son has slept with them without losing his appetite. Quite the contrary. Why does this woman have such an effect on him? She has cast a spell on him, I tell you. Have you seen her doing anything odd? Did she put any substance in his food?'

Amatbaal ignored the questioning but gave her sister a personal interpretation which might explain the intensity of her nephew's love for the young Sidonian. In so doing she tried to remain as objective as possible; her liking for Chiboulet was balanced against her fear of displeasing her older sister.

'You must remember,' she said, 'that they met under dangerous circumstances which brought them close in no time. Moreover, my nephew was her saviour and that created another bond between them.' She paused, hesitated, then added timidly, 'There's something else I should mention.'

'What is it?'

'Her courage and her virtue must also count for something, don't you think?'

Inat did not reply and changed the course of their discussion, which was interrupted once more by Tansu who re-appeared and stood silently before his mistress, prompting her to ask impatiently, 'What now? What do you want?'

'A messenger came. Master is urgently required at the king's palace.'

'Well, why don't you tell him?'

'He doesn't want to be disturbed.'

'That's important, go and tell him.'

Soon Bomilcar was on his way to the palace, having avoided being seen by his mother and aunt to spare himself endless solicitations to eat before he left. The palace was where the Council usually met. Because he was summoned there, he had to assume that either the king or his son, the crown prince, was back.

The palace stood in the south of the island, at a little distance from the southern port. It was a less sumptuous building than the temple of Melqart but more hospitable. A simple shelter covered the entrance, which was reached directly from ground level, not through any grand staircase.

Bomilcar stepped into thc hall and was directed to the vast room where the Council held its sessions. Beside the king's brother was Azemilk's son, who had arrived in the city in advance of his father, still with the Tyrian contingent to the Persian fleet. The crown prince, also called Azemilk, was a plain young man of the same age as Bomilcar and the two of them knew and liked each other. He acknowledged Bomilcar's arrival with a smile.

Most of the councillors had already taken their seats so Bomilcar did the same, placing himself at an equal distance between Chelbes and Abbarus, as he usually did. Oddly enough, this non-partisan attitude, which normally gave him a private satisfaction made him feel uneasy for the first time.

'I was in Cyprus, ' the young prince said to the assembly, 'when I heard the news of Alexander's progress towards our city and rushed back. The king, gods be with him, will need more time to return from the Aegean sea, but rest assured he will be with us soon. Upon my return my uncle informed me of the wise decisions taken during our absence and I fully endorse them.'

He turned towards his uncle and nodded appreciatively; Balator acknowledged the compliment with an imperceptible bending of the head. Civilities having been exchanged, Azemilk brought up the subject which was weighing on all minds. 'What we have to do now is to prepare ourselves to receive the Macedonian. If you have any suggestions I'll be glad to hear them. Councillor Chelbes, you may speak, I'm listening.'

'I propose to receive him in whatever place he chooses. If he wants to see us in Old Tyre we'll go to him and if he wishes to come to us here we will welcome him.'

'Why this sudden change of mind?' shouted Abbarus angrily. 'You agreed that the island should be more fortified, now, after a matter of days, you want to open its gates without a fight. Why the change? What have you been promised?'

Those words had the effect of making Chelbes furious; he jumped to his feet and was about to pounce on his insulter. He was prevented from doing so by Azemilk, who left his seat precipitately and placed himself between the two men, admonishing them. 'Are you out of your minds? This isn't a time for fighting but for serious debate and carefully mulled-over decisions. Sit down and listen. I've decided to go ahead and meet this new conqueror at the head of a delegation . I'll not wait for him to come to us but will meet him at the northern borders, at the town of Sarepta, and present him with the golden crown. He might do what he did at Aradus.

Abbarus was not appeased by the prince's plan which seemed to him a mere delaying tactic to avoid the real issue.

'What will be our response if the Macedonian demands to leave a garrison on the island? ' he asked.

'In that case I will convene the People's Assembly and ask for their view. Whenever there's a risk of war our citizens must decide for themselves.'

The prince's response was in Abbarus's view another dodging of the real issue. He persisted: 'By then it will be too late. We have to keep preparing for war. That is a decision which has already been taken.'

Those words infuriated Azemilk, for they made him appear to be reneging on earlier resolutions, ready to trade peace for any price, even the city's honour and freedom.

'We will continue to stock food and arms but we'll do that in a more discreet way in order not to antagonise Alexander, who may have more than one spy among us.'

Having said that he asked Abbarus, 'Satisfied?'

'My lord, I apologise for my insistence, but the fate of our city is at stake and that is constantly weighing on my mind.'

'Rest assured I do have the same concerns; so do all your colleagues,' retorted Azemilk, who continued for the benefit of the whole assembly. 'The moment we hear that Alexander has entered Sidon, I'll go to Sarepta and wait for him. When we meet I'll acknowledge his dominion. Councillors Chelbes, Abbarus and Bomilcar will accompany me. That's all for today.'

The members of the assembly left the palace in small groups, except for Bomilcar, who was not eager to listen to the same issues being repeated over again and again. So he rushed out in the direction of his house, paying no attention to Lysinias, who was lingering nearby.

As for Chelbes, he was in no hurry and remained by the palace entrance conversing with a group of councillors. After a while, he realised that Lysinias was trying to attract his attention. With a gesture he invited him to come closer and asked, 'Anything the matter?'

'Yes, my lord, I'm terrified. If the Greeks are resisted and they besiege and storm the island, I'm as good as dead. I came to ask for your advice. Shall I stay here or go further south?'

Chelbes shrugged dismissively and uttered words which were intended to comfort his interlocutor. 'You don't have to worry yet, because my bellicose colleagues are not prepared to open the city's gates for Alexander.'

Lysinias pretended to be horrified and cried out, 'Don't they know what will happen to all of us if they oppose the invading monster? Don't they know what was the fate of cities which didn't bend to his will? From which quarter do they expect succour when Sidon and all the Phoenician cities have already surrendered? Carthage is all that remains and Carthage is far away.'

'Carthage has pledged to help but as you said, it isn't next door. All the same, don't panic, everything could work out fine when we meet Alexander at Sarepta.'

The spy had heard all he wanted to know; he thanked his unintentional informant and left, pleased with himself, for he had completed one of his two assignments with great skill, without disbursing any money and within the minimum time.

9

Sarepta

For two of those who had left the king's palace, a word lingered in their minds: Sarepta, the name of a town located halfway between Tyre and Sidon on the northern border of the former's territory.

One of the two was Lysinias. No sooner had he extracted from Chelbes the information he needed than he started planning his way to Sarepta. From this border town he could sneak to Sidon, report the information he had gathered and return without attracting much attention.

Bomilcar was the other person who suddenly realised that the town presented the possibility of sneaking in and out to Chiboulet without being noticed; so he changed course and took the direction of Matten's forge. He found him there hammering on a piece of iron next to a fire kept blazing by an aide. Both workers were stripped to the waist, covered with sweat despite the cold weather.

Not often did Bomilcar venture outside the built-up area of the island, and his call took Matten aback. He put down his hammer, wiped his face and hands dry with a piece of cloth and looked at his friend with enquiring and worried eyes, for he expected to hear bad news.

'I made up my mind; I'm going to Sidon,' said Bomilcar.

The blacksmith was furious because of the fright that his friend's unexpected visit had given him, so he said with a note of sarcasm in his voice, 'And how do you intend to do that?'

The tone disappointed Bomilcar, who had expected to find an understanding listener. 'Don't trouble yourself with that,' he said, side-stepping the question, 'the aim of my visit is to ask you to protect mother if something happens to me and I don't come back.'

'Don't be a fool, I'm going with you. I don't need to know more. I was worried for your safety and still am, but I don't intend to wait for you here agonising. Just give me two days to make sure that the blacksmiths who promised to help remain true to their word, so the production of arms will not be interrupted during my absence.'

Bomilcar was relieved; the blacksmith's company during the hazardous trip would be invaluable. Nevertheless, he expressed a weak objection, 'I don't feel I've the right to put you in danger.'

Matten pretended not to have heard and went back to his toil with renewed ardour, trying to catch up with the time that the planned journey was going to waste.

Three days later they left by boat just after sunrise. Inat's tears had delayed them a little but she had been unable to prevent their departure, even in the last resort when she fainted.

Sarepta was a small town overlooking a broad bay, flanked by harbours on the north and south sides. Bomilcar ordered the crew not to enter the south port but to pursue their course to the next one, which was at the edge of the industrial quarter. This port's activity was significant and their arrival went unnoticed, the more so because they had taken care to wear very modest garments.

The stench emitted by dye production enveloped the whole quarter.

After disembarking, Bomilcar ordered his crew to return to base at once. The last thing he wanted was for them to hang around, draw attention to themselves, most probably get drunk and possibly let out careless words about the passengers they had brought in.

The two friends picked up their bundles and headed for a nearby inn. It was of such sordid aspect that, in normal circumstances, it would have been avoided as if plague-stricken. The innkeeper took them to a filthy room on the first floor with two straw mats in lieu of beds. The only betterment they could see was an opening overlooking the sea and the port, but it also let in the stench which fouled the area.

Matten was about to complain but a pressure on his hand by his companion made him understand that he should not.

'What can you give us to eat?' asked Bomilcar, knowing how much food counted for Matten.

'My wife is a famous cook. She will prepare a dish of lentils for you.'

The innkeeper did not notice Matten's disgusted look when the culinary promise was made and went ahead with the questions which were burning his lips. 'What's your business? What are you looking for here? Maybe I can help you.'

'Maybe you can,' said Bomilcar, who was expecting such questions and served the man a well prepared story, 'My cousin' – he indicated Matten with his hand – 'has his aged parents living in Sidon. Word came to us that they are both very ill. We convinced the proprietor of a boat to take us to them, but when we reached Sarepta the sailors forced us to disembark. They said that if they went to Sidon their boat would be seized and they would be jailed. We lost all the money we've paid them and the additional sum we promised them was to no avail.'

The innkeeper's eyes glared with cupidity when he heard that money could be earned. He tried to lure his guests with the prospect of the services he could offer. 'The moment I laid eyes on you I liked you. I might be able to help. I'll look around to find out whether I can convince a crew to take you to Sidon. This will be time consuming and difficult. I can promise nothing expect that I'll try even if, for a day or two, I'll have to neglect my livelihood and lose money.'

It was enough for Bomilcar to understand that the man expected to receive payment twice; first as an incentive to look for what they needed and then as a reward for finding it. He seized the bottom of his tunic and turned it up to his waist. From the pleats of his loincloth, he retrieved a meagre purse. He opened it and extracted a silver coin, which he gave to the innkeeper, promising him two more when the boat was provided.

The innkeeper left the room giving a more definite promise of a boat.

'Good, tomorrow we might leave this horrible place,' commented Matten.

'Don't count too much on that. Our host will not relinquish us that soon. He can make money out of our stay here and he will not hesitate to make us hang around for a couple of days or maybe more.'

This, and the prospect of skimpy meals, put Matten in a bad mood. To brighten him up Bomilcar thought of occupying his mind with something entertaining but the best he could do was to ask, 'Did I tell you precisely when I fell in love with Chiboulet?'

The blacksmith sighed and prepared himself to listen to an account he had heard several times before.

10

Abnegation

At sunset, Lysinias entered Sarepta on his mule, a day after Bomilcar and Matten had arrived by boat. The Macedonian spy spent the night in an inn in the residential area, close to the temple dedicated to Tanit-Astarte. He left the next day, early in the morning. Instead of following the coastal path, which would have taken him straight to Sidon but at great risk of being noticed, he directed his mount towards the mountainous east and crossed over to Sidonian territory inland.

After riding for more than an hour through a craggy and precipitous terrain, he reached a military post which controlled the rocky track leading to the city. The post was manned by Greek mercenaries headed by an officer. Lysinias gave him the password he had memorised before leaving Sidon and requested that a mounted soldier take him to General Hephaestion.

He was told that the general was already in Sidon and was instructed how to reach that town. Having realised that his destination was not far off, he changed his mind about his request for an armed guide and proceeded downhill in the direction of the sea, but not before he had accepted a large sip from the officer's wineskin.

Sidon's eastern gate was controlled by another military post made up of Macedonian soldiers directly under the general's command. Their officer recognised Lysinias, who was allowed within the walls without the need of any password.

He asked a shopkeeper where the mansion of Theron and Tryphon was, for he assumed that his choice of the general's accommodation had been approved. He soon found himself looking at an exquisite two-storey mansion nestled in lush greenery. The Macedonian soldiers standing guard around the garden gate confirmed that the general had his quarters there.

He asked the officer in charge to be taken to him; after being made to wait some time, he was allowed inside. He followed his guide across a vast dimly-lit hall, between two rows of life-size statues representing naked Kouroi, clear evidence that Greek influence at Sidon preceded Alexander's conquest.

From the hall he was led into a large dining room, where he found Hephaestion and his middle-aged hosts reclined on couches, conversing and drinking wine. Standing aside, Lysinias waited to be spoken to; it did not happen for some time, then Hephaestion turned his attention to the newcomer and requested that he be left alone with him. Theron and Tryphon dismissed the attending slaves and departed slowly behind them. Once at the door they turned back and sent an affectionate look at their eminent guest before leaving. They wore the same short blue linen tunics; Theron's garment had a golden border patterned with the head of a lioness, while Tryphon's golden border was embellished with the head of a lion. Both men were clean-shaven, dark skinned and had frizzy hair.

Alone with his visitor, Hephaestion listened carefully to his full report, then reiterated his order concerning Abbarus.

'I understand from your account that the man is too dangerous to be spared; deal with him.' he said.

Unwilling to leave the impression that he had been neglectful, Lysinias embarked on a long-winded explanation. The general interrupted the flood of words, showing him his appreciation.

'You did well,' he said, 'go and have something to eat, rest for the night and leave tomorrow for Tyre.'

Theron and Tryphon returned to the dining room; on their heels were slaves carrying trays filled with sumptuous food. Four musicians came as well and charmed the company with soothing songs and rhythms. Hephaestion had already been the guest of the two Sidonians for a week, fully committed to festivities and attended by a limited number of familiars. Theron and Tryphon were genuinely infatuated with Greek culture and belonged to the party that had resented Persian occupation. Alexander's victory was deemed by them as their personal triumph over King Strato, who had ignored them for a number of years once he realised that they could not be convinced to join his camp.

Theron was immensely wealthy and was not particularly affected by being kept on the sidelines of the political life; he had his own friends, and the love he had shared with Tryphon since childhood, which was all that counted for him. No sooner had the news spread that Hephaestion had made his quarters at their mansion, than visitors flocked to their door; even those they had not seen for ages and who had purposely avoided them and people who had been openly hostile to them.

Although he had no part in the social comedy, the Macedonian general was a keen observer of the comings and goings and of the behaviour of his hosts with their callers. From being appreciative of the good character of Theron and Tryphon, he became fond of them and his intimacy with the former deepened, becoming physical.

Theron's innate political leaning, his good character and wealth convinced Hephaestion that he did not have to look far to choose a new king who would rule over Sidon's territory and its population. The more so that his choice would be a death blow to the Persian party. That same evening he made up his mind to convey the good news to the two Sidonians. When they had finished their meal and were having a last cup of wine before retiring to their rooms, Hephaestion said, 'You're aware that I am here to appoint a new king. Strato has to go, not only because of his past policy but mostly because the people do not want him to stay. During the week I've been with you I have made enquiries, listened to supplicants and to their opponents, and interviewed possible candidates. None of them convinced me that he could be a good king. I realised that the person I was trying to find is here. Theron, my friend, you will be the next King of Sidon. No one else deserves the honour more than you.'

If the Macedonian expected his offer to be met with an explosion of joy he was mistaken, for nothing of the sort happened; the Sidonian left his couch and went on his knees, his arms opened, reduced to near despair. 'This mark of confidence, especially coming from you, overwhelms me, but I don't feel I'm a proper choice,' he said.

The general was vexed because of Theron's reaction. He was astounded too, for experience had taught him that most people would lie, cheat and even kill to gain a throne, or indeed a lesser distinction. His voice expressed his annoyance when he asked, 'Do you dispute my judgment?'

'Oh! My lord, how could you accuse me of having such a thought?'

By now, the Sidonian was in complete despair, for the last thing he wanted was to appear ungrateful and to irritate the man who thought of bestowing on him the highest office that any man could aspire to. 'My lord,' he repeated, 'forgive me if I did not express myself well; it isn't your judgment that is in doubt, it's me who is not qualified for such an honour. The people will not accept a king who is not of royal blood, the more so because a king is also the high priest of the city. We would have riots and maybe an insurrection, instead of the peace that you are here to establish.'

The Sidonian's words had the expected effect, Hephaestion ordered Theron to get up, and the two men hugged.

'Do you know of any worthy candidate with royal blood?' asked the general.

'I don't have a name in mind. Strato was so afraid of being deposed and replaced by someone of equal lineage that persons with royal blood were never allowed at his court. He persecuted them, prompting them either to leave the territory or to make themselves unobtrusive, condemned to an obscure life. But I'll make enquiries; in a few days I might be able to come back with a name or two.'

11

Chance Encounter

'If the innkeeper does not provide us with a boat today, I'm going to give him such thrashing that he will disgorge the silver coin you gave him and renounce any attempt to make us pay for our dreadful accommodation and horrible lentil meals; I'll also beat his wife for being such a bad cook.'

After a second day in Sarepta, waiting for their host to find a small boat to sneak them into Sidonian territory, Matten was in a state. A man of action, he was not accustomed to doing nothing; even strolling on the beach was impossible because of the persistent rain.

He and Bomilcar had spent the previous day indoors playing a dice game and drinking heavily watered wine. From time to time the innkeeper stepped out, allegedly looking for a crew adventurous and greedy enough to take them to their intended destination. Their guess, however, was that he had already found what was needed and was letting time pass to make them more appreciative of his efforts and extend their opportunity to spend on accommodation, food and drink.

Bomilcar tried to calm his friend. 'If by the end of this day we're still without transportation, I'll join you in the thrashing. Just wait a few more hours.'

Matten emitted a grumble, which Bomilcar took for assent. He rose to his feet and looked through the opening.

'The rain has stopped; let's go for a walk,' he said.

Another inarticulate sound signalled approval and one after the other they washed, using water stored in the large amphora wedged into a corner of their room.

The innkeeper welcomed them with a large smile and promising words as if he had had an inkling of the threats muttered in the intimacy of their room.

'With no more rain and a calm sea, I believe that you have a good chance of leaving this afternoon,' he said.

'If not,' Bomilcar said, 'we'll go back to Tyre immediately.'

'There will be no need for that, I promise,' the innkeeper hastened to say, also attempting to whet their appetite. 'I see that you are about to go. Come back soon to taste what my wife is preparing especially for you.'

'What is it?' asked Matten, disgruntled.

'For a change we'll have beans.'

The two friends left hurriedly. Along the shore were a dozen small jewellery workshops; now and then, they paused to admire the cross-legged artisans at work on unfinished pieces of jewellery, embossing, adding granulation or inlaying precious stones.

In one of the workshops a man was discussing prices with the jeweller. Although he was wearing local clothes, his intonation was foreign. After a moment Bomilcar recognised him as the Macedonian renegade who had warned the Council against resisting Alexander's dictates.

The man seemed to have recognised him too as the furtive but expressive look he gave him revealed. He departed in a rush, leaving the artisan who was vexed to see the bargaining game end before he had given his best price. The hasty departure surprised Bomilcar for a moment, but he did not give it another thought.

He was fascinated by the artisan's skill, he was making the final touches to a pair of gold earrings engraved with ox-heads. Bomilcar bought the earrings and a swivel ring representing a winged beetle for Chiboulet and a cylindrical amulet case for her parents.

Unwilling to have another taste of the food at the inn, they bought bread and cheese in no small quantity and went back to their room. They ate some while they waited for the news and left the rest for the forthcoming journey. Peering from the window, they saw that the good weather held and the sea was unagitated. They were so anxious to depart from the filthy place that they became oblivious to the danger they might be exposing themselves to once they reached Sidonian territory.

No sooner had the sun started its decline towards the horizon that their host shouted for them to come down, which they did in no time, expecting to see the sailor who had accepted to take them to their destination. Their host was too clever to put them directly in touch with that man before he himself had made the financial arrangements which suited him.

'Well,' said Matten, 'where is our man?'

'He's getting his boat ready and has asked me to sort out money matters with you.'

'So, how much does he want?' asked Bomilcar.

'Three silver darics for him. You may give them to me and I'll pay him.'

That was done, but before the purse was placed under Bomilcar's tunic, the innkeeper asked to be paid two darics for their accommodation and one daric for the trouble he had had trying to find them the boat.

Satisfied, the innkeeper led the way to the boat, which was waiting for them a little away from the built-up area. It was a rowboat with four oarsmen; they waded through the water towards her, soaked to their knees. They climbed on board without being seen.

The captain gave the order to start rowing, while he gave his passengers information about their journey. 'In an hour we will be sailing along the Sidonian coast and an hour after that it will be dark. Then I can steer for the shore and let you disembark. Where should that be?'

'Any place at a walking distance from the eastern gate will do.'

Bomilcar did not intend to enter the city through that gate or any other but his aim was to be able to find his way back to Abdalonymus's farm at daybreak. For that he needed a landmark and the only indicator he knew was the eastern gate. He was confident that he could easily reach the farm from there with no need to ask for directions and draw attention to him and his companion.

Fortunately, the skipper knew of a small creek with a cave in the overhanging rocky cliff where they could take shelter for the night. The creek, according to the sailor, was a short distance from Sidon's walls. The two friends disembarked and looked for the cave in the pallid moonlight. Although it was cold they did not dare start a fire, which might be seen from afar; they wrapped themselves in their cloaks and lay down at the cave mouth, trying to sleep with no great success.

12

Apparition

'Are you asleep?'

Bomilcar whispered in case his companion had been able to nod off despite their rough sleeping conditions.

'How could I?' grumbled Matten. 'Every time I change position a malicious god places a stone between my back and the soil.'

'I was thinking about the man – I forget his name – who we met at the jeweller's shop and all of a sudden, I remembered where I had seen him.'

'I know, you told me. He appeared before the Council.'

The oversight surprised the blacksmith; normally his friend was much more alert and would not have made that kind of mistake. 'Could love be the reason?' he wondered.

'I saw him somewhere else too,' said Bomilcar, 'at the palace gate just after the Council session had ended. I didn't pay attention to him then, but after seeing him in Sarepta it all came back to me.'

'That could be a coincidence,' said Matten.

'No! Remember how he fled when he saw us. I wonder whether

he was following us or someone else. That would mean that our latest encounter was a mere coincidence, unless . . . '

'Unless what?'

'Unless he's a spy and was on his way to or from Sidon. Either way he has to pass through Sarepta, like us. If he comes back to Tyre he must be closely watched.'

'Count on me. Now try to get some sleep.'

Matten's recommendation was easier to say than to follow. Not only did cold and discomfort prevent Bomilcar's eyes from closing and his mind from taking a rest, in addition his head was filled with Chiboulet's image and his heart with anxious thoughts. He had no idea how her parents would receive him. In fact it was not her parents who worried him, but the uncertainty of it all. Would Chiboulet be prepared to leave with him now that Sidon was peaceful? Would her father agree to let her go? Above all, was he prepared to take her to Tyre, possibly exposing her to deadly danger?

There was another possibility, which he would have grabbed had it presented itself a month ago. That was for him to remain in Sidon. At that time he would have had no qualms whatsoever but now he could not. It would be deserting his compatriots at a time when the city needed him.

He tried to reason with himself: he had made this trip only to see Chiboulet, make sure she was safe, make love to her once or twice in secret, and go back home. He could not, however, convince himself that this was all he expected, for he had that powerful urge to keep her beside him, publicly and forever, as his wife. He loved her body, her spirit and her mind and no furtive tryst could quench his passion and make him accept their separation.

He moaned in his pain and distress. There was no satisfactory solution to his predicament. He was not as pious as Matten, yet he took refuge in prayers to Astarte whenever he was having a personal problem or one of his ships was overdue. The goddess had been particularly venerated by Merbalos, his father, and that useful devotion passed down to him.

He closed his eyes and prayed: 'Oh Astarte! Oh celestial and marine divinity, goddess of fecundity and Melqart's companion! Guide me and help me find a way to be united with Chiboulet forever and ever.' He repeated his prayer at least a dozen times and was about to start again when a bright light illuminated the far end of the cave, revealing a naked lady seated on a throne flanked by two sphinxes. He immediately realised that he was in the presence of Astarte and threw himself on his knees, his arms wide open.

'Oh my Lady! You came to deliver me from my misery. Tell me what to do,' he implored her.

The apparition frowned in displeasure and retorted, 'You ask me a favour but you promise nothing in exchange.'

'What is your command?' His tone denoted shame and repentance.

'I desire to be venerated in this cave and visited by streams of pilgrims.'

'It will be done. I pledge this in your presence and my vow is sacred.'

Vigorously shaken by Matten, he woke up and it took a moment before he realised where he was.

'You kept repeating in your sleep "as you order, as you order", what does it mean? What were you dreaming about?'

'I wasn't dreaming, I saw Our Lady Astarte and she talked to me.'

Matten was too deeply religious to challenge the reality of the apparition.

'What did she want?' he asked.

'She wants a sanctuary in this cave and I promised to erect one for her.'

Matten's common sense won out. 'She will have to wait until peace is established. Come now, it's nearly sunrise, we must leave.'

'Not before I wash and change my clothes. I cannot present myself to Chiboulet in this state,' objected Bomilcar.

They both washed in the sea and changed their clothes, and Bomilcar shaved his face. Then they looked for a way to reach the top of the cliff and found a rough path which brought them to the ridge more easily than they had surmised. From their elevated spot the walls of Sidon came into view at a distance. The pointer they were looking for, the eastern gate, was not visible from where they stood but finding it was simple.

Invigorated, they proceeded in the direction of Abdalonymus's farm. All along the way Bomilcar was looking for a sign from the goddess which would indicate to him the way out of a difficult choice that was not entirely his. He watched the birds soaring in the sky and the frightened hare bolting and disappearing in the thicket. But being no seer, he was unable to interpret what their course meant to tell him. His real worry was that Astarte was not prepared to answer his prayer, and that feeling cast a shadow on the joy of the anticipated reunion.

13

The Making of a King

At the same time that the two Tyrians were in Sarepta waiting to be taken to Sidon, a procession was leaving that city in the direction of Abdalonymus's farm. At its head were Theron and Tryphon, mounted on two richly harnessed mules and followed by a number of slaves on foot, one of whom held the reins of another mule, also sumptuously caparisoned.

A man sent in advance to announce their visit had retraced his steps and was acting as their guide, having left behind him a flabbergasted Abdalonymus.

The farmer was not aware of who Theron and Tryphon were, but their envoy had explained that they were sent by Hephaestion, the new Macedonian governor of the city. Not only did the announced visit bewilder him, it worried him too, although he tried to conceal that feeling from his family.

'What possible business could these people have with us?' Artas's voice shivered disquietingly.

'Perhaps their visit has something to do with what took place at Eshmun temple and they are coming to arrest me,' said Chiboulet.

'Nonsense,' Abdalonymus reassured her, 'it's nothing of the sort. Tubal's death is nothing for high ranking envoys to get involved in; it is certainly not for the new governor to intervene.'

'What is it, then?' cried out mother and daughter simultaneously.

'I don't know, probably something to do with farming, a new tax or a new edict. Soon we'll be informed, but believe me, dear daughter, you needn't be concerned.'

In reality he was far from reassured, so he kept himself busy and his mind absorbed in trivial details.

The dog barked, warning of approaching callers. Chiboulet picked up Jason from the floor and with Artas hard on her heels, left for another room where the two women could follow the conversation without being seen. The farmer stepped out, followed by his slave who, as a futile means of protection, had armed himself with a shovel. With the collapse of the Persian administration, the countryside was unsafe and isolated places like the farm were easy prey for the many prowling bandits and deserters.

Chiboulet's father instantly realised that the colourful procession coming towards him was peaceful, so he discreetly ordered his slave to get rid of his improvised weapon. Relieved but still bewildered, he endeavoured with his calm demeanour to convey an impression of confidence that he was far from feeling.

'We salute you, noble Abdalonymus!'

Theron's greeting, put the farmer's mind at rest but left him more bewildered than ever. Why on earth had these two strangers made a point of mentioning a lineage that he himself had nearly forgotten?

'Can we talk inside?'

Theron's question made Abdalonymus ashamed of his shortcoming, as a host and he hastened to invite his two visitors into the house.

No city notables accompanied the two Sidonians, in keeping with Hephaestion's command. The general wanted his friends to take credit for the mission they had been sent to accomplish. Knowing their lack of interest in politics, he feared that they might be overshadowed, pushed aside by more opportunistic companions who would present themselves as the agents of the farmer's good fortune.

Abdalonymus offered his two guests wine. Craving to know the reason of their visit he said, 'If there is anything a simple farmer can do for you, I am willing and ready.' Theron did not comment but gestured to Tryphon to put on the floor the folded piece of cloth which was resting on his left forearm.

Tryphon complied, unfolded the cloth and retrieved from its layers a long robe, coloured purple and embroidered with gold, which he handed to Theron. The latter took it and presented it to Abdalonymus with the most astounding words: 'You have been chosen as the King of Sidon. Take this robe, wear it and come with us to meet and give thanks to Alexander and Hephaestion, for they are the ones responsible for your elevation.'

It took a moment or two for these words to sink in. When they did, Abdalonymus exclaimed, his voice shivering with apprehension, 'But I know nothing about affairs of state. Surely there are people of royal blood who are better qualified than me.'

'You have been singled out for more than one reason. Your people need you, you cannot let them down after the suffering they have endured under Strato.'

'I know practically no one in Sidon. Most of my life has been spent at my farm. How can I reign over people about whom I know nothing?' objected the farmer.

'Do not worry about that. In no time you will collect much more information than you ever wished for. People will be denouncing and reporting each other; charges fuelled by envy, resentment and hatred, will fly back and forth.'

'It's far from reassuring; how can I see through all that?' asked Abdalonymus.

'I told you not to have any apprehension and I mean it, for you will have wise advisers appointed by General Hephaestion at your side. They will show you the right direction. Rely on them and you cannot go wrong.'

'What about you ? Will you counsel and guide me?'

The farmer's reluctance was slowly giving way to a more positive disposition. After all, he was human. Now that he had nearly overcome his initial fear, the high office he was offered could not but exalt his self-esteem and present him with an opportunity to end a life of harsh work and little income. With his new status, not only would the future of his family be secured for good; he would triumph over those who had demeaned him, intentionally or not, throughout a life lived in obscurity.

Theron's negative answer disappointed him but his opinion of his two visitors rose because of their evident disregard for honours. He insisted, 'I'll need people like you at my side; I pray that you reconsider your decision.'

Theron remained adamant but presented Abdalonymus with a slight concession, 'We will not leave you until you have met Alexander and Hephaestion and found advisers who win your confidence. After that we'll go back to our normal life but will remain your obedient subjects.'

'You are more than that, you are my benefactors,' exclaimed the newly-appointed king.

'That's a feeling which is easily forgotten. I'll settle for friendship, if that's acceptable to you,' stated Theron.

'Of course it is,' said Abdalonymus. 'What do I do next?' he asked.

'Prepare yourself; we leave straight away for Sidon.'

14
Joy and Concern

Abdalonymus left his two visitors and went searching for his wife and daughter. From their expressions, he knew that not a word of the conversation had escaped them. The three of them looked at each other, unable to speak, then they threw themselves into each other's arms, hugging and kissing.

After the first outpouring of emotion, he freed himself from their embrace, put a finger to his lips to enjoin them to remain silent, and directed them into a far-off room.

'I can't believe it. Are you sure that these people are not playing a trick on you?' asked Artas.

'How could you utter such nonsense, woman? See this robe with the royal insignia, it's real. I'm going to put it on, then leave with our visitors to meet with Alexander and . . . ' Abdalonymus left his sentence unfinished, realising that Chiboulet was reflective and silent after the first demonstrations of surprise and joy.

'What's the matter?' he asked her, 'aren't you happy?'

'Of course, I am, father, but please take care of yourself; some people may resent your elevation. Strato has a powerful family and they may attempt to hurt you.'

'Don't worry, I'll see that I'm protected.'

Chiboulet was truly worried about her father's safety but there was another reason for her disquiet, which she had to keep to herself and hope that it would not interfere with her future plans.

As a farmer's daughter, a widow with a child, wealthy Bomilcar was more than a suitable in her parent's eyes. Would this perception remain the same now that she was the daughter of a king?

After she had heard the astounding news brought by the two

visitors, she had perceived the danger to her marital prospects and that had cast a shadow on her joy. She was also aware that this was not an opportune time for her to talk to her father and try to dispel her anguish; she must wait for a better occasion.

'I need to wash and change before I leave for Sidon. In a few days I'll send for you and we will all quit this ungrateful life. May Melqart be thanked.'

Her father's voice brought Chiboulet back to the real world and she and her mother bustled about preparing his bath. Soon after he was wearing the royal robe and riding the richly adorned mule brought specially for him. Nothing of the farmer could now be detected in him. His entire bearing was worthy of the king he had become, the more so that in no time he had convinced himself that the royal office was his due by birth and that Strato had usurped it, depriving him of what was rightly his.

'Before meeting the conqueror and the general I have a sacred duty. I must sacrifice to Astarte in recognition of her favours towards me. Also I wish to consult the oracle,' said Abdalonymus.

'We cannot let Alexander and Hephaestion wait. You will do all that after meeting them,' replied Theron.

The answer was not to Abdalonymus's liking, for it reminded him of the dependent position he had been prompt to forget, so he fell silent.

When the party came within sight of Sidon's eastern gate they noticed an assembled group of hoplites, who had put on their plumed helmets and were armed with their long sarissas, swords and round shields.

This unusual sight did not bode well. When they reached the group of soldiers, their officer, recognisable by his cuirasse, saluted them and said, 'We're here to accompany the new king to the palace.'

'Take us instead to General Hephaestion,' urged Theron.

'The general has left town to join up with King Alexander. My orders are to take you to them the day after tomorrow.'

'Tell me, why are you equipped for battle?' asked the Sidonian.

'A few troublemakers are encouraging the population to riot. So far their appeal has only been heeded by a small number and the disturbance was crushed. Our mission is to escort you.'

Theron asked a question, the answer to which he feared he already knew. 'What's the reason for this disturbance?'

For a moment the officer seemed slightly embarrassed but his rough soldierly manners returned rapidly and he gave the explanation his questioner feared. 'With due respect, some citizens are not happy with the chosen king and they make their voice heard.'

These words had an immediate effect on Abdalonymus: they mortified him salutarily but at the same time strengthened his resolve to fight to keep his newly acquired throne. He turned towards his two companions and with a perfectly calm voice said, 'My life is in the hands of the gods. It seems now that we have ample time to visit the temple, let's go there.'

Escorted by the soldiers they went to the temple of Astarte, which was located on the city's highest grounds. On their way they were hailed by a significant number of inhabitants and that was a great comfort to them. In the temple Abdalonymus offered the sacrifice of a bull to the goddess, poured out a libation in her name and then asked to see the oracle.

He was taken to a room adjoining the temple's open section. He found himself before a priestess of advanced years, frail and withered, who was seated on a chair elevated on a platform. Otherwise she could not see the visitors, unable to lift her head due to the deformity caused by her venerable age.

Abdalonymus asked to be left on his own with the priestess. When this was done, he addressed her respectfully. 'Your wise reputation reached me when I was a mere farmer. It didn't cross my mind then to consult you, for the simple reason that all I had to expect from life were the vicissitudes that a farmer must endure. As a king my duty dictates to me to anticipate events for the protection and well-being of my people.'

'Tell me what is it you want to know,' said the oracle, her voice barely audible.

'Is my reign going to last?'

'It is not your people's welfare you are preoccupied with, just your own interest. Nevertheless I will answer your question.'

Stung, Abdalonymus tried to justify himself. 'How can I take good care of my people if I am no longer a king?'

'Do not exert yourself in search of justification and hear me: because of your self-centred preoccupation, I say that you will remain king a great deal of years. Had your question been unselfish I would have had doubts. In order to last in such a high office one has to be shrewd and look at his own interest first, and you can do just that. Now I am tired; leave me.'

'One last question before I leave. What general advice do you give me?'

The oracle reflected a moment, then said, 'Be fair with your people whenever fairness does not harm your interest. If you believe it could, be merciless. Fear will ensure the perpetuation of your reign far better than a reputation for fairness.'

15

Disquieting Explanation

Getting closer to Sidon's walls, which they intended to follow at a distance before branching off in the direction of the farm, Bomilcar and Matten noticed that soldiers were standing guard by the gate. Alarmed, they moved away quickly, but no one paid attention to them and they kept going without being troubled.

After a while they decided they were out of danger and paused to get their breath back under the branches of a pine tree. Although winter was close, their brisk walk in the penetrating sun made them feel hot. They took off their cloaks, spread them on the ground and lay down on them.

Everything contributed for them to doze off. Matten turned on to one side, curled up and instinctively wrapped the whole of his body, including his head, in the pleats of his cloak. This sleeping habit had been acquired as a child, when he attempted to escape the stench which emanated from the many surrounding dye vats. This smell, which he had to endure throughout his early life, had prompted his decision never to work in the dyeing business, instead fire and iron were to be his tools and artefacts. If a grown-up Matten had been able to escape the odour which had distressed him during childhood, he still kept the habit of sleeping entirely covered from head to toe.

This saved his life and that of his friend when two bandits jumped on Bomilcar, daggers in hand, intending to rob him and kill him afterwards. They did not see Matten, hidden from their view under his cloak; or rather they believed that next to the person they were attacking was a bundle of merchandise worth taking.

Threatened by two daggers, Bomilcar could do very little. Wisely, he did not offer any resistance but tried to awaken his companion by raising his voice as if he was panic stricken and unable to control himself.

'Take whatever you want, but I beg of you don't hurt me!' he cried out.

His voice awakened Matten, who sprang up from under his cloak and charged the assailants from behind. With two synchronised thrusts he pushed them away from Bomilcar and they tumbled away from their intended victim before they could realise what had happened to them and make use of their weapons. They regained their balance and turned round to face their attacker. Seeing the red-haired giant, the fierce expression on his face and the cudgel he was brandishing, they decided, with no need for any conferring, that honesty was, after all, a much safer course than the harsh and dangerous way they made their living. They dropped their daggers, turned their backs and started running away from the demon who had popped up from nowhere.

With feigned reproach in his voice, Bomilcar said, 'I would have been dead by now had I been on my own.'

'But you're not.'

'I'm not what?' asked Bomilcar.

'On your own or dead.'

'I know I'm not dead but I meant to remind you that initially you refused to accompany me. Had I not insisted I would have been killed and who would have been responsible? You.'

'I never said I did not want to make this trip with you, I never said that.'

Matten was indignant, so Bomilcar put an end to his playful game, 'I was just teasing you. By the way, dearest friend, you saved my life.'

The blacksmith shrugged his shoulders dismissively and they prepared to resume walking.

When they reached their destination, they woke the farm dog from his habitual torpor. He lifted his head and, recognising them, came up and rubbed himself against their legs. Bomilcar caressed his back; satisfied, he went back to his spot and resumed his sleep.

His heart pounding wildly, the young lover knocked on the farmhouse door, which was opened by Chiboulet. Totally taken by surprise, she stood in the doorway, stunned and speechless. He misunderstood her lack of reaction, took it for coldness and became confused, not knowing what to say or how to behave. A cry of joy finally came out of her lips.

'Come in, come in,' she said. When they complied she threw herself into Bomilcar's arms, laughing and crying. He was baffled and was about to beg for an explanation for her confounding behaviour, when her mother came in and greeted them. She, too, appeared to be not entirely herself.

Although he was not given any sign that he was unwelcome, he felt, nevertheless, that there was something odd in their demeanour.

Artas invited them to sit down and kept them company while Chiboulet bustled in and out of the kitchen bringing cheese, bread and dried fruits. The fact that Artas had stayed with them in the absence of her husband and that Chiboulet was obviously delaying a sustained conversation, warned Bomilcar to expect unpromising news. Could it be that Chiboulet had had a change of heart? But then why had she thrown herself in his arms? Why had she cried? Where was Abdalonymus? All these questions rushed through his mind and he decided to find out the answer with no further delay.

'Where is the master of the house?' he enquired. The two women looked at each other. Eventually Chiboulet told him about the tremendous change in their fortune. Reeling from the shock of the news, he said, 'I'm glad for you and for your father. I have no doubt that he will be a just and righteous king.'

After a moment of reflection he asked, 'When did all this happen?'

'Three days ago. Alexander's emissaries visited us to inform Abdalonymus that the people of Sidon wanted him as their king. He went with them to meet the Macedonian,' replied Artas.

After another moment of reflection the difficulty that Abdalonymus's elevation might create for his intended marriage struck Bomilcar more clearly. Turning to Chiboulet, he said, 'My feelings towards you have not changed. Coming to you on this dangerous journey is, I believe, a mark of my unending love. Dear Chiboulet, do you still wish to be my wife?'

The way she looked at him left no doubt in his mind, and her answer confirmed it.

'More than ever,' she stated, keeping to herself the same apprehension which made them fear that their future plans might be thwarted because of her father's good fortune.

Artas felt it her duty to intervene to prevent the lovers from losing touch with the new reality, which might make her husband renege on his consent for their marriage. 'The King has left for Sidon and will send for me and Chiboulet before long. You could come with us and ask again for his permission.'

The invitation worried Bomilcar for it meant that the king's permission had to be obtained anew, as if the consent given when he was a farmer was now obsolete. Nevertheless, having no other choice, he declared his willingness to do what was suggested.

Matten objected, 'I cannot wait until the king summons you, I've work to do in Tyre.'

Prodded by his friend he fell silent, obviously unhappy. Chiboulet noticed his change of mood and tried to brighten him up by directing his attention to food, a topic dear to his heart. 'Mother is going to cook the young goat that our neighbour killed when he heard that father had become King. We have more delicacies brought by other neighbours. Does this dinner please you?' she asked him.

With a large smile Matten replied, 'What more can a poor blacksmith expect than to be fed by a queen?'

Everyone laughed, although Artas's chuckle was a little contrived for one of the advantages she expected being a queen was not to enter the kitchen any more. She did not object to the incongruous arrangement proposed by her only child. For the sake of her happiness she was prepared to do anything as long as appearances were respected. This brought her to broach the matter of accommodation.

'I cannot give you hospitality tonight. In the absence of the King that would be improper. Abdeshmun, our neighbour will most certainly lodge you. His farm is about two stadia from here. I'll send him a word with our slave.'

Bomilcar asked, 'Do we have your permission to visit?'

'During the day, you are welcome to stay as long as you wish but you must return to Abdeshmun for the night.'

'I long to see Chiboulet; it doesn't matter whether it's by day or by night. What would be unbearable is to be so close and deprived of her company.'

The young Tyrian's declaration was a cry of love but of frustration too; he and Chiboulet were going to be watched all the time with no possibility of intimacy between them.

Artas, unaware of his frustration, was as pleased with the intensity of his love for her daughter as any mother would be. She tried to reassure him. 'We are not barbarians. If my daughter wishes to see you, she already has her father's permission and mine, provided the proprieties are always observed. I want both of you to promise that they will be.'

'We do,' said the two young lovers simultaneously, resolved to break their promise as soon as the first occasion presented itself. Already Bomilcar was scheming.

16

Improvisation

After a hearty meal, Bomilcar and Matten were taken to Abdeshmun. He and his four grown-up sons received them warmly but displayed unwelcome inquisitiveness. Bomilcar had to be very inventive to placate their curiosity.

'We are from Sarepta,' he said. 'As soon as we heard that Abdalonymus had been chosen as king, we hurried to offer our services. Unfortunately, when we arrived he had already left for Sidon, so we decided to wait for him.'

'What is the king to you?' asked Abdeshmun, prompting Bomilcar to be even more creative. 'I'm a distant relative and my friend Matten accompanies me to propose his services as the King's bodyguard.'

'Surely,' commented Abdeshmun, 'a bodyguard has to stay close to the people he is bound to protect. During the King's absence don't you think you should keep an eye on his wife and daughter, particularly at night? The countryside is full of deserters and they have only one male slave to guard them.'

The comments caught Bomilcar unaware; yet he devised a

convincing reply, 'You are absolutely right. *Sitt* Artas is making ready the shed in their vegetable garden, where we will spend the night. In the meantime we intend to patrol the area surrounding the farmhouse after dark.'

'You don't have to worry about it. My sons started doing just that after the King left for Sidon. He asked me to look after his family. Two of my sons witnessed your arrival at the farmhouse but you didn't see them.'

During the exchange, Bomilcar was struck by the advantage that he could get out of the tale he had just improvised.

'And you, what do you do?'

'I'm a jeweller. I can trace my forefathers – who were also jewellers – to the time Sarepta belonged to Sidon.' The pedigree that Bomilcar had created was intended to gain the confidence of his hosts, whom he expected to be distrustful of anyone who was not from their own city – a characteristic common to the inhabitants of Phoenicia.

He was right; his fanciful tale was received by his hosts with beaming smiles. Throughout the verbal exchange Matten had inwardly marvelled at Bomilcar's vivid imagination.

To escape more questions, the two friends asked to be taken to the room allocated to them for the night. Their excuse for retiring earlier than normally required by good manners was exhaustion on account of their sea passage.

Lying down on the bed of leaves that had been prepared for him, Bomilcar conjured up Chiboulet's image. A powerful desire to leave his litter, go to her and make love to her took hold of him, and he had to fight hard to control this impulse. He had no way of knowing that she was in the clutches of the same lustful passion and was using all her willpower not to cause a shameful scandal by going to him. The two lovers were united in thoughts made more intense by their reciprocation, regardless of physical separation. She even considered going to her mother, telling of her torment and asking for her help. That idea was quickly dismissed as foolish and inconsiderate; for despite her strong and trusting bond with Artas, she could not decently tell her about her sexual urges.

She silently laughed at the mental image of her mother's bewildered face if she were to confide in her. At that same moment Jason cried out. Sexual desire and images of love-making were wiped from her mind while she devoted her attention to her son.

Unfortunately for Bomilcar, he did not have anything to make his phantasms disappear, so he stayed awake, tossing and turning most of the night. It was only an hour or two before daybreak that he was able to have some sleep. Not for long, for a restless Matten woke him. He was bored but afraid to leave their room in case Abdeshmun pursued his line of questioning; he did not have Bomilcar's rich imagination to provide fanciful answers and avoid saying anything that might contradict what had been said the evening before.

They washed, thanked Abdeshmun for his hospitality and left, in a great hurry, to avoid further questions. The difficult part was eluding their host's insistence on sharing his first meal of the day; they eventually succeeded but at the expense of upsetting him.

They were warmly received by Artas and Chiboulet, as if the women's earlier uneasiness had been dispelled now that they had communicated to their visitors the new factor in their lives.

'How did you spend the night? Were you comfortable?' asked Artas.

'Oh, yes!' exclaimed Matten, 'except that we had to sustain a deluge of questions. They rained on us one after the other, but Bomilcar dodged them all with great mastery, I must say.'

'That's the problem with Abdeshmun, he is too inquisitive and doesn't stop prying into other people's' affairs,' commented Artas.

Bomilcar grasped the occasion to inform the two women of the story he had concocted for Abdeshmun. The proposed use of the shed was rightly seen by Chiboulet as a prospect of keeping her lover near her after nightfall.

'What a good idea,' she exclaimed and knowing her mother's

touchiness when it came to their reputation, added, 'The story is very believable. It will silence anyone who might question the presence of two men amongst us. The bodyguard's part is a stroke of genius. I must say it is so because it's Matten who is concerned. Had Bomilcar assumed that part he would have been far less credible.'

They all laughed at the witticism.

'Mother, give orders for the shed to be made liveable and worthy of our guests.'

'Don't trouble yourself on our account,' objected Bomilcar, 'a litter on clean ground is all we need.'

'I saw how you live in your house, like a king. Now that you are in a king's house we must put all the necessary efforts to provide you with the same comfort.'

Chiboulet's repartee fell flat with Bomilcar; barely had she pronounced the words 'king's house' than concern about their planned marriage was revived. They looked at each other with consternation, realising how powerless they were. What would happen was for the gods to decide.

17

Self-serving Arguments

Following Hephaestion's instructions, the wisdom of which became apparent before long, Sidon's new king spent two nights at the palace of his predecessor, who had retired to his country estate, abandoned even by those he had believed to be his most faithful courtiers. Civil disorder had broken out the day Theron and Tryphon had left the city. The disturbance had appeared spontaneous; in fact the mob had been manipulated by Strato's clan, the greatest loser by his unseating.

Before the new king and his retinue entered Sidon, rioting had been ruthlessly crushed by the Macedonian soldiers, but discontent against Abdalonymus continued to be stirred up by the city's aristocrats and rich merchants, who were horrified to see him as their king. What they resented most was his poverty and modest occupation. They named a delegation to convey their grievances to Hephaestion's two local friends but when it became known that Abdalonymus had spent the night at the palace, the number of delegates dwindled to two diehards. No one else was prepared to bring his opposition to the newly designated monarch into the open. The two remaining members of the delegation were quickly dismissed and advised to return home, before Hephaestion was made aware of their initiative.

'You are very lucky,' Theron told them, 'that the General is not here to listen to your complaints. He would have ordered that your properties be seized and given to the King. The threat was miraculously convincing and the two delegates reported it widely. Thereafter, opposition kept quiet.

Therefore, when Theron and Tryphon presented themselves at the palace on the third day, with an armed detachment to escort Abdalonymus to Alexander, the city enjoyed complete calm. A few onlookers had gathered in front of the royal palace hoping to hail the king. Among them, doing their best to be noticed, were the two previously uncompromising members of the opposition's delegation. A night of reflection had made them see the need to atone for their misjudgement.

As gales were blowing and the sea was stormy, it was wisely decided to proceed by land to the conqueror's camp. Abdalonymus and his retinue arrived at the banks of the river Tamyras at midday.

The newly appointed king and the two Sidonians were taken to Hephaestion. He received them in his tent, glad to learn that the man who had been chosen by his two friends to be the ruler of their city was, in appearance at least, worthy of the office. He was favourably impressed by his slender body and by his white beard and hair, which enhanced the aura of wisdom emanating from his person.

Theron and Tryphon informed Hephaestion that, in general, the population had received their new king well. Satisfied with his visitors' account, the general left them and went in search of Alexander. He found him in his tent dictating a letter to Callistene.

'Listen to what mother said in her last letter,' he said to Hephaestion, who inferred that he had been engaged in answering Olympias before the interruption.

'She reproaches me for everything, from taking too much personal risk and giving away the spoils of war to my association with Barsine. Ah! My friend, she asks a hefty price for a mere nine months gestation.'

Hephaestion refrained from any comment, knowing how much Alexander loved his mother, although her constant meddling in his affairs annoyed him most of the time. Having vented his irritation, Alexander enquired, 'Anything you want to tell me?'

'The king chosen for Sidon is here.'

'Before you bring him in, tell me how you came to know of him and how his nomination has been received.' Hephaestion did so.

'What is your impression of the man?'

Alexander's question indicated that he did not accord great significance to what he had just heard, being confident that he possessed what was necessary to elevate any person of his choice to Sidon's throne. What he wanted to make sure of was that person was worthy, that he was capable of absolute loyalty and had the basic attributes of an acceptable monarch.

Hephaestion described the good impression he had had of Abdalonymus, who was thereupon brought into Alexander's tent. Theron and Tryphon were not invited to accompany him; the general did not think it proper to make them attend a meeting during which their king might be mishandled by Alexander. He need not have worried for all went well.

'Mighty King, favourite of the gods and victorious liberator, I am obliged to you forever. Command and you will be obeyed,' said Abdalonymus emphatically.

Satisfied with the way the meeting had started, Alexander invited Abdalonymus to take a seat, telling him, 'I accept your marks of deference but I will not remain here forever. I want your pledge that, after I leave, you will rule according to what you believe my orders would be.'

'Sire, I'll do my utmost to be worthy of your trust. In any event, I'll always seek instructions from the governor you will leave behind.'

'For the time being Hephaestion is that governor, but not for long. I need him by my side.'

'I will comply with the instructions of your representative, whoever he is,' Abdalonymus assured him.

His subservience pleased the Macedonian king even more. 'Have some rest before you attend the banquet in celebration of your investiture. Tomorrow you must go back to Sidon, which shouldn't be left without a master.' Having said that he turned to Hephaestion and ordered, 'The population of Sidon must rejoice for three successive days because I gave them a new king. From the roof terraces, criers will enjoin men, women and children to demonstrate their joy in the public place. Send them wine, bread and cheese to be distributed. Woe to anyone who refuses to take part in the general jubilation.'

Hephaestion was relieved because Alexander had endorsed the choice made by his friends unreservedly. Accompanied by Abdalonymus, he went back to them and they all prepared themselves for the evening banquet.

It took place in Alexander's pavilion, where some thirty guests, reclining on couches, drank wine and were entertained by musicians and dancers. Swallowing one cup after another, Abdalonymus reviewed his past life. He was a good man with no wish to take revenge on any particular human being, but he could not help feeling pleased by the idea of how shocked and frightened those who had looked down on him in the past would be.

His thoughts moved to Theron and Tryphon, who were in a different league. They had brought him to Hephaestion's attention and they must be thanked for that; but he should always keep in perspective that all they had done was to look for the most deserving candidate with royal blood. Undeniably that was him. Abdalonymus concluded that he owed the two Sidonians very little.

Having freed himself from a debt which had weighed on his mind, he looked around. Alexander was in a good mood, drinking heavily and singing with the Royal Bodyguards and Companions who attended the banquet. Abdalonymus mused. What if Chiboulet was to catch Alexander's eye? What if Ptolomey or Seleucus, or any of the Macedonian dignitaries fell in love with her – not impossible given her striking beauty – and take her for his wife? Should that happen his tenure of office would be secured forever and he would be equal to the most prominent among the conquerors.

Not for a moment did his promise to Bomilcar trouble his mind. It had been given by a different man, in another time and world. Assuming it had had any worth then, its relevance and significance had been wiped out by new circumstances.

18

Waiting Time

For two consecutive nights Bomilcar had slipped into Chiboulet's bedroom which had become the scene of passionate love-making. When dawn was about to break, he had slipped back to his temporary accommodation trying not to be seen. Although Artas did not disclose that she was aware of their nightly meetings, not only did she know about them she had encouraged them, moving Jason to her own bedroom as soon as the garden shed was ready for her guests. Chiboulet had been very persuasive; the complicity between mother and daughter worked well.

During the day the lovers had time to themselves; that was because Matten spent hours hunting in the surrounding wooded hills, while Artas was busy packing, in anticipation of their departure to Sidon. As a result the two had the blissful opportunity to be on their own most of the time. Weather permitting, they paced the grounds around the farmhouse or sat beneath the fig tree that had been witness to their love-making. When they were outdoors they had to make sure not to display any gesture or attitude which could give away their intimacy and which could be witnessed by Abdeshmun's sons, patrolling the area.

Contrary to the night hours spent in passionate embraces, which made them oblivious to anything else, and contented slumber which had exactly the same effect, days were less carefree. Both being discerning people, they were aware of the difficult situation they were in.

'Do you think your father will go back on his word?'

'I love you. I don't ever want to be separated from you,' she retorted, hoping that this display would spare her more probing.

'That does not answer my question.'

'He's a good father and he cares for my happiness.'

There was another problem, which required a lot of careful thinking before a decision could be taken. 'Your mother suggested that I go to your father and ask for his permission, as if it had not been granted already. Does she know something we don't? Has she had a discussion with your father about us?'

'Nothing of the sort. Everything happened so quickly. Why all the worry about coming with us? Are we not promised to each other?'

Her last question was less of a question than an attempt to reassure herself. He took it as such and did not insist.

'Precious Chiboulet,' he said, 'your father is a man of his word. I don't see why he should change his mind, particularly when the uncertainty that delayed our wedding has been dispelled. If I go to him now and ask for his permission, it would imply that we do not have his consent already. I'm reluctant to do that. Why don't you see him on your own and sound him out.'

'You're probably right. I'll do what you suggest; but what would you do in the meantime?'

'I believe the story I told Abdeshmun can still be very useful. Matten and I will wait here. Have we not made the trip from Sarepta to protect you and your properties?'

'Did I hear my name?' It was the blacksmith, who had just returned from the hunt, a dead deer on his back. With a powerful motion of his upper body he propelled the dead animal off his shoulders and it fell at his feet with a thud. He threw aside his bow and sat on the ground between his two friends.

'Did I hear my name?' he repeated.

'I was telling Chiboulet that you and I will wait here until she sees her father.'

'But that could take days,' objected Matten, 'don't you see we have a duty to our people. We have to prepare ourselves for a possible siege.'

Chiboulet moved closer to the blacksmith hoping to give more weight to the emotional appeal she was about to make. 'Do you realise,' she said, 'that two or three more days could make all the difference between happiness and sorrow, for the rest of our lives? I beg of you to give us this respite.'

Matten, unaccustomed to this kind of entreaty, especially coming from such lovely lips, mumbled, 'I hadn't thought of it like that; of course I'll not leave Bomilcar.'

'We are most grateful to you, are we not Bomilcar?'

The young man was not prepared to let himself be carried away by emotion. He bantered, 'Even if he wanted to leave me and return to Tyre alone, the idea of confronting Inat after his desertion will make him change his mind.'

They laughed, all of them having had a taste of the strong character of Bomilcar's mother.

'Let me tell you about the strange encounter I just had,' said Matten who was as reluctant as Bomilcar to dwell on sentimental feelings. 'You see this forest of firs?' He pointed at one of the hills overlooking the plains where the farmhouse stood. 'In the middle of the wood there is a small temple dedicated to the Baal of Mount Libanus. I went inside to pray to the god when all of a sudden, an old man materialised by my side. I didn't know from whence he came. He gazed at me with piercing eyes and said, "You are the new Heracles. The labours awaiting you are no less strenuous and dangerous than his."

'You can guess how baffled I was by this prediction,' pursued Matten, 'so I asked him whether I will successfully complete the tasks awaiting me. He replied, "You will, provided the sea is not crossed on foot." '

'Is this some sort of a proverb?' asked Bomilcar.

'Never heard of it. I believe the man is deranged.'

19

Swift Adaptation

Ahead of Abdalonymus's solemn entrance into his city, Hephaestion had sent orders for criers to mobilise the population and for food and wine to be distributed freely, in line with Alexander's orders.

The presence of soldiers from the victorious camp, drunkenness and a wish to curry favour with the new rulers contributed, along with genuine jubilation, to a widespread festive mood, when Sidon's king and his retinue reached the western gate a little before dusk. Abdalonymus entered the city riding an adorned mule, flanked by Theron and Tryphon on similar mounts and escorted by foot soldiers. An exhilarated crowd surrounded them and led them to the public place, which was lit up by a multitude of torches.

In no time Abdalonymus had adapted himself to his incredible good fortune and, as a result, he received the tribute of his subjects gracefully, as if it was long due. Success and short memory went hand in hand, as is usually the case; unlike failure, which cannot easily be eradicated from the sufferer's mind.

His mood changed when voices from the crowd hailed Theron and Tryphon as the agents of Strato's downfall. These voices were an unwelcome reminder that the king's unexpected rise was not due to his merits but had been engineered by his predecessor's foes.

While he increased his marks of friendship towards the two Sidonians, he was resolved to keep them at arm's length the moment their usefulness came to an end. Had they not turned down his invitation to make them his advisers when, in a moment of exaggerated sense of obligation, he had made his offer? In retrospect he found them very selfish, disclosing a resolve to sacrifice duty for a life of pleasure.

Waving and smiling to the crowd, he muttered, 'Let's go to the temple. I wish to offer a sacrifice to Lady Astarte to thank her for her bounty towards me.'

'Could it not wait until tomorrow?' The question surged from Tryphon, who was tired and impatient to go home.

Abdalonymus grasped the opportunity to move away from company which was making him feel uncomfortable and to show his subjects that their two compatriots were not necessarily to be seen with him at all times.

'Go home, have some rest. I cannot do the same,' he said. 'As her High Priest, my duty is to offer Lady Astarte sacrifices and libations the moment I set foot in her city. I should have done so when we passed by the temple of Lord Eshmun, but it was already getting dark and we had to move faster.'

Theron and Tryphon interpreted his words as a mark of consideration for their well-being at the end of several exacting days. They thanked him and were about to head home when he asked, 'Are you coming to see me tomorrow?'

'When do you want to see us?' asked Theron.

'Late afternoon.'

The following day, when the first rays of the sun restored nature its colours, two female slaves woke Abdalonymus as instructed. He left his comfortable bed, sumptuously inlaid with ivory, and abandoned himself to the care of the slaves who had prepared a bath. They scrubbed his body and doused him with perfumed oils; then they presented him with a choice of garments. The wardrobe was magnificent, including purple linen robes, blue tunics, white shirts, cloaks and sandals to match. He was dazzled.

'Where did you find all these clothes?' he asked.

'Ennion, son of Badbaal brought them as a gift.'

'Who is this Ennion?'

'We don't know. We used to see him in here very often.'

'Call the attendant,' he ordered.

Soon afterwards, preceded by jangling keys, a bald man of small stature and venerable age entered the room.

'Who is Ennion, son of Badbaal?' asked Abdalonymus

'Sire, he was Strato's most trusted adviser.'

'Summon him.'

'He is here waiting to be received by you.'

'Bring him in.'

The impression given by Ennion at first sight was very deceptive; the man was endowed with perspicacity and shrewdness, as unwary interlocutors often discovered. Abdalonymus thanked him for his gift, then tried to unsettle him. 'Are you not very close to Strato? What will he say when he is made aware of your visit ?' he asked.

If Abdalonymus believed that his question was going to embarrass the old courtier, he was mistaken. Ennion sighed then answered, 'Sire, friendship is one thing and politics another. Long before Strato was deposed, I warned him that subservience to the Persians was endangering the city. I advised him to pursue a more balanced policy but he was deeply engaged and did not heed my advice.'

'You did not answer my other question,' insisted the King.

'I was about to. Strato is aware of my visit; in fact I came to see you as your faithful subject but also on his behalf.'

'What does he want? Is it not enough that no one harmed him?'

'Sire, I came with a message of peace. Strato prays that you accept that he had nothing to do with the small disturbance which occurred before your arrival. He gives you his full backing and wishes you a prosperous and peaceful reign.'

Abdalonymus left his seat and paced the room, reflecting on Strato's message.

'What guarantee will he give me that he will not change his present disposition?' he asked.

'All members of the Council of Elders, including those with family and business connections with Strato, are waiting to be received by you. All are prepared to swear an oath of allegiance to you. If you wish I'll summon them.'

'Go and do that.'

'Sire, may I speak in your name?'

'You may, but only for this instance; you will have to give me more proof of your loyalty before I rely on you for another mission.'

'Sire, I'll not disappoint you.'

20

Down-to-Earth

Preceded by the loud trumpets and crashing cymbals, Hephaestion entered Sidon and was received by the King, who had hastily mobilised a small crowd to greet him. The Macedonian general took possession of the Persian governor's mansion. He had fled as Alexander drew nearer, taking with him all valuable pieces of furniture and objects and leaving behind a mostly empty edifice.

The Macedonian paid no attention to the place's bareness, accustomed as he was to leading an austere life.

The moment they learned of his arrival, his two Sidonian friends rushed to welcome him and were horrified to find out that his accommodation lacked nearly everything.

Without losing a moment, they ordered their slaves to carry from their villa enough pieces of furniture, sculptures and vases to fill Hephaestion's rooms. That task achieved, they confided in the Macedonian about a matter that had annoyed them but which would have enraged any ordinary person who felt betrayed.

Theron and Tryphon were no ordinary people, in the sense that they were devoid of any ambition, political or otherwise. Furthermore, they had no illusions about finding permanent gratitude in human beings.

After dinner, Tryphon said in a casual tone, as if the matter bore little importance, 'We are disappointed with the way Abdalonymus started administering the city's affairs.'

'What did he do?' asked the general.

'On the very day he took office, his first move was to assign an official mission to Ennion. You recall who Ennion is, don't you?'

'Is he the foxy head of the delegation that came to me to hand over Sidon?'

'Precisely. He was the first person to be received by Abdalonymus and was immediately entrusted with the task of calling the Council of Elders to swear allegiance to the king. Ennion was Strato's closest adviser and many members of the Council are related either to Strato or his creatures.'

'What do you want me to do?'

Hephaestion's question would have disappointed any person who expected him to fulminate against betrayal, but Theron and Tryphon expected none of that. All they wanted was to communicate their annoyance to their powerful host. Theron left his couch and crouched down at Hephaestion's curled up feet; his naked thighs were at the level of the Sidonian's head. He caressed and kissed them tenderly.

'Don't do anything,' he said. 'Tryphon's report is meant to keep you informed of what is going on in the city. We expect nothing from Abdalonymus and we want nothing.'

Very gently, Hephaestion stroked the Sidonian's frizzy hair.

'I know that,' he said, 'otherwise you would not have spurned the crown I offered you. No other man would have done the same. You may have willingly lost a kingdom but you have gained my fond attachment. Still, I will talk to Abdalonymus. Tryphon, go to the palace tomorrow morning, and summon him to come to see me immediately.'

'Why me?' asked the baffled Sidonian, 'why not send him a messenger?'

'I will tell you why,' the general replied, 'being the bearer of my message will tell Abdalonymus, loud and clear, that you and Theron are my most trusted Sidonian friends, that you enjoy my full confidence and rank above anyone else, in my eyes, even a king.'

Tryphon was not in the habit of leaving his bed at daybreak, often not before the midday meal, but he changed his usual practice in order to convey Hephaestion's convocation to the king. Having explained the urgency of his mission to the attendant, he was taken to the royal rooms and received by Abdalonymus, to whom he gave the message. The king was tempted to ask why the general wanted to see him at once, but he changed his mind, unwilling to disclose his apprehension to his visitor.

In actual fact, he was extremely alarmed. That sort of message reminded him of how precarious his position was; just as he had been elevated to the throne, he could be ejected from it. He dressed quickly and went to the governor's mansion.

There he was kept waiting in the vestibule, in the company of a stocky middle aged man who was obviously not a local inhabitant and probably not from Phoenicia.

Abdalonymus did not have to wait long and was taken into another room, where he was received by Hephaestion.

'I came as soon as your message reached me,' said the King, after the usual exchange of civilities.

'I appreciate your celerity. I have been told that Ennion was the first to be seen by you and that he brought to you people close to Strato.'

Abdalonymus was stricken with panic because he feared he might have given the impression he was conniving with the Persian party. He was about to apologise effusively, but Hephaestion carried on.

'I have nothing against your attempt to neutralise the opposite camp,' said the general, to Abdalonymus's great relief, 'but don't give the impression that our camp is neglected.'

'I tried to convince Theron and Tryphon to be my closest advisers, but they refused,' said the king who had grasped what the general meant.

'Theron and Tryphon do not desire any office. You should know that the crown was first offered to Theron, who refused it, so you owe your position to him. They expect nothing, but I require that they be given proper consideration.'

'This I always intended to give them,' Abdalonymus assured him, while his dislike of the two Sidonians grew.

'That's all. On your way out ask the man waiting in the vestibule to come in.'

The other visitor was Lysinias. Dispensing with civilities, the general enquired, 'Where have you come from?'

'Tyre. I have information; that is why I came.'

'Tell me what you know.'

The spy was tempted to let the information he had gathered filter out bit by bit in order to boost his image as a master spy; however, he did not dare prolong the wait in view of the general's impatience. 'Nearly all the inhabitants of Old Tyre have abandoned their homes and taken refuge on the island. The islanders store food provisions, water and weapons . . . '

'That's nothing new,' interrupted Hephaestion, 'and is to be expected from people threatened with siege. What else can you tell me?'

'Two ships bound for Carthage have left port. The message they carry is that Tyre requires urgent assistance from its colony.'

'How many vessels do the Tyreans have?'

'I believe they must have tens of war triremes, a few quadriremes, cargo and transport ships, penteconters and galleys.'

Hephaestion exhaled a deep sigh. His thoughts went to the twenty Athenian ships that Alexander had kept, mainly to carry his siege equipment but also for their crews to be held as security for Athens's good behaviour, while he was battling in Asia Minor. He turned his attention to another subject. 'This man, the one who is at the head of the uncompromising party, what is his name?'

'Abbarus.'

'Has he been dealt with?'

'Not yet,' said Lysinias meekly.

'Why not?'

'I am working on a way to have him killed without attracting suspicion. Otherwise I'll have to leave Tyre at a time I believe I'm needed there.'

No person of importance relished being reminded how much the services provided by an individual in his employ were worth. Hephaestion was no different and he dismissed his master spy.

Immediately after he regretted having discharged him in such a cavalier way and sent him, a purse and recommendations for him to rest for the night before going back to Tyre. Like any good officer, Hephaestion was very keen on the welfare of his soldiers and knew how to buy the loyalty of those who worked for him.

21

Separated

The two lovers were dreading the moment when Abdalonymus would send for his family and force them to part, even if it were for a short while, as they wanted to believe. The impending threat made their union more intense and they enjoyed six more passionate nights.

On the morning of the seventh day a messenger arrived at the farmhouse. He was riding at the head of a string of mules and a number of slaves. Two of the animals were intended as mounts for Artas and Chiboulet with her infant, and the rest to carry the belongings and personal effects they had chosen to take with them.

On their heels came Abdeshmun and his four sons to bid farewell to the family, whose turn of destiny was still hard to believe. One of the sons must have witnessed the arrival of the messenger and his train of men and beasts and alerted the rest of the family. Amidst the noisy confusion generated by the slaves carrying bundles of clothes to be loaded and fastened on the backs of the mules, the emotional parting of the lovers had to be mostly silent, the more so because Abdeshmun and his progeny were all ears and eyes.

Nonetheless, Bomilcar found an opportune moment to whisper to Chiboulet, 'I want to hear from you what your father has to say. Promise you will come back to tell me.'

'I'll try my best.'

'No. It isn't good enough. I want your promise.'

'I give it to you. Baal Shamem is my witness.'

When the time came for the convoy to depart, Artas said to Abdeshmun, 'Our guests will stay here until the king sends for them. I count on you to take care of them and keep an eye on our slave, who will be watching over the farmhouse.'

'Do not worry, your guests will be well looked after and I'll oversee your slave. May the blessings of Eshmun, Astarte and all the gods never forsake you.'

Artas thanked him and ordered the convoy to proceed; men and animals complied and made the first steps towards Sidon. The pace was slow on account of the heavy load carried by the animals. By turning her head Chiboulet was able to see Bomilcar waving farewell for a long moment.

The convoy disappeared behind a pinery, re-emerged for a short while and then disappeared for good. Although aware that he was not going to spot them again, Bomilcar remained at the same location staring in their direction long after Abdeshmun and his sons had left, until Matten shook him out of his torpor.

'Come,' he said, 'let's go inside, or for a walk, if you prefer.'

Entirely absorbed in his thoughts, Bomilcar said, 'I should have taken her to Tyre. I shouldn't wait to hear whether her father will renew his consent. After all he has already given it. Why did I agree to wait?'

'Remember, it's her mother who pressed you to go to the King.'

With childish bravado Bomilcar bragged, 'I didn't need to listen to her. Who is she to tell me what to do? Only yesterday she was a farmer's wife.'

'Calm down, it's too late now. Let's be frank, you know perfectly well that you cannot afford to go against Abdalonymus's will.'

'Why not?'

'Because Abdalonymus is the King of Sidon and we Tyrians cannot afford to give the Sidonians and their ruler an additional reason to hate us. Certainly not now, not at a time when their ships are on the high seas, Alexander is at our gate and we don't know what his intentions are. Do you wish to be the one to turn Sidon into Tyre's mortal enemy?

Bomilcar knew that Matten's rebuke was well deserved and

offered no objection or comment; instead he agreed to take a walk.

They followed an uphill path they had not trodden before, which ran in the opposite direction of the way to Sidon. The hill was not forested and they had not explored it so far, assuming it was not a good hunting area. Until then they had been under the impression that Abdalonymus's farmhouse was in the middle of nowhere, far away from any habitations other than Abdeshmun's. After just half an hour's walk, they were surprised to find themselves overlooking a hamlet nestled in a combe.

They could not see or hear any sign of life so they came closer. It was only when they entered the village that they heard a confused din, followed by what they thought to be the sound of laughter. They advanced further and discovered the reason for the racket.

The entire population of the village had formed a ring around a monkey-keeper, who was showing them the tricks that his animal was capable of performing. The man would shake a tambourine one, two or three times and the monkey would respond with the same number of somersaults. Continuous shaking of the tambourine and the animal would pretend to be dead, rising only at the sound of one drum beat. Each stunt was punctuated by a burst of laughter.

The spectacle was a welcome diversion in an otherwise dismal day; the Tyrians stepped forward to watch more closely. When he had a better view of the monkey-keeper, Matten held back an exclamation of surprise. Leaning towards Bomilcar he said, almost imperceptibly, 'I know that man; he is from Tyre.'

'Are you sure?' whispered Bomilcar.

'Oh yes, he's Abdastet, son of Abdshamesh the blacksmith. The father is helping in the manufacture of all sorts of weapons. I don't know what the son does apart from these antics.'

Barely had he relayed what he knew about the monkey-keeper than the animal leaped into the air and landed on Matten's shoulders. His master came to retrieve him and murmured, 'Wait for me by the fountain outside the village.'

Clearly Abdastet had recognised them.

They complied with his instructions and went searching for the fountain, which they found with no difficulty, rightly inferring that it must be located on the opposite side from where they had entered the village.

After a short wait, Abdastet appeared and signalled them to follow him to a more discreet place. They left the path and entered deep into a grove, pausing only when they were sure that they could not be seen or heard.

'What are you doing here?' asked Matten.

'Exactly what you saw,' answered Abdastet with a mocking laugh which implied that his activity was more than that. He carried on in a more serious tone: 'Besides gathering information, I have a message for you.'

'For us?' exclaimed Bomilcar and Matten together.

'Yes. I knew approximately where to find you. *Sitt* Inat told me what she knew. Both of you are needed back home. Bomilcar, you have to await in Sarepta for Azemilk who is due to meet Alexander after he enters Sidon. You, Matten, are expected in Tyre as a matter of urgency.'

'Who sent you?' asked Bomilcar, anxious to find an excuse to delay his departure until he had seen Chiboulet or at least heard from her.

'For you, the palace. For Matten, Councillor Abbarus. Now I must leave you. We mustn't give rise to any suspicion.'

22

Despair

'I must see Chiboulet's father, let's go to Sidon.'

'Are you mad?'

'Not at all. Haven't you heard our instructions? We cannot afford to wait any longer. I will see him and leave with Chiboulet. Going to Sidon presents no danger to us now that we have friends in the highest places.'

Despite his firm assertion, Bomilcar was far from being so assured.

'You yourself, said we cannot delay complying with our orders,' objected Matten.

'There will be no delay in taking a boat from Sidon. A few hours spent in the city will make no difference.'

Running out of arguments, the blacksmith fell silent. By the time they returned it was too late to proceed to Sidon, so they decided to leave the next morning.

When they reached Abdalonymus's palace, they were drenched from head to foot by the rain that had been pouring persistently since they had set out. The city being quiet by then, the soldiers who were guarding the gate did not pay attention to them, nor did the Macedonians standing by the palace's entrance.

They went in and requested to see the king. They were informed by the old attendant that he had left to meet Alexander, who was on his way to the city, where both were expected to receive a triumphal reception.

'I am the Queen's first cousin, take me to her. Tell her Bomilcar is here.'

The attendant believed the young man's newly found affiliation with Artas for the simple reason that he had had no time to get acquainted with all the relatives of the Queen or King. He left the two friends in the vestibule, which was poorly furnished and badly lit; they took advantage of the interval to remove their soaked cloaks and tidy their appearance as best they could. The attendant came back promptly and invited them to follow him.

They passed through several rooms without seeing anyone, as if the palace was uninhabited. They entered an antechamber where a female servant met them and took them to the Queen. She and Chiboulet were waiting, bewilderment and alarm written all over their faces. They kept silent until the attendant and the servant had left the room. When the door was closed behind them, the questions poured out. 'Are you well?' asked Chiboulet, barely able to conceal her anxiety.

'What made you change your mind and come here?' asked Artas.

Bomilcar had to fight back an impulse to take Chiboulet in his arms and reassure her. Not being able to do that, he eased the mind of his beloved one, asserting that no harm had befallen him or his companion. Then he apologised to Artas for the subterfuge he had used in order to be brought to her. After this preliminary he said, 'Remember, *Sitt* Artas, you, yourself, have recommended that I leave for Sidon in your company and see the King. After reflection I became convinced that you were right, so here I am with Matten. But maybe Chiboulet has already had his permission to leave with me.'

'You seem to forget that we came here only yesterday; we barely saw the King and this morning he had to take the road to meet Alexander. Chiboulet couldn't talk to him. She hesitated for a moment and then carried on, 'there's something else too.'

'What is it?'

'The King is not the same man. He has changed.' Artas's tone was baffled and sad.

'What do you mean?' asked Bomilcar, prompting a reply from Chiboulet. 'He's imperious, less patient. Obviously he has many problems on his mind. Seeing him like this made me refrain from opening the subject of our marriage. In any event I didn't have time. But he is expected tonight and I will talk to him, I promise, whatever mood he may be in. I am as eager as you are for us to be together.'

'Prove it, leave with me. We already have your father's permission. Why should we annoy him again? You must understand I cannot wait forever. I must go back home.'

Bomilcar's outburst worried Artas and Matten, but for different reasons. The Queen was afraid to bear the brunt of her husband's wrath if Chiboulet were to elope; while the blacksmith could not allow his friend to be responsible for raising the tension with Sidon. Both of them intervened.

'What you have in mind is unreasonable. Chiboulet must speak to her father; it's a matter of being patient for a few more hours,' said Artas.

'We must wait until she has done so,' approved Matten, displaying none of the impatience he had shown whenever confronted with the factors which had delayed their return to Tyre.

'Tomorrow everything will be made clear. Spend the night in town; my servant will take you to a nearby inn. Unfortunately, you cannot stay here, for Alexander is to honour us as our guest,' said Artas.

With a telling look she encouraged her daughter to support her suggestion; half convinced, the latter complied with a nod.

A fresh distribution of food and wine had left the Sidonians in a merry state; nearly all had closed their shops and left their homes to revel in the streets pending the arrival of the Macedonian, who had been recognised by the population as a liberator, thanks to a successful promotional campaign.

Bomilcar, Matten and the palace servant forced their way through the drunken crowd to reach the inn. Inebriated customers had taken over the public room, so the Tyrians retired to their lodgings, even though the sun was still high in the sky and their room was desperately unwelcoming.

After a while inactivity made them bored and hunger pressed them to search for food outside the stinking and noisy place they were in. They left and went in the direction of the sea, which was hidden from view by a maze of narrow streets. Surprisingly, it was only a few steps away and they reached the seashore in no time. They headed north, looking for an eating place. By the enclosed port, where a few small boats were anchored, they found what they wanted.

A fisherman was busy cleaning fish that he must have caught moments ago. A woman, seated on a stool, was tending an open fire that was protected from the wind by three slabs of stone which also served to support a grill.

Matten went to the man and asked how much he would have to pay for two cooked sea bass. The amount he was quoted was outrageous and he was about to argue but Bomilcar discreetly pinched his cloak. As Tyrians it would be unwise to draw attention to themselves. Grumbling, the blacksmith paid the asking price and he and Bomilcar were offered two stools while they waited for their meal to be cooked.

When it was ready, the woman retrieved the fish from the hot grill, placed each one on a fig leaf and handed them to her waiting customers.

Halfway through their meal they heard a commotion, which was soon drowned out by loud martial music produced by drums, trumpets and flutes.

'No doubt that's Alexander. We must see the parade,' said the blacksmith, excited.

'Alexander and Abdalonymus,' specified Bomilcar. 'We'd better avoid being seen by him while he's riding with the Macedonian. We can't predict his reaction.'

Matten silently acquiesced; they finished their meal, and returned to the inn.

Bomilcar had not mentioned Chiboulet's name all afternoon; but once in their room, he aired a dejected mood.

'I have the feeling that Chiboulet will never leave with me,' he said.

'What makes you say so? Don't you love her? Doesn't she love you?'

'That's beside the point,' answered Bomilcar with a sigh, 'it has nothing to do with us. It's on account of something I wasn't able to perceive until we came here.'

'What is it?' Matten was growing impatient; his pragmatism made him unable to fathom subtle discourse.

'At the farmhouse, I perceived Chiboulet as a farmer's daughter, even after her father became king. But here the reality is plain for me to see. She's someone else now and her father is Alexander's protégé. Do you realise what this means? He is a king in one camp, while we will probably be in the opposite one.'

'Don't despair,' said his friend, trying to cheer him up. 'Chiboulet is a clever girl and very much in love, she will find the necessary arguments to convince her father.'

'That's the only hope I have.'

23

Shattered Dream

A little earlier, Hephaestion had assigned to Theron and Tryphon the task of making the necessary arrangements for Alexander's arrival at Sidon. Both had considerable taste and means and they made use of them to ensure that the Macedonian's reception would be magnificent. A triumphal arch, made of greenery and flowers, was erected at the outer side of the northern gate and a chariot covered with palm leaves and flowers was kept ready for the conqueror's triumphal entry into the city.

Tryphon was in facetious mood and contrary to his friend's best judgment, he decided to give Abdalonymus the measure of his real importance. Instead of a noble horse as a mount, he had ordered him a mule, richly harnessed lest the scorn became too obvious.

Hephaestion was made aware of the intended mischief and found the idea greatly entertaining. It was not uncommon for a conqueror to demean the person in authority whom he had himself put into his position, should he feel that his creature exaggerated his own importance or was inclined to acquire greater independence.

Abdalonymus, Hephaestion and a small retinue were waiting for the Macedonian at the mouth of the river Bostrenus. Scouts warned them that he was approaching and they made preparations to receive him and join his parade without having to delay his progression.

He arrived riding on a horse – not Bucephalus, his beloved black charger, which he mounted during battle only. Youth, beauty and noble bearing made him look like a fair god; curls of his blond hair emerged from beneath a lionskin cap that he used as a headdress, a reminder of the representation of Heracles, his appropriated ancestor. The golden edge of his white tunic could be seen under the purple cloak that hung round his shoulders, down his back and covered part of his mount's hindquarters; he was unarmed, but at his sides rode his faithful Bodyguards in full armour and behind them came a detachment of Companion Cavalry.

The waiting party joined them and they all proceeded in the direction of the town. When they reached the northern gate, they were met by a cheering crowd and uplifting martial music. Alexander dismounted and so did Abdalonymus and the Bodyguards; their horses were taken away by stablemen who had been waiting for them.

Alexander stepped up on to the chariot made ready for him and his Bodyguards took position on foot. Abdalonymus looked for the fresh horse he expected to ride next to the Macedonian's carriage; instead he was presented with a mule and he had no choice but to accept it. Deeply humiliated, he gathered his resolve to show the happy face that circumstances dictated. They entered Sidon.

Abdalonymus tried his best to put on a brave face and to take for himself whatever share of the joyful welcome he could grab, so he mimicked the conqueror's waving of the hand, but he neither deluded himself nor the crowd, which ignored him, and he sank into dejection, which he hid behind a poor smile.

More humiliation awaited him; when the parade reached the official sector where the king's palace and the governor's mansion stood, Alexander chose the latter for his quarters. It was not that he intended to demean Abdalonymus – he had no reason to do so and was unaware of Tryphon's mischief. The choice he had made was dictated by a wish to cut short the official reception and to spend the evening among his fellow Macedonians.

All the same, Abdalonymus felt victimised, so when he went back to his family he was in a dejected state. Chiboulet realised that it was not the best of times for her to remind him that he had promised her to Bomilcar. Nonetheless, she also felt the pressure put on her by the young Tyrian, seething with impatience. Having no other option, she said, 'Father, Bomilcar is here.'

'Where? In the palace?' he yelled. The intensity of his tone frightened her. Before she could answer, he asked, 'What does he want?'

'But, father, I am to be his wife. You gave him your word.'

Abdalonymus loved his daughter dearly and hated making her unhappy; at the same time he was determined not to keep the promise made under totally different circumstances for a number of reasons, not least of which was that he had other matrimonial plans for her. Her marriage should serve to enhance his status, which needed so much strengthening just now. He undertook to make her see sense.

'Come here, near me,' he told her and gently stroked her head. 'Do you have any doubt that I want, above all, your happiness?' he asked.

'I love him and I can't be happy if I'm separated from him.'

'There are other factors to be taken into consideration,' he said.

'Such as?'

'He's a Tyrian; according to my information his city will not open its gates to Alexander. The Tyrians believe that they have nothing to fear on their island.'

'I don't see why the prospect of hostilities between the Macedonian and Tyre could be an obstacle to our marriage,' she objected.

He explained: 'If Alexander wages war against Tyre I must assist him. He expects me to repay what I owe him and is confident that I'll not let him down. With you in Tyre I will lose his confidence and most probably my throne.'

The argument perturbed Chiboulet and silenced her, but not for long. After a while she thought she had found a solution and her eyes sparkled with excitement. 'I will convince Bomilcar to remain here until the danger of war is dissipated. He will not disappoint me. That way your position will not be threatened,' she said.

Abdalonymus realised that he needed to be more straight forward, even brutal with his daughter for her to abandon the idea of her marriage to Bomilcar.

'Dear daughter,' he said, 'you must forget the young man, not only for what I just said but for an equally significant reason.'

Chiboulet's look invited him to carry on.

'How old is Jason?' he asked. The young woman was completely baffled by the unexpected question; nevertheless she replied that he was less than a year and waited to hear what was to follow.

'If something happens to me, Jason will be the next king. Being under age, your husband will want to be the regent. The Sidonians will never accept a regent from Tyre; neither will Alexander. The dynasty that I have the possibility of creating for our family will die with me.'

Abdalonymus's explanation fell like the executioner's sword. Her dream shattered, she realised that she could never marry Bomilcar. She turned towards her mother, who was staring at her with tender commiseration, as powerless as she was. The events confronting them were of great magnitude and set in action by the gods' disfavour. Chiboulet threw herself in Artas's arms, who cradled her as she used to do when she was small.

Then she freed herself and ran to her room to cry her eyes out for a love made impossible by her father's dynastic delusions.

24

Unreasonable Expectation

Artas followed Chiboulet into her room to check on her and give her more comfort. That was not her only objective; something else weighed on her mind, words she had heard from her husband which she felt she must convey to her daughter. She did not know how without seeing her anguish and sorrow increase. Realising that remaining silent would not make the matter disappear, she decided to tell Chiboulet part of what she knew.

'It would be much safer for Bomilcar and Matten if they were to leave Sidon tomorrow, at first light,' she said.

Chiboulet, who was lying face down on her bed, turned her head towards her mother and the expression of her tearful eyes changed from sadness to shocked surprise. 'Why do you say that?' she asked.

Artas did not answer but carried on, 'I will send them a word with a servant to tell them they can't stay here.'

That was too much for the young woman to accept; her barely controlled rebellion came to the surface and she cried out. 'Mother, they are not servants who can be dismissed offhandedly. I want to know what is behind this idea of yours to send them such a message.'

'Your father has threatened that if they stay in Sidon one more day, he will expel them by force.'

'That's very degrading; I cannot allow that infamy and I cannot allow a servant to warn them. I'll go myself.'

'What? In the middle of the night?' exclaimed Artas.

'I have no other choice. I must see him. I promised him, no, I pledged to him in the names of the gods, that he would hear of father's reaction from me. In any case he is entitled to an explanation from my own lips, maybe then he will read what's still in my heart. Oh Mother! I love him. What cruel fate makes fortune the cause of my misery?'

'My poor girl! Promise me that you won't elope with him and I'll let you see him, but I want your solemn promise that on no account will you leave Sidon. If you do that you will break my heart.'

'I must admit the idea had occurred to me but rest assured, I'll not do it; I can't betray father and stab him in the back. I realise how much the throne means to him, and to you, Mother – and I'd never be so selfish as to bring on our family's downfall.'

Chiboulet started sobbing and she needed some time before calming down in her mother's arms.

'My pretty one,' she said, 'a servant and a guard will accompany you. Go, and may the gods be with you.'

'Have you so little confidence in my word that you find it necessary to give me a guard for escort?'

'That's unfair; the streets are full of drunken people. You will need armed protection.'

The soldier and the palace servant who escorted Chiboulet to the inn proved invaluable assets. The servant was holding a burning torch to light their steps on the treacherous streets, and the soldier's pike kept leering drunkards at a distance. Although they did not present a real danger, they were a nuisance and had to be dealt with.

When they reached their destination Chiboulet ordered the innkeeper to tell Bomilcar and Matten of her visit. Impressed by the young woman's imperative tone and by the soldier's presence, he shook himself out of his inebriated torpor.

A short while later the two Tyrians appeared at the top of the stairs, visibly worried. Seeing them Chiboulet gestured to the servant and the soldier to wait for her and ran up the stairs. When she reached the two men she told Bomilcar, 'I wish to see you on your own.'

Matten heard the message and moved downstairs while the two lovers entered the bedroom. Once there Chiboulet burst into tears and threw herself in the arms of the young man.

'What is it?' he asked. 'What happened?'

Her mental distress was such that she was incapable of answering. His anxiety mounted, yet he tried to calm her; very gently he guided her to sit on one of the beds and sat beside her, asking, 'Why are you in such a state?'

'Because we cannot be together,' she replied between two tearful spasms.

The announcement did not take Bomilcar by surprise; when he had seen the young woman standing at the bottom of the stairs, he became almost certain that his premonition was about to be realised.

She had expected a violent reaction from him, a revolt maybe, but all he could say was, 'Tell me why.' The tone of his voice was resigned, as if he had already yielded to the dictates of fate. She reported her discussion with her father; when she had finished it took him some time to come out of his apathy. When he did he was excited, thinking he had found the answer to the impasse they were in. Totally oblivious of Matten's recommendation not to raise tension between Sidon and Tyre, he said, 'Come with me. We will leave at dawn before anyone notices.' He was fervid, full of unreasonable expectation. The sadness of her expression was eloquent enough and dispensed her from an answer.

Feeling completely powerless he exploded against those unseen powers which had destroyed their happiness. The outburst did him good; when his rage abated he was able to evaluate the situation in a more collected way. He took her hands in his and asked her.

'Do you still love me?'

'I do. What about you? You must hate me.'

'How can I hate you? I love you.'

They both fell silent, as if the assertion of their undying love had wiped out all obstacles, and they shared the same wonderful feelings for a moment.

Slowly coming out of his exalted state, he rose to his feet, paced the room twice, then stood in front of Chiboulet and said, 'We are living in exceptional times. They will not last forever. I am prepared to wait. Will you do the same?'

She did not have the courage to tell him that the obstacle to their union had more to it than Alexander's appetite for conquest; nonetheless she promised to wait for him. This was no well-meaning deception she was resolved not to marry anyone if she could not be his wife. Waiting was a state she believed she could pledge, the more so as she was blissfully unaware of her father's matrimonial plans for her.

The exchange of promises, put their minds momentarily at rest.

Suddenly Chiboulet recalled to the danger looming over Bomilcar and she made him swear to leave the following day. To make sure that no one would obstruct his departure from the port, the soldier who was waiting for her downstairs would come back early in the morning to escort him and Matten out of Sidon safely.

These arrangements made, they sat side by side, neither attempting to take advantage of their being alone in one room, for too many thoughts and worries kept their minds busy.

They repeated their vow to wait for each other and when the time came for them to part they exchanged a tender kiss. This restraint came naturally to them at that moment, a restraint they would bitterly regret with the passage of time.

Part Three

I

Second Mission Accomplished

'Have another drink.'

Laïs needed no encouragement in one gulp he emptied his wine cup before putting it down on the table before him with a bang. The alcohol made him bold and caused him to lose all restraint, so he started shouting abuse at his absent master. They were in the tavern, their habitual meeting place, and that sort of invective could draw unwanted attention. Lysinias cut it short.

'Tell me more about Crete,' he invited him.

Being reminded of his home country was enough to bring a change in the slave's mood. He buried his head between his arms, folded on the table, and started crying.

'Do you wish to see your beloved mother and your island again?' asked the Macedonian.

The slave lifted his head and from his eyes it was clear that the question had been hurtful.

'Not one day passes without my thoughts going to my mother,' he said, 'I don't know whether she's alive or dead. If she's alive, she doesn't know what happened to me after I was abducted.' His tears were accompanied by convulsive gasps.

Lysinias knew that he was emotionally ready for what he had had in mind for him all along.

'Do you know who stands between you and your mother?' he asked. Without waiting for an answer he carried on, 'Abbarus.'

'He's my master, he bought me. What can I do except curse him?'

With a motion of his hand the Macedonian dismissed what would normally be deemed a sensible reply. 'Remember what I told you when fate brought us together for the first time. I told you that if Alexander is received by the Tyrians he will liberate all Greeks from slavery. I tell you now what I said then: by exhorting resistance to Alexander, Abbarus is standing between you and your mother. And do you know where Alexander is? He's in Sidon. All he wants from Tyre is friendship, but friendship means that enslaved Greeks must go home, and that is what Abbarus and his friends wish to prevent.'

Goaded into hate, which amplified what the Macedonian was telling him, as well as by daring induced by alcohol, Laïs pledged, 'I'll kill him.'

In a matter of fact tone, Lysinias advised, 'That's what you have to do, and quickly, before he poisons the minds of other councillors and rouses the rabble.'

'He's leaving for Sarepta with the King's son. I heard him telling that to Anysos.'

'When are they leaving?'

'Tomorrow.'

'You must stop him at once; if you don't, you will never go back home.'

'What is it I have to do?' he asked eagerly.

'Wait until he sleeps and stab him with a knife. Make sure he's dead, then leave the house. Don't run; walk in your normal way and join me outside. I'll be waiting for you in the alley opposite the front door. I'll take you to Sidon as a free man, and from there you will embark on the first boat bound for Crete. Go.'

Lysinias left behind the slave. It was too early for him to go to his rented room and wait there until nightfall, so he decided to tour the island in search of information. He witnessed an unusual activity at the two harbours. He counted tens of triremes and a few bigger warships: some ships were already seaworthy; some were being commissioned; while others were hoisted on the quays and were being carened. Sailors and soldiers were everywhere, ready to take action when needed.

The two harbour mouths were guarded by triremes used as troop carriers and armed with Syracusan catapults. At the first sign of danger, fast triremes would be summoned by the piercing tones of trumpets, while archers and servers of catapults, positioned on the decks, would keep the enemy at bay until the fast ships and their formidable rams took over.

Lysinias did not linger long, lest he drew attention to himself; he went to an inn close to his rented room and ordered wine; pretending to be inebriated, he listened to the customers' conversations. That was one of his favourite ways of gathering information and one of the most rewarding, people were unbelievably careless when they had had a drink or two. When he left the inn, it was dark and it had started raining; it was also wintry cold. Bad weather would keep people off the streets and that suited Lysinias well.

He went to his lodging, wrapped himself in a heavy cloak, covered his head with a cap and headed for Abbarus's house. His destination was the alley with a direct view of the Councillor's house. Hidden behind a heap of refuse, he leaned against a wall and waited. He knew it was too early to expect Laïs, but his sense of duty made him unwilling to take any chance. He had to be at the place well in advance, in case the slave had an early opportunity to carry out his mission.

That was not to be. Lysinias waited and waited. He did not really mind; patience was an attribute he had acquired during his years of spying and the passing of time heightened tension and made the outcome more exciting.

A little before midnight the door of Abbarus's house was opened. Laïs came out and ran towards him, despite Lysinias's earlier recommendation. Although the slave could not see the spy, he knew where to find him

He arrived out of breath and shaking. The knife he was clutching dropped from his hand. Lysinias asked, 'Did you kill him?'

'He went to sleep at his usual time. I waited to enter his room until I heard his heavy breathing. I stabbed him several times, first in the back and when he turned towards me, in the chest. After a surprised yowl which I cut short by putting my hand on his mouth, he died without another sound.'

'You are a good lad and you have earned your freedom.'

Lysinias came closer to the slave, and put his left hand on his right shoulder, as if he wished to show him his satisfaction. With the speed of light, he moved that hand behind Laïs's back, drew him over and thrust the dagger he held in his right hand straight into his heart, where it remained embedded.

Laïs died instantly; his body was about to slump down heavily to the ground, but the Macedonian caught him, controlled the fall and moved away. It had never been his intention to let the slave live, for his capture would have taken a matter of hours. Under torture he would have told everything he knew including the Macedonian's name. . . That was a risk Lysinias was not prepared to take.

2

Preventative Measures

Idbal emitted a long, shrill scream. Worried about Abbarus not turning up for their daily morning meeting, he had gone to his bedroom and found him dead in a pool of blood. The scream brought Anysos up and both shouted the slave's name. When no answer was obtained, they searched the house for him but he was nowhere to be found.

Stunned partisans of the slain leader started arriving at the deceased's house. Laments and clamours for vengeance burst out sporadically, bringing the tension to its paroxysm; soon the place could not contain them all, and new arrivals filled the street.

Relieving himself in the alley, one of the partisans found Laïs's body slumped behind the heap of refuse. He reported what he had seen to Idbal, who decided not to attempt to uncover the motive for the murders of master and slave for the time being. More pressing matters needed his immediate attention.

Having conferred with Anysos, Idbal ordered the usual ringleaders to direct the crowd to the king's palace and, once there, to shout their fury, proclaim Idbal as their new head and demand that he be appointed a member of the delegation due to meet Alexander.

Everything worked according to plan; to calm the excited mob, both the king's son and brother received the hastily appointed delegation, and proclaimed Idbal a member of the City's Council of the Elders to succeed Abbarus. The newly appointed Councillor was not the scion of a family that was usually bestowed with such an honour. However, exceptional circumstances warranted Idbal's appointment as well as an invitation to join the royal delegation which was due to leave within hours.

A couple of days before Abbarus's murder, Bomilcar and Matten had sailed from Sidon without being the least inconvenienced; the presence of the soldier sent to escort them had proved a perfect deterrent. Bomilcar had disembarked at Sarepta's south port, resolving to avoid at any cost the sordid inn where he had stayed before. Instead, the young man took accommodation in an inn in the town's residential area, close to the temple.

His mood could not have been more different from that during his previous stay in Sarepta. Instead of the joyful expectation he had felt on his way to see Chiboulet, he was dejected, forcibly separated from the woman he loved with no realistic hope of being reunited with her.

Upon arriving, he had sent word to the town's governor to advise him of his whereabouts, with the request that he be immediately warned of the royal delegation's arrival. Then he locked himself in his room to grieve over his lost love. Alexander's campaign had meant very little to him until he had seen his plans to wed Chiboulet frustrated. At that point his perception had undergone a drastic change and he execrated the invaders and their king, whom he charged with the reason for his misfortune.

As for Matten, as soon as he had set foot in Tyre, he had been to the palace to let them know where Bomilcar was; after that he visited Inat to put her mind at rest. She was already aware that Sidon had had a new king but could not have possibly guessed that he was Chiboulet's father.

Informed that the wedding plans had been abandoned, her mind-set shifted from brief delight to extreme distress. In her words, Bomilcar was light-headed and unconcerned with his own interests. The daughter of a farmer had been unacceptable to her as Bomilcar's wife, and for that reason she had humiliated her; that was not the same of a king's daughter, who would have filled her remaining days with joy and pride, not to mention the heartbreak that an alliance with royalty would have brought to friends and foes.

Taking advantage of a lull in the string of moans, Matten had left on the pretext of attending to urgent business. He had gone to Abbarus who showed great pleasure at his return and urged him to work closely with Idbal and Anysos, his two faithful assistants.

The following day the blacksmith came to learn of Abbarus's murder, the shocking news having spread through town like a raging fire. He rushed immediately to the deceased's house to comfort Idbal and Anysos, who were in a state of shock, yet fully aware of their new responsibilities.

While he was in their company, the delegation chosen by the mob returned triumphantly from the palace bearing news of complete success. Jubilation replaced sadness, but not for long; the image of their murdered leader came back fast to remind them of their loss. Feeling like orphans, they turned to Idbal and confirmed him as their new leader. He must assume Abbarus's mantle and lead the struggle for the defence of the island.

Abbarus had no immediate family, so Idbal decided to carry on his new leading role from his house. While he prepared himself to join the royal delegation, he gave instructions to Anysos and Matten. The former already knew what he had to do, yet he was reminded of his duties and given new ones.

'You must intensify the physical training and weapons practice of our fighting men. In addition, I put you in charge of enlisting new recruits. Those whom you deem unfit for fighting will be kept busy fortifying and maintaining the city's walls as well as gathering a reserve of stones and boulders. That's the recommendation of the military officers I met earlier this morning. Our meeting went well; they will take over the direction of operations if we are besieged. For the time being they will provide us with their professional advice and teach us how to consolidate the fortifications of the town and develop defensive weapons. They recommend making the walls fireproof with birdlime and rawhide coverings.'

For a moment he remained silent, overwhelmed by the burden of his new responsibilities, but it did not take him long to pull himself together and resume his instruction. 'I will miss the funeral ceremony. Make sure it's an occasion to mobilise more people for our cause.'

He turned towards Matten and told him how happy he was to have him with them. He urged him to keep overseeing the manufacture of weapons, catapults and other war machinery. Then he added, 'Abbarus's murder must not remain unpunished. Our beloved leader must be avenged and we must know who killed him and why. Find out who the killers are.'

'I'll do my best.'

Matten's thoughts went straight to Bomilcar whose help, he knew, would be invaluable for that particular task; moreover, trying to find the murderers would divert the mind of his friend from brooding over his lost love and could possibly make him more engrossed in the cause.

3

Ultimatum

'I don't understand why I am not with King Alexander to receive Tyre's surrender. Am I not the King of Sidon, his loyal ally?'

Having heard that the Macedonian and the delegation chosen to accompany him were about to leave for Sarepta and that he was not part of it, Abdalonymus had gone to Hephaestion to complain. The general controlled his irritation and devised an answer likely to appease his visitor.

'It was deemed that your presence could create unnecessary tension with Tyre, in view of the old grudge between the two cities and their business rivalry, so we came to the decision not to involve you, so long as Tyre's position remains unclear.'

In actual fact, Alexander had not given any thought to whether or not Abdalonymus should accompany him, but Hephaestion could not decently tell him that.

The explanation satisfied the newly appointed king, who waited to bid farewell to Alexander and try to catch a glance, an approving nod, which would make him very happy indeed.

The Macedonian king and his retinue entered Sarepta and were met by Azemilk and the Tyrian delegation which was composed of Bomilcar, Chelbes, Idbal and a number of attendants. The Tyrian delegates had debated whether to receive the Macedonian outside or inside the town walls. Eventually, the view prevailed that a ceremony outside would intimate that Alexander was distrusted, so a formal reception was hastily arranged at the governor's house.

For most of the Tyrian delegates hopes were high that the golden crown and the precious gifts they brought to the conqueror as signs of their submission to his authority would satisfy him. They expected him to keep going for other places and other conquests. 'Why should he treat this island differently from Aradus?' they kept repeating.

Hamor and Eloeim, two career officers who were disguised as simple attendants, were less optimistic. They were aware of the strategic importance of Tyre's fortified harbours and its formidable fleet. There was also the threat they could represent in the event the Persian king decided to buy Tyre's allegiance, make use of its warships and incite trouble on the Greek mainland by encouraging the Greek cities to rise against the Macedonian while he was away from home. That threat could not be tolerated by Alexander and the Tyrian officers, knowing it, feared they might have to deal with a far less compliant conqueror than Chelbes and his partisans expected. Nonetheless they were absolutely confident in the island's impregnability; having no warships Alexander had no realistic prospect of taking the island by force. That was why the hard-liners felt secure on their island, as did the proponents of conciliation.

While waiting for Alexander's arrival, Azemilk sacrificed a ram and examined its liver, which was found complete. That and the way the animal bent its head and shivered when sprinkled with lustral water were a clear indication that the sacrifice was accepted by the gods and the augurs were favourable.

The conqueror was announced by the ear-piercing sound of trumpets.

Exceptionally, he was riding Bucephalus, which he normally did during battle only, but wore no cuirasse and had no arms. This sent a dual message of war and peace, which did not go unnoticed; accounts about the fabled horse and its master had preceded their arrival on the shores of the eastern Mediterranean.

He was surrounded by his Royal Bodyguards wearing cuirasses and Boetian helmets and followed by a squadron of Companions in full battle gear.

On behalf of the king, his father, Azemilk acknowledged Alexander's authority over Tyre's territories and presented him with the golden crown and numerous precious gifts, which were accepted. That was not the end of the matter, contrary to what the Tyrians had expected. The conqueror made a demand that stripped them of their illusions about satisfying Alexander with a nominal surrender.

'I accept your surrender,' he said, 'and because I am pleased, I intend to present a sacrifice to my ancestor Heracles in the temple of Melqart.'

The Tyrian delegates were stunned by the demand; Idbal was the first to get a grip of himself.

' My lord King,' he said, 'we will be most honoured to be with you when you offer your sacrifice in the temple in Old Tyre.'

'It's not the mainland temple I intend to go to, but the one on the island.' Alexander's tone was severe and curt.

Tension rose, for there was no doubt left that occupation was the conqueror's ultimate aim. Everything else was an act to disguise his sombre design. Before Idbal could reply with words that could anger the conqueror, Chelbes intervened. 'Sire, I am certain that Prince Azemilk will not contradict me when I say that we, the members of the delegation, welcome you on the island, in our temples and in our homes, but I must confess, to my deep regret, that our mandate is limited to surrendering Tyre to your sublime authority; for anything else we have to go back to the People's Assembly.'

Alexander was not fooled by the graceful words, nor convinced by the reason asserted by the Phoenicians to stall for time. However, a delay of a few days could do no harm. In any event, he needed that time to move his army to mainland Tyre, assemble his siege machinery and increase his pressure.

He stood up to give more weight to the words he was about to say. 'Go back home and do whatever you believe you have to do. I am prepared to wait four days but not a single hour more. That will give you time to consult the People's Assembly, but be assured I will not leave these shores before sacrificing to Heracles on the island.'

The Macedonian left the meeting without saluting the Tyrian

delegates. They and the two army officers went into a room to discuss the barely veiled threat they had received.

'I knew all the time that Alexander intended to occupy our island,' said Idbal.

'What difference does it make whether you did or didn't know that,' interjected an exasperated Chelbes, who carried on: 'if I accepted that our city prepared itself to sustain a siege, it was because I had hoped that the preparations would work as a deterrent. Apparently they have not and we are left with the same question: do we or do we not open our gates for Alexander? I say now what I said all along; we do not have to fight him. His wish is to set foot on our island. Let us welcome him there. War must be avoided at any cost.'

'Haven't you heard what he wants,' shouted Idbal. 'He wants to present a sacrifice in our temple, not to Melqart but to Heracles. Are we going to allow that?'

Azemilk was desperate to hear a view less charged with emotion; he thought that Bomilcar, who had been silent all that time, might be able to provide one.

'What's your opinion?' he asked him.

'I respect the views of both my colleagues. War must be avoided, as Councillor Chelbes said, but should we accept the hefty price that is asked? Councillor Idbal has mentioned the danger that our gods may be replaced with Greek ones and I can see from Alexander's demand that his concern is justified. There is, however, another price to pay and that is the loss of our fleet and our independence. Are we prepared to agree to that as well?'

Chelbes was disappointed with what he had just heard, having assumed that Bomilcar was still the carefree and joyous young man he knew and that the prospect of war would horrify him. He had no way of guessing the profound change of character that Bomilcar had undergone in a few days. Realising that no backing could be expected from him, he asked the officers, 'What can you tell us about the defence of the city?'

'The island is unassailable and our fleet invincible.' Was the reply he received.

It was obvious that the opinions of the members of the delegation were as far apart as ever. In any event, the People's Assembly would have the last word with regard to this vital matter; therefore Azemilk gave the order that they go back to Tyre immediately. Alexander's ultimatum should not be treated lightly.

4

Manipulation

Abdalonymus may have been a newcomer in politics; he had, however, an ingrained cunning that made him prepared to fight for the preservation of his new status. He felt that it was in danger of being eroded after a succession of events that had manifestly encroached on his position. Now he needed to react to gain back the ground that had been lost.

Before Alexander returned from Sarepta, he went to Theron and Tryphon, rightly recognising that they held the key to Hephaestion, and through him, to Alexander. Although the royal visit surprised them, the two friends received Abdalonymus gracefully. They still considered themselves indifferent to honours – a frame of mind they had taken refuge in until it became true, after years of being ostracised by the previous King of Sidon and his clan – nonetheless Abdalonymus taking the trouble to come to them did bring them a sense of satisfaction.

They were prepared to lend a favourable ear to what he would say and he was clever enough not to try to concoct any explanation as to why he had avoided their company so far. What he did was to announce the aim of his visit without any preliminary. 'It is in my mind to organise a hunt in the royal game park, to honour King

Alexander before he leaves our city. I want you to be in charge of all the preparations. My wife and daughter will greet our royal guest and oversee a banquet worthy of him.'

By involving his women, Abdalonymus intended to create an opportunity for Chiboulet to meet Alexander's Macedonian entourage. He had assumed confidently that because of her striking beauty, she would attract the attention of many: why not Ptolemy, Seleucus or any of the magnificent generals?

Theron and Tryphon had no means to find out what Abdalonymus was really after by throwing the hunting party and the banquet which was to follow. No trace of a grudge could be detected either from their demeanour or from their response to his projects.

'When does the hunt take place?' asked Theron.

That was precisely the question that Abdalonymus expected them to find an answer for, through sounding out Hephaestion, their intimate friend. 'Any time King Alexander chooses will do. Why don't you seek General Hephaestion's assistance for this matter?'

He returned to the palace satisfied with himself. He had no reason to doubt that the Macedonian, so fond of hunting, would turn down an occasion to practice his preferred pastime, particularly when on the face of it, it was his favourite general who had made the necessary arrangements.

In Abdalonymus's mind, the hunting party was to be the opportunity to get closer to Alexander without having recourse to Hephaestion's mediation each time he wished to see the conqueror. It was also the occasion for finding a husband for Chiboulet to pull her out of her depression, and by the same token strengthen his own position.

The following day Thypron came to Abdalonymus to announce that Alexander had accepted his invitation to hunt the lion, and that the hunt had to take place the same afternoon. That said, Tryphon left promptly, for he and his friend had much to do in terms of organisation.

With no time to spare, Abdalonymus sent for his wife and daughter and put them in charge of the banquet.

'My dear daughter,' he said, 'you're going to see and to be seen by the Macedonian elite. I want you to look your best.'

'I will do what you command, father.'

He took her answer for a signal that Chiboulet had most probably figured out his matrimonial project for her and that stimulated him to talk more openly about it.

'Among our foreign guests are splendid young men who have a very promising future. Keep this in mind.'

That was enough for Chiboulet to perceive what her father planned for her. 'Oh father!' she implored him, 'I don't wish to belong to any man; don't force me to take a husband. I've never disobeyed you, even when it meant I had to renounce the only person I have loved after Jason's father. Don't be so cruel as to demand that from me.'

She started crying, in silence, and the effect on her father was more effective than a loud outburst. He took pity on her, took her in his arms and promised not to marry her off without her consent.

He had lived long enough to learn that no sorrow is eternal, so he added, 'Wear your best dress for the occasion.'

5

Hunting Party

Back from Sarepta, Alexander summoned his generals to his tent; he wished to hear their views on the Tyrian delegation's evasive answer to his demand for sacrificing on the island.

Hephaestion passed on the information he had received from his informants about Tyre's state of readiness to sustain a siege. He added: 'Mainland Tyre is deserted; all its inhabitants have fled;

some took refuge on the island and the rest are scattered about the countryside. I don't see any sign that the Tyrians are prepared to comply with your demand.'

'Why can't we ignore them, keep them locked on their island and resume our campaign against Darius?'

The suggestion came from Craterus, who was immediately rebuked by Alexander. 'You want me to leave behind a powerful fleet that could sail in any direction the Persian king orders? Not being short of gold, he is in a position to buy Tyre's services as soon as I turn my back. Is that an acceptable risk?'

'I didn't see the position as my Lord has described,' retreated Craterus.

'Of course you did not, because you are not Alexander.'

With an eye in the direction of Callisthene, the chronicler who was taking notes, Alexander issued his instruction. 'Perdiccas, take the hoplites, the foreign troops and the baggage train to Old Tyre and wait for me. I will march tomorrow with the cavalry. Tyre's answer to my ultimatum should not be long in coming.'

'What about siege machinery and heavy weapons? Are they to be shipped to Old Tyre straight away or shall we wait for the Phoenician answer?' asked Seleucus.

'Ship them now,' replied Alexander, adding, 'as soon our troops become well encamped there, their cargo must be immediately unloaded and assembled. The Phoenicians must realise once and for all that I am not leaving their shores before their island is garrisoned and their fleet under my control. Nothing will make them understand that better than our siege towers, rams and catapults under their eyes. Go, carry out my instructions. Hephaestion, stay with me.'

When they were left on their own, Alexander confided in his trusted general and occasional lover, 'I don't expect to see Tyre surrendering voluntarily, so I welcome your idea of a hunting party before I fully commit myself to warfare.'

'You certainly need the little relaxation arranged for you.

Abdalonymus and his retinue are waiting for us at the game park.'

'Then you and Ptolemy will come with me. But first bring me Alistander. I want to hear from him whether Tyre will voluntarily open its gates.'

Moments later the old white-bearded seer entered the tent and stood motionless, leaning on his staff, waiting for questions to come.

'Tell me, old man, how long do I have to wait before Tyre surrenders?' asked Alexander.

Alistander did not resort to his usual preliminaries.

'Last night,' he said, 'I dreamed that you were standing on a beach all on your own. It was a late hour of the day and the sun was about to sink behind the sea. All of a sudden, you walked on water, as easily as if you were on firm ground, reached the sun, seized it and stopped it from disappearing.'

Alexander was listening, apparently pleased with the feat attributed to him, but keen to hear the precise significance of the dream.

'What does your dream mean?' he asked.

'My lord, the explanation is clear: walking on water means that the island will fall to you but not without difficulties. The Tyrians will not come willingly to you, you have to go to them and bring them under your dominion. Seizing the sun and preventing its disappearance means that Tyre will be conquered and other prestigious victories await you.'

Satisfied, Alexander dismissed the seer. With two of his generals and followed by an armed escort, he rode to the royal game park where they were received by Abdalonymus and his retinue.

With the same impetuosity he devoted to any dangerous action he undertook, Alexander threw himself into hunting the lion that had been released in the park. When the animal was tracked down and brought to bay, the Macedonian fought it, first on horseback and then on foot. The lion was pierced with spears and finished off by a well-delivered slash from Alexander's sword. Exhausted but gratified by the exercise, he retired under the huge tent that had been pitched following Theron's and Tryphon's instructions and which had its interior decorated with flowers and garlands.

Abdalonymus presented his wife and daughter to his eminent guests. Alexander showed them great courtesy but his two companions were totally indifferent. Then the women retired to oversee the preparation of the meal, leaving behind a disappointed Abdalonymus.

His consolation, however, was to have attained his other objective. That was a proud achievement that he would literally take to his grave; his first deed when Alexander left Sidon was to order for himself a sarcophagus made of marble and engraved with scenes of this same hunt.

6

Mainland Siege

'No, Mother, Chiboulet is not coming back.'

'My poor son, you must be terribly unhappy. What can I do for you? Shall I tell Tansu to hire musicians and singers for the evening?'

They were in the family room trying to warm themselves by the fire that was burning in a large brazier. Inat's offer surprised Bomilcar; he wondered whether his mother was unaware of the difficult time lying ahead for them or whether she feigned ignorance in order not to add worry to his heartbreak. Whatever the case might have been, his duty, in view of the critical situation they were in, was to hold a serious discussion with her and not try to fool her or pretend to have been fooled by her out of love.

'Mother', he said, 'there's a serious risk that Alexander's army will occupy the mainland. The situation may deteriorate further. I want you to leave. We have relatives at Byblos; go to them.'

'I will not leave without you; either we go together or we stay together.'

He knew how determined she could be, but he tried to make her change her mind. 'I beg of you, go for a few days, if for nothing else but my own peace of mind; you know that it's my duty to stay,' he implored her.

'And my duty is towards you. I'll not leave you.' She fell silent as did Bomilcar, their thoughts filled with a less than reassuring vision of the future. Eventually she shook herself up and said unconvincingly, 'The People's Assembly may decide to open the city's gates for Alexander.'

'You're right, they may well do that,' approved Bomilcar who harboured even less faith than she. He knew that Idbal's ringleaders were, at that very moment, manipulating the population and urging them to resist the Macedonian. He himself needed no persuasion to endorse the policy that denied the conqueror's demands. Besides being fully convinced that the island was impregnable by force, he had a personal reason for loathing the Macedonian, whom he blamed for the break of his ties with Chiboulet. He refused to see the irrationality of this feeling and the artificiality of its target, because he had conveniently closed his mind to perceiving Abdalonymus as the guilty party; his instinct, or rather his fancy, told him that, one day, Chiboulet's father might change his mind. Feeling compelled to blame someone, he had shifted his resentment on to Alexander, whom he also charged with having forcibly subdued the highly civilised Greek cities. Even though accounts of Alexander's refined culture and manners had reached Phoenician shores ahead of the invasion, he remained, in Bomilcar's eyes, a northern tramontane, a neighbour of the barbarian Illyrians and Thracians and not much better than them.

At that juncture Matten entered, dripping wet; he was in such an excited state that he forgot to greet Inat. 'Come with me,' he said to his friend.

'What's the matter?'

'Come. From the parapet walk you will see Macedonian soldiers setting up camp in and around Old Tyre.'

Bomilcar wrapped himself in a cloak and followed the blacksmith. They climbed a flight of stairs located inside one of the corner towers and reached the parapet which rose 150 feet above sea level. The rain had stopped and several onlookers faced towards the mainland, which was the scene of intense activity. Soldiers were exercising or pitching tents, while engineers were assembling what appeared to be huge siege towers. With the passing of time, Old Tyre's walls had progressively crumbled with no incentive to restore them. The population had moved to the island or the countryside leaving a ghost town behind them. The mainland was a mere 2,400 feet away, habitually across calm seas with ripples gently ruffling the water. On the face of it this distance could be easily crossed but the apparent tranquillity hid treacherous undercurrents and a depth of 600 feet close to the island.

Neither Bomilcar nor Matten were unduly worried by what they saw; they expected a siege but they were also confident that it would come to nothing. Siege towers and war machinery were useless if they could not be brought near the city's walls; moreover, with no fleet under Alexander, Tyre's harbours could not be forcibly entered.

Nevertheless, the activity developing not far from them generated a feeling of uneasiness that was very understandable under the circumstances. Although the sea was still open to the Tyrians, the fact that a threat from the mainland was perceptible with the naked eye was unsettling.

Bomilcar and Matten stood, fascinated by the spectacle, incapable of tearing themselves away, until the blacksmith mentioned, 'We should be going.'

The People's Assembly was due to meet to vote on a reply to Alexander's demand to visit their island. The previous day, the palace had sent criers all over the town, inviting all men old enough to carry arms to assemble at noon the following day, in the public place located by the sanctuary of Agenor, the mythical King of Tyre and father of Europa. The sun had reached its peak, so the two friends hurried down the stairs and rushed towards the meeting place, joining a stream of people going in the same direction.

The King's son, his brother and members of the Council of the Elders were seated on an elevated platform covered with an awning. Bomilcar sat among the Councillors and Matten joined Idbal's clan, which had gathered in one corner at the foot of the platform, facing Chelbes's clan in the opposite corner.

As priests of Melqart, Azemilk and Balator had donned the costume of their religious function. Their heads were covered with truncated conic headpieces, their tunics were white and the cloaks covering their shoulders were red. Each of them held in their left hands a staff crested with a golden bull.

Azemilk gave the floor to successive Councillors, who perorated for much longer than the crowd could bear. They started shouting Idbal's name and the opposite clan felt obliged to respond with Chelbes's name. The cacophony became unbearable, so the King's son stood up, gesturing for silence. The shouts died down progressively and he was able to make himself heard. 'We will listen first to Councillor Chelbes because he is an elder of the Council, then it will be Councillor Idbal's turn. In the event that there is not enough time for all would-be speakers and for casting the votes, we will reconvene tomorrow.'

Chelbes stood up, bowed in the direction of the two royal persons and delivered a well prepared speech. It was also well balanced; he presented the crowd with the prospect of a peaceful resolution of the crisis against a price that was no heavier than the price paid so far to the Persian king. He scared them with his description of the dreadful fate of the cities did not voluntarily surrender to Alexander. He finished late so Azemilk asked Idbal whether he wished to speak right away or start the next day.

Idbal realised that the crowd was tired and wanted only to go back to their homes. Nonetheless, he sensed it was wrong to send them away under the sole effect of Chelbes's speech, so he decided to strike a few cords until such time as he delivered his major address.

'Tyrians,' he said, 'Councillor Chelbes wants you to believe that Alexander's yoke is no different from Persian rule. He even mentioned that the price demanded by the new lord will not be unlike the price we have been paying. That's untrue and totally perverse. Darius did not set foot on our island, did not sacrifice to his god in our temples or seize our ships. The Macedonian is determined to do all that. He said it plainly and clearly. Are we going to let him?'

A furious roar of horror came from the crowd. Satisfied, Idbal indicated that he had finished for the day. Azemilk instructed the crowd to come back the following day at the same time to conclude the procedure.

7

Speculation

The crowd vacated the public place, all engaged in impassioned discussions about the merits and dangers of the two options they were presented with. Bomilcar took leave from the royals and joined Matten, who was waiting for him at the platform's foot.

'Come home with me.'

The blacksmith walked alongside Bomilcar towards the proposed destination. Although never talkative, his muteness drew his friend's attention.

'What's on your mind?' he asked.

'Could it be that Chelbes gave the order to murder Abbarus?'

'Chelbes is the wealthy owner of transport ships; he's very shrewd and would go to any lengths to keep the sea open for trade, but I don't believe for a second he would resort to murder. No, Abbarus was not killed on his orders.'

'Then who killed him and why?'

It was Bomilcar's turn to remain silent; having reached their destination, he felt that this matter deserved a more comfortable place to be explored. In the dining room they lay on couches, holding out their cups to be served wine.

'Are you going to address the Assembly?' asked Matten.

'I'll say a word,' replied Bomilcar, adding to the delight of his guest, 'yielding to Alexander's demand is out of the question. This island cannot be taken by force, he will soon realise that and leave. The activity we saw on the mainland was intended to put pressure on us but I will not be intimidated.'

'I'm so happy to hear you have joined our ranks. That's wonderful news that I will take to Idbal. He was anxious to know how you would be casting your vote.'

'Alexander cannot be trusted. Everywhere he goes he brings havoc with him. Remember how peaceful our cities were before he turned up. His thirst for new conquests has disrupted our lives and kept Chiboulet away from me.'

Matten was careful not to try to put the record straight by reminding his friend that Alexander was only indirectly responsible for his heartbreak. The blacksmith was elated that Bomilcar had acceded to his own political view; his reasons were irrelevant, and Matten was not prepared to engage in a purposeless discussion. He was also keen to fulfil his mission to find out who killed Abbarus and why, so he brought the conversation back to its starting point, putting faith in Bomilcar's cunning, to help him unravel the mystery of the two deaths.

'Remind me where the bodies were found,' said Bomilcar.

'Abbarus was killed in his bed and the slave's body was found in a nearby alley.'

Getting involved in the mental exercise, the blacksmith added without being asked, 'Both men were killed as a result of knife wounds.' His eyes reflected the expression of someone satisfied with himself, but it was replaced by bewilderment when he heard the next questions.

'What kind of knives were used? Where were they found?'

Matten made a mental effort to recall those details. 'Abbarus was killed with a kitchen knife taken from the house. The murder weapon was found beside the body of the slave, himself killed with a dagger which was left embedded in his chest.'

Bomilcar rose to his feet and paced the dining room, immersed in his thoughts. Suddenly, as if struck by illumination, he stood still. 'The slave killed his master; he himself was dispatched by the person who instigated the murder.'

'How do you know that?' asked a baffled Matten.

'The other possibility is that an intruder entered the house, went to Abbarus's room and killed him. The slave woke up – maybe he was alerted by Abbarus's shouts – pursued the murderer into the street and was dispatched by him. On reflection, I disregarded this hypothesis.'

'Why? It's as conceivable as the thesis you've retained.' There was a hint of a challenge in Matten's tone.

Bomilcar picked up on it and immediately rose to it, expounding, 'The kitchen knife taken from the house is the weapon used for murdering Abbarus. If this dreadful deed had been carried out by the man who dispatched the slave, he would have used on the master the dagger we know he had on him. He did not do so, so the only assumption left is that the slave used an improvised murder weapon found in the house to kill his master, fled to join the person waiting for him outside and was killed by that person with his own dagger.'

'But why?'

'Why what?'

'Why did the slave kill and why was he killed?'

'That we have to find out. I exclude robbery as a motive, I will tell you why before you ask. You said earlier that nothing from the house is missing. If the slave's motive was theft, he would have chosen a moment he was in the house alone to gather what he had an eye on and disappear.'

'What motive did he have then?' asked Matten.

'It can't be because of a murderous grudge against his master because the murderer was killed immediately after by an unknown person. That does not happen when resentment leads to murder. You don't need an accomplice to settle a private score and assuming you need one, he is not supposed to kill you.'

The blacksmith muttered, 'If the motive is neither robbery nor homicidal hatred what's left is politics.'

'You said it,' confirmed Bomilcar.

'But who is behind it? I was right to suspect Chelbes.'

'No, no, I told you he is not capable of murdering or ordering the murder of anyone. We have to look elsewhere to find out who persuaded the slave to kill his master. Why don't you ask around about who the slave was seen shortly before the murder took place?'

'I'll feel more confident if you ask the questions.'

'I'll do that. The man who has the ability to manipulate a slave and convince him of killing his own master is really dangerous. We must catch him. That's not all.'

Matten's curiosity was aroused. 'What else?' he asked.

'How could I let down the dear friend who defied danger and accompanied me to Sidon making possible my reunion with Chiboulet?'

Matten sighed; he knew perfectly well that the last words had nothing to do with a sense of obligation but were intended to allow the young lover to mention the name of the person he loved and make her the subject matter of their conversation – or rather, his monologue – for most of the evening and probably a good deal of the night as well.

He was not mistaken and he had to listen to Bomilcar talking about Chiboulet until it was too late for him to return home. He stayed at his friend's house for the rest of the night.

8

Extreme Resolve

Alexander reached Old Tyre on horseback at the head of his Companion Cavalrymen, surrounded by his Bodyguards. Two of them displayed the shield and set of weapons attributed to Achilles and taken by the Macedonian, at the start of his Asian epic, from the temple erected at Troy to commemorate the mythical hero.

An abandoned house had been prepared for his accommodation but before he took any rest, he demanded to know the Tyrians' response to his barely veiled ultimatum.

'We haven't heard a word from them,' Perdiccas told him.

'The four days granted to them have elapsed.'

'Today's the fifth day,' confirmed the general, who added, 'I was waiting for your instructions.'

'Send envoys to the island now. I must get an immediate reply from these sly people.'

Six trumpeters, standing at the edge of the water and facing the island, produced loud, high-pitched sounds which drew the islanders' attention. Many rushed to the parapet walks, curious to know what was to come next.

Moments later they saw a rowing boat heading in their direction. When it came nearer, the onlookers were able to count four men standing at the boat's fore-end, each holding a palm leaf, an indication that they were emissaries coming in peace.

The palace was immediately informed of their imminent arrival and the king's brother sent orders to the officer guarding the eastern wall to allow them in and escort them to the palace.

When the boat carrying the envoys was within earshot, the Tyrian officer leaned over the parapet and shouted instructions to the rowers to cast anchor at the foot of the wall. They complied and waited most uncomfortably in the craft, which was jolting at the mercy of the swell.

It was out of the question to allow the boat into one of the ports and give the envoys the opportunity to inspect the system of defence put in place, and the occasion to see the number and type of moored vessels.

From the height of the eastern wall a wicker basket with enough room for two was lowered down and hauled up twice, transporting the envoys to the top of the walls. There, an armed escort was waiting to take them to the palace, but the soldiers were prevented from carrying out their duty by a group of bystanders who started a scuffle with them, for no apparent reason. As a result the envoys were left with no protection and were seized by another gang. In an instant their throats were slit and their still panting bodies thrown over the parapet into the sea.

It was obvious that the butchery had been carefully staged. As for the instigator of the outrage, a finger could be decisively pointed in one direction, namely Idbal's clan. It was that clan which was against any compromise with the Macedonian and must have resorted to the extreme means of a savage murder to frustrate any conciliatory efforts.

After the killing the mob surged through the streets chanting its triumph and threatening those who showed signs of disapproval. The same day, while immersed in such atmosphere, the People's Assembly reconvened and the vote it produced went overwhelmingly in favour of rejecting Alexander's demands.

After the vote the mob went berserk and attacked Chelbes who was on his way home; he was saved by Matten's intervention, at Bomilcar's request. What contributed to calming the rabble and allowed him to go free was the promise he made from behind the blacksmith, to bestow a tenth of his fortune for the defence of the island. He was prompt to forget when calm was restored.

Alexander had realised that something wrong had happened when he saw from afar what seemed to be human bodies falling into the sea. The distance was too great to be absolutely sure so he had waited for the boat to return. Eventually the terrified sailors had confirmed what the king had already suspected but refused to believe, for the killing of envoys was considered a most heinous crime, seldom committed because every army knew of the benefit of conducting negotiations through intermediaries when there were chances of avoiding the spilling of blood.

Seething with rage, Alexander was more determined than ever to take possession of the island and teach its mercantile population a lesson that would make them realise the cost of defying him. He summoned his Royal Bodyguards and officers of a lesser rank and told them of the infamy perpetrated by the Tyrians and his determination to avenge the envoys' murder. He ended his speech saying, 'I am aware that some of you believe that a mainland siege is all we can do in the absence of a fleet, that I am losing time here and would do better to move away and leave behind an army corps to maintain the blockade. I have never shared that view, least of all after Tyre's abominable outrage. I have explained my reasons more than once and I don't see the need to repeat them. I am more determined than ever to capture the island.'

He looked at his audience in a way that could be interpreted as an encouragement to hear the objections he knew would be coming. After a moment's hesitation, Craterus said, 'My lord, we are prepared to follow you anywhere you go but there's one feat we can't do and that's walking on water. How do you expect us to take the island when we have no warships?'

Many of those present murmured in a way which showed their support for what seemed to be a sensible objection. The King let them, noting in the process who shared Craterus's view. His intention was not to punish the dissenters but to rely on his habit of classifying members of his entourage in categories and then watching them move into the class he wanted them to be in, either because of the potency of his arguments and charisma or because he was able to bribe them, in some way.

He waited until the murmurs and comments died down. 'I'll ask no one to walk on water but I will pave the way to the island for your sake,' he said, then proceeded on a more serious note. 'My orders are to build a causeway to link the island and the mainland. Perdiccas, send surveyors under the cover of darkness to gauge the depth of the water between the shore and the island. Stones from Old Tyre and wood from the neighbouring forests will provide the materials for the causeway. Craterus, you are in charge. Everyone else has a duty to assist in mobilising, motivating and overseeing the men.'

He dismissed the officers and sent for his favourite seer. When Aristander presented himself he ordered him to spread among the soldiers the account of the latest dream he had had about Alexander and his interpretation of that dream.

9

Meaningful Olives

Conflicting feelings swept the islanders during the days that followed the killing of Alexander's envoys. For a large part of the population it was justified and they condoned the deadly reply to the invader's impertinent demands and anticipated his withdrawal from the mainland once he realised that the Tyrians were not going to hand over their island. Worlds apart stood a limited number of people who had a worrying vision of what was to come and feared the Macedonian's wrath.

Inat and her sister Amatbaal were among those who expected the worst, despite Bomilcar's efforts to reassure them. His repeated reminders that Alexander had no means of reaching the island and his promises that before long, the prospect of easier conquests would lure him away were met with the most disquieting comments. 'For someone about to leave he's very much present.' They referred to the intense activity that could be seen from the island. With no means of figuring out the use they were intended for, the tearing down of Old Tyre's houses and the felling of trees from neighbouring forests were ascribed to Alexander's desire for retribution.

Most afternoons were spent by Bomilcar and Matten discussing the development of the situation, or rather the lack of it; the Macedonian had not yet given any indication that he was about to lift the mainland siege or start anything else. Although the siege did not much disturb the islanders' daily life – except for the overcrowding of their city with large numbers of refugees from the mainland – it was irritating to see the enemy so close and have no capability to dislodge him. The one positive factor was the Tyrian fleet still enjoyed the freedom of the sea and used this latitude to bring more storable foodstuffs and raw materials needed for the manufacture of weapons.

During one of those afternoons, the two friends found themselves short of new arguments, so Matten turned to a subject still much on his mind.

'We haven't yet found the person who was behind Abbarus's murder,' he said. 'You've stated that we must know who he is lest his evil influence instigates further killing. Have you changed your mind?'

'No, I haven't. Under the circumstances we can't afford to overlook the matter. We must know why Abbarus was killed, otherwise no master will ever feel safe.'

'You said also that we should ask around whether the slave was seen shortly before he was killed with someone new. Where do we start?' asked the blacksmith.

'Did it not occur to you that Abbarus may have been killed by a person who was close to him?'

The question took Matten by surprise and left him speechless; this allowed Bomilcar to respond to his own question. 'We know that the motive for the assassination was political. Your suspicions went straight to Chelbes. Knowing the man, I told you he is incapable of having a hand in a murder. Idbal is of a different league. Look what happened to the envoys. Besides, let's not forget that he benefited from Abbarus's death.'

'So it's Idbal,' said a dejected Matten.

'Not so fast. He was a possibility I entertained for a while, before dismissing it.'

'You see me relieved. But tell me, out of curiosity, what made you clear him of suspicion?'

'His colleague Anysos was Abbarus's lover. With Idbal, the three of them were together every day. Should Idbal have harboured murderous thoughts and plotted to get rid of Abbarus, it would have been most extraordinary if Anysos's suspicions had not been aroused. One word that may have slipped from Idbal, one impatient gesture he may have made, would have taken on a different meaning. There's something else that is even more telling.'

'What is it?'

'Why should Idbal need anyone to carry out the killing? What's more, would he actually rely on an unsteady house slave? Would he confide in him? It's far from believable, the more so that he himself had plenty of opportunities to perpetrate the crime. He and the victim were practically inseparable.'

'Where do we go from here?' asked the blacksmith.

'We do what I first suggested, we ask around whether the slave was seen shortly before the murder with anyone he had had no dealings with before. Come, the best place to start from is the food market.'

When they reached their destination, Bomilcar interrogated one stallholder after the other. All they could get was a description of the urchin, until after a while, a vendor of olives came up with the piece of information they were looking for.

'Oh yes, I remember the poor devil. He was most appreciative of my olives until that man came along and denigrated them.'

'What man?' asked Bomilcar.

'I saw him several times, he is not from here. Can you believe that he had the nerve to say in front of me that olives from Crete are better than mine?'

'To whom did he tell such an appalling lie?'

Bomilcar's attempt to ingratiate himself with the stallholder worked wonders. 'That's what he told Laïs, Abbarus's slave,' said the stallholder, who added, 'You see, I heard them say that they were both from Crete or something like that, then the older man took the slave away to celebrate their chance encounter.'

'Where did he take him?' pressed Bomilcar.

'In there.' The vendor indicated with his extended arm a nearby drinking place.

'Now, describe the older man to me.'

The stallholder frowned, trying hard to think back. Bomilcar came to his assistance.

'Was he old or young? Short or tall? Thin or stout?'

'Oh, he was middle-aged, not tall but strongly built.'

'That's very useful,' Bomilcar encouraged him. 'Have you seen that man recently?'

'Now that you mention it, no I haven't.'

The two friends thanked the stallholder and headed for the tavern, where they ordered wine and invited the keeper to join them. He well remembered the slave and the older man who had visited his establishment on several occasions. He even knew the name of the latter, which he communicated to the two friends.

'That's the man who testified before the Council of Elders as to Alexander's mercilessness if resisted. That's the same man we saw at Sarepta and wondered whether he was a spy. He's definitely in Alexander's pay and must be detained.'

Matten needed no encouragement to take on that task; before Bomilcar had finished speaking, he was on his feet.

'I'll find him,' he said and left hurriedly.

10

Volunteering

A couple of hours later, Matten went back to Bomilcar to report that Lysinias was nowhere to be found. His landlord had not seen him for several days and had rented the room he had previously occupied to a family of refugees who were desperate to find vacant accommodation on the overcrowded island.

The landlord had also confirmed that his previous lodger left no personal belongings behind. It was unthinkable that Lysinias could be hiding on the island, for there was no way he could stay unnoticed in such a crammed place; the only logical explanation was that, having successfully fulfilled his mission, he had become nervous because of the notable tension on the island and had left.

With recent events firing up most of the population and making them support the unflinching determination of Idbal's clan, the motive for the assassination became less obvious. An effort of mind was needed to revert to the time when the Tyrians were divided in two clans, more or less of equal importance – one in favour of peace, at any price, and the other for the rejection of Alexander's demands, at any cost. While the two friends were busy speculating about what Alexander expected to gain from Abbarus's death, Inat entered the room with an urgent message from the palace. The Council of Elders was convened for that evening and Bomilcar was required to attend. He immediately left for the palace while Matten went searching for Idbal to report on their findings.

Habitually, the member of the royal family who was to preside over a Council session waited until most Councillors had assembled in order to make his official entrance. Not this time; Bomilcar found Azemilk and his uncle already engaged in conversation with a handful of Councillors surrounding them.

'Does anyone have any idea why the Macedonian takes apart the Old Town's houses or why he cuts so many trees that he has sent parties to the mountains to get more?' asked Azemilk, baffled.

One after the other the Councillors ventured an explanation, all of which appeared unsatisfactory under close examination. If Alexander intended to build a fleet why should he make his men lose time and energy demolishing houses? If his intention was to wreak vengeance for the crime perpetrated by the Tyrians and for the rejection of his demands, why not lay waste to the surrounding agricultural fields, instead of razing a town that had been deserted by its inhabitants?

Realising that most of the Councillors were now present, Azemilk put an end to private discussions and addressed the whole assembly.

'The reason I called this urgent meeting,' he said, 'is because I have been informed that Sidon's fleet is due to return home at the beginning of spring. If the ships enter the town's ports they will necessarily fall into Alexander's hands. We must do whatever is in our power to prevent it. I want to hear your suggestions how may we achieve that.'

Some Councillors were in favour of engaging and destroying the Sidonian fleet when it was close at hand; others advised secret negotiations with the new Sidonian king to convince him to sail the fleet away.

Bomilcar saw an occasion to be reunited with Chiboulet, and jumped at it. 'I know the new king, and I'm prepared to go and see him,' he said.

'We heard that he was no more than a farmer when Alexander chose him,' said Balator.

'Indeed he was. I knew him before his elevation and after,' confirmed Bomilcar.

'Go and speak to him in my name but be very cautious lest you end up in trouble,' recommended the King's son. 'We ought to promise the King a consideration should he accept to send the fleet away. I propose to offer him Sarepta, to be added to his territory once Alexander leaves the region. Any other ideas?'

After a lengthy discussion the Council of Elders empowered Bomilcar to offer Sarepta to Abdalonymus in exchange for denying the Macedonian access to the Sidonian fleet.

With no time to spare, the young man took leave from the King's son and Balator to prepare for his trip. He was accompanied to the door by a number of Councillors; some patted him on the shoulders to signal approval and encouragement and others gave him words of advice to remain cautious and vigilant.

He went home and sent Tansu to look for Matten and deliver a message urging him to return immediately to the villa. The slave was also instructed to summon Zaccho, the pilot of a merchant galley that was part of Bomilcar's business enterprise.

At that late hour, both men were found at home. Made aware of the message that Tansu brought him, the blacksmith responded straight away and was told of the intended trip to Sidon and of its aim. Unlike his reaction when the young lover had confided his plan for both of them to sneak into Sidon, this time he raised not a single objection but considered himself unreservedly part of the planned mission. He had been prompt to grasp its significance.

The exchange between the friends was short and to the point, aware as they were of the seriousness of the situation and the danger of their mission, good reasons to not allow themselves to lose time on vain words.

When Zaccho was ushered in, Bomilcar ordered him to have his sailing ship ready to leave from the northern port before dawn the following day. The twenty rowers needed to propel the ship when there was no favourable wind or when precise manoeuvring was needed, all had to be known to Zaccho and enjoy his full confidence. He nodded to pledge compliance, which was enough to reassure Bomilcar. Zaccho had been tried and tested on several occasions.

Left on their own, the two friends elaborated on the details of their cover, for it was out of the question for them to go to Sidon as official emissaries, not when the Macedonians were on the alert and hungry for revenge after the murder of their envoys.

11

Frustration

Just before the dawn of a foggy and rainy day, Bomilcar and Matten went on board the bowl-shaped sailing ship. Her single broad sail was kept lowered, but twenty oarsmen were in position waiting to be ordered to take the vessel out of Tyre's northern port. At daybreak, when it became possible to distinguish between a black thread and a white one, Bomilcar signalled to Zaccho to proceed.

The crew had been warned ahead to make as little noise as possible, so they toiled over their oars in silence; only the cadenced sound produced by the oars when they went in and out of the water could be heard.

The boat, propelled by the rowers, left the harbour and took the direction of the high seas to escape the attention of any Macedonian lookouts on the shore.

Once she was out of sight, her sail was billowed, but she maintained a northward course. Then, in keeping with Zaccho's calculations, which indicated that Sidon had been passed, she was turned around and pointed in the direction of that town. When she appeared on the horizon she seemed to be coming from the north and that was exactly the impression her passengers wished to give.

At midday she entered Sidon's port and lay at anchor. In comparison to Tyre's port, the number of ships there was very modest, a comforting confirmation that the Sidonian fleet had not yet returned home.

Bomilcar and Matten wished to avoid being recognised, so they sent Zaccho to the palace to request an audience with the King for two envoys sent by the Elders of Byblos. That was their cover. The pilot reported back that they were expected by the King.

They wrapped themselves in their cloaks, pulling down their hoods to hide their faces. If Matten's ginger hair was left uncovered, he would run the risk of being recognised, for the colour was most unusual among Phoenicians.

They arrived safely at the palace and were introduced into the King's rooms where they had to take off their cloaks. A stunned Abdalonymus paused for a moment, undecided about what to say or to do. Eventually he realised that if the two Tyrians had taken the risk of travelling to what had become an unfriendly territory, using a subterfuge to be received by him, they must have had good reason. He dismissed all the persons who were in attendance and invited his two visitors to take a seat. While they complied Bomilcar apologised, 'I beg of you to forgive us for the stratagem we have used.'

'You must have a justification, which I'm eager to hear.'

The King's tone was serious and his demeanour cold, so Bomilcar hastened to explain. 'We are sent by Azemilk and the Council of Elders.'

If the young man had expected the King to be impressed, he could not have been more mistaken. Abdalonymus had just started feeling more secure on the throne and the last thing he wanted was to get involved in the quarrel between the island and Alexander. He was determined not to take sides if possible and most certainly not to provide any assistance to Tyre, the more so that Sidon and Tyre had never been the best of friends, having much to compete for commercially. He was too cunning to reveal his thoughts or show any signs of annoyance, so when he invited Bomilcar to convey the contents of the message he had brought with him, his tone had softened to sound almost friendly.

'Sire,' said the young man, 'Azemilk has received information that your ships are due back in spring. He prays you not to allow them in. As long as they remain at a distance from these shores, they will comply with your orders, otherwise they will have the Macedonian voice to obey.'

'I can see that Azemilk is well informed about the course of our fleet,' commented Abdalonymus.

'He has to be; the fleet must in no circumstances fall into Alexander's hands and that's precisely why we came to implore you to send it away before it's too late.'

Having delivered the message in one breath, Bomilcar disclosed the consideration promised by Tyre, 'Azemilk and the Council of Elders will add Sarepta to your territory the moment Alexander leaves.'

The King stood up and paced the floor, giving the impression he was deep in his thoughts. In reality he had made up his mind the moment Bomilcar had made him understand what was expected from him. Under no circumstances was he going to endanger his throne, himself and his family by complying with Tyre's request, but he had to remain cautious until Alexander made his next move. Should the Macedonian appear to be pulling out as unexpectedly as he had arrived, any assistance promised to the Tyrians would turn to be most advantageous for him as it would be devoid of any relevance. On the other hand, should Alexander continue to show determination to take the island by force, he would give him all the assistance required from him. Until he knew more, he had to remain on his guard but keep all his options available and for that he had to stall.

'What I can promise you is to convene the Council of Elders and prompt them to decide on the course of the fleet. I will even back your request,' he said.

Despite this promise the two Tyrians were deeply disappointed; they had expected to King to take it upon himself to send the fleet away, lured by the prospect of adding the wealthy town of Sarepta to his territory. Bomilcar tried to find more arguments in favour of Tyre's request. He pleaded that Alexander would tire before long of the island's stubbornness and quit; his departure would be to the advantage of Abdalonymus for it would deliver him from the Macedonian presence that impeded his freedom of action. An unconquered Tyre would make him more valuable in Alexander's eyes, while Tyre would be grateful for the assistance he had extended when it was needed. The young man even used the argument of brotherhood against a foreign conqueror which sounded hollow to Abdalonymus because of the commercial rivalry between Sidon and Tyre.

Taking his time, the King explained to his two young visitors that a decision of such importance could not be taken unilaterally.

Eventually Bomilcar accepted that a courageous decision concerning the fleet might have been conceivable from the King, but it would be entirely unrealistic to expect it from the Elders. These people would never stand against Alexander. Bomilcar had to recognise that his proposal had been turned down and that Abdalonymus had no intention of convening the Council of Elders. He decided to call his bluff, unwilling to leave the impression that he had been fooled or that Tyre was in any way indebted to Abdalonymus for having tried his best to assist.

'I would like to address the Elders and explain the situation,' he said.

The King was taken aback, forced to forsake the seemingly promising disposition he had devised for himself.

'You can't do that,' he said, 'you will put yourself and Matten in great danger; most of the Elders are loyal to Alexander and will demand your arrest.'

Bomilcar did not insist. He refrained from showing his disappointment and said, ignoring Matten's reproving look, 'You're right; we will leave the matter to your skilled diplomacy and return home. Before we do that, I have a personal favour to ask from you.'

'What is it?' enquired the King who had already guessed the kind of favour he was about to be asked.

'I would like your permission to see Chiboulet. With enough

warships at his disposal, Alexander will besiege us from the sea, wiping out any prospect for Chiboulet and me to meet again. That is my last chance to see her and I beg you not to take it from me. I have accepted your decree that we should not marry but don't deny me a final look at her.'

It was uncomfortable enough for Abdalonymus to listen to Bomilcar telling him indirectly that he had been equivocating; he was not going, in addition, to allow another oblique charge of being a heartless father. If Chiboulet were to learn that Bomilcar had been in the palace and had left without seeing her, she would have no one to blame except her father. He relented and announced to an overjoyed lover, 'I will send for her. But you have to leave immediately afterwards for I cannot guarantee your safety if you are recognised.'

12

Heartbroken

She was standing in the doorway, in total disbelief of what her eyes were telling her. The young man she still loved, who she had never expected to see again, was a few feet away, as moved as she was. Behind her, her mother gently pushed her forward. The two lovers came closer and remained still, intimidated by her parents' presence and by a sense of withdrawal generated by the passing of time.

They were face to face and he could smell Chiboulet's perfume, a mixture of olive oil and Arabic gum. Bomilcar closed his eyes and reeled back, simultaneously overwhelmed by feelings of joy because of the opportunity he had been given to see the person he loved, and sadness because he knew that their separation was to follow inexorably.

All he could utter was a platitude which did not even sound

right. 'I can see that you are well,' he said, when she looked drawn and had lost weight.

'I'm fine,' she said but the sorrow in her eyes belied her words.

'I miss you,' he timidly ventured and she gave him a poor smile in lieu of a reply.

Abdalonymus stepped in to prevent more emotion taking grip of the two young people who were obviously still in love. 'Our two friends here should be going now. They must take advantage of the few hours of daylight left to sail away,' he said.

Chiboulet's eyes sent a desperate call for help in the direction of Artas, who instinctively reacted.

'Let's leave these two young people on their own, for a moment,' she said. Abdalonymus's only reaction was to move towards the door and leave the room; she and Matten followed.

Left by themselves, the two young lovers remained motionless, until Bomilcar opened his arms and Chiboulet threw herself against his chest; he held her, kissing her head. His right hand slipped under her chin and gently lifted her face to reveal that her beautiful eyes were filled with tears. Engulfed with emotion, he covered her with kisses and she gave herself to the sweet feeling of shared love.

Neither wished to interrupt their silent communion, for both were aware that words would bring them back to the real world to face the same circumstances that had kept them apart.

Assuming that he could convince her to leave everything behind and elope with him to Tyre, he would be putting her life in danger; he knew that the island would come under attack sooner or later. It was out of the question for them to run away to another place, for he would never envisage deserting his own people at a time of danger.

Silence, which intensified their feelings and fed their imaginations, was definitely preferable to words likely to destroy fanciful images of the mind. Eventually he felt the urge to make her renew the pledge they had given each other during the fateful evening at the inn.

'Are you still prepared to wait for me?' he asked.

In lieu of a reply she gave him a look, exuding tenderness and gentle reproach for having doubted her. He pressed her tighter against him. They just had time for their lips to touch, before they hurriedly separated, hearing the door creak. The return of Chiboulet's parents and Matten denied them the prolongation of their daydream.

Abdalonymus's demeanour made the Tyrians understand that it was time for them to leave. Artas put a hand round her daughter's shoulders and directed her towards the way out. At the door Chiboulet turned her head back to cast an ultimate glance at Bomilcar, who was shattered by the sadness emanating from her eyes, and a sense of powerlessness.

As if being heartbroken was not enough, he and Matten felt utterly frustrated all the way to their boat, because they had failed to make a success of their mission. They moved quickly to be able to take advantage of the remaining daylight hours, which were needed to sail away from this hostile and unhappy place. They ran no risk of being recognised because their faces were again partly covered and few people ventured outside, on a cold wintery evening.

Their ship was kept ready to leave port at no notice, the oarsmen having been ordered to remain on board in case a precipitate flight was necessary. Another reason was to prevent sailors getting inebriated and letting out indiscreet words that might give away their city of origin.

The two friends were about to embark when Matten, always on the lookout, saw Lysinias, who was preparing to enter a nearby inn that was popular with sailors and impoverished travellers. He seized Bomilcar by his sleeve to stop him stepping on to the gangway, and passed on what he saw.

'We have, at most, a couple of sailing hours before it's dark and we are forced to seek shelter for the night. I propose that you wait for me on board; I will join you at sunrise,' he added.

Bomilcar needed no further explanation to understand that

Matten intended to dispose of Lysinias during the night. He did not oppose the plan, having interpreted the blacksmith's glimpse of Lysinias not as a chance occurrence but as a gift from the gods and their command to avenge Abbarus.

He nodded to convey his approval and whispered, 'Baal Shamem be with you. Don't take any risk. You're going to be much needed in Tyre.'

Matten entered the inn, his hood still hiding much of his face, in case he were to come upon the man he was after. The Lord of the Heaven and other gods were definitely on his side; all he could see was a couple of drunkards and the innkeeper, as inebriated as they were. There was no sign of Lysinias. 'He must have gone to his room,' he thought.

'I need your best room for the night,' enjoined Matten.

The man, too unsteady to leave his chair, shrugged as if to make his interlocutor understand that his request was that of all those who sought shelter in his inn. Matten extended his left hand and seized the man by the neck forcing him to stand.

'Do I understand that your best room can't be made available to me?' he uttered menacingly.

'It's already occupied, but I can give you the next best,' pledged the innkeeper, trembling from the effects of fear and alcohol.

'How do I know you are not lying to me,' insisted Matten.

'By Eshmun, I'm telling the truth. You see this room, on the left, at the top of the stairs? It's already rented to a customer who is in it now. The three other remaining rooms are empty; you choose whichever you want.'

That was all the blacksmith wished to know; he released his grip on the neck of the poor man, who slumped into his chair.

Once upstairs, Matten entered the room adjoining the one that he presumed to be Lysinias's and waited, paying attention to the surrounding noises. His plan was to carry out the mission he had assigned to himself during the advanced hours of the night, when sleep is at its deepest. Gradually, the sounds coming from downstairs and from outside faded away and Matten knew that the time he was waiting for had come.

Taking great care not to make the wooden floor creak, he left his room, closed the door behind him, stood at Lysinias's door and listened. After a while he was able to hear regular breathing and occasional grunting. He entered the room, remaining still for a moment to make sure that he did not awake the sleeper. When he was satisfied that his entry had gone unnoticed, he went closer to the figure lying down on a mattress, in one corner of the room.

Before he struck he had to be absolutely positive that the person sleeping at his feet was Lysinias; for that he needed time for his eyes to adjust to darkness. He knelt beside his intended victim and when he had no doubt, he stabbed him in the heart while obstructing his mouth and nose with his left hand, to muffle and smother his breathing and agonised cries. Lysinias was a strong man and it took a moment before he ceased beating the air with his legs. When Matten was sure he was dead, he slowly removed his hand, retrieved the dagger, wiped it off with the bed cover and left the room, closing the door behind him to delay the discovery of the dead man.

He went downstairs, where he found the innkeeper alone and asleep in one corner. He left the inn as the first shafts of sunlight started giving shape to his surroundings, so he had no difficulty finding his way.

The boat was at a distance of a few steps, which he crossed rapidly but without haste, in order not to draw attention to himself in case he was to meet an early riser. He went on board without seeing anyone and was welcomed by a much-relieved Bomilcar, who ordered Zaccho to cast off immediately.

13

Strategic Committee

The sailing ship that took Bomilcar and Matten back to Tyre covered the distance in little more than three hours, the oarsmen having been promised a reward for redoubling their efforts.

They reached Tyre's northern port before midday, but had to wait at the harbour entrance to get permission to enter. Access was obstructed with a huge chain extended across, with a number of boats sunk in a way that left only a narrow passage for one ship at a time. On the sunken boats was disposed an artillery of catapults and composite crossbows and more of the same were deployed along the walls and turrets.

These measures had not been in place when they left the previous day, indicating new developments.

Bomilcar had to satisfy the officer in charge of the identity of passengers and crew before they were allowed in. A mooring space for their boat was found with difficulty because most of the Tyrian fleet had taken refuge in the port. They surmised that the southern port must be as congested for the same reason. Having realised that Tyre was unquestionably in a state of war, Bomilcar felt a lump in his throat; not that the seriousness of the situation had passed him by, but because until then he had kept a glimmer of hope that war could be averted, that the Macedonian would go away and everything would return to normal. Although not taken by surprise, he was psychologically unprepared and was left with a feeling of fear that he had never experienced before and which he hated.

He looked furtively at Matten, trying to read his thoughts, and was amazed to see him solid as a rock with a smile at the corner of his mouth. Not only was fear an emotion unknown to the blacksmith, he seemed to enjoy the prospect of action and danger.

For the first time in his life Bomilcar envied the strong spirit and physical strength of his childhood friend who until then had had every good reason to envy him, if that feeling ever crossed his mind.

Even before the boat was securely hitched, the friends jumped on to the quay; Bomilcar rushed towards the palace to report on his mission and Matten went to Inat to reassure her of their safe return and await further instructions.

The palace was buzzing with excited tumult; high dignitaries were shouting orders and soldiers, servants and slaves were running along the corridors that took Bomilcar to Azemilk's rooms. Immediately introduced, he was invited to participate in a War Council held by the King's son and his uncle and attended by Idbal, Chelbes and a handful of councillors. Hamor and Eloeim, the two army officers who had joined the delegation to Sarepta, were also there.

Azemilk invited Bomilcar to communicate the outcome of his mission. When he did, silence fell on the room. Although the expectation of seeing the new King of Sidon take a bold decision with regard to the fleet had always been far-fetched, confirmation of the mission's failure was received with disappointment. The only piece of good news was of Lysinias's execution which made the members of the War Council sigh with relief, for they were presented with conclusive evidence that no Tyrian had had a hand in Abbarus's murder.

Following an exchange of comments Azemilk said, 'When we last met, we were all puzzled, asking ourselves why Alexander had ordered the felling of entire forests and the razing of Old Tyre's houses. Do you know why? Do you know what this madman intends doing?' He did not wait for an answer. 'Boulders, rocks and stones are dumped in the sea and timber is packed down on top because he is filling up the sea, yes, he is building a causeway.'

'We shouldn't be unduly alarmed,' intervened Balator. 'If the water is shallow close to the mainland, it isn't the same by the city's walls. He will have to fill in a depth of six hundred feet before he reaches the surface of the waters. In the meantime, we will not stay idle and watch him.'

'I'm still convinced we should attack the Sidonian fleet before it's too late and they take shelter in their harbours,' asserted Idbal.

'We can't take the risk of sending the fleet away, see it destroyed and be left without protection. What else do you suggest?' asked the King's son to no one in particular.

'The strategy for the defence of the island must be entrusted to a committee, which will devise proposals in keeping with the prevalent circumstances at the time to be submitted to us for a final decision,' proposed Balator.

'That's exactly what I have in mind,' said Azemilk. 'I nominate Councillor Idbal and officers Hamor and Eloeim as members of that committee.'

'Excellent,' approved his uncle who added, 'Councillor Chelbes's advice would be most useful. I propose that he also be a member.'

It was clear that in Balator's eyes, the conservative councillor would be a moderate element needed to create a proper balance within the committee. His proposal was accepted without discussion and the War Council was adjourned.

At the palace gates Idbal caught up with Bomilcar.

'Brother Bomilcar,' he said, 'I was told by Matten that through reasoning alone you were able to find out who murdered Abbarus and why. Your insight has prevented a dangerous rift among the population and put an end to one faction pointing an accusing finger at another. Would you agree to advise me?'

'I do.'

'Fine. Bring Matten and follow me to Abbarus's place. We ought to outline a defensive plan of action and submit it to the War Council.'

'We won't be long,' Bomilcar assured him.

14

First Encounters

The following days were spent by the members of the Strategic Committee in devising ways and means of holding back the construction works on the causeway. Once a plan was in place, Idbal and Bomilcar took it to the War Council for approval, and when that was secured, the plan was put in action. Matten sent for Abdastet the monkey-keeper, and instructed him to sneak on to the mainland, go up to the villages of Mount Libanus and mobilise them against the Macedonians and their Phoenician helpers. Bomilcar started assembling a flotilla of skiffs. As for Idbal, he ordered Anysos to select fifty of his most able fighters and prepare them for action.

Abdastet waited for a night when moon and stars were hidden by thick clouds. When this happened, he and his monkey, which had been an effective cover so far, boarded a sculling-boat. Thanks to a password he was allowed to leave the northern port; he maintained a course parallel to the coast, which was sprinkled with fires, an indication of the presence of many Macedonian sentries. Leaving them behind, he headed for the dark line of the mainland; a lighter strip of the coast drew his attention and he knew it must be a sandy beach. He rowed in that direction until his boat banged against the shore. With the monkey perched on his shoulder, very much frightened by pitch blackness, he leaped into the water and pulled the boat on the sand. He did not know where he had landed but he was disabled until sunrise. He chose not to venture away from the boat, which gave him a sense of security that his dark surroundings would not provide him.

He tried to get some rest lying on the sand, the monkey snuggled against his chest. A faint daybreak found him on the alert and ready for action; he hid the boat beneath a cluster of nearby shrubs and started his march towards the foot of Mount Libanus whose great dark shape he perceived yonder. He stumbled several times, not being able to see his way properly. Then the tip of the sun came up from behind the mountains, almost immediately emerging in full view.

Abdastet's eyes blinked as he looked around to make sure that there was no unwanted presence in the vicinity. He saw no one and proceeded on his way. The first village he arrived at was in the heart of a pine forest. The inhabitants gathered round him expecting to watch the monkey's act. To their disappointment, all Abdastet wanted was to be told who the head of the village was. When the latter made himself known, he took him aside, gave him an account of the situation including the building of the causeway by the Macedonians and explained what was expected from the villagers.

After a short rest, the monkey-keeper resumed his climb towards the villages nestled in forests of fir, oak and cedar trees, which he visited as he progressed in the direction of the summit. Everywhere he was well received and found the inhabitants of the villages willing to carry out the part devised for them.

In the meantime, the members of the Strategic Committee were waiting for Abdastet's return to activate the whole plan. He had been given twenty five days to carry out his mission and come back. If after that time he did not, he would be deemed either killed or detained against his will and the remaining parts of the plan would be implemented regardless.

Four days before the end of the waiting time, the monkey-keeper reappeared and reported that his mission had been a success. He confirmed that in about seven days, the inhabitants of the mountains were going to attack the Macedonians who were supervising the tree-cutting.

A flotilla of skiffs had been assembled in the Southern port together with Zaccho's sailing ship, hidden from the mainland by an elevated screen made of hides and sails. Seven days after Abdastet's reappearance, at first light, Anysos's fifty fighters were taken to the port and split up. Thirty men under his command went on board the sailing ship, which had been stripped of her rig to make room for them, and would be propelled by the crew pulling with the oars. The remaining fighters were divided between the ten skiffs. All were armed with bows and javelins.

The boats sneaked out of the harbour, but while Zaccho's rowers headed for the mainland, the skiffs encircled and attacked the workers who were engaged in the construction of the causeway that had taken shape close to the seashore where the water was shallow.

A few soldiers were standing guard on the projecting part of the causeway. They were all killed by sudden volleys of arrows and javelins, as were most of the workers. Those who escaped the first volleys jumped into the sea or ran towards the mainland but they were hunted and killed one by one, either with missiles or by the rowers knocking them out with their oars.

The fighters on Zaccho's boat were just as successful; having disembarked close to an army camp; they engaged the enemy soldiers, who were taken by surprise and promptly disabled. Before the general alarm could be sounded, the Tyrians returned to their ship, which sped towards the island. The skiffs were already there. The Tyrians had not lost a single man and were elated by their success.

A few days later, news reached the island that at about the same time the boats were conducting their attacks, the villagers on Mount Libanus had fallen on the Macedonians and killed thirty of them.

Tyrian victory was total, but instead of lessening Alexander's resolve it increased it. He summoned his officers to his shelter and reproached them bitterly for their weakness. He was aware that he shared responsibility but he could not admit it when Callisthene was taking notes for posterity. Eventually he gave practical orders to deal with the disastrous situation.

'Bring two siege towers to the tip of the causeway and equip them with soldiers and artillery,' he ordered Perdiccas.

'But the towers are not completed,' objected the general.

'I'm aware of that but they can be completed on the causeway; until they are they will serve a defensive purpose, but when we get closer to the island walls and they stand higher than those walls, the Tyrians will be in for a surprise.'

15

Matchmaking

'Mother! I don't believe what I've just heard. Do you really mean that Sosipatros and his wife are paying us a social visit today? Haven't they heard that we are besieged by a ruthless enemy? Don't they know we have other things in mind than socialising?'

'Calm down, Bomilcar, of course they know that but life goes on. By the way, Zarka their daughter will accompany them.'

'Ah! Now I understand; it's one of your ploys, your way of presenting me a girl of marriageable age.' Inat knew her son and what to expect from him in given circumstances. If she were to deny the obvious, he would clam up, making any dialogue impossible; so she decided to be open.

'What's wrong with that?' she said, 'It's time for you to consider taking a wife. I long to see my grandsons. If you wait too long I might die before my dearest wish is realised.'

Bomilcar felt sorry for his mother, yet he was not prepared to give her false hopes, as long as he himself had not completely despaired of marrying the woman he loved. He went closer to Inat, took her hands in his. 'Mother,' he said, 'I can't stop thinking of Chiboulet; I yearn for her. I promised to wait for her and made her promise to wait for me.'

'Wait for what?' exclaimed an exasperated Inat.

'A change of circumstances that could lift the obstacles from our path. Events of enormous bearing loom ahead, one never knows what could happen next. Abdalonymus may lose his throne, he may relent . . . anything could happen.'

'My poor son, I see you are still enthralled. Tell me, how long are you prepared to wait before you start a family with a real person and not with illusions. At least promise me one thing – receive Sosipatros, his wife and their daughter with social grace and the hospitality due to guests.'

'Of course, mother, I do, but you have to promise me something in return.'

'What?'

'You will not open the subject of marriage with these people. Their visit must remain without any ulterior motivation.'

'Promised.'

Early in the afternoon the expected guests arrived. Sosipatros was diminutive and slender; to make up for his bald head he had grown a beard long enough to reach his navel and broad enough to cover his chest. This disproportionate accessory would have appeared ridiculous on most men, but not Sosipatros; his piercing eyes and confident bearing would make anyone intent on mocking him baulk and retreat. By contrast, his wife, also small but rotund, was self-effacing, as if she wished to apologise for existing. Zarka, their daughter, was a graceful fifteen year old; with her features not fully delineated, it was difficult to guess whether she would remain pleasant to look at or develop into a beauty.

'Your late father and I did business together. In addition, we became friends,' said Sosipatros, commandeering the most comfortable seat in the room. Bomilcar emitted a brief 'I know,' immediately complemented by Inat's effusive detail about the relationship between their guest and her late husband. Despite the promise she had made to her son, she could not prevent herself from adding, 'My dearest wish is to see the old relationship perpetuated and strengthened with my son and your family.'

Her words would have normally sounded innocuous but not under the circumstances. Bomilcar controlled his anger and pretended to have understood his mother's words as being strictly related to business.

'I will be honoured if we were to revive your business association with my father,' he said. 'We should talk about it when Alexander leaves us in peace.'

'You must have a view on that at the Council of Elders. Do you believe that the Macedonian will get tired and will turn his back?' asked Sosipatros.

Bomilcar hesitated; on the one hand he did not wish to appear over-optimistic in view of the seriousness of the situation, but on the other he did not want to be responsible for spreading panic amongst an already frightened population. His answer was a measured one: 'We have already scored a big victory; if we continue in that direction it is possible that Alexander will realise the pointlessness of his enterprise. But we have to be prepared to pay the price for that and it will be a hefty one.'

'I am too old to be of any use as a fighter, but I can still help. I have a stock of iron which I am prepared to give the Council for a very good price. Why don't you act as the middleman for that transaction?'

Bomilcar was revolted by his guest's proposal. It disgusted him to find out that even in times of mortal danger, people like Sosipatros would not miss any opportunity for getting richer. He was about to give him a sharp rebuke when his eyes met his mother's expressive look. She had read his aversion, was afraid of an outburst and was begging him not to. He complied with her silent plea and changed the course of the conversation once more. He could not refrain from teaching his guest a lesson, albeit in a circuitous way.

'It's very fortunate,' he said, 'that there are so many volunteers prepared to fight and die, so many craftsmen manufacturing weapons in their workshops, and so many ordinary sailors drilling for war.'

If Bomilcar had in mind to make his guest ashamed of himself, he could not have been more mistaken. Sosipatros was totally unconcerned by the allusion and commented with a straight face, 'These poor people have no other means of being useful.'

At that juncture, Inat realised that her matchmaking had not the least chance of succeeding.

16

Fireboat

Day after day, the Tyrians used psychological warfare and a full panoply of stratagems to hamper the construction of the causeway. From the height of their walls and on board their boats, they insulted and taunted the besiegers, who had discarded their weapons to carry loads on their backs, like pack animals. Riding their fast skiffs, they also harried the improvised labourers, hurling arrows and javelins while divers swam undetected to the structure, and with the assistance of hooks, pulled out the branches of the trees which were used as elements of the foundations. They were often successful and in the process took much of the building material into the water.

Despite all these efforts and the casualties on the Macedonian side, the work went ahead; the huge unfinished siege towers, which had been rolled on to the causeway on Alexander's orders, provided a degree of protection thanks to the firing points on several levels. Nonetheless, the besieged did not feel immediately threatened, for they remained out of reach of the giant enemy catapults and composite crossbows. It was unthinkable that these machines could be brought closer, for the city walls dropped into such deep water that the construction of the causeway would necessarily cease at that point.

Every now and then Bomilcar and Matten would climb the stairs to one of the corner towers to inspect the progress of the construction work on the causeway. One day towards the end of winter, they went to their lookout post and remained there longer than usual, despite bitter cold and pouring rain. The causeway seemed much closer than their recollection told them. They eventually realised that the construction of the two siege towers stationed there had been completed and that they stood taller than the city's walls.

Suddenly, a leather curtain screening the twentieth level of one of the siege towers was pulled back and a volley of arrows was fired in their direction. Fortunately none harmed them but they remained as paralysed as if they had been hit. Once they had pulled themselves together, they rushed down the stairs and went straight to Idbal to report what they had experienced.

'Impossible,' he exclaimed, 'the towers must be at a distance of about 1,200 feet and no crossbow has that range.'

'That's what we thought before being on the receiving end,' commented Bomilcar.

'Very strange, I don't understand it. I think we should meet with the two army officers to review the situation. I will summon them and Chelbes straight away.'

Barely had he finished these words that Anysos came running in. 'The eastern walls are under bombardment,' he shouted, 'stones are being launched against them, but with no damage.'

With that fresh confirmation there was no more reason to doubt that the Macedonians had found a way of doubling the range of their artillery, something that no one else had done before.

A counter-attack plan was set out by the Strategic Committee, approved by the War Council and work on its implementation begun. An old and enormous penteconter, which was moored in the southern port, was commandeered by Anysos's men, who loaded her stern with rocks and sand until her bow emerged high out of the water. The remaining cargo space was filled in with inflammable material of all sorts, and the whole was daubed with bitumen and sulphur. Across the mast was rigged a long yard, which protruded from the prow, from which hung large cauldrons filled with naphtha.

When all was set, commenced the waiting for a favourable wind, while the boat was closely guarded. A couple of days later the wind blew in the right direction and order was issued to start the planned operation.

Four triremes, one of them with Matten on board, escorted the penteconter. With acquired speed and deft manoeuvring her raised prow hit the target with great force and came up on to it at the exact point where one of the siege towers stood. She was quickly ignited by the crew, who jumped into the escorting triremes.

The ship blew up and the cauldrons fell into the fire, which was ferociously kindled by their discharged contents; a furious blaze spread to the two towers and anything nearby. Soldiers and workers were burnt to death or succumbed when the giant structures collapsed. Those on the causeway who escaped and tried to put out the fire were prevented from doing so by the Tyrians, who threw arrows and javelins at them, tossing firebrands to fuel what was already burning and ignite what had been spared until then.

In no time a large portion of the structure and everything on it was engulfed in flames. Those who did not die instantly hurled themselves into the sea. With their oars the crew of the triremes beat the hands of the swimmers to disable them, so they could be taken on board.

Strict orders had been issued to take prisoners and Matten was there to make sure that they would be complied with. Those orders were not the result of any humanitarian disposition but were motivated by the need to know how the Macedonians had been able to double the range of their artillery. The only way to solve the puzzling question was to take prisoners and make them talk.

The four triremes headed for the city's port, leaving behind fire and destruction. The crowd that had been watching the operation from the parapet walks climbed down to receive the returning heroes with tumultuous joy, shouting 'May the gods bless you. May Melqart protect you and your families as you've protected us.' A great number of animals, big and small, were sacrificed and a number of offerings were made, to thank the gods for being on the Tyrian side. A sickly smell of blood invaded the city.

Matten and his men had difficulty extracting the prisoners from the hands of the crowd, grown dangerously threatening. He took them to Idbal's house where they had to suffer rough interrogation.

Two of the prisoners were engineers; they were persuaded to explain that their catapults and composite crossbows were powered by springs made of twisted animal tendons which doubled their range. They promised to teach their captors how the springs were made and fitted and as a result their lives were spared. The remaining prisoners were taken to the top of the walls, slain and their bodies thrown into the sea while the Macedonians watched from afar.

That was not all; the following day an unusually high wind hurled underwater currents and waves against the mole whose substructure had already been weakened by fire. Repeated battering created more than one rupture and a large segment of the structure crashed into the water, causing the collapse of the whole.

17

Intrigues

'Tyre's latest victory has seriously dented Alexander's prestige. What is he going to do, Ennion? Do you have any idea?'

Abdalonymus's new trusted advisor replied without hesitation. 'He will not rest until he takes the island. What you call Tyrian victory is a simple setback for him.'

'But what more can he do than he has already done without success?' insisted Abdalonymus.

Ennion was amazed by his interlocutor's lack of insight, but then he remembered that only a few months ago he had been a simple farmer lacking political experience. He did not realise that cunning Abdalonymus was carrying out a loyalty test regarding his person and the new regime established by the Macedonian. Had Ennion said anything indicating that, in his appraisal, Alexander had suffered a decisive defeat, he would have concluded that his advisor had his mind set on going back to the Persian king.

Ennion, however, was a too skilful politician to forsake a master for a new one, as long as no drastic events decided otherwise. As a matter of principle he would not contribute to a change of regime, but when such a change occurred he would be among the first to try to find accommodation with the new reality. 'Sire,' he said, 'Alexander has no warships. Wait until the fleet returns and see what he can do. Now that winter has ended it's only a matter of days.'

'You're right, I shouldn't worry unduly and give Tyre's feat more significance than it deserves.'

'Sire, it's my duty to make you aware of a matter which can still give some concern.'

'I don't understand. On the one hand you seem confident that Alexander will eventually win, and on the other you tell me he might not.'

'With all due respect, I didn't say that. What I feel I should bring to your attention is that factions that believe that Darius can still be victorious have taken heart from Tyre's latest success and interpreted it as Alexander's complete defeat.'

'Who are they?' asked Abdalonymus, furious as well as alarmed.

'Eshmun's priests for one. They have received money from the Persians and are poisoning people's minds. The pro-Persia faction is growing restless.'

'What about Strato, is he with them?'

'He has promised you his full backing and wished you a prosperous and peaceful reign. He stands by his words.'

'Why have the priests turned against me? What did I do to them?'

'They are furious because you haven't sacrificed in their temple yet, which you did on several occasions in Astarte's. That's the pretext. Persian gold is the real reason; there is something else . . . an absurd allegation.'

'What is it? Speak,' enjoined the King.

Ennion faltered but complied with the injunction. 'Some time ago,' he said, 'their chief priest was killed in mysterious circumstances. They allege that a member of your family was present but fled instead of staying and giving an account of what exactly took place.'

'That's not only absurd, it's insane. They must be shut up. What's your advice?'

'Promise them gold and your imminent visit, but keep them waiting for some time; they will remain quiet in case you change your mind and forsake your promises.'

'Where do I find the gold? My coffers are empty.'

'Leave the matter with me. All my business partners and a few wealthy acquaintances will be happy to oblige. With your permission I'll take my leave and get hold of them.'

'Do that.'

Left on his own, Abdalonymus paced the room, engulfed in his thoughts. A single setback inflicted on Alexander and his throne had started shaking beneath him. He had to accept that his fate was inextricably linked to Alexander's fortune and the information received from Ennion confirmed it. How fortunate that he had not listened to Bomilcar. Had he fallen for the attractive Sarepta offer, he would have been left without protection, at the mercy of his political opponents, whose ranks Eshmun's priests had joined. That menacing alliance ought to be tackled and dismantled before it was too late. Ennion's plan was perfect, except that it would put him under obligation to his advisor and his friends. Too bad; the priests must be contained, the more so because Tubal's death was being used to embarrass him by insinuating Chiboulet's involvement. He was less worried by that – for as long as he remained king no harm could befall his daughter – than by being indebted to Ennion.

To reduce that obligation he took the decision to appeal to Theron and Tryphon. He sent a word inviting them to dine with him that evening. Although he had not seen them for a while, he knew that was not a factor which could be held against him, for the two young men were not particularly interested in being associated with powerful people.

They answered his invitation readily and a magnificent feast was served, although no other guests took part in it. Towards the end of the meal, while they were sipping wine from Samaria, the king dismissed the slaves who had been serving them, straightened up on his couch and said, 'Sidon owes you a lot for ridding it of a king who was a Persian puppet. However, you should know that our enemies have not given up.'

'Tell us more,' Theron encouraged him.

'Eshmun's priests have received gold from Darius, which happened concomitantly with the destruction of the causeway by the Tyrians. The priests' venomous preaching and the Macedonian's temporary setback are having a dangerous effect on some segments of the population, which still regard Darius as a possible victor.'

'What do you suggest?' asked Theron.

'With regard to the priests, a distribution of gold, an official visit at the temple and a ceremonial sacrifice will suffice. As for the troublemakers among the pro-Persia faction, prison or exile for a handful will frighten the rest. That I can do, but gold is a problem. I don't have enough to give away.'

'We are prepared to contribute and ask prominent pro-Greek champions to do the same,' promised Theron.

'Those who refuse will live to regret it,' added Tryphon.

'I didn't expect less from you,' declared Abdalonymus, who had been careful not to mention his trusted advisor's promise to do exactly the same but with a different faction. Because the two Sidonians and Ennion revolved in different circles, he expected their endeavours to remain concealed from each other. If, at the end of the day, more gold than needed was collected, he would know how to make good use of the surplus. He also kept quiet about the veiled threat against Chiboulet because he did not wish to give his guests the impression that his concern was personal rather than in the interest of the pro-Greek faction.

18

Self-Delusion

One day in early spring, Sidon was buzzing with excitement; news had reached the city that its warships were heading for their home ports. The sailors' families, who had been separated from their loved ones for months on end, started scanning the horizon, in spite of being well aware that they had to wait a little longer before the much anticipated reunion took place. The elating news had been brought by the crew of a Sidonian merchant ship, which had called at Cnossos to load a cargo of Anatolian tin. In that Cretan port the Sidonian war fleet had sheltered for repairs and the fleet's commander-in-chief had made the master of the merchant ship privy to his intention to defect from the Persian naval forces and take his men home. He was determined to do that the moment his ships were ready to sail again.

Hephaestion was told of the good news and immediately sent a word to Alexander, who was still in Old Tyre, engaged in supervising the rebuilding of the causeway. His engineers' advice had been to aim the structure directly into the headwind instead of making it run parallel; by doing that it was expected that the tip of the mole would shelter the rest of the work behind it. They had also advised him to increase the width of the causeway to two hundred feet and to array siege towers and pieces of artillery in the middle of the construction, where they would be less vulnerable to another assault from the sea.

Leaving the construction work in the hands of his engineers and generals, Alexander moved quickly to Sidon to wait for the much needed warships. Abdalonymus was informed of his arrival but was disappointed once more by the Macedonian's decision to stay at the governor's mansion and not the royal palace. Nevertheless, he found solace in the prospect that the young conqueror would have to remain several days in the city, during which time their rapport would necessarily be strengthened.

Having welcomed Alexander, Abdalonymus returned home in excellent mood and disclosed the reason for his high spirits during the family lunch.

'He was extremely considerate towards me and bestowed on me many kindnesses,' he said, looking at his wife and daughter to see the effect of his words. He was disappointed, for Artas was busy with the food before her and Chiboulet's eyes were as sad as they had been since she was told that she could not be Bomilcar's wife. Because of their apathy, he persisted and conveyed more good news in the hope that he might raise the interest of the two women.

'He himself asked me to arrange for another hunting party to keep him busy and fit while he is waiting,' he said. Artas felt it was her duty to feign interest, so she stopped eating and asked, 'Waiting for what?'

'Warships, ours, are on their way home. I'm relieved, for I'll be able to repay my debt to the Macedonian.'

'What do you mean, father?' asked Chiboulet, vaguely worried by what she had just heard.

Happy to find her prepared to listen, he explained: 'Tyre continues to have free access to the sea, but not for long; my ships, which I will give to Alexander, will block this access and the siege will be complete.'

Engrossed in the illusion of having the free command of the fleet, which he certainly had not, he did not notice the tears running down his daughter's cheeks. Artas saw them, left her couch and put her arm round Chiboulet's shoulder. 'What's the matter?' she asked prompting more tears and no reply. 'Tell me, why are you crying?' she insisted and eventually received an explanation, broken by sobs.

'Bomilcar is to be trapped in a siege made possible by father's vessels. He's going to die because of that.'

'Nonsense,' exclaimed Abdalonymus, 'the moment the Tyrians realise they are surrounded from all sides, they will surrender. By giving my ships to Alexander, I'm doing them a favour and making them understand that resistance is meaningless. Bloodshed will cease immediately and Bomilcar will have a better chance of staying alive . . . Mind you, the fate of this young man should be of no concern to you. I thought I'd made myself clear.'

Abdalonymus was not unlike other rulers put in office by foreign volition. Not only did he need to create for himself the illusion of being able to take decisions freely; in addition, he had to present the unwarranted deeds he had no choice over as being for the good of those who would suffer from them. Those rulers often ended up believing in their fallacies and were to be counted among their own most gullible victims.

Chiboulet ignored her father's last words and put her faith in his optimistic prediction about Tyre's bloodless surrender, for it met with what her heart desired. Father and daughter finished their meal in a gratified mood, but for different reasons.

The following day Abdalonymus went to the governor's mansion to pay his respects to Alexander, to be told that he had left the city. Asking to see Hephaestion, he was received by the general in Theron's and Tryphon's company.

'Yes,' he confirmed, 'the King has left, he went after the villagers who had attacked the tree-cutters. They must be taught a lesson. He will be back in time to receive the fleet.'

The moment Abdalonymus saw the general's two visitors, he surmised that they must have reported to him the conversation he had had with them on the intrigues of the pro-Persia faction. Although it had not been his intention to reveal the existence of those intrigues to the Macedonian – lest it weakened his status in his eyes – he instantly adapted to what he believed was the actual position.

'I need to see you about an important matter . . .' Lacking diplomacy, Hephaestion interrupted him, having no wish to listen to what he already knew. He had been briefed by Theron and Tryphon about every single incident, political or social, which had taken place in the city.

'I'm aware of what you wish to tell me,' he said, 'and I approve your plan how to deal with the situation. But when you approach the priests and those who hastily believe that a temporary setback is a defeat, do in your own name. Don't bring mine into it. I must be seen as the last resort and refuge for those who repent and see the foolishness of their options, but are too proud to mend fences with you. After all, we want results and that's the best guarantee to get them.'

'I will do exactly as you wish,' said Abdalonymus, who was sampling a taste of what was expected from him whenever the situation turned to be unpleasant. Obviously his role was to bear the brunt of unpopularity; in this instance, to allow Hephaestion to appear as the mediator, if not the saviour. The general, like any head of an occupying army, wished to leave to Abdalonymus the responsibility and blame for the suppression of local disturbances. If matters were not resolved, he would intervene with might if necessary.

'I will do exactly as you wish,' repeated Abdalonymus meekly.

'Good. With regard to the gold promised by our two friends here, it will be delivered to my mansion and distributed with my knowledge.'

'I didn't see the matter otherwise,' said Abdalonymus, adding precipitately, 'Ennion also promised to get gold from his business partners and friends. I will bring it to you.'

'It will be much simpler if you tell Ennion to bring the gold straight to me.'

'Of course, I didn't think of that,' said Abdalonymus, in the nadir of dejection.

'Well, that's settled, maybe you wish to go about your business.' Having said that, Hephaestion realised that he had been rather rude to his visitor, so he added, 'Why don't you come back and have the midday meal with us?'

'Oh, I'd be delighted.'

Abdalonymus left the governor's palace as poor as when he had arrived in terms of gold, yet richer in disingenuous signs of friendship; he was not prepared to question them lest he destroyed the illusory world he had created for himself.

19

Sailing Season

Taking advantage of the sailing season, King Azemilk returned to Tyre. His people received him with relief, as if his mere presence on the island would be enough to repel the assailants. His son and his brother informed him of the situation, and during a lull in the bombardment he went up to the parapet walk to inspect the construction of the causeway, which was getting closer and closer to the city's eastern walls. The population was in the grip of a paralysing fear; missiles had landed within the walls, killing and injuring a few victims and making everyone realise how precarious their defences were. The king convened the Council of the Elders in close session, to listen to the members' views. Nothing much came of the meeting, for they argued and squabbled most of the time. Nevertheless he kept the session permanently open in view of the seriousness of the situation.

While the politicians were engaged in their favourite pastime and the people were on the verge of panic, the monkey-keeper returned to the island from another mission on the mainland. He went straight to the palace but to his frustration, was told that his controller was unavailable and that Idbal, who was attending the Council session, could not be disturbed. The information he had brought with him was of prime importance and he was keen to transmit it without delay. He went in search of Matten, the next person he would trust, and found him at his smithy surrounded by fellow workers, among them Abdshamesh, his own father.

Matten was telling them that enough swords and shields had been manufactured for the time being, and that they should start producing harpoons, crows and spearheads, all needed to repel attempts to storm the city's defences. This was expected to take place sooner or later.

The monkey-keeper went to his father, bent over his hand and kissed it; straightening up, his eyes met Matten's, who read a pressing need for them to talk. He dashed off his demonstration and dismissed the blacksmiths. Alone with Abdastet he uttered a single word. 'Well?'

'Sidonian warships are expected in port any day now.'

'Are you sure?'

Matten's insistence vexed the monkey-keeper it looked as if his skill was distrusted. Nevertheless, he endeavoured to allay his interlocutor's doubts.

'The crew of a Sidonian merchant ship brought the news to the city,' he said. 'The fleet's Commander-in-Chief asked them to announce his imminent arrival.'

'Come with me,' said Matten.

They went to the king's palace where Matten's authoritative tone and impressive stature convinced one of the attendants to go into the Council Room and tell Bomilcar that two persons waiting outside needed to talk to him urgently. The young man followed the attendant. Moments later, he returned to the Council Room with the dreaded news, which he communicated to the king and to his colleagues.

This was a renewed occasion for the Councillors to air conflicting views and plans. As expected, the pugnacious party was for engaging the Sidonian fleet before it reached port. As their leader, Idbal advocated an immediate sortie of the fleet. 'We have more warships than they. We must give battle in high seas and destroy them.'

'That would be a dangerous gamble, which could end up being a disaster,' objected Chelbes. 'Imagine that our vessels leave their shelter to find that they are confronting a superior number of enemy craft. That's not a far-fetched conjuncture. The Sidonian fleet might be joined by vessels coming from other Phoenician cities or from further afield.'

Eventually the Council decided to yield to the voice of reason and not to expose the fleet to a danger that was impossible to evaluate.

In the meantime the eastern walls, which faced the mainland, were subjected to intermittent bombardment from Macedonian catapults. The missiles were getting closer and therefore more destructive by the day, for construction of the causeway was in full progress and the area won over the sea had increased steadily. By then, both sides were well versed in what they had to do to achieve their objectives: the Macedonian artillery and siege towers were strongly defended and protected against a surprise assault, while the besieged had demonstrated great inventiveness in protecting their walls. They had invented a cushion against the strength of the incoming boulders by hanging leather bags stuffed with seaweed along the battlement and sails were suspended behind the walls to catch incendiary missiles; in addition they had continued to send underwater swimmers by night, on a mission to damage the structure under construction as much as they could. What havoc the Tyrians were able to wreak during the night was rebuilt in daytime, and the parts of the walls which were damaged by the Macedonian artillery were immediately mended by free labourers and slaves. In addition, an inner wall was started. Just the same, with more projectiles landing within the walls the death toll among the Tyrians increased and a blanket of grief and fear descended on the city.

All signs indicated that the siege would be protracted unless Alexander was given the means to launch a simultaneous assault from the sea and from the causeway. No such means were available for the time being, and Tyre's northern port afforded free passage to and from the high seas whenever the obstacles put in place by the islanders were briefly removed to allow access.

Through this northern port, only a few days after the return of King Azemilk, came a Carthaginian vessel from the African colony with a messenger on board.

The message he brought was delivered to the king, who discussed its implications with the Council of Elders and then sent for the Carthaginian delegation, which had turned up just before winter to commemorate the burning of the effigy of Melqart, and had remained on the island to celebrate the god's spring resurrection.

The King addressed Magon, the head of the delegation, and the tone of his voice was marked with sadness, even dejection.

'Listen to the messenger sent by our African brothers,' he said. Azemilk's demeanour did not portend good news, so the priest of Baal Hammon waited anxiously to hear what the messenger had to say.

'The Suffetes offer their unreserved allegiance to the King and pay him their most devoted homage. They pray Tanit and Hammon to bestow on him and on his people signs of their favour and . . . '

The King could not bear more in terms of an introduction, he interrupted the messenger. 'Tell him what you told me,' he ordered.

'At home we are fighting the Syracusans for survival; they are nearly under our walls. The Suffetes regret but they cannot send any reinforcements.' Having said these words in one breath, he fell silent, his head bent on his chest as if he were the author of the negative communication he had passed on. Azemilk dismissed him but invited the delegation to stay.

'Voices within the Council press me to send our children and women to Carthage,' he said. 'I have agreed and ordered the fitting of ten transport ships to take most of them. The boats will be ready in a few days. For you and the entire delegation it is time to go back home. Our city is a dangerous place for anyone to stay. It could well become deadly.'

'Sire,' replied Magon, 'all the members of the delegation, including your humble servant, have already deliberated and decided to stay. The decision was taken well in advance, to be carried out whether or not assistance should come from home. In fact, in the absence of such assistance, our presence takes more significance. Alexander, who must respect our neutrality, will fear our eyewitness account, if he fell into the grip of the same murderous rage which made him lose control at Thebes and Halicarnassus.'

Reminding the members of the assembly of the carnage perpetrated by Alexander's soldiers when the two cities were stormed left them tongue-tied with fear, while the blood turned ice cold in their veins.

20

The Brook's Spirit

As he entered the garden, Bomilcar was met by his dog's joyous barking. He expected his mother to emerge from the house and stand by the main door, between the two columns, as she used to do when his approach had been announced. Not this time. Vaguely worried, he entered the house, shouting, 'Tansu! Lula! Tansu!'

The old slave materialised immediately but the young girl was nowhere to be seen. Bomilcar did not pay much attention to her absence; she seldom answered a call if she and the caller were not in the same room. She knew that sooner or later, somebody else would respond and take the orders and instructions which she would otherwise have to carry out herself. By being persistently unresponsive she had made her masters accept her the way she was.

'Where is your mistress?'

Tansu's reply came in his customary laconical way. 'Bedroom,' he said.

'Is she ill or what?' Without waiting for an answer, which anyhow was unlikely to come, Bomilcar rushed into his mother's room and found her lying in bed, her sister Amatbaal by her side.

'What's the matter?' he asked, 'where's Lula? Why isn't she tending you?'

'Dear son, it's good to see that you have my well-being at heart. Don't you worry, I am not ill.'

'But why are you in bed in the middle of the day?' he insisted.

Engulfed in a fit of crying, she was unable to answer. Amatbaal came to her rescue.

'Do you remember who Nasea was?' she asked.

'Of course, I do. I can't count the number of times I heard mother pronounce that name. She's a childhood friend, isn't she?'

'Yes. She was killed this morning.'

'How was she killed?'

Having recovered, Inat took over from her sister. 'You don't know where she lived, do you?' she asked. Without waiting for a reply, she told him: 'just by the eastern ramparts; her modest place is part of the inner wall. She ventured outside and a boulder thrown by a catapult fell on her and smashed her. She died instantly.'

'But, Mother! You haven't seen her for ages. It doesn't mean you shouldn't feel sorry for her, but don't put yourself in that state.'

'It's precisely because we haven't seen each other enough that I feel guilty. Now it's too late.' She shed new tears.

'Are you sure there isn't something else which makes you unhappy?' Bomilcar knew his mother well and had surmised that she had not been telling him all the reasons for her anguish.

'You're right,' she admitted, 'there's something else that we women are not ashamed to talk about. Nasea's terrible death is not the only casualty of the bombardment. The difference is that we knew her and that has brought home the frightening image of Thanatos, the personification of death who lurks around us. Are we to sit passively and wait for him? I can't stand our helplessness any longer, it drives me mad and makes me feel sick.'

'This discussion couldn't have come at a more opportune time,' he said. 'In actual fact, I came back from the palace to tell you that you, Amatbaal and her son are to leave for Carthage. The king has ordered the evacuation of free women and children. You must go before it's to late and the trap closes more tightly. Prepare yourself to leave at very short notice.'

Inat jumped out of the bed. 'I'll never leave without you, either we travel together or we stay together. Do you believe I'm afraid to die? No! It's you I'm worried about. Its for you I fear. I want you to leave this unfortunate place. Take one of your boats and go. Go! I don't mind staying, I don't mind being killed. I'm an old woman and I don't expect much from what's left of my life.'

'Mother, calm down and listen. It's out of the question for me to flee at a time when the city and my fellow-citizens are in danger, and I can still be useful to them. For you it's different; you are a woman, you can't bear arms, you can't lift stones and you would be a burden for us in close combat. Please go and I'll follow you, I promise.'

Inat gave herself a short respite for reflection. 'I'll think about it.' A gasp of disappointment escaped, Amatbaal who saw the prospect of saving her son's and her own life diminish.

Bomilcar was relieved by his mother's apparent relent. 'I must go to the palace,' he said. 'I'll come back when I can.'

After he left the room, Inat read in her sister's eyes the disappointment she did not have the courage to vent. A brief smile in her direction was followed by disheartening words. 'I haven't given up, contrary to the impression I may have conveyed,' she said.

'What will you do? What can you do? Bomilcar seems very determined. Knowing him and his pride, he will never desert the city in time of danger.'

'I don't know exactly what I'll do, but rest assured I'll not sit idle. Leave me and come back tomorrow.'

The following day Inat woke up early, washed with Lula's help, and chose the best dress and the best cloak she had.

When she was ready, she summoned Tansu and led their steps in the direction of the palace. It was early in the morning, very cold and the streets were nearly deserted except for groups of refugees who had built makeshift accommodation on street corners, having been unable or too poor to find a proper shelter. From time to time a loud bang could be heard, signalling that the unnerving, often deadly bombardment had resumed with daylight.

At the palace gate she asked to be taken to the king and when the guards enquired about her name, her response was, 'The Brook's Spirit.'

They did not dare challenge the name they were given by the richly dressed and very assured woman and they dispatched one of them to check whether Azemilk would receive her, despite having presented herself in such a peculiar way. To their amazement, the emissary came back running. With marks of reverence, he invited Inat to follow him. No sooner was she in the presence of the king than he jumped from his armchair with the agility of a youth, and came to meet her with a broad smile on his face.

'You didn't forget, then?' she said coquettishly.

'How could I? I gave you that nickname myself.'

They fell silent, their memories taking them back to a time when they were no longer infants nor yet grown up. At that time her parents had been invited by his to an outdoor meal in their orchard, north of Old Tyre. The two children had played together and strayed away from where they were supposed to remain. Disconcerted, they had stood still under a canopy of intertwined branches to get their bearings; the murmur of running water had caught their attention and they had walked hand in hand in the direction of the inviting sound. Although slightly frightened, they had nevertheless kept going, in the grip of a strange emotion never felt before. Being together in an enchanting surrounding, with no parents or minders around, had been a source of ambiguous gratification.

Their steps had taken them to the bank of a murmuring brook. No sooner had Inat seen it than she disengaged her hand from his, ran to the bank, sat on its edge and dipped her feet in the water, still wearing her sandals. She gestured to him to do the same. He hesitated a little, then joined her but not before he had taken off his footwear and placed them carefully on a dry spot.

Progressively he had let himself go, flapping his lower legs in the water as she had been doing. In the action their skin had touched more than once and an outburst of impulsive, yet innocent desire, took hold of him. He kissed her on the cheek, telling her, 'You're the Brook's Spirit.'

'Please take a seat.' He broke their silent reminiscence, indicating an armchair next to his. She complied but still could not bring herself to make plain the reason for her visit. He realised that and tried to put her at ease.

'I kept abreast of your well-being from poor Merbalos and after his premature demise, from Bomilcar. He's a fine young man.'

'I also had your news from them. I am proud of you, you are loved by your people.'

He nodded, acknowledging the compliment. 'What can I do for you?' he asked.

'I heard that it's your behest to send women and children to Carthage. Bomilcar wants me to leave with the evacuees.'

'That's what you should do. Although the situation is not desperate, it could well turn for the worse.'

'I will not leave without him and he refuses to move from here.'

Azemilk's attitude stiffened; he had no wish to intervene against Bomilcar's decision, which he could not but condone. The change did not escape Inat, so she resorted to extreme measures, throwing herself to her knees before him and begging. 'He is my only child. I don't want him killed.'

Against his best judgement, he heard himself asking, 'What can I do? I can't force him to leave with the women and children.'

She had obviously thought long and hard. 'He will not be a simple evacuee among women and children but the person put in charge for the journey and responsible for the convoy's safe arrival at Carthage. His experience with boats and sailors will be invaluable.'

Won over by her stratagem, he smiled, and she knew she would obtain what she wanted.

21

Abjuration

'Triremes and transport ships, more numerous than one can count, congest our harbours. Sailors and their families are jubilant at being reunited after a lengthy separation. There's not a single person in Sidon who does not rejoice except me, Mother.'

Artas clasped Chiboulet to her bosom, caressing her sleek black hair and wiping tears from her eyes.

'Don't cry,' she said, 'things might turn out for the best. Your father believes that with our ships at Alexander's disposal, Tyre will seek an arrangement with him. It means you could see Bomilcar safe and sound, much sooner than expected.'

'Oh, Mother! I hope this could be true. I wish that the dream I had last night will never materialise. The message I got is so dreadful, so frightening.'

'It's not easy to understand the actual message sent through a dream. You'd better tell me yours I'll try to interpret its meaning,' said Artas.

'I saw myself on the beach in my night raiment, standing at the edge of the water. There appeared from nowhere a boat with one person on board, Bomilcar. He was standing by the prow. The craft headed in my direction, but I couldn't see any sail unfolded or anyone rowing. Each time she came close to me, she was pushed back by an invisible and irresistible force. Bomilcar and I were unable to make a move or exchange a word, and we remained still, as if we were made of stone. All of a sudden the boat disappeared from view, as if dragged down by the marine god. I wanted to enter the waters to fathom what happened, but I still couldn't move. I woke up with tears in my eyes.'

'My poor girl, don't you know that sometimes dreams must be interpreted contrary to their apparent message. That's the gods' malicious way of playing tricks on us. Sometimes the message delivered by a dream is unclear or hidden and requires an apt interpreter. You told me that in your dream you saw the boat disappear, as suddenly as her earlier apparition. You didn't see what happened to Bomilcar. That's the most important part of the dream and it should mean something. Don't you agree? Let me tell you what it means: the boat being an object, not a living being, it relates to the obstacles which separate you from Bomilcar. These obstacles will disappear in the same way the boat did.'

'Oh, mother, I wish you're right, but I've a foreboding which tells me otherwise. I have come to accept I will never be his wife; all I pray for is his safety.'

At that juncture Abdalonymus entered the room, very excited.

'Go to the roof terrace and admire the view,' he said.

'What is there to see?' asked Artas.

'Go, you will never see ships in such great numbers.'

'I know Chiboulet has told me the Sidonian ships returned to their home port.'

'There's much, much more. From the roof terrace you will have a full view of a spectacle such as you have never contemplated. As for me, I must join Alexander; together we'll proceed to the beach to receive the ships officially.'

Mother and daughter climbed to the spot indicated by Abdalonymus and were dazzled by the sight laid out before their eyes. Some forty Sidonian ships, mostly triremes, were at berth in the two harbours, while probably four times that number were at anchor in the open sea. They were told later, that Aradus, Byblos, Rhodes and Cyprus had all sent their warships to Alexander. A few vessels stood taller than the others; they were the quinqueremes, flagships of the Cypriot kings. More quinqueremes and quadriremes had been provided by the Phoenician cities. All the ships had defected from the Persian camp and joined the Macedonian in the rush for Tyrian blood. Some were driven by a feeling of Greek solidarity against anyone who was not a Greek or Macedonian; others were glad to see the prospect of getting rid of Tyrian competitors, others again felt it was high time to join the ranks of the likely victor; and all had one wish, to make Alexander forgive them for having supported the Persian king.

From where they stood, the two women saw Alexander slaughter two bulls in honour of Poseidon; one animal was to thank him for the safe arrival of the vessels and the other a propitiatory offering before imminent military action, to win over divine favour. They also saw Alexander pouring libations to Thetis and other sea-nymphs, before he retired to the governor's mansion with his Macedonian generals.

The magnificent and formidable sight of the naval forces and the thought of how they were about to be used overcame Chiboulet. She nearly fainted, and she had to lean on her mother while they climbed down the stairs to their rooms. 'What I saw convinced me that I read correctly the ominous message of my dream,' she said.

'Why do you say that? Don't you know you may bring bad luck on yourself?' Artas made that reproach despite having realised that nothing would stop Alexander from conquering the island-city by force. He had been taunted and challenged over several months and he was not going to accept a peaceful settlement or even unconditional surrender, assuming that the Tyrians were prepared to offer him one, an unlikely prospect.

'Let's go to your father and see what he has learned during the ceremony.' Artas wanted to give her daughter another opportunity to listen to her father's optimistic views and perhaps learn a piece of information which would alleviate the disastrous impression they had been left with. They found Abdalonymus in great spirit, as always when he had been in Alexander's presence.

'Do you know what he told me?' he said. 'He told me that victory over Tyre will also be mine.'

Engrossed in his exhilaration, he did not pay any attention to the mental agony he was causing Chiboulet. Artas came to the rescue and tried to make her husband see the anguish of his daughter. First she had to assure him that his refusal to let her be Bomilcar's wife would not be defied. She then added, 'All Chiboulet wishes is for you to use your influence and make sure that Bomilcar comes out of the war unharmed. You're the King of Sidon, and if you so desire, you can guarantee his safety. Remember that he saved Chiboulet and Jason from Tubal's clutches, risking his life.'

Abdalonymus was a good man who hated to see his joy not shared by his household. Should he do nothing, his daughter's dejection and his wife's grumbling would prevent him from revelling in his good fortune. He was also a practical man who saw an opportunity and grasped it. 'Is it true that's all you wish is this young man's safety?' he insisted.

'Father, that's all I'm allowed to hope for,' she replied, sounding bitter; these, however, were the words he wanted to hear from her mouth.

'Do you promise to be the wife of the man I choose for you?'

Chiboulet hesitated a moment, for she still felt bound by the promise she had exchanged with Bomilcar to wait for each other. Yet what would be the worth of a promise if the man she loved perished during the impending encounters?

'Have I ever disobeyed you, father?' she said with a heavy heart.

'Then I will see what I can do.'

Having extracted his daughter's promise he was careful not to tell her that what he could do was negligible, unless Bomilcar was to be captured alive. If that were to happen, he would probably be in a position to secure his freedom; otherwise he could do very little indeed. He saw no point in telling his family the truth and dispiriting them more than they already were, so he left them with an empty promise.

22

Substitution

King Azemilk's spies reported that the naval force assembled by Alexander at Sidon was being made ready to blockade Tyre from the sea. This was expected to take place in a matter of days. The spies brought more worrying news. They reported that reinforcements of four thousand mercenaries, recruited from the Peleponnese, had reached Sidon.

Azemilk ordered that work on the ten ships due to transport women and children to Carthage be carried out non-stop, day and night. They should sail in five days at the most, to avoid Tyre's utter annihilation.

The island-city was in the grip of intense agitation and emotion; children and women were selected for the journey by the drawing of lots, and a privileged few were designated by the King and assigned to one of the vessels. Amidst the great confusion, families, that were about to be separated became nearly hysterical: they hugged, kissed and cried their eyes out, all day and all night. They knew they had little chance of being reunited.

Bomilcar was ashamed of having been ordered by the King to accompany the evacuees, of being compelled to leave his compatriots at a time of great danger. In preparation for their departure Inat had put their house into turmoil, giving orders left and right and collecting the items she had chosen to take with her, only to change her mind moments later and replace them with others.

The atmosphere of the household was unbearable, so Bomilcar decided to escape it and go in search of Matten, whom he had not seen for two days. He decided to start with his place of work, which he seldom left in these times, because his skill and leadership were much needed. As expected, he found him at his forge, surrounded by a few apprentices who were watching him at work.

When he saw Bomilcar, he entrusted his teaching role to his best apprentice and came out to meet his friend. They took a stroll, searching for a peaceful spot in the otherwise agitated city.

'I haven't seen you for a while,' said Bomilcar. 'Are you angry with me? Maybe you believe I'm happy to leave Tyre. If that's the reason, I'll be really disappointed for I thought you knew me better.'

'What's this nonsense?' thundered Matten. 'I know you better than you know yourself! How can I think ill of you? In fact I was kept very busy but I intended to come around tonight.'

'Do you realise that after bidding farewell we might not see each other again. I had hoped to spend every hour left with you and what do you do? You avoid me. Why?'

'You're right in a sense. I've a message for you, a message that part of me tells me to deliver and part tells me not to.'

'What is it? Speak.'

'Idbal asked me to approach you to see whether you would be willing to give up your mission.'

'I don't understand,' said Bomilcar, puzzled. 'Why does he want me to stay? Did you ask him why?'

'He had in mind to sail in your stead, but before he goes to the King to ask his permission, he wants to know that you don't mind.'

The reply stunned Bomilcar, who could not believe what he had just heard. He vented his astonishment. 'You're telling me that Idbal, the fierce enemy of any compromise with Alexander, the staunch supporter of armed resistance, is afraid and wants to flee?'

'It's not exactly that,' protested Matten timidly. 'He wishes to go himself to Carthage and meet with the Suffetes. He believes he can convince them to help. At least that's what he said.'

'Maybe that is his real reason. But tell me why did you find difficulty transmitting me his message?'

'Don't you see we are doomed? We're all going to die. I wanted you to leave and live.'

Matten's outburst took Bomilcar by surprise. Until then he had thought that his friend's considerable courage derived from his imperviousness to the danger of any given situation. He was astounded to find out that he had been completely wrong. The explanation he had created about Matten's bravery was only to exculpate his own occasional weaknesses and constant calling into question matters that seemed obvious to Matten. For the first time since they had grown up, Bomilcar felt that his less fortunate friend had an edge on him. The fortitude of Matten's character, which knew no indecision, and his bravery, which never wavered, were the moral pillars left unimpaired at a time when everything else, human beings and buildings alike, were marked for destruction.

'My friend, my dear friend, between dying in shame in Carthage and being killed in Tyre fighting beside you, I choose the second option. Tell Idbal that I welcome his initiative. But I have one condition,' said Bomilcar, his voice still trembling with emotion.

'What is it?'

'He must keep the substitution secret until the last minute. I don't want my mother to change her mind and refuse to leave because I'm not with her. Just before her boat breaks moorings, I'll inform her of my decision to stay.'

On the day the evacuees were summoned to the northern port, Inat and her sister, holding her son in her arms, were accompanied to their assigned vessel by Bomilcar, Amatbaal's husband, Zarkat, and a host of slaves carrying the travellers' belongings. They had great difficulty forcing their way through the crowd, which was going in the same direction and with same purpose. Women and children were in tears while their men tried to wear brave faces and to reassure their loved ones with unrealistic promises about a forthcoming reunion. The less fortunate ones, who were to stay behind, followed the exodus in complete silence. Their resentment was tempered by the sight of the distressing ripping apart of the evacuees' families.

Just when the boat was about to leave harbour, Inat was told of

Bomilcar's decision to remain behind. She shouted, cried and demanded to be disembarked, but her son jumped out of the boat and ordered that the gangplank be removed. Helpless and broken-hearted, she stood on the deck leaning on her sister, who was in no better state; she was leaving behind a husband. He and Bomilcar remained on the quay to avail themselves of the last sight of their loved ones. When the boat disappeared from their field of vision, Bomilcar returned home, which seemed to him eerily quiet. He went to his room, closed the door and cried.

A few days later, the Tyrians, whether those who had been traumatised by the dramatic separation from their women and children, or those who were resentful for not having been given a chance to send theirs away, were united in fear. From the parapet walks the population witnessed the progression of warships, never seen in such numbers before. They advanced in two columns at a speed estimated at around seven knots. Each trireme had on her deck ten hoplites, four archers from Crete and one catapult. The sound of hundreds of flutes beating out the rhythm filled the population with dismay.

The Tyrians ordered their vessels, which were patrolling the seas, to return immediately to port. Engagement was impossible; the imbalance between Tyrian forces and the assailants was too great.

When the ships were close enough to the city's walls but out of range of Tyrian artillery, they encircled the island completely. Then the formation was broken and a number of vessels cast anchor by the mainland and each side of the causeway, while enough craft were left on the lookout to keep up the siege from all sides.

23

Obstinate Resistance

Alexander had neither the time nor the patience to wait until the island-city surrendered out of hunger and thirst. He took the decision to attack it on all fronts. The construction of the causeway was near completion; despite fierce Tyrian counter-attacks, and the damage caused by occasional rough seas, the walls of the besieged city were brought within javelin range. Macedonian artillery poured continually from the siege towers erected on the causeway, and missiles rained on and inside the eastern walls. The death toll and casualties mounted.

With his newly acquired fleet, Alexander was now in a position to assail the walls from the sea. On the advice of his engineers, several boats were lashed in pairs and decks were erected on the coupled surfaces. On these improvised platforms, powerful battering-rams were suspended, covered with rawhide roofs to protect the operators from arrows and cauldrons of boiling oil emptied from above. When several of the paired boats were so fitted, their crews rowed them up to the city walls, cast anchor and the battering-rams went into action.

The Strategic Committee appointed by Azemilk held an urgent meeting to discuss the new situation. Matten and Bomilcar attended that meeting as substitutes for Idbal who had nominated them as such before he started his journey. A plan of action was put in place, approved and immediately implemented. As part of the plan Matten was put in charge of the defence of the southern port.

Tyrian counterattacks were carried out through various means which proved extremely effective; besides the usual defensive weaponry, such as throwing boulders on to the boats anchored by the foot of the walls, and pouring boiling oil and sand on their crews and the operators of the battering-rams, the besieged invented several other deadly means to kill and repel the besiegers.

Their new array comprised undetected underwater swimmers, who approached the boats anchored by the walls, and cut the ropes from which the anchors were suspended, setting the boats adrift; tridents fitted to long ropes to harpoon the attackers; and giant fishing nets to trap anyone who dared step on to the siege towers' drawbridges. Those pierced by harpoons or caught in nets were hurled against rocks or drowned in the sea.

Tyrian inventiveness was met with Macedonian resolve. Neither adversary could afford to give up; for the Tyrians it was a matter of life or death, while Alexander, could not allow himself to leave Tyre's navy unscathed while the Persian fleet threatened southern Greece. In addition, the Macedonian would never acknowledge that he had been beaten by a city of merchants.

As a result, a war of attrition dragged on for weeks; constant danger and persistent hunger made the Tyrian mob very receptive to alarmist rumours, which were plentiful. One baker dreamed that Apollo was about to abandon the city; he told his dream to a friend who reported it to another friend; so in a matter of hours the rumour was wide-spread and a number of people gathered in the empty space around the temple of Melqart. In the temple Apollo had a statue next to Melqart's; it was a gift from the Carthaginians who had taken it from Syracuse. The crowd became restless, prepared to listen to absurd suggestions. At the ringleaders' instigation, a party entered the temple, bound the statue with golden chains and attached it to the altar, to prevent the god from fleeing.

Day after day, security inside the island-city deteriorated. No one was available to do anything about it, for every able man had been given a specific defensive duty. The shortage of hands was such that slaves, who did not normally participate in armed conflict, were required to fight. No one being left to maintain order on the streets, bands of pillagers and marauders took control.

The situation became intolerable and the Council of Elders met to see what could be done. Many Councillors were racked with fear and it was difficult to make any sense of their speeches.

'We have offended the gods by allowing the Israelites to worship their own god in our city. Their god is very jealous of his authority and refuses to accept any other deity in his Olympus. His followers should not be allowed to stay among us,' said one Councillor.

'I don't know why we have tolerated them so long,' added another, 'I was told by one of our priests that a prophet of theirs has cursed our city and prophesied its destruction. I, like my colleague, believe that the Israelites living here must be expelled.'

The King was annoyed; he was not in favour of such a drastic measure, yet there was a danger that if the mob were to hear of the accusations thrown by the Councillors and realise they had been ignored, they might take the matter into their own hands. Should this happen, expulsion would not satisfy the rabble, which might resort to mass murder. Anyone with a grudge against anyone else, Israelite or not, would seize the opportunity to settle the score. Instability and insecurity would increase to a level impossible to control.

'Shame on you,' he thundered, 'Do you wish to give our enemies more reason to call us barbarians? Besides, how could you say that the handful of Israelite families living with us are responsible for our predicament? Remember, their ancestors were already with ours when we built the temple of Jerusalem for their King Solomon, when Carthage was founded and our business empire flourished. If their presence did not offend our gods then, why should it offend them now? I don't want to hear these absurdities.'

'The King is right,' said one Councillor. 'We mustn't make anyone but ourselves responsible for our misfortune. Instead we should revive the worship of Molock and sacrifice our dearest possessions, offering him free-born male children.'

A clamour of horror emanated from the councillors, silencing the speaker.

The King dismissed the assembly but asked Chelbes and Bomilcar to stay. 'We have to try something that will occupy the minds of the people and show them that we haven't lost the initiative,' he said to them.

'What do you have in mind, Sire?' asked Bomilcar.

'I don't know. We still have our ships, don't we? Maybe it's time to use them.'

24

Last Throes

An unexpected attack against enemy ships was devised by the Strategic Committee. Taking the initiative was necessary to boost the morale of the population and possibly deliver the assailants a blow from which they might not recover.

Behind the rigged sails that hid the northern docks, thirteen of Tyre's best warships were fitted: three quinqueremes, three quadriremes and seven triremes. About three hundred oarsmen were needed for each large vessel and one hundred and seventy for each trireme. To guarantee the success of the operation it was essential to choose the crews from the most able men, those renowned for their courage and experience in naval warfare.

Bomilcar sought the assistance of his aunt's husband, an experienced mariner, to help him choose the right oarsmen. Not only did Zarkat's knowledge of the sea prove invaluable; he also volunteered to command one of the triremes.

Speed and manoeuvrability were essential for the operation, so it was decided to supply each warship with only a handful of armed men.

'I'm fed up waiting for the Macedonian's blows,' said Bomilcar, bringing a hint of a smile to Matten's face.

'What do you have in mind?' he asked.

'Exactly what you have guessed. I want to be in one of the boats.'

'It's amazing,' said Matten. 'I want exactly the same.'

'I don't think you should, You are a most valuable warrior and you are needed to stimulate others. For me it's different, I'm not much of a fighter, but I know about navigation. You must stay.'

The blacksmith had to accept the soundness of his friend's words, so he did not object when Bomilcar was put in command of one of the quinqueremes, while he was given no part in the operation.

All the preparations having been completed, the Strategic Committee waited for a favourable sea to allow the raiding party to leave harbour.

One morning towards the end of July, a squadron of thirteen warships slipped silently out of the harbour; no flute called the rhythm and not a sound came from the men, who held their breath and rowed in silence. The northern harbour was under a blockade by a number of warships belonging to the Kings of Cyprus. When the raiding party came within sight of them, it split into two columns. One column, which included Bomilcar's quinquereme, charged the blockading vessels at high speed. The six foot bronze ram fitted to each Tyrian ship was driven into the hull of a chosen prey. Pursuant to a technique acquired through experience, the ram had to be swiftly retrieved, a manoeuvre made possible by the strength of her oarsmen's arms; otherwise attacker and attacked would sink in a deadly embrace.

The other column charged the vessels anchored by the causeway and sank a number of them. The carnage was stopped by Alexander himself who happened to be in Old Tyre's southern port and witnessed it. He immediately boarded his quinquereme. Followed by a number of triremes which had their crews on board, he attacked the Tyrian squadron. Some managed to return to port, but many were sunk. All in all, the raid had been more damaging to the Tyrians – who could not afford to lose smart ships and able crewmen – than to their enemies, more numerous and better equipped.

Bomilcar's quinquereme avoided engagement and owing to her speed returned undamaged to port. He was received by a relieved Matten, who had rushed to the northern harbour, anxiously awaiting news. The joy of both friends was marred by the failure of Zarkat's trireme to return, and an ominous feeling that warned them that the end was nigh.

They were not mistaken. A few days later a fierce onslaught came from different places, all at once, the assailants making use of various methods and means. From the siege towers erected on the causeway, artillery rained missiles; battering-rams, hauled on ships, ringed the island and were put into action to break points in the walls. Ship-borne siege-towers, armed with catapults, moved around the fortifications, giving cover to the rams' operators and driving the defenders from the parapet walks. At the same time two naval forces tried to force the two island harbours, and more ships cruised the island to demonstrate that the threat could come from any point.

After several days of the same treatment, the walls started to totter and the exhausted defenders saw their numbers dwindling. No one remained under any illusion about the city's imminent fall. The King and his family took refuge in the Temple of Melqart and were joined by the members of the Council of Elders and their families as well as by the Carthaginian delegation. One after the other messengers came with more bad news.

'Sire, allow me to leave and fight,' said Bomilcar, who was pushed to the limit. He felt that this time was not for words and that the non-stop session of the Council of Elders had lost all significance. He was stared at with disapproval by most of his colleagues, for they refused to contemplate any participation in his pointless design and were unhappy to have their shortcomings exposed. Others were too despondent to react.

'I forbid you to leave the temple. You have accomplished more than your duty.' The tone of the King was firm and categorical and the assembly sighed with relief. He added, 'In the temple we have a chance of staying alive. King Alexander is a wise young man; I don't expect him to wish to rule over ruins and I don't see him willing to offend the gods by spilling human blood in their house. Don't leave my side. I need all of you; together we'll rebuild our city and restore its greatness.'

Tears ran down the King's face and an oppressive silence fell on the assembly; some were crying, some were praying and others were prostrated, lost in their thoughts. All dreaded the moment when the gate of the temple would be violently opened and the Macedonians and their mercenaries would pour inside the building. Despite Azemilk's reassuring words, no one knew how they would react or what their orders would be.

In the meantime fierce fighting was taking place on one breach in the walls, which had been reached through a drawbridge dropped from one of the siege-towers. Alexander, very conspicuous in his steel helmet that gleamed like polished silver, was in the heat of the battle; he established control of some of the towers and sections of the walls connecting them. Then he and his shield-bearers descended down into the town, wiping out all armed resistance in their way.

About that time Cyprian warships gained control of the northern port and Phoenician warships smashed access into the southern one. Hoplites and mercenaries poured out from their transport vessels and fought their way into the heart of the city, despite a last stand made by Matten and a handful of his armed companions who had vowed to die fighting but never surrender.

Shrines and temples were a safe refuge for those who entered them; that was the promise made by the invaders. Nevertheless most fit Tyrians refused to take advantage of the pledge; they chose to die in combat instead of being enslaved, for that was the lot awaiting those who were taken alive. Others shut themselves in their homes and perished with their families by their own hands.

When Alexander became confident that the winged goddess of victory was definitely on his side, he went to see Azemilk, who he treated with courteous consideration.

'You and those with you are pardoned,' he declared to their immeasurable relief.

'Sire,' said Azemilk,' your clemency is worthy of Aristotle's teaching and of your reputation as a great and merciful leader.'

During the exchange of civilities, the massacre of thousands of ordinary people and the enslavement of thousands more went on.

'You and your retinue will be taken to your palace. I restore you in your kingship,' said the Macedonian. With a motion of the hand, he stopped a flood of thankful words.

'The envoys from Carthage,' he added, 'will be sent back home. They will be provided with transportation. Their journey will start from Sidon, where they will be taken tomorrow.'

He ignored the envoys' manifestation of hearty thanks and told Azemilk, 'Your son will be my guest; he and a small retinue of his choice will leave for Sidon, with the envoys. In the meantime I advise you not to venture outside the palace.'

Despite the semblance of trust which had been established in Azemilk, Alexander required a guarantee of his loyalty. The son, taken as a hostage, was deemed a satisfying one.

25

Reunited

King Azemilk, his son and the members of his family were escorted to the royal palace by hoplites and placed under the command of an officer who had been instructed by Alexander to show them respect and consideration. The same instructions also applied to the Councillors, their families, and the Carthaginian envoys, who were all to be given temporary shelter at the palace, until carnage and looting died down and those due to leave Tyre were shipped to Sidon.

The dejected convoy crossed the short distance separating the temple from the palace. During that interval, they had a terrifying glimpse of the ravages which went with the fall of the city. Dead men, women and children littered the ground, a guilty reminder of the privileged fate of those still alive.

Bomilcar was particularly broken-hearted; he wished he had died with a sword in his hand and not been singled out because of his privileged status, which seemed obscene when so many had perished. Above all, the thought of Matten's fate distressed him. He knew that if he had survived the fighting, he would by now be enslaved. It was that idea he could not bear, although he had no doubt whatsoever that Matten would not be held in bondage for long; he would always find a way to avenge his dead companions before being killed. His thoughts went also to Tansu, Lula and the rest of his household. Tansu was too old to have a market value or serve in a new household, so most probably he had been murdered. As for Lula, he did not dare dwell too long on her fate.

When they reached the palace, the King's son took him apart. 'I want you to come with me to Sidon,' he said.

The invitation awakened Bomilcar from a morbid lethargic state and a foolish hope rushed into his mind. Accepting the offer would give a chance to see Chiboulet and maybe convince her to elope with him; in a split second he worked out details which would make of a seemingly insane dream, a feasible design; he even identified where their new home would be and how to get there, if only he was able to make contact with her and she was willing.

'Well?' insisted Azemilk.

'Forgive me, I was lost in thoughts,' apologised Bomilcar, who hastened to add, 'Oh yes! I will come.'

'That settles it.'

He was tempted to tell the King's son of his plan, to warn him that he might leave him soon for a new home. He refrained from saying anything. An inner voice was reminding him that she had once declined to defy her father's decision against their marriage.

Now he was destitute, he had not much to offer to induce her to change her mind. Awareness of his present condition deflated Bomilcar's earlier exhilaration. Once more, sombre thoughts took hold of his mind and made him feel guilty, not only for being alive, but also for working out self-serving plans.

The tragedy was so great and the disaster so enormous that everyone at the palace remained prostrated and kept to himself. No comments or exchange of views took place, because there was nothing left to speculate about and no hope left to build a future on.

The following morning, the officer who had escorted them to the palace came back to accompany Azemilk, his small retinue and the Carthaginian delegates to their ship anchored in the canal. On their way they saw more bodies strewn everywhere and houses burnt to the ground. No one had been on hand to put out the fires. Objects, discarded from looting, were scattered where they were not supposed to be, almost more indecent than the motionless bodies. The house that Bomilcar's father had built suffered the same fate; a smouldering ruin was all that was left and tears came to the eyes of the young Tyrian when he passed by with the others on their way to the ship.

Sidon was reached at midday; Azemilk and his attendants were led to the governor's mansion and the Carthaginian envoys were sheltered in tents erected for them on the beach. Knowing he was close to Chiboulet revitalised Bomilcar; the knotty point, however, was for him to get in touch with her without her father's knowledge. He was aware that he might not have much time, for the transport ship earmarked for Carthage might cast off any moment Alexander ordered. The African colony was going to be his new home. He had no doubt that Azemilk, if asked, would secure for him and his loved one a passage with the Carthaginian delegation. In the African colony he would be reunited with his mother and he would start a new life with Chiboulet, if only she was willing to accompany him. To find out he must see her on her own; but how?

He needed time for quiet reflection; for that, he had first to get away from the heavy atmosphere of the governor's crammed mansion. He left the building and walked in the direction of the beach, where he expected to benefit from a marine breeze which would alleviate the unbearable heat of midsummer and contribute to the clear thinking he badly needed.

A gentle wind brought him some relief but also the waft of grilled fish. That made him realise that he had had nothing to eat since the day before. Guided by the smell, he walked down the sandy beach in the direction of a man and a woman who were busy broiling fish on an open fire. Getting a little closer, he thought they might be the same couple who had sold him and Matten expensive fish when they came to the city to see Abdalonymus after he was appointed king.

Indeed, they were and they were not alone. In the shock of his life he recognised Matten lying next to them on a blanket stretched out on the sand; an improvised shelter made of palm leaves protected him from the sun's rays. Bomilcar could not believe his eyes, not until he knelt beside his friend and touched him to make sure he was not dreaming.

Laboriously Matten lifted himself up and the two friends hugged, which made the blacksmith groan with pain.

'Are you alright?' asked Bomilcar.

'Now I'm better knowing you are alive and free. I was struck with a sword here.' He pointed at his right shoulder before he carried on. 'I don't know how I did not lose my head in the process. This man' – this time he pointed at the fisherman, who was standing above him smiling – 'this good man rescued me.'

Too tired to continue the account of his rescue, he stretched out on his blanket and invited his saviour to take over from him. The Sidonian needed no further encouragement.

'My boat, like all fishing boats, was commandeered to transport rocks to serve the catapults, so when the orders came, we followed the warships.' he said, 'I and my three brothers, who make up my crew, did exactly that and we entered the southern port, where fierce fighting was taking place. When it died down we disembarked, driven by curiosity . . . '

He was interrupted by Matten roaring, 'Don't believe him, they were intent on looting, but I love him even though he's ugly.'

The fisherman seemed not to mind either the charge or the judgment on his looks, but laughed and proceeded with his story. 'Among the dead and dying a giant of a man with ginger hair drew my attention. He was wounded and unconscious but not yet gone. I recognised him as the man who had been my customer. When he made a move and opened his eyes, I felt I couldn't leave him to die. We carried him to the boat. Mind you, he isn't the only Tyrian who has escaped with his life and I'm not the only one who has helped. Many others were smuggled to safety in our boats.'

'These people are unbelievable,' interjected Matten. 'They brought me here, tended my wound and took care of me. Enough of me, tell me what happened after our resistance was broken up.'

Bomilcar told him what he knew and what he had witnessed. Recalling the tragic events of the previous day left the two friends mute, while they reflected on their hapless condition and on the unknown fate of those left behind.

Finally Matten broke the silence and asked the one question which was burning his lips. 'Have you seen or heard of my parents?' he said, with no real hope of getting a positive answer.

'I'm sorry to say I have not.'

'I must go back and find out,' said Matten. 'What about you? What do you intend to do?'

'I want to see Chiboulet and convince her to run away with me and settle in Carthage. I have no idea how I'm going to get in touch with her without her father knowing.'

'I know how,' said the blacksmith who called out to the fisherman's wife, 'Go and fetch over your niece.' It was obvious that the blacksmith had succeeded in exercising full control over his benefactors, in spite of his many handicaps. To the bewildered

Bomilcar he explained, 'Her niece is a maid at the palace. She will transmit whatever message you wish to send Chiboulet.'

They did not have to wait long for the fisherman's wife to come back with her niece. With his appropriated authority, Matten asked the young girl with his thundering voice, 'Do you know the King's daughter?'

'Of course I know her. I am one of her servants,' she replied, not in the least impressed either by the voice or the size of the man lying at her feet.

'Then go and tell her . . . '

He was cut short by Bomilcar who had instantly realised from the girl's demeanour that she should be treated in a more genteel way, otherwise her co-operation could not be guaranteed.

'I can see that you are a bright girl besides being very pretty,' he said, lying through his teeth, at least with regard to the latest part of his compliment.

Her face brightened and he knew that with the help of a promised reward she would do what was expected from her.

'See this piece of silver,' he said, 'it's yours if you come back with your mistress. What you have to tell her is simple, tell her: Bomilcar is waiting for you on the beach. Remember well: Bomilcar. Convey the message the moment you are alone with her and don't tell anyone else what the message is. This is a very urgent matter. Go.'

The girl left, running in the direction of the King's palace, leaving behind a restless Bomilcar. His torment came to an end after an hour or so when Chiboulet, crying with emotion and joy, threw herself in his arms.

'I thought I would never see you again. Echoes of the carnage which took place in Tyre have reached us and I thought I had lost you forever.'

'I am here and look who is with us.'

She disengaged herself from their embrace and saw Matten smiling at her. She knelt beside him and hugged him cautiously, having realised that he was wounded.

They sat cross-legged beside Matten, barely believing their luck in being reunited despite the turmoil which spared nothing and no one.

Knowing that a decision had to be taken immediately if the plan had any chance of success, Bomilcar explained the arrangements he had in mind for their future, ending the explanation with an anxious pleading. 'I've lost everything but I'm not prepared to lose you. In Carthage we will build up a future together. Come with me, I beg you. I realise I'm asking much of you and I've very little to offer . . . '

She interrupted him, determined to let him realise her desperate state of mind before their magical reunion. 'When I heard what befell Tyre, I thought I'd lost you forever. I wanted to die and only a faint hope of seeing you alive again prevented me from taking my own life. Now that I've found you I'll never leave you.'

'Go, prepare yourself and prepare Jason. I have to talk to Azemilk for our passage. We will meet in one hour's time at this place and we will hide in the boat being ready to sail for Carthage. Don't be late and don't say a word to your mother, the prospect of losing you and her grandson might make her thwart our plan.'

'Wait for me,' she said. She did not need to tell him more; the love in her eyes was enough to pledge her determination.

GW01605257

--

WEATHER LORE
OF THE
ENGLISH COUNTRYSIDE

RED SKY AT NIGHT
SHEPHERD'S DELIGHT?

--

WEATHER LORE
OF THE
ENGLISH COUNTRYSIDE

BY

PAUL J. MARRIOTT

First Published by

Publishers of
History, Country and Biographical Books.
(Member of Independent Publishers Guild)
31 DASHWOOD RISE,
DUNS TEW,
OXFORD, OX5 4JQ
Tel. Steeple Aston (0869) 40615

First Published 1981

ISBN 0 9505730 5 1

Reproduced from copy supplied
printed and bound in Great Britain
by Billing and Sons Limited and Kemp Hall Bindery
Guildford, London, Oxford, Worcester

INTRODUCTION

The two years taken in collecting, testing and editing this collection of English countryside weather lore has been both stimulating and exhausting. I have tried to embrace the scientific/academic end of the subject with the old country weather knowledge and blend together a readable but sound reference book. It contains nearly 1,900 adages covering all weather types from the famous "red sky at night, shepherd's delight," to the "ash before oak, you'll get a soak". 88 percent of these were star rated (the remainder being obvious statements). The chance of a weather saying being very good or excellent in the truth stakes was 14.6 percent or 1 in 7.

All old English county names are retained with Victorian and earlier sketches of birds, trees and flower motifs, to keep a country atmosphere in the book. No barometer maxims appear.

A star rating system is used for the reader as an instant assessment of the validity of each weather maxim. Also exhaustive tests were carried out on the sayings which appear in the format 96/169 (57). This example means that of 169 times the saying was tested 96 were correct or 57 percent of occasions were true. Further explanations can be seen at the beginning of the first chapter.

The data and techniques used in the tests are accounted for on pages 354-355 . Briefly they cover nearly 37,000 daily airstream patterns of the U.K. from 1861-1971; monthly and seasonal temperatures for Central England 1698-1971 and rainfall for England and Wales 1727-1971; tree figures 1776-1935 and animal and crop records for 1866-1966.

References to occlusions, cold and warm fronts and warm sectors in the book are now generally accepted phrases which denote sharp changes between different airstreams.

I would like to express my sincere gratitude to all those concerned with this book, especially to Ray Pitts for his collection of West Oxon rook weather lore and H.A. Poskitt for many Yorkshire sayings. Acknowledgements are made to the Royal Meteorological Society for permission to use material from Richard Inward's 1898 collection of *Weather Lore*. If any acknowledgements have been omitted, then apologies are now rendered.

Finally all opinions expressed and test figures quoted in this book are entirely those of the author.

Paul J. Marriott
Duns Tew
Oxon
March 1981

CONTENT

STAR RATING SYSTEM AND TEST EXPLANATION

A large number of weather sayings are tested and all appear in the same form. For example 39/116 (34) means that the maxim was correct 39 times out of 116 or a 34 percent true rating. The star rating goes a stage further enabling the reader to make an instant assessment of each weather maxim - whether it is true or false. Of the 1,880 sayings 224 received no stars as they were obvious statements of fact. A star rating with no test results are the author's judgement. All percentages were taken to the nearest whole number.

Percentage in Test Result	*Rating*	*Star Rating*
1 - 16 percent	Very Poor	*
17 - 32 "	Poor	**
33 - 48 "	Fair	***
49 - 64 "	Good	****
65 - 80 "	Very Good	*****
81 -100 "	Excellent	******

JANUARY

January usually begins with a stormy period with the year's highest frequency for westerlies, lasting about two weeks - roughly 5-17th January with a peak date on the 8th. A quiet and frosty interlude normally follows with anticyclonic weather - about 18-24th, peaking 20-21st. However January returns to a stormy end as depressions cross England from the south-west - around 24th Jan-1st Feb, peaking on 31st Jan.

Froze Janiveer,
Leader of the year;
Mince pies in van,
Calf's head in rear.

The blackest month in all the year
Is the month of Janiveer.

An observation of the coldest and sometimes bleakest month of the year.

A favourable January brings us
a good year. **

It depends on how one defines "a favourable January". A very cold and dry one can be suitable for lack of disease, since low temperature and a hard frost kills land virus and germs which will give sheep and cattle a good start to the year. On the other hand a mild dry January helps winter seeds for the grain farmer.

In Janiveer if the sun appear,
March April pay full dear. **

March in Janiveer,
Janiveer in March, I fear. **

These types of weather lore are all too common where the countryman believes in a compensating balance in weather. A sunny January has to be matched against a sunless March or April.

JANUARY

January warm, the Lord have mercy! **

If grain grows in January, there
will be a year of great need. **

If birds begin to whistle in
January, frost's to come.

A January spring
Is worth nothing. **

The maxims mean that a warm January brings on plant growth which should be retarded by February and March frosts. The figures are tested for warm Januarys, hay and wheat from 1885 to 1966 giving poor results of 30 and 25 percent. The fourth maxim hails from Rutland. A mild January often leads to a mild February and March producing a better harvest than normal.

6/20 (30)
5/20 (25)

Dry January, plenty of wine.
A wet January, a wet spring. ***

More English vineyards were in operation in the medieval period than any other time showing the age of the maxim. The most important ingredient for growing grapes is warm excessive sunshine which is not forecast from a dry January. The second line contains little truth with a 36 percent correct result.

29/81 (36)

Is January wet? - the barrel
remains empty. **

January wet, no wine you get. **

In January much rain and little
snow is bad for mountains,
valleys and trees. **

Much rain in January, no blossom
to the fruit. **

These similar sayings infer that a wet January will play havoc with winter seed, erasing topsoil and generally rendering disaster to farming. Certainly damage will be done and unless the rains continue into February and spring harvests will vary in quality.

Always expect a thaw in January.

A thaw is always experienced in January, although only slight ones occur in severe winters.

Fog in January brings a wet spring. ***

Fog is mainly connected with cold anticyclones or high pressure systems in winter (in summer they produce hot, hazy dry periods). The foggiest Januarys from 1861 to 1971 were compared with their corresponding springs but unfortunately only 42 percent were wet. 16/38 (42)

If there is no snow before January, there will be the more in March and April. **

Another compensating adage this time dealing with the balance of snow. Poor results evolved when tested against March and April above average snow from 1882 to 1974. 4/20 (20)

January freeze the pot by the fire,

A kindly, good Janiveer
Freezes the pot by the fire.

As the day lengthens,
So the cold strengthens.

These are well-established saws dealing with the coldest month of the year and are mainly pure observation and of little forecasting use. In the second maxim January daily temperatures start to slowly increase as daylight lengthens.

JANUARY

Jack Frost in Janiveer
Nips the nose of the nascent
year. ****

This rhyme refers to a cold January continuing into a cold February or "nascent" (beginning or young) part of the year. The persistence of similar monthly temperatures is one of the few true striking features to emerge from this book. Unfortunately it is only an evens chance that a cold January passes onto February. 54/110 (49)

Hoar frost and no snow is
hurtful to fields, trees,
and grain. **

When oak trees bend with snow in
January, good crops may be
expected. **

Sound advice here as hoar frost will injure seed and plant life at any time but a covering of snow will act as an insulator against frost and cold winds. The top line of the second adage refers to very deep snow. Snowy or very snowy Januarys 1885-1966 were tested with hay and barley figures. Low returns of 25 and 26 percent respectively occurred. In theory the insulated snow over seed should help towards a bumper harvest but with further months to go with varied weather in practice the picture is different. 10/39 (26)
9/39 (23)

Thunder in January signifyeth
the same year
Great winds, plentiful of corn
and cattle, peradventure. *

I suppose this very old weather lore was based on the idea that thunder, storms and great winds occurred together and if thunder erupted out of season in January the trend would continue.

Who in January sows oats
Gets gold and groats;

January

Who cows in May
Gets little that way.

An old-style farming maxim determining the best time to sow seed.

January commits the fault and
May bears the blame. *

Again any extreme weather in January is supposed to have an effect on crops in May but really the only truth it contains is when applied as a metaphor to human affairs.

A warm January, a cold May. ***

Another country balance lore with only satisfactory results. 21/49 (43)

December frost and January flood
Never boded husbandman good.

This weather sequence, especially a wet soggy January, plays havoc with cattle and seeding operations for the farmer or husbandman.

25 December to 5 January

These twelve days are said to be
the keys of the weather for the
whole year. *

This is a pleasant thought, having each day ruling the corresponding months of the coming year. Similar results to those in the section 1-3rd January would be expected.

1 January

Morning red, foul weather and
great need. *****

The above can be applied to any day of the year. For further reading turn to the chapter on sky colours.

If New Year's Day happen on a
Saturday the winter will be mean,
and the summer hot. *

The day of the week measures time not weather in this North Riding of Yorkshire saw.

2 JANUARY

As the weather is this day so it
will be in September. *

No logic can be seen in this saying. The tested result of 11 percent, covering the temperature and rainfall of this day from 1861 to 1971 and the corresponding September, proves it. 12/105 (11)

1-3 JANUARY

The first three days of January
rule the coming three months. **

Low test values occur in this adage. 69/312 (22)

12 JANUARY

If on January the twelfth the
sun shine, it foreshows much
wind. ***

Another saying which expects wind if the sun shines on this particular day - the results prove different. 25/57 (44)

13 OR 14 JANUARY - ST HILARY'S DAY

The coldest day of the year. *

January the forteenth, Saint Hilary,
Coldest day of the year. *

January the forteenth will either be the coldest or the wettest day of the year. *

Named after Hilarius, Bishop of Poitiers who died in 367 AD. The Anglican festival lies on the 13th but the second Yorkshire and third Hunts maxims refer to 14th January. This is the first of many fixed religious days that weather lore latches onto. Before clocks the countryman used natural times of the year such as harvest, start and end of seasons, first cuckoo call and so on, and also religious days. The three saws refer to this part of January as the coldest of the year. In fact the coldest night of the year at Kew and Greenwich (1841-1964) occurred in the last week of December (26-31st).

17 January - St Anthony's Day

After Saint Anthony's death there fell no rain from Heaven for three years. *

22 January - St Vincent's Day

Remember on Saint Vincent's Day,
If that the sun his beams display,
Be sure to mark his transient beam,
Which through the casement sheds a gleam;
For 'tis a token bright and clear
Of prosperous weather all the year. *

St Vincent, born around Huesca in Spain and died from torture in 304 AD, became the patron saint of wine growers and drunkards, hence the connection in the third maxim. The mean-

ing of "prosperous weather all the year" was difficult to define as a mild wet year would suit fruit growers and not others. So average temperature and rainfall conditions were thought best and were tested for sunny 22nd Januarys covering 1861-1970, but as expected the results were as appalling as the saying.
21/280 (7)

If the sun shine on January the
twenty-second, there shall be
much wind. ***

If Saint Vincent Day the sky is
clear,
More wine than water will crown
the year. **

Poor results occurred when excess wind blew on at least four days of the seven after a sunny 22nd January. One could nominate sun to shine on any day of the year and emerge with similar figures. 20/56 (36)

22 AND 25 JANUARY - ST VINCENT'S AND ST PAUL'S CONVERSION DAY

If Saint Vincent's has sunshine,
One hopes much rye and wine;
If Saint Paul's is bright and
clear,
One does hope a good year.

25 JANUARY - ST PAUL'S CONVERSION DAY

Saint Paul fair with sunshine
Brings fertility to rye and
wine. ***

Fair on Saint Paul's conversion
day is favourable to all fruit. **

If Saint Paul's Day be faire and
cleare,
It doth betide a happy yeare; **

But if by chance it then should rain,
It will make deare all kinds of graine;
And if ye clouds make dark ye skie,
Then neate and fowles this yeare shall die;
If blustering winds do blow aloft,
Then wars shall trouble ye realm full oft. ***

If Saint Paul's Day be fair and clear, it indicates plenty; if cloudy or misty, much cattle will die; if rain and snow fall that day, it presages a dearth; if windy, it forebodes wars, as old wives do dream. *

If the sun on Saint Paul's Day, it betokens a good year; if rain or snow, indifferent; if misty, it predicts great dearth; if thunder, great winds and death of people that year. *

Saint Paul's Day, very good: a good yeare. **

Clouds on Saint Ananias's Day portend floods. **

This is St Paul's Conversion Day, sometimes called St Ananias Day after the Bishop of Damascus, who restored Paul's eye sight and baptised him after being blinded on the road to Damascus. Ananias died by being stoned in c70 AD. Most of the sayings concern a fair bright 25th January with a prosperous year - a stereotyped pattern for most of the saints' days. The fifth adage comes from Oxford.

The 25th January was tested for mist, rain and fair weather. Wheat and hay figures are the annual yield per acre for England and Wales (1885-1966), weighted to arrest the acceleration in growth from c1948 due to the introduction of chemical fertilizers. The final yields were divided into three groups, poor, average and good. Cattle figures (1861-1971) were similarly grouped. The following poor results range from 14-37 percent.

Fair and sunny 25th January = good year. (Wheat) 14/44 (32)
(Hay) 16/44 (36)
(Spuds) 16/43 (37)

Rainy 25th January = poor grain and indifferent year.
(Poor grain) 12/36 (33)
(Low number in cattle) 17/46 (37)
(Indifferent wheat) 9/36 (25)

Misty 25th January = great dearth. (Poor wheat) 3/14 (21)
(Low number in cattle) 3/22 (14)

26 JANUARY

If the weather be dry and bright
on the twenty-sixth of January
the year will generally be the
same. *

This North Riding (Yorkshire) maxim follows the pattern of the previous sayings. 7/53 (13)

26-31 JANUARY

The last twelve days of January
ride the weather for the whole
year. *

Very like the lore covering 25th Dec - 5th Jan. Logically the same falsity and poor test outcome would apply.

FEBRUARY

After the early storms of February - 24 January to 1st February peaking 31st - comes a quiet anticyclonic period usually occurring 8-16th February reaching a maximum around the 13th giving cold, frosty and foggy weather. Another cold spell is experienced during 21-25th February peaking 22nd. A late cold stormy number of days - 26 Feb to 9 March peaking 1st - brings a northerly airstream (the time near the annual peak).

Februeer
Doth cut and shear.

Double-faced February.

There is always one fine week in
February. ****

February, like other months, experiences fast changing weather. A couple of days of mild wet weather can quickly alter to a bitter cold easterly. The contrast is felt more during the winter months. The good result of 59 percent came from a test which searched for at least 7 dry days in February from 1861 to 1971. 66/111 (59)

Warm February, bad hay crop; **
Cold February, good hay crop. ***

All the months in the year
Curse a fair Februeer.

When gnats start in February,
the husbandman becomes a beggar. **

If in February the midges dance
on the dunghill, then lock up
your food in the chest. **

A February spring is not worth a
pin.

The first saw implies that in a warm February grass grows quickly and is receded by early spring frosts (bad results of 20 percent). The theory continues for cold Februarys and good

hay crops (final figure of 38 percent). In practice poor results show little faith in the adages. The third Cornish saying reiterates the first maxim. Gnats and midges dancing again refer to warmth and disaster for the husbandman. 3/15 (20)
5/13 (38)

Isolated fine days in February are known in Surrey as "weather breeders", and are considered as certain to be followed by a storm. ****

The fact that this Surrey saying restricts fine weather to only one day greatly increases the odds for sudden storms to follow.

February singing,
Never stints stinging.

A real tongue-twister meaning that a mild February ("singing") always has days of sharp frosts never limiting its sting.

If bees get out in February, the next day will be windy and rainy. ***

Whenever the bees get about at this time (February), we are certain to get wind and rain the next day. ***

February rain is only good to fill ditches.

February fill the dykes,
Weather either black or white.

February fill dyke, be it black or be it white;
But if it be white, it's better to like.

FEBRUARY

February fill ditch,
Black or white, don't care which;
If it be white,
It is the better to like.

February fill dyke;
March lick it out.

February fill dyke
With what thou dost like.

February fill the ditch,
Black or white we don't care
which.

Rain in February is worth as
much as manure.

One of the most famous of English weather lore. White refers to snow and black means rain. Unfortunately most people fail to grasp the real meaning. Basically it is a command by the farmer wanting February to fill the dykes (in East Anglia) and ditches elsewhere with rain or snow. The latter is more preferable as it gives insulation against sharp frosts and cold winds. The maxims do *not* mean that February always fills dykes. The first adage hails from France and is included to show the wide coverage of this famous saying. Hampshire provides the home for the seventh saw. Please note the subtle differences in all of the weather lore.

When it rains in February, all
the year suffers. **

This applies to the annual crop to suffer, not the year's weather. Wet soggy topsoil ruins corn seed.

In February if thou harvest
thunder,
Thou will see a summer's
wonder. *

Thunder in February or March,
poor sugar maple year. *

FEBRUARY

The first saying is similar to the January saw about thunder. A "summer's wonder" is supposed to occur because thunder in February is out of season. Not enough occasions happened to test the saw.

When the cat in February lies in
the sun, she will creep behind
the stove in March. ****

When the north wind does not blow
in February, it will surely come
in March. *****

The first part proclaims a warm February will be followed by a cold March. When tested only a 49 percent result emerged. The second part gives a very good 69 percent figure but before accepting this a 70 percent value also occurs when the saw is changed to include a northerly in February. The great annual maximum in northerlies happens in spring with a gradual build up in February and March. 21/43 (49)
31/45 (69)

February makes a bridge, and
March breaks it. **

The building of a bridge in February means a bridge of ice or a very cold period followed by a mild March thaw which will "break" the bridge. The test result was poor. 22/107 (21)

Fogs in February mean frosts in
May. *

There is little meaning in this saw. Certainly high pressure areas will produce fogs in February (also frost) and sometimes night ground frost in May but that is as far as the connection goes - no continuous sequence through March and April occurs. Poor results of 12 percent evolved. 5/41 (12)

For every thunder with rain in
February there will be a cold
spell in May. *

February

Another piece of wild weather lore containing no truth.

If February gives much snow
A fine summer it doth foreshow. **

A favourite balance saw - a snowy February will produce a fine summer. Cold reality begs differently. 9/30 (30)

If February brings no rain
'Tis neither good for grass nor grain. ***
**

A dry February (look at the February fill dyke maxims for pleas of water or snow) is supposed to be the husbandman's nightmare. But there are further months to go before harvests which often have favourable weather improving the crop. The low results say that the various harvests were good.

(Hay) 11/30 (37)
(Wheat) 7/30 (23)
(Barley) 7/30 (23)

A warm day of February is a
dream of April.

Taken literally, a warm February day when one is near the end of winter must feel easily like a foretaste of April spring.

There will be as many frosts in
June as there are fogs in
February. *

By now it should be plainly obvious that high pressure areas can contribute to February fogs and frosts in later months but are unconnected in sequence. Therefore testing would prove unsatisfactory and time wasting.

Violent north winds in February
herald a fertile year. ***

February

The theory that a cold snap in February brings forth warm weather to produce good harvests is incorrect. Hay and wheat returns showed 47 and 33 percent. 14/30 (47)
10/30 (33)

1 February - St Bridget's Day

Bridget's feast-day white,
Every ditch full.

In Ireland the first day of February is named after St Bride or St Brigid who was born c450 AD probably in Louth or Armagh and died c520. Snow falling on this day or any other in February does not always signify that a great depth has accumulated.

2 February - Candlemas Day

The most prolific day of the year for weather lore. By the mid-5th century the day was celebrated with lighted candles to commemorate Simeon's comment about Jesus as "a light to lighten the gentiles". Also on this day candles are thrown away to end Christmas.

Snow at Candlemas
Sign to handle us.

At Candlemas
Cold comes to us. **

The first hails from Rutland. Tests on the second showed no favouritism to cold weather falling on the 2nd.
33/108 (31)

Candlemas Day! Candlemas Day!
Half our fire and half our hay.

On Candlemas Day
You must have half your straw
and half your hay.

They mean that when one is halfway through winter one should have stored half the season's fuel, hay and straw.

On Candlemas Day
The good goose begins to lay.

If it neither rains nor snows on Candlemas Day,
You may straddle your horse and go and buy hay.

If Candlemas Day be fine and clear,
Corn and fruit will then be dear. **

The second adage comes from Lincs. The test used poor grain harvest figures, but achieved sad results. 11/34 (32)

If Marie's purifying daie,
Be cleare and bright with sunnie raie,
Then frost and cold shall be much more
After the beast than was before. ***

When on the Purification the sun hath shined,
The greatest part of winter comes behind. **

If it be bright and clear on February the second there will be a long continuance of cold wintry weather.

Candlemas Day or the Purification of the Virgin Mary has various forecasts to make. The first maxim receives 47 percent and the third hails from Yorkshire. 21/45 (47)

You should on Candlemas Day
Throw candle and candlestick away. ***

FEBRUARY

Candlemas Day is when candles should be thrown away to denote the end of Christmas.

As far as the sun shines in on
Candlemas Day,
So far will the snow in afore
old May. *

As far as the sun shines in at
the window on Candlemas Day, so
deep will the snow be ere winter
is gone. *

On Candlemas Day, just so far as
the sun shines in,
Just so far will the snow blow
in. *

More ridiculous weather balance lore.

The hind had as lief see his wife
on the bier,
As that Candlemas Day should be
pleasant and clear. *

A very odd maxim. Possibly the meaning is as follows - a hind in this case is a farm workman; the phrase "had as lief" means to do one thing or another and a bier is a movable frame on which coffins are placed. Since this line comes first one therefore must assume that if a farm labourer's wife dies on 2nd February it will be "pleasant and clear". What a morbid saying!

If Candlemas Day be mild and gay,
Go saddle your horses, and buy
them hay;
But if Candlemas Day be stormy
and black
It carries the winter well on its
back. ****

FEBRUARY

If Candlemas Day be gay and bright,
Winter will have another flight. ***
But if Candlemas Day brings clouds and rain,
Winter has gone and won't come again. ****

If Candlemas be fine and clear,
We've half the winter to have or more. ***
But if Candlemas be cold and wet,
A little more winter we shall get. ***

Probably the most famous and important of the Candlemas proverbs. The last part contains good results (57 percent) for a wet cloudy 2nd Feb continuing in the main for the rest of the month. The third maxim from Kennington (Berks) produces only average results. 31/54 (57)
4/9 (44)

After Candlemas Day the frost will be more keen,
If the sun then shines bright, that before it hath been. ***

On Candlemas Day, if the thorns hang a-drop,
Then you are sure of a good pea crop. **

Sow or set beans in Candlemas waddle.

Sussex provides the first saw. The second is an example of sowing bean seeds by the moon - "waddle" means the moon's wane.

If a storm on February the second, spring is near; but if that day be bright and clear, the spring will be late. **

If it snows on February the second, only so much as may be seen on a black ox, then summer will come soon. *

If on February the second the goose finds it wet, then the sheep will have grass on March the twenty-fifth. **

When drops hang on the fence on February the second, icicles will hang there on March the twenty-fifth. ***

When drops hang on the fence on February the second icicles will hang there on March the fourteenth. ****

The long saw has little to offer in fact. The connection of 25th March with 2nd Feb is Mary. The former is St Mary's or Lady Day and latter the Purification of the Virgin Mary. Poor results of 10 percent refer to snow on 2nd Feb followed by an early summer. Also ice after a wet 2nd Feb boasted 46 percent. The second maxim from North Riding (Yorkshire) contains surprisingly good figures of 63 percent.

1/10 (10)
27/59 (46)
35/56 (63)

When the wind's in the east on Candlemas Day,
There it will stick 'till the second of May. *

Easterlies total from 7 to 15 days over the 95-day period from 2nd Feb to 2nd May. 0/9 (0)

When Candlemas Day has come and gone,
The snow lies on a hot stone.

This is particularly true when referring to ground temperatures now at their lowest. This allows a snow covering to melt only slowly during the daytime. Besides at night warm daytime stone or concrete surfaces rapidly cool to freezing temperatures.

A windy Christmas and a calm
Candlemas are signs of a good
year. *

There were only a small number of occasions to test but one would expect a negative result.

If the sun shines on Candlemas
Day,
We shall have snow in May. *

This hails from Kennington, Berks, but is totally false.
4/43 (9)

Candlemas shined, on the winter's
behind. *

Most fine Candlemas Day proverbs refer to more of winter to come - this one is different.

6 FEBRUARY - ST DOROTHEA'S DAY

Saint Dorothea gives the most
snow. *

In a quick survey over 1875-1975 the risk of snow was marginally higher for January and February than December and March. To give an actual day for the deepest snowfall seems too brash. Any time during Dec-March, a severe snowstorm could occur.

7-14 FEBRUARY - BUCHAN'S FIRST COLD SPELL **

This is known as Buchan's First Cold Period. Dr Alexander Buchan, once Secretary of the Scottish Meteorological Society,

established in 1867, to his own satisfaction, 6 cold and 3 warm periods during the year in Scotland. His fame came after his death when in 1928, Lord Desborough presented a bill for fixing Easter's date in Parliament. The suggested Easter date coincided with Buchan's Second Cold Period (11-14 April). The bill was defeated but public interest was aroused. In the following year, by sheer chance, the 9 Buchan periods were nearly all correct so his name became a household word - popularity he did not deserve. 7-14th February was tested for average temperature from 1861 to 1971. Poor results of 28 percent show unreliability in the spell. Infact if Buchan had called the period a warm spell he would have increased the result to 50 percent.
31/111 (28)

14 FEBRUARY - ST VALENTINE'S DAY

Saint Valentine,
Set thy hopper by mine.

To Saint Valentine, the spring
is a neighbour.

St Valentine's Day was named after two saints. One was a Rome priest decapitated c269 AD and the other a person, who saved a patient from an incurable disease, also beheaded in c273 AD. In medieval times birds were believed to pair probably leading to the sending of "valentines". The two weather saws render as milestones in the old farming calendar. A hopper was a machine for spreading seed.

MID-FEBRUARY

Winter's back breaks about the
middle of February. *

On reflection one would have thought that the beginning of March would be more the time for breaking "winter's back".

22 FEBRUARY - ST PETER'S DAY

If cold on Saint Peter's Day,
it will last longer. *****

The saying proves to be an excellent one. On average a cold St Peter's Day lasts about 5½ days in the test, coinciding with the cold snap normally found at the time of the year (see the start of the chapter). 41/55 (75)

The night of Saint Peter shows
what weather we shall have for
the next forty days. *

Unfortunately this saw is the first of many saint day ones with 40-rain days occurring afterwards. It is likely that they have a common origin with Noah's flood. The test result fails dismally. 0/106 (0)

24 FEBRUARY - ST MATTHIAS' DAY

Saint Matthias,
Sow thy leaf and grass.

This is the husbandman's old style date for first sowing.

If it freezes on Saint Matthias'
Day, it will freeze for a month
together. *

Another miserable result. 0/43 (0)

Saint Matthias breaks the ice; *
If he finds none, he will make **
it.

A warm 24th February following an icy spell and a very cold 24th following a non-icy period yield poor figures of 11 and 20 percent respectively. 5/45 (11)
9/46 (20)

Saint Matthy
All the year goes by.

At Saint Mattho
Take thy hopper and sow.

Saint Matthie
Sends sap into the trees.

28 FEBRUARY - ST ROMANUS' DAY

Romanus bright and clear
Indicates a goodly year. ***

Further old time expressions to date the beginning of farming chores. When tested for wheat and hay low 35 and 33 percent results evolved. 16/46 (35)
15/46 (33)

MARCH

March normally starts with a cold stormy period (21st Feb to 9th March, peaking on 1st) where the northerly almost reaches its annual spring maximum. This is followed by a very quiet time in the middle of the month with early spring anticyclones (12-19 March, peaking 13-14th). Finally a return to cold stormy weather is experienced (24-31 March, maximum 28th) with another predominance of northerlies.

March, many weathers.

March many weathers rained and blowed,
March grass never did good.

In beginning or in end
March its gift will send.

March yearns the lammie
And buds do form,
And blows through the flint
Of an ox's horn.

These maxims are all a testimony to the varied weather to be expected in March. The last saw hails from Northumberland.

A peck of March dust is worth a king's ransom. ***

A peck of March dust is worth an earl's ransom 'when do vall and thornen leaves.' ***

Dust in March is worth a king's ransom. ***

March dust on an apple leaf
Brings all kinds of fruit to grief. ***

A bushel of March dust is a thing
Worth the ransom of a king. ***

MARCH

A bushel of March dust on the
leaves is worth a king's ransom. ***

A peck of March dust and a
shower in May,
Makes the corn green and the
meadows all gay. ***

The March wind causes dust and
the wind blows it about.

These are some of the most famous of English weather sayings with the second from Dorset, third from Kennington in Berks and fourth hailing from Herefordshire. Basically they are promising that any dry March is suitable in the soil preparation and sowing of spring cereal and vegetable seed. Also a very wet soil after a wet February would be dried by a dusty March. On the other hand a wet March would cause chaos with heavy topsoil.

March dry, good rye;
March wet, good wheat. **

This Suffolk saying differs from others especially in the second line. Most other wet March maxims are supposed to produce poor harvests. Poor results of 19 percent occur.

6/31 (19)

Better to be bitten by a snake
Than to feel the sun in March.

March grows,
Never dows.

March flowers
Make no summer bowers. **

March damp and warm
Will the farmer much harm. **

A damp rotten March gives pain
to farmers. **

The first maxim originates in Wilts and the second from

Yorkshire. All basically imply that a wet or wet and warm March bring on plant life too quickly which is often checked by late spring frosts. Also spring seed has too muddy a soil for a firm beginning. The poor results apply to the last two saws.

Wheat 3/14 (21)
Spuds 6/14 (43)

A wet March makes a sad August. ***

March water is worse than a stain on a cloth. ***

However agreeable the theory might seem in practice the results are bad. Later months with their varied weather will influence, to a great extent, the final crop state.

Wheat and spuds 12/31 (39)

The March sun raises, but dissolves not.

The above saw refers to the weak sun of March having enough heat to raise mist or fog into low cloud but lacking enough energy to dissolve or evaporate it. A late June sun could quickly tackle the complete clearance of dense fog.

March, black ram
Comes in like a lion and goes out like a lamb. **

March comes in with an adder's head and goes out with a peacock's tail. **

March snow hurts the seeds.

Presumably "black ram" is similar to a black sheep referring to the oddity and variation in March's weather. Of course ram is used to rhyme with lamb. To come "in like a lion" or "adder's head" refers to March beginning stormy with gales (54 percent result). A "lamb" and "peacock's tail" means March ends quietly and serene (19 percent correct). Normally March comes in and goes out like a lion. A lion start to be followed by a lamb ending produced only 22 percent. 60/111 (54)

MARCH

21/111 (19)
13/60 (22)

March comes in like a lamb and
goes out like a lion. ****

This reverses the previous two adages, but receives a better combines test result of 56 percent. 14/25 (56)

As March hasteneth all the
humours feel it.

I think this means that as one goes through March experiencing its extreme weathers one can liken it to the human good, bad or ill humours.

A dry March, a wet April, a dry
May and a wet June,
Is commonly said to bring all
things in tune. ***

This rare pattern of dry, wet, dry and wet months only occurred once in 1935 during the period 1885-1971. In that year good wheat and barley harvests and a poor hay crop happened.

A windy March and a rainy April
will make a beautiful May. *

A windy March foretells a fine
May. *

Conditions gave a disastrous result. 2/19 (11)

March wind and May sun
Make clothes white and maids dun.

The combination of March wind and May sun is supposed to induce good drying weather for clothes and sun-tan for young ladies.

March

Fogs in March, frost in May. *

So many mists in March you see,
So many frosts in May will be. *

As many mistises in March, so
many frostises in May. *

These sayings (the third one hails from Wilts) are similar to one in the February chapter. The same meteorological reasons apply and the results are very poor. 6/46 (13)

As many days of fog in March, so
many days of frost in May, on
corresponding days. *

This Hampshire maxim is even more daring expecting corresponding monthly days to experience March fog and May frost. Even worse results emerge with only 7 percent. 3/46 (7)

So many frosts in March, so many
in May. *

Another hopelessly incorrect adage. More frosts occur in March than May by virtue of its earliness in the year.

Mists in March bring rain,
Or in May frost again. **

Only the top line is tested - that after a foggy or misty day the following one will have rain. Poor figures evolved. 58/289 (20)

March winds and April showers
Bring forth May flowers.

March search, April try;
May will prove if you live
or die.

MARCH

The first is the most famous saying of the two, both having similar meanings.

A dry March, a wet April, and
cool May
Fill barn, cellar, and bring
much hay. **

Only three years during 1888-1971 fulfilled the maxim's conditions - all with poor crop harvests.

As it rains in March, so it
rains in June. **

The test was executed by comparing the three rainfall categories (dry, average and wet) of March against those of June from 1727 to 1971. Bad figures emerged. 79/245 (32)

Fog in March, thunder in July. ***

A ridiculous saying with poor results. 4/10 (40)

As much fog in March, so much
rain in summer. **

This was tested with high frequencies of March fogs having wet summers. This proved similar in content and result to the previous saw. 14/49 (29)

A wet March makes a sad harvest. *

A "sad August" is taken as a wet and cold month but the only sad occurrence is the results. 17/80 (21)

As much dew in March, so much
fog rises in August. *

March

This is a weather and 6-month balance maxim. As one would expect the test proved fatal. 13/111 (12)

A frosty winter and a dusty
March, and a rain about Averil,
Another about the Lammas time,
when the corn begins to fill,
Is weel worth a pleuch o'gowd,
and a'her pins theretill. ***

In March, and at all seasons of
the year when the judges are on
circuit and there are criminals
to be hung, storms prevail. *

This Lincolnshire saying escapes the author's comprehension although itself is a fascinating piece of weather lore.

In March is good graffing, the
skilful do know,
So long as the wind in the East
do not blow:
From moon being changed, 'till
past be the prime,
For graffing and cropping is very
good time.

A dry March never begs its
bread! **

A March without water,
Dowers the hind's daughter. **

The idea of a dry March producing a good wheat harvest is fine for the early stages of crop growth but weather in later months determines the end product. It is opposite in meaning to the earlier Suffolk saw. The last maxim probably means that a bumper harvest from a dry March will increase the hind's (farm labourer) wages enabling him to afford a dowry for his daughter.

March buys winter's cloak and
sells it three days afterwards. ****

A simply marvellous saying stating that a spell of cold weather in late winter is always short. The excellent results showed that on 78 percent of occasions the cold nip lasted under 4 days. 230/296 (78)

When it thunders in March, one
may say alas.

Presumably March thunder means heavy showers which in turn could erode away top soil and harm young root crops.

1 MARCH - ST DAVID'S DAY

Upon Saint David's Day
Put oats and barley in the clay.

The traditional saint's day for early spring sowing.

2 MARCH - ST CHAD'S DAY

Saint David and Chad,
Sow pease good or bad.

David and Chad,
Sow peas good or bad;
If they're not in Benedick,
They had better stop in the
ricke.

Another early-style sowing day. St Chad was born in Northumbria, became Abbot of Lastingham in North Yorkshire and died of the plague there in c672 AD. Benedick refers to St Benedict's Day on 21st March.

1-3 MARCH

First comes David, then comes
Chad,

March

And then comes Winneral as though
he was mad. ***
White or black **
Or old house thack.

Here we have three saints, St David on 1st, St Chad on 2nd and St Winnold on 3rd, which were milestones in the old weather calendar. White means snow and black rain, as in the February filldyke set of sayings. House thack refers to house thatch and Winneral being mad means stormy. The windy results in the test of three days comes out best.

Windy	55/110	(50)
Snow	16/110	(15)
Rain	39/110	(35)

Late February and Early March

Whenever the latter part of
February and beginning of March
are dry, there will be a
deficiency of rain up to
Midsummer Day. *

Midsummer Day is the 24th June. 2/14 (14)

11-28 February and 1-10 March

If the eighteen last days of
February be
Wet, and the first ten of March,
you'll see
That the spring quarter and the
summer too,
Will prove too wet, and danger
to ensue. *

This saw produces terrible results. 0/111 (0)

1-10 March

If the first ten days of March
are cold and rainy, so will the
spring and summer be. ***

MARCH

There was only one year (1916) when all 10 days were cold and wet. If one takes 5 days or more as cold and wet then 40 percent of the following spring and summer seasons continued this pattern. 4/10 (40)

10 MARCH

If it does not freeze on the tenth, a fertile year may be expected. ***

Mists or hoar frosts on this day betoken a plentiful year, but not without some diseases. ***

All very disappointing figures.

Above freezing	= good wheat	14/46	(30)
on 10th March.	= good hay	16/46	(35)
Misty on	= good wheat	9/17	(53)
10th March.	= good hay	7/17	(41)
Hoar frost	= good wheat	15/35	(43)
on 10th March.	= good hay	10/35	(29)

17 MARCH - ST PATRICK'S DAY

Saint Patrick's Day, the warm
side of a stone turns up, and the
broad-back goose begins to lay.

19 MARCH - ST JOSEPH'S DAY

Is't on Saint Joseph's Day clear,
So follows a fertile year. ***

Another balance saying with grim results.

Wheat	15/48	(31)
Hay	19/48	(40)

21 MARCH - ST BENEDICT'S DAY

Saint Benedict,

March

Sow thy peas or keep them in thy rick.

Whatever the weather is on March the twenty-first that weather will continue until twenty-first of June. *

Where the wind is at twelve o'clock on the twenty-first of March, there she'll bide for three months afterwards. *

This means that one should sow peas on 21 March - if left later then a failure would occur. This is another old spring equinox milestone adage. The second saw hails from Yorkshire and third originates in Surrey and Hants. Terrible test results apply to the last two weather sayings. 0/106 (0)

Vernal Equinox - About 21 March

When the wind blows from the north-east, a uniformly dry quarter during the week of the vernal equinox, it is an all but unfailing guide to the general character of the ensuing season. **

The test was confined to a north-easterly on the 21st to see if a dry week then occurred (26 percent) or a dry season (16 percent). 5/19 (26)
3/19 (16)

20-27 March

If a storm arise from the east on or before the spring equinox or if a storm arise from any point of the compass about one week after the spring equinox the summer is generally dry four out of five times. ***

March

If a storm arise from the south-
west or west-south-west on or
just before the spring equinox
summer is generally wet four out
of five times. **

These three saws with their confident high forecast success rate are not confirmed in the tests.

Eastern storm around 20 March	9/27	(33)
Any storm 25-27 March	15/47	(32)
SW or WSW storm 19-21 March	5/16	(31)

25 March - St Mary's or Lady's Day

Is't on Saint Mary's bright and
clear,
Fertile is said to be the year. ***

Again poor results on a saint's day.	Wheat	18/44	(41)
	Hay	15/44	(34)

29-31 March - The Borrowing Days

The last three days of March are
called the Borrowing Days; for as
they are remarked to be unusually
stormy, it is feigned that March
has borrowed them from April to
extend the sphere of his rougher
sway. ***

March borrows of April
Three days, and they are ill;
April borrows of March again
Three days of wind and rain. **

The warst blast comes in the
borrowing days. ***

March borrowed of April, April
borrowed of May,
Three days, they say:
One rained, and one snew,
And the other was the worst day
that ever blew. *

MARCH

March borrowed from April.
Three days, and they were all ill:
The first of them is wan and weet, ***
The second is snaw and sleet, **
The third of them is a peel-a-bane, **
And freezes the wee bird's neb to
the stane.

High winds on these days, a dry
summer to follow. ***

March does from April gain
Three days, and they're in rain, **
Returned by April in's bad kind,
Three days, and they're in wind. ***

The fourth saying hails from Staffs. The basic meaning of Borrowing Days is the stormy period which often occurs at the end of March and extends into April. So March "borrows" the first three days of April to extend March. The reverse is also true when April lengthens its beginning. However in reality all test figures are unsatisfactory.

First saying		48/111	(43)
Second saying		25/111	(23)
Fifth saying	= 1st April	41/107	(38)
	= 2nd April	18/104	(17)
	= 3rd April	23/104	(22)
Sixth saying		17/42	(40)
Seventh saying	= Rain	33/111	(30)
	= Wind	13/33	(39)

APRIL

Usually April experiences a cold stormy period in the middle (10-15th, peaking 14th) of the month with the annual maximum of Northerlies. A similar weather type is repeated from 23rd to 26th peaking on 25th.

A dry April
Not the farmer's well.
April wet
Is what we should get.

April showers bring summer flowers.

April showers bring forth May flowers.

An April flood carries away the frog and his brood.

In April Dove's flood is worth a king's good. ***

Moist April, clear June. **

April wet, good wheat. ***

April rains for men, May for beasts.

Although it rains, throw not away thy watering pot.

April has thirty days, and if it rained on thirty-one, no harm would be done.

All of these sayings refer to wet Aprils. With temperature now high enough and rainfall more or less plentiful continual crop growth is assured. The fifth maxim originates in Derbyshire where the river Dove is situated. The eighth saw means that a rainy April is good for corn and a wet May for grass crops. The results for the latter can be seen in the May chapter. The last saw implies that April rain is welcome, that sowing is completed and young crops need water. The poor test figures of 17 percent refer to the sixth saying. 14/80 (17)

A cold April
The barn will fill. **

April cold and wet fills barn and barrel. *

April wears a white hat.

The belief here is that a cold April, although temporary stunting growth, will bring mild and wet weather the following months and produce a good wheat or barley harvest.

A cold April = Wheat and barley	8/34	(24)
A cold and wet .. = ...	2/13	(15)

A sharp April kills the pig. ***

This intriguing snippet alas receives poor figures when tested with the number of pigs in England and Wales 1866-1966 (specially weighted) of 33 percent. 11/33 (33)

April snow breeds grass.

Snow in April is manure; snow in March devours.

Till April's dead
Change not a thread.

Changeable as an April day.

April weather,
Rain and sunshine, both together.

True observations of the changeable weather to be experienced in April.

April

Plant your 'taturs when you will,
They won't come up before April.

Whatever March does not want April
brings along.

What March will not
April brings always.

Both applicable to the two varied weather months of March and April.

April for me, May for my master.

After warm April and October, a
warm year next. ***

No real truth in this adage. 16/49 (33)

Thunderstorm in April is the
end of hoar frost. ***

When April blows his horn,
'tis good for hay and corn. *

Thunder in April,
Floods in May. ***

"Blows his horn" in the second saw means thunder but emerges with unsatisfactory results. 2/13 (15)

1 April - All Fool's Day

If it thunders on All Fool's Day
It brings good crop of corn and
hay. *

So few cases occur here that no test was instigated.

APRIL

1-3 APRIL

If the first three days in April
be foggy,
Rain in June will make lanes
boggy. **

I'm afraid this Huntingdonshire saying falls on stony ground. 2/10 (25)

6 APRIL - LATTER LADY DAY

On Lady Day the latter
The cold comes on the water. **

This does *not* mean that water temperature of our rivers and coast reaches its annual minimum (which occurs in February and March) but refers to the supposed cold weather (result of 29 percent) expected around 6th April. 32/109 (29)

LATE MARCH OR EARLY APRIL

There are generally some warm
days at the end of March or
beginning of April, which bring ****
the blackthorn into bloom, and
which are followed by a cold
period called the Blackthorn
Winter. **

Beware of the Blackthorn Winter. **

Tis always cold when the black-
thorn is in bloom. The blossom
generally appears in March. **

These are famous weather sayings. The Blackthorn flowers on average on 30 March in S.W. England through to 4th April in S.E. England, 9th in Midlands and later as one goes further north. The period to test for cold weather during the "Blackthorn Winter" was 6-12th April (centred around the Midland's flowering date of 9th). The first maxim refers to a warm spell in late March and early April which was tested 27 March to 5

April. Average figures of 53 percent were returned for three or more consecutive warm days. Similar conditions were applied to the 6-12th April for a cold spell falling *after* a warm 27 March to 5 April - only 31 percent emerged. The Blackthorn Winter occurring in its own right failed miserably on 21 percent.

59/111 (53)
18/59 (31)
23/111 (21)

11-14 April - Buchan's Second Cold Spell **

The Blackthorn Winter is sometimes extended beyond 6-12th April which nicely slots into Buchan's second cold spell, but when tested proves to be false. 34/111 (31)

23 April - St George's Day

When on Saint George's rye will hide a crow, a good harvest may be expected.

At Saint George's the meadow turns to hay.

Two old-style farming sayings which are perfectly true.

Saint George cries "Goe!"
Saint Mark cries "Hoe!"

Presumably on St George's Day crops and vegetation grow quickly and on St Mark's weeding and hoeing are the order of the day. St Mark's Day is 24th April.

25-28 April

If from the twenty-fifth to the twenty-eighth of April the full moon come with serene nights and no wind (at which time the dew commonly falls a great plenty), the ancients, from

their experience, held it
certain that the crops of grain
would suffer. **

Unfortunately the full moon occurred only once during 25-28 April in the tested years 1959-71. Regardless of the moon, nights of heavy dew can form at any random time in April.

MAY

Often a pleasant month. Usually the period 29 April to 16 May attracts Northerly airstreams alternating with some anti-cyclonic intervals - the Westerly being at its annual minimum. 21 - 31 May is recognized for its fine dry weather with anti-cyclones and Southerlies predominating.

The merry month of May.

This mainly refers to May Day and maypole activities and similar celebrations during the month.

A hot May makes a fat churchyard. *

For a warm May
The parsons pray. *

These old adages, like their winter counterparts, prophesy death (mainly of the old and young) caused by mild Mays which are supposed to bring on disease. Weighted death figures per 1,000 head of population for Oxford were tested covering April to June with very poor results. 1/13 (8)

Blossoms in May
Are not good, some say.

Flowers in May, fine cocks of
hay. *****

These are sayings referring to mild winters and springs which accelerate blossoms or flowers to appear early in May. The same process is supposed to occur with hay in June. Logically the results should be very good and indeed are with a 70 percent correct rating. 16/23 (70)

The month of May seeks warmth

to exchange for bread. ***

This confirms the previous adages.

If May will be a gardener, he
will not fill the granaries. ***

Dry May brings nothing gay. **

A dry May is followed by a wet
June. ***

A dry May is bad for grain crops - a mixture of warmth, sun and rain is ideal. Little confidence was held for the third saying which is born out with poor results for all three.

First saying	= Wheat	5/12	(42)
	= Barley	6/12	(50)
Second saying	= Wheat	8/23	(35)
	= Barley	6/23	(26)
Third saying		27/82	(33)

March wind and May sun
Makes clothes white and maids
dun.

The combination of spring wind and sun is supposed to be helpful in drying clothes and sunburning the gentle sex.

When May is dry, the following
September is apt to be wet. ***

No relationship can be established here. 29/81 (36)

Many thunder storms in May,
And the farmer sings "Hey!
hey!" ****

The more thunder in May, the less
in August and September. ****

These two adages have surprisingly good results. Close conditions and heavy rain associated with thunderstorms would help crop development. The first set of figures refer to six or more thunderstorms in May. 5/8 (63)
4/7 (57)

May damp and cool fills the barns
and wine vats. ****

A May wet
Was never kind yet.

A May flood
Never did good.

A shower of rain in May
Is worth a load of hay. ***

A wet May
Makes a big load of hay. ***

A wet May
Makes a lang-tailed hay. ***

A rainy May marries peasants. ***

Rain in May makes bread for the
whole year. ***

The fourth saw hails from the Kentish Weald; fifth from West Shropshire and sixth from Whitby, North Yorkshire. Varied results appear throughout, the highest with 62 percent from barley in the first maxim. The seventh saw possibly means that peasant smallholders would normally own a small number of cows instead of a large acreage of wheat which is supposed to benefit from a wet May.

First saying = Wheat 6/13 (46)
= Barley 8/13 (62)
Fifth saying 11/24 (46)

Betwixt April and May if there
be rain,
'tis worth more than oxen and
wain. ***

May

The hay figures are good.

Hay	16/29	(55)
Wheat	7/29	(24)

For an east wind in May 'tis
your duty to pray. ****

A windy May makes a fair year. *

These two maxims tend to differ in meaning. An Easterly wind in May is always dry which can be said to persist to play havoc with crop growth.

A cold May is kindly,
And fills the barn finely. ***

A cool May and a windy
Barn filleth up finely. ***

A cold May and a windy
A full barn will find ye. ***

A cold May is good for corn and
hay. **

Cold May brings many things.

Cold May enriches no one.

Cool and evening dew in May
brings wine and much hay. *

If May be cold and wet, September
will be warm and dry, and vice
versa. *

Frost in May
Frost in September. *

Berks, Hants and Wilts provide the ninth adage. A minimum of 17 days in May with a good wind was used as a basis for some of the tests. Nearly all figures are disappointing. The last two weather balance saws follow the usual poor return pattern.

First saying	= Wheat	10/29	(34)
	= Barley	12/29	(41)

Second saying = Hay	9/16	(56)
= Wheat	7/16	(44)
Fourth saying = Wheat	3/14	(21)
= Hay	4/14	(29)
Seventh saying	2/14	(14)
Eighth saying	2/17	(12)
"Vice-versa"	2/25	(8)
Ninth saying	0/18	(0)

A snow storm in May
Is worth a waggon load of hay. *

The reasoning behind the saying is baffling. 2/11 (18)

He who sows oats in May
Gets little that way.

The latest for sowing spring oats used to be February to March in the South and April in Northern England.

Those who bathe in May
Will soon be laid in clay;
They who bathe in June
Will sing a merry tune;
They who bathe in July
Will dance like a fly.

Presumably this is a reflection on the water temperature in relation to man's bathing capabilities.

A swarm of bees in May
Is worth a load of hay; *****
A swarm of bees in June
Is worth a silver spoon; ****
But a swarm in July
Is not worth a fly. ***

Towards the end of May or beginning of June it becomes favourable for bee swarming. The saying means that early colonies will collect surplus pollen for beekeepers and late ones will not gather sufficient food to survive.

May

Shear your sheep in May,
And shear them all away.

If sheep are sheared too early in May after which a real cold snap is still likely survival problems occur. The usual time for sheep shearing is in the warmer months of June/July.

Go and look at oats in May,
You will see them blown away;
Go and look again in June,
You will sing another tune.

Sound old-style advice the farmer used.

Be it weal or be it woe,
Beans blow before May doth go.

Good or bad, one should always expect a few days of strong wind in May.

What April cannot do
May will do all day.

The May sun is stronger and warmer than in April and can disperse fogs quicker and help plants grow faster.

May makes or mats the wheat.

A cold or warm and wet May can make or dull (mat) wheat.

1 May - St Philip's and St James' Day

Hoar frost on May the first
indicates a good harvest. ***

Little can be expected from this maxim. 12/27 (44)

The later the blackthorn in bloom after May the first, the better the rye and harvest. *

A late blackthorn bloom depends on previous seasons and the present May weather.

8 MAY

If on the eighth of May it rain,
It fortells a wet harvest, men sain. **

Since harvest for grass is in June and cereals in any of the three months July to September only June and September were tested. Poor results prevail. June harvest 12/46 (26)
Sept harvest 15/46 (33)

9-14 MAY - BUCHAN'S THIRD COLD SPELL ***

Hopeless results for the so-called Buchan third cold spell (see index for remaining spells). 47/111 (42)

11-13 MAY - ST MAMERTIUS', ST PANCRAS AND ST GERVATIUS' DAY

Who shears his sheep before Saint Gervatius' Day loves more his wool than his sheep. **

These three saints' days are known as the "Three Icemen", but like the previous cold spell, are a myth. 97/333 (29)

MIDDLE OF MAY

In the middle of May, comes the tail of the winter. **

The "middle of May" was taken as 11-20th. The results are based on the *number* of cold days in the period. The highest frequencies of cold days were 9, 12, 15 and 19th. There is no continuous cold spell but individual days of low temperature. 323/1110 (29)

17-19 MAY - ST DUNSTAN'S DAY (19 MAY)

Saint Dunstan was a brewer and was sold to the devil who blighted all apple trees from the seventeenth to the nineteenth of May. Hence the cold blast which usually comes about this time. **

St Dunstan's Day (19th May) showed the highest total of cold days in the three-day period. The test was carried out in the same way as the previous saying. 102/333 (31)

17-23 MAY

Storms from the east or south-east, between the seventeenth and twenty-third of May, indicate a wet summer. ***

This saw promised much but cold reality proved otherwise. The 39 percent refers to wet summers after a storm from the East or Southeast occurs on at least two days. The 37 percent similarly applies to a minimum of four days. 12/31 (39)
3/8 (37)

19-21 MAY

Easterly winds on May the nineteenth to the twenty-first indicate a dry summer. ***

This adage might prove fruitful but unfortunately only 4 years of the tested 111 supplied a cold spell 19-21 May.

Franklin's frost strikes on nineteenth, twentieth or twenty-first of May. **

This Devon adage states that a frost occurs on at least

one of these three days. The unknown gentleman called Franklin has probably remained forgotten because of the falsity of the maxim - certainly the 27 percent result bears this out.

89/333 (27)

24 MAY - ST URBAN'S DAY

Saint Urban drives his mother from the fire.

Urban brings summer.

Hopefully by now all night frosts have ceased and warmer weather has arrived, so "mother" can venture outside instead of remaining by the fire.

END OF MAY

Cast ne'er a clout 'till May be out.

'till May out leave not off a clout.

"May" refers to the month and *not* the May blossom.

JUNE

The most frequent weather pattern affecting England during June is a stormy one. Usually during 1-4 June the first wave of cool stormy summer weather occurs with frequent cyclonic disturbances. Fortunately a dry spell 5-11th, peaking on the 7th, with anticyclones helps to change the trend. However the 12-14th is usually associated with a second phase of wet cool stormy weather followed by the third and final onslaught from about 20th into early July with a very noticeable return of the Westerlies.

When it is hottest in June, it will be coldest in the corresponding days of the next February. *

The result speaks for itself. 5/113 (4)

Mists in May and heat in June
Bring all things into tune. ****

Mist in May, heat in June,
Make the harvest come right soon. ****

If June be sunny harvest comes early. ****

A calm June
Puts the farmer in tune. ****

Calm weather in June
Sets corn in tune. ****

There is no doubt that a calm or warm June which would give plenty of night-time dew could combine and help towards an acceleration in crop and plant growth.

JUNE

A dry May and a leaking June
Makes the farmer whistle a
merry tune. ****

A dry May and a dripping June
Bring all things into tune. ****

The combination of a dry May and wet June gives good results (57 percent) for barley. The second maxim hails from Bedfordshire.

Wheat	3/7	(43)
Barley	4/7	(57)

A cold and wet June spoils the
rest of the year. ***

A wet June makes a dry September. **

A leak in June brings harvest
soon. ****

A leaky May and dry June keep a
poor man's head abune.

A leaking June brings harvest
soon. ****

June damp and warm
Does the farmer no harm. ****
A good leak in June
Sets all in tune.
A drip in June
Brings all things in tune. ****

Cornwall gives rise to the second saw. Even though wet weather brings a crop to a certain growth level, warmth and sunshine are also much-needed ingredients.

Second saying	25/79	(32)
Sixth saying = Wheat/hay (lines 1 and 2)	3/6	(50)
= Wheat/hay (rest of rhyme)	11/20	(55)

Wheat or barley 'll shoot in
June
If they bain't no higher'n a
spoon.

June

This West Somerset saying would be true if the June weather had large amounts of sunshine, rainfall and warmth.

In the hay season, when there is
no dew, it indicates rain. *****

Unfortunately this saw has not been tested but doubtless very good results would emerge. The reasoning is obvious - dewless nights are associated with moderate to fresh winds with or without low cloud. These are often the forerunners of rain. The only exception is with a very dry night (low humidity) accompanied by a breeze.

If north wind blows in June,
good rye harvest. **

Rye is a rugged crop which can grow in almost any soil and under any diverse weather conditions.

A swarm of bees in June is
worth a silver spoon. ****

A swarm of bees in June is not
worth a silver spoon. **

Mainly included as an example of two maxims with completely opposite meanings. Refer to the May section for the complete bee verse.

As June, so next January. **

This saw is basically a half-yearly comparison test between June and January. Unfortunately temperature only scores 20 percent and rainfall 43. 54/273 (20)
83/194 (43)

Early June

When the wind goes to the west

early in June, expect wet
weather 'till the end of August. **

The first summer storms normally begin in early June and often with Westerly winds, but for the pattern to continue till the end of August occurs only on a few number of occasions.
20/69 (29)

8 JUNE

If it raineth on the eighth of
June a wet harvest men will see. **

Testing the extreme months of the harvest period, June and September, one arrives at poor results. June 12/41 (29)
Sept 11/41 (27)

11 JUNE - ST BARNABAS DAY

On Saint Barnabas
Put a scythe to the grass.

Rain on Saint Barnabas' Day
good for grapes. *

Barnaby bright, Barnaby bright,
The longest day and the shortest
night.

Barnaby bright
All day and no night.

Saint Barnabas mow your first
grass.

Joseph Barnabas was born in Cyprus and died about 80 AD. June is the hay harvest month and farmers always used St Barnabas Day as the time to commence scything grass.

15 JUNE - ST VITUS' DAY

If Saint Vitus's Day be rainy
weather,

It will rain for thirty days together. *

Oh! Saint Vitas, do not rain, so that we may not want barley.

If Saint Vitas's Day be rainy weather, It will rain for forty days together. *

St Vitus or St Guy was a martyr from the 4th century AD and is the protector of epileptics. Here we have another of the rainy saints' days but this time expecting 30 wet days to follow instead of 40. The results apply to the first and third saws. 0/41 (0)

21 AND 24 JUNE

June the twenty-first, summer begins; June the twenty-fourth Midsummer Day. *

Extremely poor figures emerge here. 1/111 (1)

If the cuckoo does not cease singing at midsummer, corn will be dear. ***

Cuckoos usually remain till July/August before they migrate. Unfortunately no records of the last-heard cuckoo are available

23 JUNE - MIDSUMMER'S EVE

Camomile flowers or St John's Wort gathered on St John's Eve and hung up in the house will provide protection against storms. *

If it rains on Midsummer Eve, the filberts will be spoiled. *

The first maxim is true of many flowers that afford protection against storm and thunder. The plant chapter provides many examples of this. Nuts (filberts) being spoilt by rain on this eve is pure myth.

24 JUNE - ST JOHN'S OR MIDSUMMER'S DAY

Before Saint John's Day we pray for rain; after that we get it anyhow.

Rain on Saint John's Day, and we may expect a wet harvest. **

Previous to Saint John's Day we dare not praise barley.

If Midsummer Day be never so little rainy, the hazel and walnuts will be scarce, corn smitten in many places; but apples, pears, and plums will not be hurt. ** ***

Rain on Saint John's Day, damage to nuts. **

Cut your thistles before Saint John,
You will have two instead of one.

Never rued the man
That laid in his fuel before Saint John.

If a cuckoo sings after Saint John's Day the harvest will be late. ****

The first saw was obviously originated by an extreme pessimist although contains the seeds of truth. The ancient day was one of the milestones of the old farming calendar, even before it became a Christian saint's day. The range of subjects it covers in weather lore is a testament to its great age. Infact a type of rye called St John's Day or Midsummer Rye was introduced being a rugged crop grown in the most inferior soil and under extreme weather conditions. The fourth maxim has the horrible phrase "never so little rainy" which is interpreted as meaning extreme rainfall. Only the corn part is tested.

Second saying	12/42	(29)
Fourth saying = Wheat	10/31	(32)
= Barley	11/31	(35)

27 JUNE

If it rains on June the twenty-seventh, it will rain seven weeks. *

Another example of meaningless weather lore. 0/45 (0)

29 JUNE - ST PETER'S DAY

If it rains on Saint Peter's Day,
the bakers will have to carry
double flour and single water; ***
if dry, they will carry single
flour and double water. ***

This of course means that a wet 29 June will produce little wheat and a dry St Peter's Day plenty of wheat. However both tests came up with unsatisfactory results.

Wet 29 June	13/33	(39)
Dry 29 June	20/50	(40)

Peter and Paul will rot the
roots of the rye.

Presumably this refers to rain on both St Peter's and St Paul's Day (25 January).

29 JUNE - 4 JULY - BUCHAN'S FOURTH COLD SPELL ***

Again another of the fatal Scotsman's cold weather periods which gains a meagre 44 percent accuracy rating. (Refer to the index for all 9 Buchan periods). 49/111 (44)

JULY

The usual weather of July begins with the late June Westerlies and storms for the first week. Then follows a warm mid-July period 10-24th. The last week 23-30th July continuing into August normally suffers a return to thundery, cyclonic weather. The highest annual mean daily temperatures are reached at the end of July into August.

No tempest, good July,
Less the corn but look ruely.

A valid observation of corn, now reaching maturity, which would be flattened by any violent summer thunderstorm - especially in the last week of July.

When the sun enters Leo, the
greatest heat will then arise. *

The sun enters Leo on 24 July. The "greatest heat" was tested as the year's highest temperature to fall during 24-28th - poor results of 4 percent arose. Just for warm weather to occur in this period during this notoriously wet time only 6 percent was conjured up.

5/124 (4)
7/111 (6)

In July
Shear your rye.

In July
Some reap rye;
In August,
If one will not, the other must.

Further old-style farming rhymes covering rye.

A shower of rain in July, when
the corn begins to fill,

Is worth a plough of oxen, and
all belongs theretill.

Much thunder in July injures
wheat and barley.

These are more subtle observations than first meets the eye. A shower means rain and sunshine - the perfect weather blend for July corn. The second maxim mentions thunder which means heavy or violent showers which can flatten whole fields of corn with terrific downdraughts of rain and hail.

As July so the next January. **

No truth emerges when comparing similar rainfalls of July and January with 39 percent and temperature offering 21 percent.

96/244 (39)
58/273 (21)

Whatever July and August do not
boil, September cannot fry.

Culinary metaphors explaining that the excessive heat of the summer months of July and August is reduced in power when September comes along.

When the months of July, August,
and September are unusually hot,
January will be the coldest month. ***

Normally January is the coldest month of the year occurring on 43 percent of occasions. After a hot summer it only increases to 45 percent. 5/11 (45)

A swarm of bees in July is not
worth a butterfly. ***

A pretty saying meaning that a late July bee swarm would collect very little pollen to produce honey for the beekeeper.

July

As the days begin to shorten
The heat begins to scorch 'em.

The days begin to shorten in July and although one would expect a slight decrease in the sun's heat the year's highest mean daily temperatures occur in late July. So the crops would be scorched. The maxim's counterpart can be seen in the January section.

The English winter ends in July
and begins in August.

A pessimistic piece of weather lore that must have been formulated during a wet, cold miserable late July day when the summer looked as if it would never begin.

1 July

If the first of July be rainy weather,
It will rain more or less for four weeks together. *

There is absolutely no truth in this adage. 2/40 (5)

First Friday in July

The first Friday in July is always wet. ***

As expected the result is unsatisfactory. 49/111 (44)

2 July - St Mary's Day

If it rains on Saint Mary's Day,
it will rain for four weeks. *

Another disastrous result. 0/52 (0)

3 July to 11 August - The Dog Days

July

As the dog-days commence, so
they end. *

If it rains on the first dog-day,
it will rain for forty days after. *

Dog-days bright and clear
Indicate a happy year;
But when accompanied by rain,
For better times our hopes are
vain.

July, to whom, the dog-star in
her train,
Saint James gives oysters and
Saint Swithin rain.

The Dog Days are the 40 days during which the Dog star, Sirius, rises and sets with the sun. The general country belief was that it added heat to the sun. I'm afraid there is no truth in the adages.

First saying 7/111 (6)
Second saying 0/57 (0)

10 July

If it rains on July the tenth,
it will rain for seven weeks. *

This saying never works. 0/52 (0)

12 July

To the twelfth of July from the
twelfth of May
All is day.

This weather saying must date before 1752 when the present style calendar was introduced (on 2nd September 1752). Then 11 days were added so the 3rd Sept. became the 14th. This would put the old 12 June around the summer solstice or the longest day in today's calendar. Hence an equal period either side of this date would constitute a time when "all is day".

14 JULY - ST PROCESSUS' AND ST MARTIN'S DAY

If it rains on the feast of
Saint Processus and Saint Martin,
it suffocates the corn.

The Norfolk adage is correct in saying that any heavy rain in July could seriously damage corn.

12-15 JULY - BUCHAN'S FIRST WARM SPELL **

Further bad figures for Buchan's first warm spell. (Refer to index for the remaining spells.) 25/111 (23)

15 JULY - ST SWITHIN'S DAY

If about Saint Swithin Day a
change of weather takes place,
we are likely to have a spell
of fine or wet weather.

If Saint Swithin weep, that
year, the proverb say,
The weather will be foul for
forty days. *

Saint of the soakers. *

Saint Swithin's Day if it do
rain
For forty days it will remain. *
Saint Swithin's Day on it be
fair
For forty days t'will rain
nae mair. *

How, if on Saint Swithin's
feast the welkin lours,

July

And every penthouse streams
with hasty showers,
Twice twenty days shall clouds
their fleeces drain,
And wash the pavements with
incessant rain. *

In this month is Saint Swithin's
Day,
On which if that it rain they
say,
For forty days after it will
Or more or less some rain
distil. *

Saint Swithin is christening
the apples.

St Swithin's Day is the most famous of the saints' days for weather lore, still held very dearly and stubbornly believed in. Unfortunately a different story emerges when the facts are checked. The majority of the sayings concern a wet St Swithin Day followed by 40 similar ones. However there is an exception in the first saw. Swithin, who was an Anglo Saxon bishop of Winchester c852-c862 AD, originated the rain legend by wishing to be buried in a churchyard where rain from the church eaves might fall upon his grave. When he was removed to Winchester Cathedral on 15 July 971 it poured for 40 days (15 July to 23 August) or so legend has it.

During 1861-1971 none of the sayings became true but an average of 21.1 raindays out of the 40 were independantly wet after a wet 15 July. Similarly 20.8 dry days occurred after a dry 15 July. Identical results were observed by Mirrlees in 1929 and Brazell in 1968.

Wet 15 July then wet for 40 days	0/55	(0)
Dry .. .. .. dry	0/55	(0)

All the tears that Saint Swithin
can cry
Saint Bartlemy's dusty mantel
wipes dry. ****

This is interesting since St Bartholomew's Day is the 24th August 41 days after. It is a sudden dry ending to the supposed 40-day wet spell. Results are average. 28/55 (51)

20 JULY - ST JACOB'S DAY

Clear on Saint Jacob's Day,
plenty of fruit. *

If it rains on Phillip's and
Jacob's Day, a fertile year may
be expected. *

More nonsensical pieces of weather lore. Philip's Day refers to the 1st May.

20 JULY - ST MARGARET'S DAY

So much rain falls about this
day that people often speak of
"Margaret's Flood". ***

The figure of 43 percent suggests nothing special about rain on this day. 46/107 (43)

22 JULY - ST MARY MAGDALEN'S DAY

Alluding to the wet usually
prevalent about the middle of
July, the saying is: "Saint
Mary Magdalen is washing her
handkerchief to go to her
cousin Saint James' fair." ***

The results are barely satisfactory - anyhow the middle of July is often frequented by a warm period (10-24th).
21/56 (37)

25 JULY - ST JAMES' DAY

Till Saint James' Day be come
and gone,
You may have hops and you may
have none.

Ancient country-style weather lore.

AUGUST

The thundery, cyclonic weather of late July normally continues into the first week of August. The most dramatic change, after a mixed weather pattern for mid-month, is the beginning of the late August or first storms of autumn. 20-30th August covers this weather type with a peak on 28th.

Dry August and warm
Doth harvest no harm.

Extreme weather in the form of strong gales, thunderstorms or heavy rain is a great disadvantage to a mature crop. Hence quiet late summery-type conditions are most welcome.

So many August fogs, so many
winter mists. *

After the fiasco of the poor results from the saws dealing with fogs in March, frosts in May and the like, one suspects that this adage will be closely related.

A fog in August indicates a
severe winter and plenty of
snow. *

This old saying is similar to the fog lore of March. The basis is the belief that August anticyclones, causing the fog, will continue as a trend into winter. By then frost, low temperatures and fog will be the norm. Little truth is born from the results. 3/19 (16)

When the dew is heavy in
August, the weather generally
remains fair. ***

The first sentence is certainly true. To produce heavy dew at night the most favourable conditions needed are clear skies

and a calm wind which are often associated with anticyclones and fair weather. August thunderstorms are on the decline after the summer July maximum but still remain frequent. The last part of the maxim possesses no real truth with 44 percent.
8/18 (44)

As August, so the next February. **

Another balance saw of August's weather against February's with hopeless results of 34 percent for rainfall and 19 per-cent for temperature.
83/244 (34)
52/273 (19)

A rainy August
Makes a hard bread crust. ****

Heavy rain should have an effect on the final wheat crop yield. There is slight evidence for this in the 55 percent rating.
15/27 (56)

None in August should over the land, in December none over the sea.

It is assumed this proverb applies to fog which is a rarity inland in August but common over the sea and coastal waters. The reverse is true in December.

It is always windy in barley harvest; it blows off the heads for the poor.

A poetic ditty, possibly with a religious flavour, forgiving the stormy weather in August, which causes barley damage, by compensating the needy poor.

1 AUGUST - LAMMAS OR LOAF-MASS DAY

After Lammas corn ripens as

much as by night as by day.

1-7 AUGUST

If the first week in August
is unusually warm, the winter
will be white and long. **

A compensating saw with disastrous test figures.
4/20 (20)

6-11 AUGUST - BUCHAN'S FIFTH COLD SPELL ***

Again consistent with results from the other Buchan periods (refer to other Buchan periods for their dates in the index).
50/111 (45)

12-15 AUGUST - BUCHAN'S SECOND WARM SPELL **

Disastrous results for Buchan's second warm spell.
26/111 (23)

15 AUGUST - ST MARY'S (ASSUMPTION) DAY

On Saint Mary's Day sunshine
Brings much and good wine. *

Another silly maxim of the type where one day's weather decides the fate of a year's crop.

24 AUGUST - ST BARTHOLOMEW'S DAY

If this day be misty, the
morning beginning with a hoar
frost, the cold weather will
soon come, and a hard winter. *

At Saint Bartholomew
There comes cold dew. ***

AUGUST

Bartholomew
With the heavy dew. ***

If Saint Bartlemy's Day be fair
and clear,
They hope for a prosperous
autumn that year. **

As Saint Bartholomew's Day, so
the whole autumn. **

Thunderstorms after Bartholomew's
Day are more violent. **

The usual connection with St Barthomew's Day is dew. Although still summer the nights are becoming longer with minimum temperatures lower. The extra cooling period allows more dew to form which consequently delays harvesting in the morning until the sun is strong enough to evaporate it. In the first saw hoar frosts are rare in August let alone on the 25th so no investigation could be held, even so the result would have been poor. Prosperous autumn in the fourth saying can mean wet or dry depending on the country business it involves, but both offer poor returns. The fifth adage was tested by taking the general airstream of the day and comparing its temperature and rainfall categories with following autumn. Poor results.

Fourth saying = dry autumn 9/53 (17)
= wet autumn 11/53 (21)
Fifth saying 18/109 (17)

SEPTEMBER

The most frequent weather pattern associated with September is the three dry periods known as the "Old-wives summer" which in turn are followed by wet stormy days. The dry spells normally occur 7-10th, 16-21st and 30th as travelling anticyclones move east across the U.K. into the Continent. The most common time for gales and depressions is around the 24th.

When September has been rainy,
the following May is generally
dry; and when May is dry, the
following September is apt to
be wet. **

Only the first part is tested. Conclusions for the second half can be seen in the May chapter. 24/75 (32)

September rain is much liked
by the farmer.

September rain good for crops
and vines.

Crop maturity and land preparation for winter ploughing are helped by September rain which has the distinction of coming in short periods.

If the storms in September
clear off warm, all the storms
of the following winter will be
warm. *

A storm or depression crossing the country clearing "off warm" refers to it taking a track across Scotland or further north so as to avoid the full force of its cold rear northerly winds. The trend of cyclonic movement in high latitudes might continue into October but no longer.

SEPTEMBER

When a cold spell occur in
September and passes without a
frost, a frost will not occur
until the same time in October. *

Although not tested the saying fails because of dates. To assume that one weather type occurs exactly one calendar month after a cold September spell is pure folly. In fact a cold September spell is no guarantee to any following weather sequence.

Thunder in September indicates
a good crop of grain and fruit
for next year. ***

Nonsensical saw supported by bad test figures.
Wheat, barley and oats 6/15 (40)

September blows soft till the
fruit's in the loft.
November take flail, let ships
no more sail.

Dry mild September will make
cellars full of good ale.

Countrymen hope September will be a quiet month without the full blast of gale force winds (notable in November) to ruin late harvesting.

Many haws, many sloes,
Many cold toes. *

A heavy crop of berries foretells
hard weather ahead. *

This is the time-honoured period when people firmly believe that a plentiful crop of red berries or haws prophesy a severe winter to follow. This is based on the myth that nature provides an abundance of berries for birds to eat and survive the cold winter. Pleasant weather lore, but in truth a surplus of berries is the result of good growing seasons in the previous year. The poor result bears this out. 3/16 (19)

SEPTEMBER

September dries up wells and **
breaks down bridges. ***

This means that after a summer flood or drought, September often continues the sequence putting in the finishing touches. In reality there is little evidence.

Dry September 9/42 (21)
Wet September 31/84 (37)

Stooks leave to stand for three
Sundays.

This Yorkshire (North Riding) old farming maxim refers to a stook or a number of sheaves (usually 6 to 12) of grain stacked for drying. The stook is angled to face the prevailing wind and positioned to catch the maximum amount of sunshine. The period they are left depends on the location and weather conditions. The suggestion of a minimum of 14 days (three Sundays) in the saying is probably correct.

The harvest late, garden stuff
good and cheap; honey, flax and
hemp abundant.

True farming facts from the North Riding of Yorkshire.

1 SEPTEMBER

Fair on September the first,
fair for the month. **

Another fable that has fallen by the wayside.

12/53 (23)

8 SEPTEMBER

As on the eighth of September,
so for the next four weeks. *

A completely useless maxim. 0/111 (0)

14 SEPTEMBER - HOLYCROSS OR HOLYROOD DAY

If dry be the buck's horn
On Holyrood morn,
Tis worth a kist of gold; ***
But if wet it be seen
Ere Holyrood e'en,
Bad harvest is foretold. **

This Yorkshire adage is pleasant when read but disagreeable in result.

Dry 14/41 (34)
Wet 12/38 (32)

MID-SEPTEMBER

There are generally three
consecutive windy days about
the middle of September, which
have been called by the Midland
millers the windy days of barley
harvest. *****

This maxim was tested for three consecutive windy days during the period 11-20th September (mid-month). The peak was 12-15th (refer to beginning of this chapter). The result obtained a high rating of 66 percent. 73/111 (66)

15 SEPTEMBER

This day is said to be fine six
years out of seven. ****

To obtain a dry 15th September 6 times out of 7 times is to do so on 86 percent of occasions. When tested the figure returned was 55 percent. 58/105 (55)

19 SEPTEMBER

If on September the nineteenth
there is a storm from the south,
a mild winter may be expected. *

This Derby saying, like the majority of daily weather maxims, falls flat upon its face. 1/10 (10)

AUTUMN EQUINOX - ABOUT 21 SEPTEMBER

A quiet week before the autumn
equinox and after, the temperature
will continue higher than usual
into winter. **

A well-established high pressure system rapidly changing to stormy conditions is the normal weather sequence around the time of the autumn equinox. The test gave only a rating of 21 percent. 5/24 (21)

20-22 SEPTEMBER

These three days of September
rule the weather for October,
November and December. *

Another "key days" maxim ruling future monthly weather, in this case the early days of the autumn equinox commanding October to December. The temperature and rainfall of each day's airstream were tested against their corresponding month. Only 10 percent were correct. 33/318 (10)

21 SEPTEMBER - ST MATTHEW'S DAY

St Matthee,
Shut up the bee.

St Matthew
Brings on the cold dew. ***

Matthew's Day bright and clear
Brings good winde **

Saint Matthew,
Get candlesticks new.
Saint Mathi,
Long candlesticks buy.

SEPTEMBER

St Matthew brings the cold rain and dew. *

Most of the St Matthew Day rhymes are concerned with the approach of cold weather and the first ground and air frosts of autumn.

Cold dew	50/106	(47)
Cold rain	4/106	(4)

A southerly wind on September the twenty-first indicates that the rest of the autumn will be warm. **

Only a very few examples of a Southerly wind on this day occurred so the saw could not be tested.

29 SEPTEMBER - ST MICHAEL'S DAY (MICHAELMAS)

So many days old the moon is on Michaelmas Day, so many floods after. *

If Michaelmas brings acorns, Christmas will cover the fields with snow. **

Michaelmas rot
Comes ne'er in the pot.

A dark Michaelmas, and a light Christmas. **

If Michaelmas Day be fair, the sun will shine much in the winter; **
though the wind in the north-east will frequently reign long, and be very sharp and nipping. ***

This set of diverse poetic sayings are difficult to test apart from the last one.

Fair 29 September then a sunny winter	12/46	(26)
Fair 29 September then NE'ly in winter	18/55	(33)

September

There is a superstition about examining the oak apples on the twenty-ninth of September, and auguries are inferred from their condition.

Weather and other prophecies are made from the condition of oak apples on this day (Oak Apple Day is 29 May).

OCTOBER

Normally the third Old-wives summer dry period at the end of September continues into early October (till 4th). Then it becomes stormy 5-12th peaking 8-9th, returning to quiet anti-cyclonic weather in mid-month 16-20th, peaking on 19th. The see-saw pattern continues when the late autumn rains and storms appear 24 October to 13 November peaking on 29th.

Dry your barley in October,
Or you'll always be sober.

If barley is not properly dried then malt and consequently liquor are not available, so the farmer will always be sober.

There are always nineteen, some say twenty-one, fine days in October. *

This Kent saying is untrue.

19 fine October days	10/94	(11)
21	3/94	(3)

Much rain in October, much wind in December. **

Another maxim with poor results. 10/34 (29)

When it freezes and snows in October, January will bring mild weather; ****
but if it is thundering and heat-lightening, the weather will resemble April in temper. **

The first part is a balance saw which surprisingly works with 64 percent results. Poor figures greet the second part.

October

7/11 (61)
2/9 (22)

If October brings heavy frosts and winds, then will January and February be mild. *

If October brings much frost and wind, then are January and February mild. *

Similar balance sayings with little to offer. 4/33 (12)

Now that it is October, don thy woolly smock.

Certainly by the time October comes frost will be becoming more frequent.

A warm April and October, a warm year next. ***

An unusual blend of a mild April and October (6 months apart) forecasting a warm year to follow. 16/49 (33)

Warm October, cold February. **

Another balance maxim with no truth. 10/58 (17)

For every fog in October a snow in winter, heavy or light according as the fog is heavy or light. *

This type of pedantic weather lore has entered the realms of fiction.

October

A large number of foggy days in October indicates a hard winter. **

Based on the theory that October anticyclones producing fogs will persist into winter to give very cold weather.
6/36 (17)

If in the fall of the leaves in October many of them wither on the boughs and hang there, it betokens a frosty winter and much snow. ***

If the oak wears its leaves in October you may expect a hard winter. ***

Dry quiet weather in October allows leaves to stay on the trees. For the test 13 or more anticyclonic days in a dry Oct were checked against any following cold winter. The results were unsatisfactory. 9/27 (33)

Full moon in October without frost, no frost till full moon in November. *

Warm cloudless weather in October hardly lasts into November.

If the October moon appears with the points of her crescent up, the month will be dry, if down, wet. *

This is a famous saying with no scientific basis. The moon is shaped like this because of its odd elliptical orbit around the Earth catching the sun's light.

If the deer's coat is grey in October there will be a severe winter. **

October

If the hare wears a thick coat in October, then lay in a good stock of fuel. *

If foxes bark much in October they're calling up a great deal of snow. *

The Carrion Crow
Creeping back again
With October wind and rain.

The Carrion Crow is involved in partial migration but the remainder of the family are residential. The maxim emphasizes October's storms aptly illustrated by the Crow.

As the weather in October, so it will be in the next March. **

Rainfall (27 percent) and temperature (20 percent) figures showed little comparison. 66/244 (27)
55/273 (20)

A good October and a good blast,
To blow the oak, acorn and mast.

The average periods of October's stormy and windy weather can be seen at the beginning of the chapter.

If there is thunder in October, January will be wet. ***

One cannot see the reasoning behind this saw. 3/9 (33)

29 September and 16 October - St Michael's and St Gallus' Day

If it does not rain on Saint Michael's and Gallus, a dry spring is indicated for the next year. **

If it does not rain on Saint Michael and Gallus
The following spring will be dry and propitious. **

Weather lore incorporating two saints' days. 11/34 (32)

18 October - St Luke's Day

Saint Luke's little summer. ***

There is often about this time a spell of fine, dry weather, and this has received the name of Saint Luke's little summer. ***

An Indian Summer often occurs in October or November.

This is one of the most famous English weather sayings and is adamantly believed by countrymen. However the figures tell a different story. The period 15-21st October was tested for dry sunny weather. Also a minimum of three days allowed for a "little summer" to occur. A 31 percent chance of this happened when the 18th was one of the three days. The 41 percent result refers to any consecutive three-day period happening during 15-21st. In fact the driest days were the 18 and 19th which also coincide with our Indian summer (strictly an Indian summer is a lengthy dry sunny spell from late Sept. into November). The name is probably derived from the N. American Indians who relied on a similar fine spell in late autumn for harvesting. The third saying proves it. 34/111 (31)
45/111 (41)

28 October - St Simon's and St Jude's Day

This day was anciently accounted as certain to be rainy. ***

These figures give an evens chance of rain on 28 October. 52/108 (48)

October

On Saint Jude's Day
Then oxen may play.

On Saint Simon and Saint Jude
winter approaches at a gentle
trot. ***

The first month of winter (December) is very near and the end of October could easily feel colder weather. However the result of 44 percent for a cold 28th Oct was nothing special.
47/108 (44)

NOVEMBER

The late autumn storms and rains usually continue until 13th, peaking 9-12th. In mid-month one sees a brief quiet foggy anticyclonic interlude covering 15-21st peaking 18-20th. The return in late Nov and early Dec to unsettled rainy weather is the first of the early winter storms. These are almost certain to occur 24 Nov through to 14 Dec with two separate maximums on 25 Nov and 9 Dec.

When in November the water
rises, it will show itself
the whole winter. ***

November rains replace the dry soil of the previous summer. Also with the drop in evaporation loss drains and well levels soon rise. Unfortunately the rains do not continue over winter. 30/81 (37)

October and November cold indicate
that the following January and
February will be mild and dry. *

There is no relationship here. 0/15 (0)

If there's ice in November that
will bear a duck,
There'll be nothing after but
sludge and muck. **

The saying was tested for a mild wet winter. 9/52 (17)

Ice in November
Brings mud in December. *

Further hopeless test figures. 4/52 (8)

NOVEMBER

A cold November, a warm Christmas. ***

A 41 percent result tells the usual story. 14/34 (41)

A cold November signifies a cold winter. ****

This has an evens chance of being correct. 53/106 (50)

Thunder in November, a fertile year to come. *

One can see no logic in this maxim. 0/6 (0)

As November, so the following March. **

Unfortunately the comparison of rainfall (35 percent) and temperature (15 percent) proves to be useless. 85/244 (35)
41/273 (15)

If the November goose bone be thick, so will the winter weather be. *

Another dainty morsel to whet the appetite of fiction lovers.

When the hoar-frost is first accompanied by easterly winds, it indicates that the cold will continue a long time. ***

These figures are based on the cold continuing for at least three days. They are disappointing since Easterlies should normally prevail at this time. 9/27 (33)

1 NOVEMBER - ALL SAINT'S DAY (HALLOWMAS)

Farewell, thou latter spring;
Farewell, thou All Hallow'n
summer. **

In this Shakespeare quote the period 30 Oct to 1 Nov was tested for a dry spell. Only 18 percent were totally dry and any two consecutive day dry spell won a 32 percent rating. The 31st was by far the driest. 20/111 (18)
35/111 (32)

If on All Saints' Day the beech
nut be found dry, we shall have
a hard winter; but if the nut *
be wet and not light, we may
expect a wet winter. **

Here a dry mild October was tested for a severe winter (13 percent) and a wet month against a wet winter (29 percent).
4/32 (13)
23/80 (29)

If ducks do slide at Hallowtide,
At Christmas they will swim; ***
If ducks do swim at Hallowtide,
At Christmas they will slide. ***

Little to recommend this adage. The duck rhyme applies to sayings in most winter months.

Icy 1st Nov. then wet Xmas	20/46	(43)
Wet .. .. .. icy ..	18/50	(36)

On the first of November if the
weather hold clear,
And end of wheat sowing you do
for this year.

Old-style farming lore.

November

Early November

When you see gossamer flying,
Be sure the air is drying.

Gossamer is the web of a small spider often spun on foliage. This light mass of thread will float in calm air or spread over grass. Gossamer literally means "goose summer" referring to early November (11th Nov is St Martin's "little summer") when geese were eaten - the time when gossamer was plentiful.

Late October to Early November

If the latter end of October
and beginning of November be
for the most part warm and
rainy, then January and
February are like to be
frosty and cold, except after
a very dry summer. **

Unfortunately this famous "Shepherd of Banbury" balance saying number 25 is untrue. 2/7 (29)

10 November - St Martinmas Eve

Where the wind is on Martinmas
Eve, there it will be through
the coming winter. *

The weather on Martinmas Eve is
an index to the barometer for
some two or three months forward. *

The first saw originates in Atherstone, Warwicks, and the second hails from the Midlands. Both are hopeless. 0/106 (0)

11 November - St Martin's Day (Martinmas or Hollandtide)

If ducks do slide at Hollantide,
At Christmas they will swim; ***
If ducks do swim at Hollantide;
At Christmas they will slide. ***

A familiar period representing St Martin's summer - similar to October's St Luke's summer. The adage reverts to a well-known theme relating icy weather to wet and the reverse. As one would expect the results are poor.

Icy 11th Nov. then wet Xmas	16/43	(37)
Wet .. .. .. icy ..	20/47	(43)

If it is at Martinmas fair, dry
and cold, the cold in winter
will not last long. ****

This saying is supposed to show the trend of the next winter, unfortunately it does not succeed. 11/22 (50)

When the wind is in the quarter
from the south-south-west at
Martinmas, it keeps mainly to
the same point right on to the
old Candlemas Day, and we shall
have a mild winter up to then
and no snow to speak of. *

If the wind is in the
south-west at Martinmas, it
keeps there till after
Candlemas, with a mild winter
up till then and no snow to
speak of. **

The two maxims are similar with the second coming from the Midlands. In this 96-day period the S.W. quadrant ranges from 10 to 27 days. The first part up to Candlemas has a 0 percent rating and a mild winter renders 24 percent. 0/29 (0)
7/29 (24)

Wind north-west at Martinmas,
severe winter to come. *

This Huntingdonshire saw is another pointer to the following winter's weather, but with disastrous results. 2/17 (12)

Expect Saint Martin's summer,
halcyon days. **

Saint Martin's summer lasts
three days and a bit. ***

Here we have the first real reference to St Martin's summer, mentioned by Shakespeare in the first maxim. Both were tested along similar lines to St Luke's summer (18 October). The period chosen was 8-14th Nov. The 24 percent refers to three consecutive dry days including the 11th. 35 percent involves any three consecutive dry days in the week period. Unfortunately St Martin's summer is a myth - even the date with the highest total number of dry days was the 10th. 26/110 (24)
39/110 (35)

If the wind is south-westerly
at Martinmas,
It keeps there till after
Christmas. *

The Midlands provide the first saying, but both are extremely misleading. 0/106 (0)

If Saint Martinmas ice can
bear a duck,
The winter will be all mire
and muck. ***

Another icy/wet duck theme with little truth. 19/43 (44)

6-13 NOVEMBER - BUCHAN'S SIXTH COLD SPELL **

A further disastrous result which completes the set of cold spells. (Refer to index for the rest of Buchan's spells.)
31/110 (28)

21 NOVEMBER

As November the twenty-first,
so is the winter. *

Each airstream's temperature and rainfall categories occurring this day were checked for similar combined results in winter. Only 9 percent was returned. 10/108 (9)

22 NOVEMBER

Wherever the wind is at
midnight before Deddington
Fair,
There it will stay till the
end of the year. *

This refers to Oxfordshire's old Deddington Martinmas Fair held on this day. Very poor figures emerged. 0/106 (0)

23 NOVEMBER - ST CLEMENT'S DAY

Saint Clement gives the winter. *

St Clement was St Peter's third successor in Rome and died c100 AD. Identical testing was carried out as on the 21st Nov. 17/106 (16)

25 NOVEMBER - ST CATHERINE'S DAY

As at Catherine foul or fair,
so will be the next February. ***

St Catherine was born in Alexandria and is the patron saint of grinders, millers and spinners. 36/106 (34)

LATE AUTUMN

Flowers in bloom late in autumn
indicate a bad winter. *

NOVEMBER

A balance maxim which was tested for a very mild November and a severe winter to follow. 5/54 (9)

If October and November be snow and a frost, then January and February are like to be open and mild. *

The Shepherd of Banbury's 26th adage but is completely untrue. 0/44 (0)

DECEMBER

On average the early winter storms and rains continue into December till about 14th, peaking around 9th. A quiet frosty period occurs usually 18-24th, peaking 19-21st with frequent South and East winds. A most reliable weather trend is when the old year sees a dramatic change to storms bringing a post-Christmas thaw 25 Dec to 1st January, peaking 28th. Here cyclonic and Westerly winds are most predominant.

Thunder in December presages
fine weather. **

First Sunday in December

If it rains on this Sunday
before Mass, it will rain for
a week. *

A religious weather saying related to the day of the week and unlikely to have any sound weather reasoning. Refer to the chapter on weekdays and Sunday's weather.

3-14 December - Buchan's Third Warm Spell ****

At last a good result for one of Buchan's 9 periods. This ties in with the early winter cyclonic storms which produce mobile depressions and mild Westerlies. A 60 percent rating confirms this. (Refer to index for other Buchan spells.)

67/111 (60)

13 December - St Lucy's Day

Lucy light, Lucy light,
The shortest day and the
longest night.

Refer to the sixth adage of 21st December.

21 DECEMBER - ST THOMAS' DAY

Look at the weathercock on Saint Thomas' Day at twelve o'clock, and see which way the wind is, for there it will stick for the next lunar quarter. *

St Thomas was the "doubting apostle". 8/111 (7)

Frost on the shortest day is said to indicate a severe winter. **

This Lancashire saying is a combination of frost occurring on the winter solstice and its hopeful inspiration to the rest of the winter. But alas the test contains terrible results.
8/44 (18)

If it freeze on Saint Thomas' Day, the price of corn will fall; if it be mild, the price will rise. *** ***

The price of corn was measured as wheat being abundant or scarce in the following year's crop, but ratings are low.

Frozen 21st Dec.	= good wheat	14/35	(40)
Warm	= bad ..	17/44	(39)

If the ice will bear a goose before Christmas, it will not bear a duck after. **

If ice will bear a man before Christmas, it will not bear a mouse afterwards. **

The goose and duck theme produces another low rating.
5/22 (23)

DECEMBER

Saint Thomas grey, Saint Thomas grey,
The longest night and the shortest day.

This is a statement of fact.

BEFORE CHRISTMAS

Sharp frosts before Christmas mean much rain afterwards. **

Similar themes failing miserably. 20/87 (23)

25 DECEMBER - CHRISTMAS DAY AND NIGHT

The weather lore for Christmas is prolific, being the most significant religious event of the Christian year. It must be emphasized that the following saws in this sub-section deal with Christmas Day and Night only.

A clear and bright sun on Christmas Day forteLleth a peaceable year and plenty; but if the wind grows strong before sunset, it betokeneth sickness in the spring and autumn quarters. ***

This first saw offers little hope. 16/40 (40)

If the sun shine through the apple tree on Christmas Day, there will be an abundant crop in the following year. *

If windy on Christmas Day, trees will bring much fruit. *

December

It is difficult to believe that one day's weather will influence the following year's fruit crop.

If it snows during Christmas
Night, the crops will do well. *

Snow on Christmas Night, good
hop crop next year. *

Presumably this means that snow covering young seeds will be protected from cold blasts and sharp frosts by the snow's insulation properties. Only five incidents of snow were found to fall on Christmas Night, so could not be tested, even so poor results would be inevitable.

If Christmas Day on Thursday be,
A windy winter ye shall see;
Windy weather in each week,
And hard tempest strong and
thick,
The summer shall be good and dry,
Corn and beasts shall multiply;
The year's good for lands to
till,
Kings and princes shall die
thy skill. *

If Christmas Day on Monday be,
A great winter that year you'll
see. *

If that Christmas Day should
fall
Upon Friday, know we all
At winter season shall be
easy,
Save great winds aloft shall
fly. *

When certain weekdays coincide with Christmas Day and are then used as a basis for weather forecasting one might as well relate the number of pints of beer the author drinks on Christmas Day to the weather of the following spring.

December

A dull Christmas Day with no
sun bodes ill for the harvest. ***

Reaffirmation using test figures of the falsity of this weather saw. 15/41 (37)

24-26 December

Reference to *Christmas* in English weather lore must be treated as the whole of Christmas and not the two specific times of Christmas Day and Night, in the previous sub-section. It must also be remembered that the modern Christmas includes Boxing Day which was originally one of the four holidays that bank employees took due to the Bank Holiday Act of 1871. Soon after, Boxing Day was observed as a Public Holiday. So at the time of the *Christmas* weather lore, Boxing Day did not exist. The author has chosen 24-26th Dec as a reasonable period for the "old-time" Christmas.

A green Christmas makes a fat
churchyard. **

Another enjoyable maxim. Green Christmas of course means a mild wet period when green foliage temporarily grows. A fat churchyard is the fatal effect of this on old and young people. The results are poor in fact a severe cold Christmas was the major weather cause in "killing off" people through hypothermia. The 25 percent rating was based on January to March deaths and a mild Christmas. 2/8 (25)

A green Christmas brings a
heavy harvest. **

Disappointing results for this Rutland maxim. 10/32 (31)

At Christmas meadows green,
at Easter covered with frost. *

Christmas in snow, Easter in
mud; *

DECEMBER

Easter in snow, Christmas in mud. *

The fact that Easter is a movable feast gives no weather credence to these two sayings, only a religious connection.

Light Christmas, light wheat-sheaf; *
Dark Christmas, heavy wheat-sheaf. *

The meaning of light and dark refers to a full and new moon.

Christmas wet, empty granary and barrel. ***

An unreliable adage. 9/25 (36)

If at Christmas ice hangs on the willow, clover may be cut at Easter. ***

A pleasant saying meaning that a cold Christmas will eventually turn the winter mild and wet accelerating early clover growth to be cut in the spring (Easter). In reality there is little truth. 7/21 (33)

If Christmas finds a bridge, he'll break it; *
If he finds none, he'll make it. ***

To find a bridge and break it means dry weather will be followed by torrential rain or vice-versa. There is a similar maxim in the September chapter. Tested for Christmas (3 days) and afterwards (27-29th) with poor results.

Dry Xmas = wet 27-29th 1/29 (3)
Wet .. = dry .. 13/33 (39)

If the beech shows a large bud

at Christmas a moist summer
will probably follow. ***

A mild Dec is tested for a wet summer. 16/48 (33)

Thunder during Christmas week
indicates that there will be
much snow during the winter. *

Very few cases arose. Anyway it is difficult to understand the relationship between thunder and snow.

28 DECEMBER - CHILDERMAS OR HOLY INNOCENT'S DAY

If it be lowering and wet on
Childermas Day there will be
scarcity; while if the day be **
fair it promises plenty. ***

The usual bad returns. Scarcity is taken as loss in crops but the usual poor results prevail.

Wet 28th Dec. = scarce harvest	12/47	(26)
Dry .. .. = plentiful ..	13/38	(34)

31 DECEMBER

If New Year's Eve night wind
blows south,
It betokeneth warmth and
growth; ***
If west, much milk and fish in
the sea; ***
If north, much cold and storms
there be; *
If east, the trees will bear
much fruit; **
If north-east, flee it man
and brute. ***

The last day of the old year is supposed to determine the weather of the new. Winter and spring were combined with temperature and rainfall categories. Only South, West and North winds on 31st were tested with poor returns; not enough cases occurred with an Easterly.

South wind	5/11	(45)
West ..	4/11	(36)
North ..	0/6	(0)

NOVEMBER AND DECEMBER

Thunder and lightning early in winter or late in fall indicate warm weather. ***

Not enough data found to research any test.

LATE DECEMBER

If the old year goes out like a lion, the new year will come in like a lamb. **

Although December often ends like a lion (meaning roaring gales), the new year to follow like a lamb (quiet weather) seldom occurs. Refer to the March chapter for a similar theme.

12/68 (18)

MOVEABLE FEASTS

EASTER

All the Christian movable (i.e. no fixed calendar date) feasts are commanded by Easter Day (Sunday) which can fall from 22 March to 25 April. Today Easter covers four days Good Friday, Saturday, Sunday and Monday. The latter was introduced as a bank holiday in 1871. Periodically a series of bad Easters with wet cold weather experienced under the fluctuating date system, has provoked Parliament to pass laws to give Easter a fixed date. In 1928 such a proposal was observed for Easter Sunday to fall on the second Sunday in April. (Refer to the 7-14th February in that month's section for further information.)

Using this fixed day a comparison was made using temperature and rainfall figures from 1829-1928. Two facts emerged; that on average the later the date of Easter the better the weather and that there was no weather advantage for a fixed or movable Easter.

SHROVE OR PANCAKE TUESDAY

So much as the sun shineth on
Pancake Tuesday, the like will
shine every day in Lent. *

When the sun is shining on
Shrovetide Day, it is meant
well for rye and peas. *

Lent, lasting for 40 days, begins on Ash Wednesday. The main difficulty in testing weather lore associated with movable feasts was the hard-slogging job of working their dates during the years 1861-1971. All of the sayings showed nothing.

Thunder on Shrove Tuesday
foretelleth wind, store of
fruit, and plenty. *

Lent

Ash Wednesday

Wherever the wind lies on Ash Wednesday, it continues during all Lent. *

As Ash Wednesday, so the fasting-time. *

Both maxims were completely false. 0/94 (0)

Lent (40 Days from Ash Wednesday)

Dry Lent, fertile year. **

When applied to wheat a 25 percent rating is returned. 7/28 (25)

Never come Lent, never come winter.

Presumably this Herefordshire adage means that a late Lent during April is into spring but a late cold snap can still occur.

Palm Sunday

If the weather is not clear on Palm Sunday, it means a bad year. **

Another bad saying where one day's weather rules the year's crop. 10/35 (29)

From whatever quarter the wind blows on Palm Sunday, it will continue to blow for the greater part of the coming summer. *

This Hampshire saw is poppycock. 0/94 (0)

HOLY OR MAUNDY THURSDAY

Fine on Holy Thursday, wet on
Whit Monday; fine on Whit **
Monday, wet on Holy Thursday. ***

A Huntingdonshire saying which produces sad figures.

Fine on Holy Thursday wet on Whit Monday	16/53	(30)
Fine on Whit Monday wet on Holy Thursday	20/58	(34)

If a piece of hawthorn is
gathered on Holy Thursday
and kept in the house it
will never be struck by
lightening because:
Under a thorn
Our Saviour was born.

Quaint piece of weather lore with religious connotations. Similar thunder/lightning saws can be found in the plant chapter.

GOOD FRIDAY

Rain on Good Friday,
foreshadows a fruitful
year. ***

The result speaks for itself. 11/33 (33)

EASTER DAY (SUNDAY)

A wet Good Friday and a wet
Easter Day
Makes plenty of grass, but
very little hay. **

A wet Good Friday and a wet
Easter Day

Easter

Makes plenty of grass, but
little good hay. **

Leicester supplies the second saying but both follow the usual false pattern. 5/23 (22)

If the sun shines on Easter Day,
it shines on Whit Sunday
likewise. ***

One wouldn't expect this to be true. 23/51 (45)

A good deal of rain upon
Easter Day
Gives a good crop grass,
but little good hay. **

If it rains on Easter Day,
There shall be good grass
but very bad hay. **

Both saws, the first one hails from Herts, look more sensible at first glance with rain around late March or April bringing on grass in June, but results state otherwise.
Poor hay 11/35 (31)

Such weather as there is on
Easter Day there will be at
harvest. *

The general airstream flow for Easter Day was tested for August and September harvests.
Aug. harvest 16/88 (18)
Sept. .. 13/88 (15)

Easter (4 Days)

Late Easter, long, cold spring. ***

This Sussex maxim involving a late Easter provides a poor result. 11/30 (37)

EASTER

Past Easter frost,
Fruit not lost. ***

Not entirely true, especially if an early Easter (late March or early April) occurs when frost is still feasible to attack fruit blossom.

Easter come early, or Easter come late,
Is sure to make the old cow quake. **

This Herefordshire saw refers to cold weather implying that when Easter comes along it will always be cold. Not true.
20/63 (32)

Easter in the snow, Christmas in mud, *
Christmas in snow, Easter in mud. *

This is pure myth.

PASTOR SUNDAY

If it rains on Pastor Sunday,
it will rain every Sunday until Pentecost. *

Applied to the five Sundays until Pentecost and tests show a 3 percent chance of success. 1/38 (3)

ASCENSION DAY

As the weather on Ascension Day,
so may be the entire autumn. **

Another saying stuffed with nonsense. 23/89 (26)

EASTER TO WHITSUNTIDE

Whitsuntide

If fair weather from Easter to Whitsuntide, the butter will be cheap. **

This relates to cheap or abundant amounts of butter which in turn means excess cow's milk. This is connected with plentiful grass caused by high rainfall in June and July. July rainfall was tested but with poor results. 24/85 (28)

Corpus Christi

If it rains on Corpus Christi Day, the rye granary will be light. *

Another maxim where one day's weather rules a year's rye harvest.

Whitsunday

Whit Sunday bright and clear
Will bring a fertile year. ***

If Whit Sunday bring rain, we expect many a plague. ***

Whit Sunday wet, Christmas fat. ***

I'm afraid no truth can be found in these saws.

19/49 (39)

Pentecost - Whitsuntide

Strawberries at Whitsuntide indicate good wine. ***

Rain at Pentecost forbodes evil.

Whitsuntide is Whit Sunday plus a few days.

SEASONS

Spring

A late spring
Is a great blessing.

A late spring never deceives.

A late spring certainly helps crops after a cold start, but sometimes its nett effect is felt too late.

Better late spring and bear
than early blossom and blast.

This applies to fruit growers. Early blossom will often be checked by late winter frosts. So it is better to be over the major frost period in a late spring and accept a below average blossom and fruit harvest.

If the spring is cold and wet, then
the autumn will be hot and dry. **

A neat balance saying for spring and autumn, but in reality has little to offer. 7/32 (22)

A wet spring, a dry harvest. **

Again little to offer. August harvest 29/84 (35)
Sept. .. 25/84 (30)

In spring a tub of rain makes a
spoonful of mud. **
In autumn a spoonful of rain makes
a tub of mud. ***

SPRING

If this maxim means that in spring the soil water evaporation is greater than in autumn - hence a large spring rainfall would leave little in surface mud, then it is correct. However it could also mean a heavy spring rainfall would be followed by a dry period and vice-versa in the autumn. For testing a high or low month's rainfall was checked for the correct rainfall in the following month in spring and autumn. Poor results emerged.

Wet spring month followed by dry	75/231	(32)
Dry autumn .. .. .. wet	83/241	(34)

The spring is not always green.

The spring although often sunny can be cold and dull. Crops and plants only grow when continual hourly temperatures are above about 6°C (43°F).

Thunder in spring
Cold will bring. **

Spring thunderstorms only indicate that heavy showers are about at that time. 12/39 (31)

First thunder in spring - if in
the south, it indicates a wet *
season; if in the north, a dry
season. *

The same sentiments apply as in the previous adage - the direction is a misfit.

Early thunder, early spring. ***

Test figures show this to be incorrect. 5/12 (42)

Lightning in spring indicates a
good fruit year. **

One would have thought that this maxim would follow the usual trend of poor results.

Spring

If there's spring in winter, and
winter in spring.
The year won't be good for anything. ****

There is some truth in as much that a warm winter can accelerate seed which is often checked or ruined by cold spring frosts.

Long winter and a late spring are
both good for hay and grain, but *****
bad for corn and garden. ***

The hay results are marvellous with 73 percent but the bad corn harvest only yields 45 percent. 8/11 (73)
5/11 (45)

The spring she is a young maid,
who does not know her mind.

A reminder that spring from March to April possesses some of the most variable weather of the year.

Spring is here when you can tread
on nine daises at once on the
village green.

A lovely poetic saying which is appealing and very true.

A dry spring - a rainy summer. **

This balance saw is unfortunately incorrect. 24/81 (30)

Early blossoms indicate a bad
fruit year. ****

Indicating that an early spring with good fruit blossoms will be tragically affected by late spring frosts, adding up to a bad fruit year.

Summer

Generally a moist and cool summer
portends a hard winter. **

This Bacon balance saw has poor results. 11/42 (26)

A wet summer almost always precedes
a cold, stormy winter. **

The summer be rainy, the following
winter will be severe. **

Note that these two sayings relate only to a wet summer. 14/82 (17)

Midsummer rain
Spoils hay and grain.

Midsummer rain is often of the violent thundery type and the cold down draughts associated with these hail showers can ruin hay and flatten grain fields.

Happy are the fields that receive
summer rain.

Opposite in meaning to the previous adage. When summer rain is gentle it is often warm and this combination is good for a reasonably fast growth rate.

A dry summer never made a clear peck. **

Meaning a dry summer produces a low crop yield or weight (peck) because of lack of rain. Warmth, sun and rain are the perfect weather blend for a bumper crop. The results are poor. Summer weather is only a part of the long 9-month growth of a winter crop. 9/33 (27)

A dry summer never begs its bread. **

This Somerset maxim has an opposite meaning to the previous saw. 7/33 (21)

Who so hath but a mouth
Will never in England suffer drought.

This means that although long dry summer droughts occur once every decade or so (remember 1959, 1975 and 1976!) eventually autumn or late summer rains return.

Drought never bred dearth in England.

Similar to the preceding maxim where a drought never really lasts long enough to starve people to death in this country.

A very hot and dry summer is sometimes followed by a severe winter. **

The classic example of one extreme season balancing another. Notice the word "sometimes" has crept in, but even so only a 23 percent success is assured. 6/26 (23)

An English summer, two hot days
and a thunderstorm.

A real pessimistic version of an English summer - sometimes correct. One feels total agreement especially on holiday when all it does is bucket down with rain.

After a famine in the stall,
Comes a famine in the hall. **

A famine in England begins in the horse-manger. **

The first adage refers to a bad hay crop in the first line and poor corn harvest in the second. The chance of two such harvests in succession is 23 percent. The last saying refers to a poor hay yield. 6/26 (23)

Summer

One swallow does not make a summer. ****

Summer goes with the swallows. ****

The first is a gorgeous famous saying repeated in the bird chapter. True swallow migration often sees the lonely leaders arriving first in the country - it's a few days later when the main flocks arrive that one hopes the warmer weather has come. The second maxim marks the end of summer for a countryman as the swallow seeks warmer climes.

In summer a fog from the south, ***
warm weather; from the west, rain. ***

A summer fog is for fair weather.

Grey mists at dawn,
The day will be warm.

These three maxims are placed together because it is felt that all too often people believe summer fog/mists presage a dry warm day. The crux is to determine the *type* of fog or mist occurring in the morning. Poor visibility originating after a clear calm night will quickly evaporate and clear. Fog and mist caused by a change of air mass say to a warm moist airstream, often remains all day in summer.

A cool summer and a light weight
in the bushel. **

Poor test figures show that winter and spring weather are also important seasons in the final crop success or failure.

Wheat	12/34	(35)
Barley	10/34	(29)

A mild, wet winter always follows
an unproductive summer. ***

"Unproductive" means poor harvest. The best result was for a mild wet winter to follow a poor hay harvest.

Wheat	10/24	(42)
Barley	11/28	(39)
Hay	14/27	(52)

Summer

T'is not the husbandman but the good weather that makes the corn grow.

Although the husbandman has special skill and knowledge, the weather ruled the success or failure of farming - even today with modern machines and land chemicals.

The greater the haze, the more settled the weather. *****

Summer haze, especially when thick, is the sign of a temperature inversion above the ground (usually below 2,000ft). These are associated with anticyclones which in turn can be related to quiet dry summer spells. In the test haze guaranteed at *least* three settled days on 71 percent of occasions.

At least three dry days	201/283	(71)
.. .. four	171/283	(60)
.. .. five	150/283	(53)

Winter is summer's heir. **

The balance saw was tested with equal temperature and rainfall categories to be persistent in each season.

Temperature	45/273	(16)
Rainfall	70/254	(28)

What summer gets, winter eats. **

The maxim means that summer's weather will produce the opposite effect in winter. Again temperature and rainfall categories were tested.

Temperature	32/214	(15)
Rainfall	43/169	(25)

Autumn

Clear autumn, windy winter; **
Warm autumn, long winter. **

Only the second line was tested with poor figures.

21/111 (19)

AUTUMN

A wet fall indicates a cold and early winter. **

Again poor results here.

Cold winter	17/80	(21)
Early ..	10/80	(13)

Much fog in autumn
Much snow in winter. ***

A "see-saw" maxim which follows the usual pattern. 3/7 (43)

Thunder in the fall indicates a mild, open winter. *

An illogical adage with a bad outcome. 2/14 (14)

Short harvests make short addlings.

The Yorkshire saw is obvious but earthy.

If during the autumn, the winds have been mainly from the South-east, or if the temperature has been lower than usual, it generally rains a great deal about the end of the year. ***

The end of the year was selected as 26-31st December (6 days) but results showed little.

4 days out of 6 wet	19/36	(53)
5 .. .. .. 6 ..	10/36	(28)
6 .. .. .. 6 ..	7/36	(19)

A hot and dry summer and autumn, especially if the heat and drought extend far into September, portend an open beginning of winter, and cold to succeed towards the latter part of the winter and beginning of the spring. **

This balance saw from the ancient pen of Bacon sounds full of promise but that's all. 2/10 (20)

If on the trees the leaves still hold,
The coming winter will be cold. **

A saw with similar cousins in the October and November chapters.

WINTER

Winter never died in a ditch.

Even though a winter, say by the middle of February, has been favourably mild it can still rapidly turn cold and snowy until real spring arrives.

Winter finds out what summer lays up. **

It is difficult to know whether winter experiences the type of weather that summer saves for the future.

Abundant wheat crops never follow a mild winter. ****

This is really a good result but is against reasoning as a mild winter should bring on winter wheat and even an average spring shouldn't affect its abundant crop potential.
29/41 (71)

A green winter makes a fat church-yard. **

Refer to the Christmas section in the December chapter for a full meaning.

When there is a spring in the winter, or a winter in the spring, the year is never good. ****

Winter

Similar to an adage in the spring section.

Summer in winter, and a summer's flood,
Never boded an Englishman good. ****

Excess weather of this type plays havoc with growing nature.

A warm and open winter portends a hot and dry summer. *

Classic balance saw from Bacon's pen, but offering only a 10 percent success rating. 5/48 (10)

One fair day in winter makes not birds merry.

One fair day in winter, impersonating the false beginning of spring, often catches birds out of their normal winter singing and feeding habits.

A fair day in winter is the mother of a storm. ***

It is always difficult to define a "fair" day; it is one of those loose adjectives like nice. But the author used it as meaning a clear dry sunny warm or hot day with a slight or moderate breeze. The test figures are not really any good.

Storm to follow "fair" day within	24 hours	36/121	(30)
.. ..	48 ..	55/121	(45)

An unusually fine day in winter is known as a 'borrowed' day, to be repaid with interest later in the season, known also as a 'weather-breeder'; and by sailors as a 'fox'. *

The terms "borrowed day" and "weather breeder" occur in other periods of the year. Excellent weather lore poetry but poor in the truth stakes.

Winter

When winter begins early, it ends early. ***

This is also untrue with a 46 percent result.

25/55 (45)

An early winter,
A surly winter.

An early winter is surely winter.

It is interesting to note that a difference of one letter in "surly" and "surely" completely changes the meaning. An early cold frosty or snowy winter in November is the most dangerous to a farmer.

Winter thunder,
A summer's wonder. ***

Winter thunder
Bode's summer's hunger. ***

Two balance maxims. Extracting winter thunder out of the June and July summer is supposed to help towards a warm sunny summer or abundant crop. Unfortunately the meaning falls by the wayside. (Refer to the February chapter for similar adages.)

Wheat and barley	3/9	(33)
Hot/dry summer	4/9	(44)

Winter thunder and summer flood
Never boded an Englishman good. ***

Any extreme weather conditions such as flood and thunder play havoc for the husbandman.

Winter thunder,
Poor man's death, rich man's hunger. **
Winter thunder,
Rich man's good and poor man's hunger. **

The saying is supposed to mean that winter thunder is good for fruit and bad for corn.

Winter

Sudden frosts in winter, after
rain,
Soon bring back more rain again. ***

Apparently this does not always happen in fact only on 47 percent of occasions. 38/81 (47)

When the Winter Solstice (about 21
December) has not been preceded
nor followed by the usual storms,
the following summer will be dry
at least 5 times out of 6. **

Usually 18-24th December has a quiet frosty period peaking 19-21st, around the winter solstice. Storms normally occur *before* 18th and *after* 24th. The test applies to 15-27th Dec. where times were viewed when no more than 2 days of gales blew. In the saying 5 out of 6 dry summers followed or 83 percent but the test only came up with 25. 4/16 (25)

As the days grow longer,
the storms grow stronger. *

As daylight starts to grow longer from late December the storms do grow stronger but a quiet period usually reigns in February. In March the gales return but from April into summer and autumn this saying is totally false.

After a frosty winter there
will be a good fruit harvest. ***

If the drop do freeze in the
cup of the blum
Surely there will be no plums. ***

These two sayings are contradictory.

A winter fog
Will freeze a dog. ****

Winter freezing fog is the coldest of the year. It is often associated with an anticyclone producing extremely low temperatures. And of course freezing fogs are notorious for producing rime deposits which with temperatures of -5 to -12°C prove the point.

Under water, dearth;
Under snow, bread. ****

Under water famine, under snow bread. ****

This again is the explanation of snow affording an insulation for plant life, seeds etc, against frost and cold winds. Water or rain will freeze, kill or rot vegetation.

Too fine a winter will swamp the summer. **

Another balance saw with poor results. 5/24 (21)

A good winter brings a good summer. *

A good winter, a good summer. *

It is difficult to know the dubious meaning of good winter and summer in these two maxims. A warm wet winter is good to some and not others. In the end a good winter and summer was defined as one with average temperature and rainfall.

1/21 (5)

A persistently hazy atmosphere in winter is a sign of cold raw weather. *****

A true saying that needs no testing. The majority of winter hazy conditions imply long dry days around anticyclones. The winter anticyclones differ from the summer ones in as much that they experience extreme frost and really cold conditions tending to worsen as the hazy days continue.

Expect the frost to increase in severity, and the weather to become drier and crisper, if, in winter, the wind veers from north-west to north-east. *****

WINTER

The results are very good and are tested on dry clear days under winter conditions at least two days after a North Easterly has set in. The cases for NW to NE winds are short-lived often occurring with depressions traversing Southern England or the English Channel and hence this part of the saying is false. 34/50 (68)

A wet autumn followed by a mild winter is the forerunner of a dry, cold spring. *

A moist autumn with a mild winter is followed by a cold and dry spring, retarding vegetation. *

An exact set of figures which look impressive but in reality are untrue. 1/12 (8)

Predict fog in autumn and winter when (1) the sky is clear (or clears) at sunset; (2) there is no more than a mere breath of wind; (3) when the air is fairly damp. *****

All true. Here we have the basic ingredients for fog formation. I like the "not more than a breath of wind", if it was calm then only shallow fog patches would form. A light wind is needed to produce the turbulence to mix the fog so it becomes widespread. This country adage is indeed very shrewd.

YEAR

A dry year never starves itself.

Presumably this means there are clear nights with dew to help in the annual moisture total.

After a wet year a cold one. **

Poor figures emerge here. 4/19 (21)

YEAR

Wet and dry years come in triads. *

A fanciful idea that pays poor dividends. 1/19 (5)

A snow year, a rich year. **

Snow year, good year. **

A snow year is a good year. **

Seeds and vegetation are insulated against frost and bitter winds by snow in the winter half-year.

Barley	9/32	(28)
Hay	13/32	(41)
Wheat	8/32	(25)

A good nut year, a good corn year. *

A good hay year, a bad fog year. *

Again the significance of this saw is baffling.
6/38 (16)

A pear year,
A dear year. ****

A cherry year,
A merry year. ****
A plum year,
A dumb year. ****

In the year when plums flourish
all else fails. ****

The second adage originates from Kent and the third from Devon. Plums are hardiest of all stone fruit and apart from being susceptible to damage by spring frosts can live in all varieties of weather. Hence the poor harvests of other fruit crops. Cherry is one of the earliest to begin so an abundant year signifies a mild wet spring, good for most crops.

Year

A serene autumn denotes a windy winter;
A windy winter, a rainy spring;
A rainy spring, a serene summer;
A serene summer, a windy autumn;
so that the air on a balance is
seldom debtor to itself. **

Spring. Slippy, drippy, nippy.
Summer. Showery, flowery, bowery.
Autumn. Hoppy, croppy, poppy.
Winter. Wheezy, sneezy, breezy. *****

A wonderful brief description of the year's seasons.

Extreme seasons are said to occur
From the 6th to the 10th year of
each decade, especially in alter-
nate decades. **

Extreme seasons were added to each decadal year. The most frequent year for extreme seasons was the 2nd (ie say 1891, 1901, 1911 and so on) followed in order by 10th, 3rd, 9th, 1st, 4th, 6th, 8th, 5th and 7th year. From the maxim the 6th to 10th years are supposed to have the bulk of extreme seasons which of course is untrue. Alternate decades are also a folly.

The first 3 days of any season
rule the weather of that season. *

Another "keys of the season" type saw where the weather on the first three days of any season dictates the following three month's weather. Similar maxims prove useless when tested.

The general character of the
weather during the last 20 days
of March, June, September or
December will rule the following
seasons. **

The saw looks promising but a quick glance at the results shows little confidence in it.

YEAR

Last 20 days of March	= spring	63/245	(26)
.. .. June	= summer	54/245	(22)
.. .. Sept.	= autumn	90/245	(37)
.. .. Dec.	= winter	48/244	(20)

A year of grass - good for nothing else.

This means a year of excess rain, and although crops need rain, too much is disastrous.

There can never be too much rain before mid-summer.

Rain is always needed from April to June when crops begin to accelerate in growth.

The harvest depends more on the year than on the field.

Like all things, farming was dependant on the random effects of the English *weather* rather than soil consistency.

A windy year is an apple year. ***

WEEKDAYS

There is no logical reason why a day of the week should affect the weather. Nearly all results bear this out. The wettest weekday (figures for Teddington Oct 1953 to Sept 1968) is Thursday (with 47.9 percent chance or rain) then Saturday (44.8) followed by Wednesday (44.4), Friday (43.7), Sunday (43.4), Tuesday (42.7) and finally Monday (41.5) falling perfectly as the recognized washing day. The order can be reversed for the driest days of the week. Thursday as the wettest is appropriate as it stems from the Scandinavian Thor - the god of thunder.

WEDNESDAY

When the sun sets clear on
Wednesday, expect clear
weather for the rest of the
week. ****

Wednesday clearing, clear till
Sunday. *

These two maxims are similar with surprisingly good results for the first one of 58 percent.

63/109 (58)
1/16 (6)

THURSDAY

On Thursday at three
Look out, and you'll see
What Friday will be. **

This Devon saw can be applied to any day.

FRIDAY

Friday's a day as'll have his
trick,
The fairest or foulest day o'
the wik. ****

Weekdays

Friday is the best or worst
day of the week. ****

As the Friday, so the Sunday. ***

If on Friday it rain
Twill on Sunday again; ***
If Friday be clear
Have for Sunday no fear. **

If the sun sets clear on a
Friday, it will blow before
Sunday night. **

The relationship between Friday and Sunday may have been influenced by the Christian Good Friday and Easter Sunday. The first adage hails from Shropshire and shows Friday to be the 4th wettest and 3rd driest weekday with figures to prove it. The third saying was tested on similar airstreams for both days. Poor results for the fourth and fifth saws occur.

Wettest Friday	342/783	(44)
Driest ..	441/783	(56)
Third saying	41/177	(23)
Wet Friday then dry Sunday	33/77	(43)
Dry .. .. wet ..	25/99	(25)

Saturday

There is never a Saturday
without some sunshine. *

There is never a Saturday in
the year
But what the sun it doth appear. *

The sun appears on 44 Saturdays out of a 100.

Saturday change, and Sunday
full,
Is always wet, and always wull. ***

A Northants saw, not particularly true. 14/36 (39)

WEEKDAYS

SUNDAY

If it rains on Sunday before
Mass, it will rain all week. *

Rain afore church
Rain all the week, little or
much. *

Sunday clearing, clear till
Wednesday. **

Low ratings for this adage. 3/14 (21)

Saturday's moon, Sunday seen
The foulest weather there ever
hath been. *

Too ridiculous to contemplate (see Moon chapter).

If sunset on Sunday is cloudy,
it will rain before Wednesday.

A safe obvious bet. Once the weather trend becomes changeable with Westerlies and depressions bringing rain fronts across the UK, the chance of rain, even within two days, is very high. So whether the cloudy sunset appears on Monday, Thursday or Sunday, the consequence is factual. 57/76 (75)

When it storms on the first
Sunday in the month, it will
storm every Sunday in the
month. *

The last phrase refers to the remainder of Sundays in the month. 2/21 (10)

Weekdays

The last Sunday in the month indicates the weather of the next month. *

Usual pattern of useless test figures. 6/44 (14)

A wet Sunday, a fine Monday, wet for the rest of the week. *

This saw from Winchester has little to offer. 3/21 (14)

Any Day

A misty morning may have a fine day. ***

It all depends on the type of mist - whether valley, hill or frontal. (Refer to the fog/mist chapter.)

Too bright a morning breeds a lowering day. *****

This is absolutely correct. A brilliant clear morning inland with excellent visibility always occurs with a cold polar airstream which is often potentially unstable or showery. So as the temperature of the day increases shower clouds form (cumulus) and rain showers often occur in afternoon/evening.

When there are three days cold, expect three days colder. ***

One would expect this saying to be true with cold weather persisting but surprisingly only 38 percent are correct.
107/282 (38)

A warm and serene day, which we say is too fine for the season, betokens a speedy reverse. ***

Any Day

A similar saw with ratings can be seen in the winter section.

A blustering night, a fair day. ***

For morning rain leave not your journey. ***

These two should have an evens chance. Blustery nights can continue throughout the next day and equally can abate to produce fine gentle weather.

A bad day hath a good night. ***

This is really only true with daytime showers which frequently cease inland overnight. This of course is mainly due to the falling night temperature allowing little energy to produce them.

Twilight looming indicates rain. ***

Twilight looming indicates a cloudy or overcast sky after sunset or before sunrise. It hints at a certain amount of cloud or mist/fog. The question is what type of cloud is capable of producing wet or dry conditions.

A day in England is generally much like the one before. **

This is a test of persistence of weather which is probably the best forecasting tool for this country. It is certainly better than chance conjecture. Results were based on the same type of airstream for two consecutive days. 234/729 (32)

Between the hours of ten and two
Will show what the day will do. ****

Between twelve and two

ANY DAY

You'll see what the day will do. ****

A cloudy morning bodes a fair afternoon. **

The second adage is Cornish. They contain a large amount of truth. They are subtle and hint of the situation where cumulus or cottonwool clouds form during the morning and by two o'clock (afternoon), which is the usual time of maximum temperature, one can decide by the cloud depth the severity of the showers, if any at all. Also mist, fog or low cloud can be decided to clear or remain by 1400 hours depending on the state of the sky and time of year. For example in winter if fog has not dispersed by early afternoon it will remain all day. Unfortunately the passage of rain belts is not really affected by the time of day.

A wet morning may turn into a dry afternoon.

It's the use of the word "may" which renders the saw as useless.

BIRDS

In west Oxfordshire at the morning bird chorus if they begin and then stop after ten minutes, then resume ten to fifteen minutes later, the day will be unsettled. ****
If they continue throughout the chorus the day will be more settled. ****

If the birds be silent, expect thunder. ****

This first West Oxon saying has the ingredients of truth. Around dawn more birds sing than any other time of the day often lasting 20 to 40 minutes. Daylight is an important factor affecting bird-song. Therefore if dark heavy clouds hang around morning twilight, the dawn chorus of birds can be late or intermittent. Often rain and storms follow such an overcast beginning to the day. The opposite is also often true.

The second saw could be correct as a thunder cloud (see cloud chapter under cumulonimbus cloud) often darkens the daylight, of great consequence in bird song.

If birds begin to whistle in the early morning in winter, it bodes frost. **

In west Oxfordshire if birds play tag in the air, it is a sign of unsettled, thundery weather. ***

If birds that dwell in trees return eagerly to their nest, and leave their feeding grounds early, it is a sign of storms. **

If birds return slowly to their nest, rain will follow. **

If small birds seem to duck and wash in the sand, it is held to be a sign of coming rain. **

When summer birds take their flight, summer goes with them. ***

Land birds are observed to bathe before rain. **

The second West Oxon lore is most probably connected with bird behaviour. Bacon wrote the third law.

BLACKBIRD

When blackbirds sing from the tree tops a fine day is promised but from bottom branches, beware. ***

If a blackbird sings with its tail straight down it is "waiting to shoot the water off". *

One of our most beautiful songsters with numerous voice facets. His warning cry of "pink, pink" and long continuous note at dusk are examples. In the last saw there seems to be no connection between tail down and forthcoming rain. The Blackbird often vocalizes with erratic up and down tail movements.

CRANE

Whenever migrating birds, especially the cranes, take flight earlier than usual, a cold winter may be expected. *

This is a rare migrant to England from Scandinavia.

CROW

When crows go to the water, if they beat it with their wings, throw it over them, and scream, it foreshows storms. *

The continual prating of the crow, chiefly twice or thrice quick calling, indicates rain and stormy weather. *

If the crow hath an interruption in her note, like hiccough, or croak with a kind of swallowing, it signifies wind and rain. *

Crow

The wicked crow aloud foul weather threats. *

If starlings and crows congregate together in large numbers, expect rain. *

The hoarse crow croaks before rain. *

One crow does not make a winter. ***

Bacon penned the first maxim leading the way to the many sayings concerning the Crow. Its most frequent weather asset is its voice, normally a hoarse "kaaah", usually repeated three times in succession. Although the Carrion Crow is a solitary bird it will gather in family parties in summer and in large roosting flocks in autumn and winter. The last saying is difficult to understand. Although the Carrion Crow is involved in partial migration it basically remains in this country (see a similar saying connecting Swallows and summer).

Cuckoo

In East Riding of Yorkshire a cuckoo's frequent calling is a sign of rain. **

Cuckoo

There seems to be no relationship between the Cuckoo's famous call and following rain except for the rain and strong wind theme, common in bird weather lore.

When the cuckoo comes to the bare thorn,
Sell your cow and buy your corn; **
But when she comes to the full bit,
Sell your corn and buy your sheep. ***

Bad for the barley, and good for the corn,
When the cuckoo comes to an empty thorn. **
If the cuckoo sings when the hedge is brown,
Sell thy horse and buy thy corn. **
If the cuckoo sings when the hedge is green,
Keep thy horse and sell thy corn. **

The first and second (Shropshire) sayings are subtle and need to be explained. The male Cuckoo mainly arrives in the second or third weeks of April from its winter quarters in Africa. This time is the normal start of spring and the countryman has blended the cuckoo's arrival and spring together in the rhymes. "Bare thorn" and "empty thorn" refer to a late start to spring; "hedge is brown" is the beginning of an average season and "full bit or "hedge is green" an early spring. Now the state of the season has been established related forecasts are made for following harvests. A good or bad grass harvest in June will affect sheep, horses and cows since this is their basic food. So to "sell your cow" means a poor grass harvest and "buy your sheep" applies to good grass or hay. The barley and corn harvests in August and September are similarly treated. In precis, early spring brings a good grass but poor corn harvest. Average springs forecast bad grass but good corn harvest and late springs allow bad grass but good corn to follow. The six possibilities were tested, all with poor results.

Early spring = good hay harvest	9/20	(45)
Early spring = poor wheat harvest	6/20	(30)
Average spring = bad hay harvest	7/20	(35)

Average spring = good wheat harvest	5/20	(25)
Late spring = good wheat harvest	2/15	(13)
Late spring = bad hay harvest	5/15	(33)

If a cuckoo can be penned up in
an enclosure of hedges and trees,
to prevent it flying away, then
summer will never end. *

Country weather lore believed that if a Cuckoo brought fine weather and was penned or imprisoned in a bush or hedge it was a guarantee to keep the fine conditions. Over a dozen English place names include the word Cuckoo - Cuckoo Bush Hill in Gotham, Notts, which may refer to this ancient activity.

DOTTEREL

When dotterel do first appear,
It shows that frost is very near; *
But when the dotterel do go,
Then you may look for heavy snow. **

This Wiltshire saying applied to the times when these members of the Plover family were widespread throughout England. Now less than 100 pairs nest here arriving in May and leaving in October.

Duck

If ducks or drakes do shake and flutter their wings when they rise, it is a sign of ensuing water. *

When ducks are driving through the burn,
The night the weather will take a turn. *

If a breast bone of a duck be red, it signifyeth a long winter; if white the contrary. *

Divers and ducks prune their feathers before a wind; but geese seem to call down the rain with their importunate cackling. *

If ducks and geese fly backwards and forwards, and continually plunge in water and wash themselves incessantly, wet weather will ensue. *

Fieldfare

The fourth maxim hails from Bacon's pen which like the rest contains little fact. The lore about breastbone colouring can be related to a similar one in the Goose section.

Fieldfare and Redwing

Larger than usual flocks of fieldfare or redwings indicate very cold weather and a long, hard winter. *

The huge flocks of Fieldfare and Redwing appearing from September to April (winter visitors from Northern Europe) have no connection with forecasting weather. When a severe winter occurs the large numbers are vastly reduced.

Finch

When the finch chirps, rain follows. *

Domestic Fowl

If fowls huddle together outside the henhouse instead of going to roost, there will be wet weather. *

Domestic Fowl

If fowls grub in the dust and clap their wings, or if their wings droop, or if they crowd into a house, it indicates rain. *

If fowls roll in the sand,
Rain is at hand. *

Hennes resorting to the perche or rest covered wyth dust declare rayne. *

If the cock moult before the hen,
We shall have weather thick and thin; *
But if the hen moult before the cock,
We shall have weather hard as a block. *

If cocks crow late and early, clapping their wings unusually, *rain is expected.* *

If the cock crows during a down-
pour it will be fine before night. *

If the cock goes crowing to bed,
He will certainly rise with a
watery head. **

Days lengthen a cock's stride
each day after Christmas.

Pea-fowl utter loud cries before
a storm, and select a low perch. **

There is probably little truth in all of the Domestic Fowl sayings. The seventh maxim originates in Devon and the penultimate one provides another way of saying that daylight has passed its shortest span and is now lengthening.

Guinea Fowl

The guinea fowl called the 'come-
back' in Norfolk, is regarded as
an invoker of rain. It often
continues clamorous throughout
the whole of the rainy days. *

Guinea-fowls squall more than
usual before rain. *

This bird was introduced into England in 1550 for domestic usage but is now on the decline.

Water Fowl

Water-fowl meeting and flocking
together, but especially seagulls
and coots flying rapidly to shore
from the sea or lakes, particularly
if they scream, and playing on the
dry land, foreshow wind; and this
is more certain if they do it in
the morning. ****

If the feathers of water-fowl be thicker and stronger than usual, expect a cold winter. *

Among East Coast folk there is a pretty belief, very widely held, that in May, when the sea-fowl are hatching out on the saltings, providence checks the spring tides so that they do not rise high enough to interfere with the birds. These they call by the appropriate name of "bird tides". *

The widely held view that Sea Gulls and Sea Fowl fly inland to shelter from gales and storms raging at sea may contain a certain amount of truth. Fish would be more difficult to acquire in rough seas, and today with water pollution and lack of natural food, many Sea Fowl have taken to feeding and nesting well inland from their coastal habitat. The last East Coast saw is quaint showing one of the many appealing facets of bird weather lore but unfortunately the saying contains fiction not fact.

Goose

Goose

When the goose-bone, exposed to air, turns blue, it indicates rain; when it retains its colour, expect clear weather. *

Breast-bone of goose to dark-coloured after cooking, no genial spring, and vice versa. *

The whiteness of a goose's breast-bone is superstitiously thought to indicate the amount of snow during winter. *

The goose and the gander
Begin to meander;
The matter is plain,
They are dancing for rain. *

Geese flying out to sea is a sign of good weather. ***

Early arrival of winter migrants such as ducks, geese and swans, indicate very cold weather and a long hard winter. **

The first three maxims (the second hails from Lincoln) deal with the colouring of the Goose's breastbone when exposed to air. It states that a dark colour provides harsh weather and a light colour proclaims mild conditions. It is difficult to find the exact connection and is probably lost in time. Possibly the breaking of the "wish-bone" of Domestic Fowl has some relationship. Migratory Geese usually arrive in October.

Marsh Harrier

The marsh harriers, or dunpickles, alight in great numbers on the downs before rain. **

The saying refers to the Marlborough Downs in Wiltshire.

HERON

When a heron stands melancholy on the sand it only denotes rain. *

A heron, when it soars high, so as sometimes to fly above a low cloud, shows wind; but kites flying high show fair weather. ***

When the heron or bittern flies low, the air is gross and thickening into showers. ***

Herons in the evening flying up and down, as if doubtful where to rest, presages some evil-approaching weather. ***

If the heron stand melancholy on the banks, it portends rain. *

If the heron cry in the night as she flies, it presageth wind. ***

The first Bacon and fifth saying presumably refer to the Heron's usual role of waiting in silence ready to strike with its sharp bill at fish, frogs or water vole. Its preying stance is to rest on one leg with half-closed eyes, hunching its head between its shoulders. The Heron high or low in flight does not seem to have any pre-knowledge of weather.

JACKDAW

When three daws are seen on St Peter's vane together,
Then we are sure to have bad weather. *

St Peter's church, like the saw, comes from Norwich.

KINGFISHER

A dead kingfisher hung up by the legs even inside a house is said to turn its beak to windward. *

Kingfisher

A foolish but interesting saying.

Magpie

For anglers in spring it is always unlucky to see single magpies; but two may always be regarded as a favourable omen. And the reason is, that in cold and stormy weather one magpie

alone leaves the nest in search of food, while the other one remains sitting with the eggs or young ones; but when two go out together, it is only when the weather is mild and warm, and favourable for fishing. *

Magpies flying three or four together and uttering harsh cries predict windy weather. *

When Magpie eggs are incubating it's the lonely female that stays on the nest (for about 21 days in April or May). After this both parents are seen flying together during the 28-day feeding period of their young. So in April to June the pattern is naturally set for single or pair Magpies proving there is no relationship with cold or mild weather. From the second saw the only time the bird is seen in threes or fours is when it partakes in ceremonial gatherings - otherwise they fly alone or in pairs.

MARTIN

When martins appear winter has broken. ****

No killing frost after martins. ****

Martins fly low before and during rainy weather. ***

The Sand Martin arrives at the end of March, the House Martin not till the end of April. Winter is nearly over by mid-April but not all frosts. Apart from frost hollows, like Rickmansworth in Herts, which can have night ground frosts nearly the whole year through, May is the last month for general frost. If killing frosts mean severe air frosts then the second is true.

MOORHEN

When moorhens fly at night to a distance from their usual water, and utter discontent cries during their flight, expect rain. ***

When moorhens build their nests high above water it is the sign of a wet summer and vice versa. *

The last maxim is similar to one in the Swan section.

Owl

In England the owl's calling heralds hailstorms. *

The screeching owl indicates cold or storm. *

If owls hoot at night expect fair weather. *

The whooping of an owl was thought by the ancients to betoken a change of weather, from fair to wet, or wet to fair. But with us, the owl when it whoops clearly and freely, generally shows fair weather, especially in winter. *

An owl hooting quietly in a storm indicates fair weather, and also when it hoots quietly by night in winter. *

If owls scream during bad

weather, there will be a change. *

The dirt-bird sings, and we
shall have rain. *

There is little or no truth in the Owl's hoot or cry leading to ensuing weather. The famous screech is from the Barn Owl; the eerie hoot (mentioned in the third Bacon saying) comes from the Short and Long-Eared Owl but more probably from the Tawny Owl. The Little Owl was only introduced into Northants in the late 19th century so can be discounted as Owl bird weather lore is much older. As most Owls are nocturnal hunters they are frequent night callers producing hoots and shrieks which are connected with hunting and anger at breeding time - not weather.

PARROT

Clamorous as a parrot against
rain. *

Parrots whistling indicate rain. *

It is said that parrots and
canaries dress their feathers
and are wakeful the evening
before a storm. *

These saws relate to the caged or domestic Parrot. Shakespeare was responsible for the first one.

PEACOCK

When the peacock loudly bawls,
Soon will have both rain and
squalls. ***

If peacocks cry in the night,
there is rain to fall. ***

The strutting peacock yawling
'gainst the rain. ***

When the peacock's distant voice
you hear,
Are you in want of rain? ***

Rejoice, 'tis almost here.
And with his voice prognosticates
all weathers. *

The Peacock calls throughout the day and night. When dark it has a frightening voice which, like the Green Woodpecker, can be heard louder in a strong wind often prevailing before rain. It seems unusual that the four sayings apply to the call and not the Peacock's famous fan of bright coloured feathers so striking when fully displayed.

PHEASANT

If pheasants roost late in
evening and are up with the sun
in the morning, a good day is
promised but if early to perch
and to feed, the weather will
break up. ***

Known to have been in England for over 900 years, this most colourful of birds (the cock Pheasant), unfortunately has only one piece of weather lore.

PIGEON

Pigeons wash before rain. *

Doves or pigeons coming later home to the dove house in the evening than ordinary, is a token of rain. ****

If pigeons return home slowly, the weather will be wet. ****

These maxims are common to many bird species. There may be a plausible link with weather. In Pigeon racing it was observed that faster return times occurred on cloudless days. The Pigeon was using the sun for navigating and positioning, but on a cloudy day when a layer obscured the sun above the bird's flight level, slow times prevailed and sometimes even loss of life. In the last saying a Pigeon late in returning to the medieval dovecote would have miscalculated possibly because of increase in cloud cover, often a forerunner of rain.

PLOVER

When the plovers fly high and then low, making their plaintive cry, expect fine weather. ****

Similar in meaning to the Rook weather lore.

RAVEN

If a raven stalks about, it only denotes rain. *

When the crow or rayen gapith, agaynst the sonne, in somer, heate foloweth. *

Ravens, when they croak continuously, denote wind; but if the croaking is interrupted or stifled, or at longer intervals, they show rain. *

When ravens sit in the sun, expect fine weather to last. *

If ravens croak three or four times and flap their wings, fine weather is expected. *

If a raven is observed in the morning soaring round and round at a great height and making a hoarse croaking sound the weather will be fine. **

If the raven makes several different cries in winter, it is a sign of a storm. *

The first and third prophesies are from the prolific pen of Bacon. The Raven, the largest of the Crow family, used to be a familiar common bird in this country but has now been driven to South-West and Northern England, Wales and Scotland. It is renowned for deep croaking or "pruk-pruk-pruk" but more for its flying acrobatics. In spring Raven pairs tumble in the air, rolling sideways, nosediving and even flying upside-down. Unfortunately there seems to be no relationship between the Raven's antics and his prowess as a weather forecaster.

ROBIN

If the robin sings in the bush,
Then the weather will be coarse; ***

ROBIN

If the robin sings on the barn,
Then the weather will be warm. **

On a summer evening, though the weather may be in an unsettled state, the robin sometimes takes his stand on the topmost twig or housetop singing cheerfully and sweetly - a primose of succeeding fine days. *** *Sometimes, though dry and warm, he may be seen melancholy, chirping and brooding in a bush, or low in a hedge: this promises the reverse of his merry lay and exalted station.* ***

If robins are seen near houses, it is a sign of rain. *

Robins indicate the approach of spring. * *Long and loud singing of robins in the morning denotes rain.* * *Robins will perch on the topmost branches of trees and whistle when a storm is approaching.* **

Robins sing from hedge or bush, storms are near; when they sing in the open, good weather is expected. ***

The above weather lore is mainly confined to the Robin singing in high trees and barns delivering us future warmth (although the fifth saw has the opposite meaning) or chirping in low branches predicting rain or cold weather. One must remember both the male and female Robin look very similar uttering their famous "tic, tic", "tsweee" or "tsit" throughout the year (except in July when moulting) mainly in territorial defence. However there is a time in mid-winter, when most of the Robin weather lore applies, certainly in the first East Anglian saying, when the female hunts the male. While the cock sings in the high trees, the hen remains in the undergrowth hoping to be accepted as a mate after a few weeks. Although there seems to be little connection between the Robin and weather, one cannot help but feel joyful and friendliness towards the bird when he suddenly appears with his distinctive redbreast.

I'm sure the countryman would wholeheartedly agree with the choice of the Robin as Britain's national bird.

Rook

When birds of long flight, rooks, swallows, or others, hang about home, and fly up and down or low, rain may be expected. ***

When rooks seem to drop in their flight, as if pierced by a shot, it is said to foreshadow rain. ****

This 'tumbling' of rooks is amongst the best-known signs of rain in places where those birds are found. ****

When rooks fly sporting high in air,
It shows that windy storms are near. ***

If rooks stay at home, or return in the middle of the day, it will *rain; if they go far abroad, it will be fine.* *

It is believed in some parts of Yorkshire that when rooks congregate on the dead branches, there will be rain before night; if *
they stand on the live branches, the day will be fine. *

Rooks will not leave their nests in the morning before a storm. ***

If rooks feed in the streets of a village, it shows that a storm is near at hand. *

If rooks or blackbirds sit on the top-most branches looking in one direction (mainly in afternoons) for long periods, bad weather can be expected from that direction. *

If rooks fly low, it means rain; if they feed busily and hurry about together, a storm is likely; if they sit about on fences, or dart down and reel about, expect wind. *

If rooks fly from their nests in a straight flight around dawn, a dry day will occur. ****

If rooks twist and turn on leaving their nest, rough weather is approaching, ****
if they stay by their nest, screaming raucously, gales are on the way. *

When rooks are late leaving the rookery in the morning and hurry about feeding on the roadside, it will rain. ***

High rook nests mean a good summer. *

Rook

Rook weather lore is prolific and varied with the fifth maxim hailing from Devon. Their very advanced communial life has been the foundation for much country belief, such as the supposed Rook parliaments and Rook circles sitting in judgement on criminal Rooks. Complete understanding of Rook's social rules is lacking. Certainly the "peck order" or the hierarchy position where the highest in the social order eats first is comprehended (probably evolution has allowed the strongest to survive in times of food shortage. The real reason for the Rook's autumn tumbling, twisting and diving display in free air is unknown. The sixth Yorkshire maxim about dead and live branches is intriguing, probably an older non-meteorological origin to it. The seventh saying originates in Cornwall; eighth from Durham and the remainder hail from West Oxon. With his famous continuous tree-top "cawing" in the rookeries and acrobatic aerial display no wonder much Rook weather lore has emerged.

This famous West Oxon saw about rookeries positioned high in trees foretelling a good summer is of course based on the myth that the Rook can foresee no storms or gales which would demolish the nests. The truth is different. Rookeries are normally permanent features and a pair of Rooks use the same nest each year adding material and repairing it. If winter gales did destroy the rookery then new nests would be sited where tree branches were strongest whether high or low.

Seagull

Seagulls in the field indicate a storm from the south-east. *

Sea-mews early in the morning making a gaggling more than ordinary foretoken stormy and blustery weather. *

When sea-mews appear in unwanted numbers, expect rain and high south-west winds. *

Seagull, seagull, sit on the sand;
It's never good weather when you're on the land. ****

The Sea-Mew is a general name meaning Gull. Strong onshore

SEAGULL

gales often make Sea-Gulls venture inland for food, indeed some Gulls remain there most of their life.

SKYLARK

When larks fly high and sing long, expect fine weather. ****

Field-larks congregating in flocks indicate severe cold. *

When larks rise before they sing at dawn, with an overcast sky, expect rain; but when they fly ****
very high, singing as they rise, expect a fine day. ****

If the skylark hovers and glides during its descent, the weather will remain fine, but if it drops straight to ground it will rain. ***

The songs but mainly the flying antics of the Lark dominate the sayings. In the second saw Skylarks only gather in flocks to feed and migrate. The third saying is a sharp and accurate record of the bird. It can sustain its warble up to five minutes most frequently when flying high, almost out of sight. It's the only English bird to sing while ascending and descending vertically.

Sparrow

The chirping of the sparowe in
the morning signifyeth rayne. *

If the hedge sparrow is heard, before the grape-vine is putting forth its buds, it is said that a good crop is in store. *

Sparrows chirping excessively as a sign of forthcoming rain (there are many similar bird weather saws) may have some deep hidden significance but on the face of it possess little truth.

STARLING

If starlings and crows congregate together in large numbers, expect rain. *

Starlings roost or sleep at night in flocks numbering thousands. Who hasn't seen and heard the deafening mass blackening the sky as they follow their familiar flight path in the countryside to some safe wood, to return along the same route the following morning. It is such a daily routine, weather forecasting can hardly play any part.

SWALLOW

In England swallows flying low foretell rain. ***

Swallow

When swallows fleet, soar high,
and sport in air,
He told us that the welkin would
be clear. ****

If swallows touch the water as
they fly, rain approaches. *

If there are many more swifts
than swallows in the spring,
expect a hot and dry summer. *

Low o'er the grass the swallow
wings; 'twill surely rain. *

If swallows fly high the weather
will be fine. ****

Swallows high,
Staying dry. ****
Swallows low,
Wet 'twill blow. *

The majority of the Swallow weather lore are confined to the bird's flight - high flying predicts good weather, low soaring rain. The Swallow is a migrant remaining in the country from late March to October returning to South Africa for our winter. The saying "one Swallow does not make a summer" (to be found in the summer season section) is true because at the end of March and during April they arrive in ones and twos, only coming in force from mid to late April. Presumably when

Swallows fly low they are avoiding the strong winds aloft (which often bring rain) and when they decide to venture up to high levels the wind is light (usually a sign of settled conditions). But it must be emphasized the evidence points to the Swallow experiencing only *present* weather conditions.

SWAN

If the swan flies against the wind, it is a certain indication of a hurricane within twenty-four hours, generally within twelve. *

The swan is said to build its nest high before floods come up but lower when there will not be unusual rain. *

Swans are hatched in thunder-storms . *

There is no doubt that swans have an instinctive prescience of floods, for it is a well-known fact that before heavy rains the birds whose home is on the banks of the Thames raise their nests so as to save their eggs from being chilled by the water. *

The maxim from the Thames Valley about the Swan or Moorhen building her nest high in the reeds well above water level in anticipation of wet weather to come is a pure myth. The same applies to the low built nest and follow up of fine weather. The third intriguing Hampshire adage is difficult in finding a suitable explanation, unless the hatching time, which is May or June, vaguely corresponds to the most thundery month of July.

SWIFT

When there are many more swifts than swallows in the spring, expect a hot and dry summer. *

Swift

When swifts and swallows fly high, eating insects, the day will be fine; although sometimes this occurs during thundery weather. ***

This late migrant (arriving from late April) virtually remains flying all the time. The countryman also called it the "Devil Bird" because it flew around houses screaming during late spring and early summer evenings. With flying insects the general rule is that any good breeze or strong wind will allow them to rise to reasonable heights. They will manoeuvre near the ground in calm or gentle conditions (often associated with temperature inversions - a shallow layer above the ground where temperature increases with height). The Swift therefore will feed on flying insects depending on wind profile - often a good strength foretells rain, calm denotes settled weather (these are in opposition to the second maxim and many other sayings).

Thrush

The missel thrush or the storm cock sings particularly loud and long before rain. **

When the thrush sings at sunset, a fair day will follow. **

When this bird perches itself

Thrush

upon the topmost bough of a tree
and remains there for some time,
singing loudly, expect rain. *

Again most of the lore is concerned with the famous Thrush voice. In the first and third adages the Missel Thrush (named after its fondness of mistletoe berries) is called the Storm Cock because it sits in the topmost tree branches singing its loud harsh "churr" quickly followed by a sharp "click" through all kinds of weather even raging January storms. So instead of presaging rain it remains oblivious in song to all severe weathers.

The second maxim probably refers to the Song Thrush, aptly named, having a much more wholesome song than the Missel Thrush. He begins vocalizing in January (unless severe weather prevents it) for the whole year except for a break July to September.

Titmouse

The titmouse fortells cold, if
crying, 'Pincher'. *

The saw-like note of the great
titmouse fortells rain. *

The Great Titmouse, better known today as the Great Tit, has a call in the spring like "tea-cher, tea-cher" or "pincher, pincher". His other song sounds like the sharpening of a saw.

TURKEY

Turkeys perched in trees and refusing to descend indicate snow. *

Turkeys were introduced to England in 1521 by Turkish traders (hence the name) from North America.

WAXWING

The arrival of the waxwing from
Scandinavia means a severe winter. **

This is one of the "finds" of weather lore. For centuries the erratic arrival of large numbers of Waxwings from Scandinavia in September to our East Coast was the excuse for countrymen to call the forthcoming season a "Waxwing Winter". The reason for the huge flocks is that Waxwings eat mainly berries, especially the rowanberry. A failure of the latter in Northern Europe leads to the mass migration of Waxwings to this country. In 1679 they arrived here and also for four consecutive years 1956-9. Unfortunately severe winters did not follow. The reason for poor Scandinavian rowanberry harvests lies with poor weather in seasons *prior* to the sad harvest.

WOODCOCK

Cuckoo oats and woodcock hay
Make a farmer run away.

The saying refers to the migrating arrival date of the Cuckoo (second to third week in April) and the Woodcock (October to November) from across the North Sea. By these dates the farmer should have sowed his spring oat seed and gathered the after crop of summer hay.

WOODPECKER

The green woodpecker's
frequent calling is a
sign of coming rain. ***

When woodpeckers are much
heard, rain will follow. ***

In Shropshire the green wood-
pecker is called 'storm-cock' ***

The country people doe divine
of raine by their cry. ***

In Shropshire the call of the
heigh-ho forbodes rain. ***

When the woodpecker leaves,
a hard winter is expected. *

When woodpeckers peck low on
the trees, expect warm weather. *

The yaffel, or green wood-
pecker, cries at the approach
of rain, and is described as
'laughing in the sun, because
the rain is coming.' ***

The bird is famouse for its cry of "ha-ha-ha" or "hellew-hellew-hellew" which can at times sound like laughter, so country people nicknamed him the Yaffle. The third and fifth saws are from Shropshire and the reason why the Green Woodpecker is also known as the Rain or Storm Bird is probably because his call can be more clearly heard in strong winds, which often precede rain. The origin may go back further. In Continental bird lore it is said that the Green Woodpecker refused to hollow out rivers and pools at the time of the Creation so was punished by God to drink only rain water.

ANIMALS

When animals seek sheltered places instead of spreading over their usual range, an unfavourable change is probable. ***

If animals crowd together, rain will follow. ***

When animals between sunrise and eight to nine o'clock in the morning assemble in bunches or in one corner of a field, expect a very unsettled day. ***
If after this time they are spread out all over the field, expect a fair day. ***

The last saw comes from West Oxfordshire. An extensive observational programme has been carried out by the author in Yorkshire in the summer of 1980. It mainly covered cows and sheep. The figures and close studies showed that these animals *do* adjust their behaviour pattern to different types of weather *after* the change has taken place and not *before*. For example cows did huddle or crowd together during gale force winds and moderate or heavy rain, but also in fine settled conditions.

ASS AND DONKEY

If asses having their ears downward and forward, and rub against walls, rain is approaching. *

If asses bray more frequently than usual, it foreshows rain. *

Hark! I hear the asses bray;
We shall have some rain today. *

It is time to stack your hay and corn
When the old donkey blows his horn.

Rutland provided the third saw. The pattern of fanciful but untrue weather prophesies continues.

BAT

If bats abound and are vivacious, fine weather may be expected. ***

It will rain if bats cry much or fly into the house. **

If bats fly abroad after sunset, fair weather. ***

When bats appear very early in the evening, expect fair weather; but when they utter *** *plaintive cries, rain may be expected.* **

The favourite food of the Common Bat is the moth which when frequent at night usually signifies fine conditions. Since the bat is a nocturnal creature hunting at night, it uses its very highly developed ultrasonic system. A high-pitched squeak is given which rapidly bounces off objects including the moth and is received instantaneously by the bat. The method helps him to determine the size, speed and distance of his prey. The system is also used for navigation. So excess numbers and bat cries point to abundant moths which of course in turn refers to settled weather conditions.

BULL

If bulls lick their hoofs or kick about, expect much rain. *

If the bull lead the van in going to pasture, rain must be expected; but if he is careless, and allows the cows to precede him, the weather is uncertain. *

In the second saw the "van" is a cow herd. Sometimes bulls lead or hang behind - they are unpredictable beasts. Both sayings have little to offer.

CAT

The cardinal point to which a cat turns and washes her face after a rain, shows the direction from which the wind will blow. *

Cat

*When a cat sneezes, it is a
a sign of rain.* *

*When the cat lies on its brain,
Then it is going to rain.* *

*An old woman promised a fine
day on the morrow because the
cat's skin looked bright.* *

*When the cat scratches the
table legs, a change is coming.* *

*While rain depends, the pensive
cat gives o'er
Her frolics, and pursues her
tail no more.* *

*When cats wipe their jaws with
their feet, it is a sign of
rain, and especially when they
put their paws over their ears
in wiping.* *

*If the cat washes her face
o'er the ear,
Tis a sign of weather'll be
fine and clear.* *

The third adage hails from Kent and last from Northern England. Unfortunately all of these well-known habits of the feline bear absolutely no relationship to forthcoming weather. In fact the last two saws have opposite meanings.

Cockle

*Cockles, it is said, have more
gravel sticking to their shells
before a tempest.* *

Again here is further falsity.

Cow

*When cows fail their milk,
expect storm and cold weather.* ***

Cow

When cows bellow in the evening, expect snow that night. If they stop and shake their feet, or refuse to go to pasture in the morning, or when they low and gaze at the sky, or lick their forefeet, or lie on the right side, or rub themselves against posts, or lie down early in the day, it indicates rain to come. **

Cows like any other animal are sensitive to cold, gales, wet and snow. They will avoid such hindrances by sheltering, huddling and generally shunning such horrid weather. A close Yorkshire study of cows by the author (1980) showed that although they did react to weather type there was no indication that they could forecast it even as little as one to two hours ahead. The above maxim covers most of the ridiculous relationships between a cow's antics and subsequent weather. The first line unfortunately excludes milk and thunderstorms but see in Thunderstorm chapter.

When cattle lie down in light rain, it will soon pass. **

Cows and sheep lie down before rain to keep a dry place to lie on. ***

Cow

Wiltshire provides the first saw. The very famous theme of cows lying down indicating rain to follow because they are keeping a dry patch is partly true. Cows stand to eat grass and sit to chew the cud. They will sit in any type of weather although very rarely in heavy rain or very wet grass. The Yorkshire test shows variable results with the cow more prone to lie down in dry overcast conditions (68 percent) and sheep in moderate or heavy rain (44 percent).

Cows lying down in:-

Moderate or heavy rain	99/261	(38)
Slight rain	39/165	(24)
Dry overcast weather	153/234	(65)
Partly cloudy weather with sunny intervals	0/99	(0)
A clear sky	81/225	(36)

Sheep lying down in:-

Moderate or heavy rain	72/165	(44)
Slight rain	54/237	(23)
Dry overcast weather	6/405	(1)
A clear sky	27/414	(7)

When cattle remain on hilltops,
fine weather to come. **

When cows sniff the air and
walk down hill towards the
farmyard, then rain or storm
will follow. **

Derbyshire provides the first maxim. Again cows feed on high or low ground depending on the *current* weather conditions.

When cows huddle in the corner
of a field and stand with their
tails to the wind, rain is
expected. ***

This well-known behaviour pattern of the cow, especially the tail against a cold or wet gale force wind (to protect her sensitive head), are conditions of present weather. Cows seem to huddle a lot but less so in dry sunny weather. The Yorkshire test defined "huddled" as two cows within a maximum range of three body lengths of each other. Results with cows near hedges produced sporadic hopeless figures. In fact the availability of grass seems to be the obvious reason.

Cows huddled in:-		
Moderate or heavy rain	121/261	(46)
Slight rain	84/165	(51)
Dry overcast weather	112/234	(48)
Partly cloudy weather with sunny intervals	30/99	(30)
A clear sky	87/225	(39)
Cows near a hedge in:-		
Moderate or heavy rain	90/261	(34)
Slight rain	51/165	(31)
Dry overcast weather	36/234	(15)
Partly cloudy weather with sunny intervals	48/99	(48)
A clear sky	12/225	(5)

He taught us erst the heifer's tail to view;
When struck aloft that showers would straight ensue. *

When a cow tries to scratch its ear,
It means a shower is very near. *

When cows stampede with their tails in the air it tells of forthcoming rain and thunder. ***

The number of adages concerned with the cow's tail and ensuing weather probably stems from the warble fly. This horrible little creature lays its eggs in the cow's hide during warm humid weather, which can sometimes precede thunderstorms or heavy showers.

Dog

Dogs making holes in the ground, howling when anyone goes out, eating grass in the morning, or refusing meat, are said to indicate coming rain. *

When dogs eat grass, it will be rainy. *

If spaniels sleep more than usual, it foretells wet weather. *

Dog

If dogs roll on the ground and scratch, or become drowsy and stupid, it is a sign of rain. *

If dogs do much barking in the night the weather is about to change. *

One of the most popular dog weathers saws is the eating of grass to be followed by rain. Dogs frequently eat long grass mainly for medicinal purposes. They can hear sounds beyond the human receiving range. So in thundery conditions the high pitch of static and certain thunder tones can be detected about one to two hours before a thunderstorm is imminent. The other dog activities described above are due to natural and obvious causes.

Fish

When the wind is in the east,
then the fishes do bite the least;
When the wind is in the west,
then the fishes do bite the best;
When the wind is in the north,
then the fishes do come forth
When the wind is in the south,
It blows the bait into the fish's mouth. ****

Fish

If, during damp weather, fish bite readily and swim near the surface, an improvement is likely, or, if it remains cloudy, it will be quiet rather that windy. **

Fishes rise more than usual at the approach of a storm. In some parts of England, they are said not to bite so well before rain. **

When fish bite readily and swim near the surface, rain may be expected: they become inactive just before thunder showers. **

Fish bite the least
With wind in the east. ****

Fish can forecast cold weather for they keep to the cooler, lower water and are reluctant to take hook. **

Supposedly there is a relationship between the biting rate of the freshwater fish and the subsequent weather. Again, fish certainly react to water temperature change but there is such a time lag between say the start of a cold easterly wind and the cooling of the river water by 0.1°C that it is often hours before the fish's biting rate is reduced. If conditions are normal then the biting is also normal but a prolonged South or East wind will eventually increase or decrease it. Raindrops on a water surface reoxygenate the water resulting in the fish becoming more active increasing the biting rate.

When trout refuse bait or fly,
There ever is a storm a - nigh. *

If eels are very lively, it
is a sign of rain. *

When pike lie on the bed of a
stream quietly, expect rain or
wind. *

Good fish weather lore but contains little truth.

FOX

When foxes bark and utter shrill
cries expect a violent tempest
of wind and rain within three
days. *

An interesting but untrustworthy maxim.

GOAT

The goat will utter her
peculiar cry before rain. *

If goats and sheep quit their
pasture with reluctance, it
will rain the next day. **

Flocks of goats graze down the
mountains before the approach
of a storm, and upwards before
fair weather. ***

Should you notice a goat graze
with his head to the wind,

expect a fine day; but if he crops with tail to the wind, look out for rain during the day. *

The reader will notice the same pattern of weather saws for goats, sheep and cows - presumably for all domestic grazing animals. The same invalid relationship equally applies here.

HARE

When hares move from low to high ground, very heavy rain and floods are expected. *

Another high to low ground for bad weather theory.

HEDGEHOG

Observe which way the hedgehog builds her nest,
To front the north or south, or east or west;
For if tis true that common people say,
The wind will blow the quite contrary way. **

The hedgehog commonly has two holes or vents in his den or cave, the one towards the south and the other towards the north; and look which one of them he stops - thence will great storms and winds follow. **

Similar maxims can be found in the Mice and Mole sections. Again it is dubious whether such operations are related to warm and cold weather.

HORSE

If horses stretch out their necks and sniff the air, rain will ensue. *

Horses sweating in the stable is a sign of rain. *

If they start more than ordinary and are restless and uneasy, or if they assemble in the corner of a field with their heads to leeward, expect rain. **

If young horses do rub their backs against the ground, it is a sign of great drops of rain to follow. *

Horses and mules, if very lively without apparent cause, indicate cold. **

When horses lie on their heads upon the ground, it is a sign of rain. *

All six sayings have no truth in their weather connections. As in the Cat section, the various horse's actions are due to natural causes or health reasons.

LEECH

A leech confined in a bottle of water is always agitated when a change of weather is about to take place. Before high winds it moves about with much celerity. Previous to slight rain or snow it creeps to the top of the bottle, but soon sinks; but if the rain or wind is likely to be of long duration, the leech remains a longer time at the surface. If thunder approaches, the leech starts about in an agitated and convulsive manner. **

LEECH

The Medicinal Leech *(Hirudo Medicinalis)* used by old-style apothecaries for sucking human blood was often agile when placed in water. This observation inspired a certain Dr George Merryweather (a most appropriate name), a general practitioner of Whitby, North Yorkshire, to conceive an apparatus for forecasting tempests. He described the invention seen in the figure as "an atmospheric Electromagnetic Telegraph, conducted by Animal Instinct. The Tempest Prognosticator - two words expressive enough to all foreigners to understand." The illustration is from his original machine exhibited at London's Great Exhibition of 1851 expecting that "our Whitby pigmy temples" would be distributed all over England.

The machine (a copy is on view in the Whitby museum) consisted of 12-pint bottles of clear glass distributed around the base of a circular wooden stand. At the top was a bell surrounded by 12 hammers. Each bottle with a metal tube in its neck had a piece of whale bone and wire attached to a small chain which in turn was connected to the upper hammers. Then "into each bottle was poured rainwater to the height of an inch and a half, and a leech was placed into every bottle, - when influenced by the electromagnetic state of the atmosphere a number of the leeches ascended into the tubes; in doing so they dislodged the whalebone and caused the bell to ring." Dr Merryweather was so convinced of the leech's prognostic powers that he besought the Government to establish leech-warning stations, which needless to say were turned down.

MOUSE

If mice run about more than
usual, wet weather may be
expected. **

When the field mouse makes its
burrow with the opening to the
south, it expects a severe
winter; when to the north, it
apprehends much rain. *

The first saw is similar to the Rat saying. Wiltshire comes up with the last adage and is identical in meaning to one of the Hedgehog maxims. A Field Mouse to purposely build his home entrance facing south for warm weather or north for cold seems highly unlikely. The convenience of food and lie of the ground are more likely factors.

MOLE

Moles plying their works, in
undermining the earth, foreshows
rain; but if they do forsake
their trenches and creep above
ground in summertime, it is a
sign of hot weather; but if all
of a sudden they do foresake
the valleys and low grounds, it

foreshows a flood near at hand; but their coming into meadows presages fair weather, and for certain no floods. *

Previous to the setting in of winter the mole prepares a sort of basin, forming it in a bed of clay, which will hold about a quart. In this basin a great quantity of worms is deposited; and, in order to prevent their escape, they a partly mutilated, but not so much as to kill them. On these worms the moles feed in the winter months. When these basins are few in number, the following winter will be mild. **

If moles throw up their earth more than usual, rain is indicated. *

When the mole throws up fresh earth during a frost, it will thaw in less than forty-eight hours. *

When moles dig holes as usual but build no hills on the surface, a long dry spell is expected. *

It is almost tempting to believe some of these weather saws, they appear to include undeniable facts. Unfortunately there is little truth in the mole's prowess as a weather forecaster. This likeable "gentleman in velvet" is a loner with a great appetite for earthworms. His nest chamber or "fortress" is joined by numerous escape and feed tunnels. The key to the meaning of the saying is the availability of the earthworm. The adult mole is constantly on the move, capable of devouring 50 or 60 worms or grubs each day. If he leaves off hunting for 10 hours death is certain. So if previous seasons have produced an excess or deficite of worms appropriate methods have to be employed by the mole. The second saw is perfectly true - the mole always stores worms for winter. In fact *during* a very cold winter, since he does not hibernate, he burrows deeper into the ground, as do other grubs and worms, thus the same feeding pattern continues but at a lower depth.

PIG

Hogs crying and running
unquietly up and down with hay
or litter in their mouths
foreshadows a storm to be
near at hand. *

When pigs carry straw to
their sties, bad weather
may be expected. *

When pigs carry sticks,
The clouds will play tricks;
When they lie in the mud,
No fears of a flood. *

Hogs rubbing themselves in
winter indicate a thaw. *

The usual set of animal quirks related to weather. All are false being caused by medical, hunger or other obvious reasons.

Swine are so terrified and
disturbed when the wind is
getting up, that countrymen
say that this animal alone
"sees the wind", and that it
must be frightful to look at. *

This Lord Bacon pig (it had to happen!) weather maxim renders further investigation. There is obviously little truth in the adage but it is interesting to wonder how the relationship between pigs and winds evolved. Is the phrase "pigs might fly" connected?

RABBIT

When rabbits are out at strange
times of day rain is expected. *

No meteorological connections occur here.

RAT

If rats are more restless than usual, rain is at hand. *

Although rats are experts of conditioning, the "more restless" habit is really old hat.

SHEEP

If old sheep turn their backs towards the wind, and remain so for some time, wet and windy weather is coming. *

When sheep turn their backs to the wind, it is a sign of rain. *

Sheep

Sheep act similarly to cows in that they are susceptible to adverse weather conditions. It was closely observed by the author (in Yorkshire 1980) that sheep reacted only to *present* weather types.

All shepherds agree in saying
that before a storm comes sheep
become frisky, leap and butt
or "box" each other. *

If sheep gambol and fight, or
retire to shelter, it presages
a change in the weather. *

Again excess or lack of sheep activity seemed to occur *during* a particular weather condition.

Old sheep are said to eat more
greedily before a storm, and
sparingly before a thaw. When
they leave the high grounds, and
bleat much in the evening and
during the night, severe weather
is expected. In winter, when
they feed down the hill, a snow
storm is looked for; when they
feed up the burn, wet weather
is near. ***

If sheep feed uphill in the
morning, a sign of fine weather. ***

When a moorland shepherd meets
his sheep on a winter's night
coming down from the hill-tops
(where they prefere to sleep)
he knows that a storm is brewing. ***

When sheep begin to go up the
mountains, shepherds say it
will be a fine day. ***

Derbyshire provides the second adage. Sheep do feed on hills or in valleys when warm or cold weather prevails. It was observed that at least 12-24 hours of the appropriate weather had to occur before sheep took up their relevant residence. Not forgetting that areas of new grass would also influence their move.

When sheep do huddle by tree
and bush,
Bad weather is coming with
wind and slush. ***

Sheep huddle together, more in wet weather than dry, Their sheltering against fences or walls in foul weather is a fallacy.

Sheep next to hedge in:-		
Moderate or heavy rain	21/165	(13)
Slight rain	16/237	(7)
Dry overcast weather	21/405	(5)
A clear sky	81/414	(20)
Sheep huddling in:-		
Moderate or heavy rain	57/165	(35)
Slight rain	78/237	(33)
Dry overcast weather	102/405	(25)
A clear sky	54/414	(13)

In a long cold spell, pregnant
sheep will hang on to their
lambs, with rain and higher
temperatures they all lamb
at once.

Lambing is in full swing in February. On the whole ewes drop their offspring after the normal 145-150-day gestation period. February can have cold snowy or warm dry days.

SQUIRREL

When squirrels lay in a large
supply of nuts, expect a cold
winter; but: **
When he eats them on the tree,
Weather as warm as warm can be. **

This adage is like the "red berries, severe winter" theme. Abundant nuts due to a previous good weather winter, spring and summer are the reasons for the squirrel's avarice.

WORM

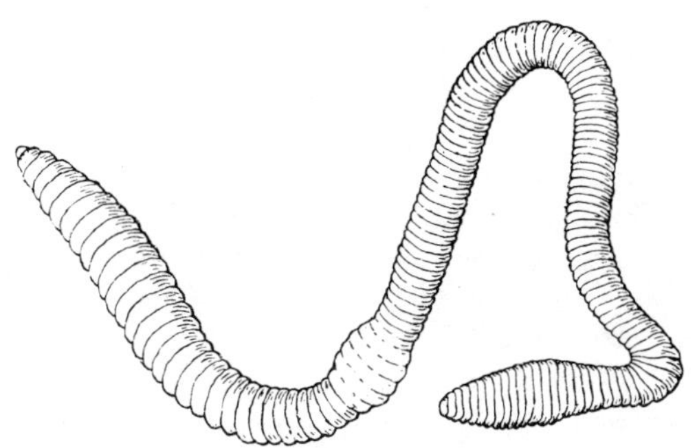

If many earthworms appear, it presages rain. **

What reader has not seen earthworms appear at night under a heavy dew on the lawn and when digging to find them for fishing bait. They are always found in moist soil. The earthworm experiences 75-90 percent of its body weight made up of water so consequently has to keep to wet earth. But the main reason for the night appearance of many earthworms is temperature and light. They are most active when the soil temperature ranges 2-10.5°C with rain to have fallen within the previous four days. It also possesses a diffuse light sense which attracts it to *dim* light. All these factors account for the above saw which contains no forecast value.

When the common garden worm forms many "casts", rain or frost will follow according to the season of the year. Where they appear in the daytime, expect rain; but when early in the evening, it indicates a mild night with heavy dew and two days fine weather. **

Worms descend to a great depth before either a long drought or a severe frost. **

The earthworm descends low into the ground because of *present* soil conditions. That is it becomes too dry with near-surface temperature falling low.

REPTILES

Almost any of the reptiles which pass the winter in a semi-dormant condition show signs by their attitude when any marked weather change ensues.

This is perfectly true. Semi-dormant reptiles on encountering long periods of warm weather in winter or early spring will normally react as if official spring had arrived.

FROG

Croaking frogs in spring
We'll be three times frozen in. *

Male frogs croak at night in March to attract females. So chances are they could be frozen three or more times. All frogs make noises which mainly relate to social intercourse.

The louder the frog, the more the rain. *

If frogs make a noise in the time of cold rain, warm dry weather will follow.

Noise often travels quicker in stable windy conditions, often to be experienced before rain, so a male frog's croak would carry far (see Sound chapter). The second adage seems ludicrous.

Yellow frogs are accounted a good sign in a hay field, probably as indicating fine weather. *

If frogs, instead of yellow, appear russet green, it will presently rain. *

The Common male Frog is olive grey or brown and female a light buff to reddish olive, but both can to some extent vary their shades according to the colour of the background. So the reason is due to camouflage not meteorology.

Great quantities of frogs, small and great, appearing at unusual times and in unusual places, presage great dearth of corn or great sickness to follow: where they appear. **

Female frogs produce thousands of tadpoles but as easy prey to other animals, birds and fish, only a steady number survive as frogs around June (three months of evolution from spawn to frog). So a great quantity shows some upset in the natural sequence.

Tree-frogs piping during rain indicate a continuance. *

The green tree-frog becomes very unquiet before rain. *

Tree-frogs crawl up to the branches of trees before a change of weather. *

The last saw is interesting. In olden times, especially in Germany, the Common or Green Tree Frog was kept as an animal barometer in tall glass cylinders with tiny ladders inside and water at the bottom. When the tree frog sat on the top rung it was a sign of "set fair" weather - to return to the water signified an approaching thunderstorm. Like the leech the tree frog unfortunately does not react to atmospheric pressure.

SNAKE

Snakes are out before rain, and are therefore more easily killed. *

Snake

When snakes are hunting food, rain may be expected; after a rain they cannot be found. *

Snake trails may be seen before houses before rain. *

Rain is foretold by the appearance and activity of snakes. *

If snails and slugs come out abundantly, it is a sign of rain. *

The predominant theme of snakes and rain may be connected with the three English snake's great fondness of water and swimming. Certainly the Viper, Grass and rarer Smooth Snake will bask or rest in warm sunny weather, so it is quite possible the countryman has related the snake's active feeding time (May to October - they hibernate in winter) to rain. Unfortunately snakes are bad weather prophets.

Toad

When the toad is of a browner colour than usual, expect rain. *

If toads come out of their holes in great numbers, rain will fall soon. **

Both similar to saws in the Frog section.

Tortoise

Tortoises creep deep into the ground, so as to completely conceal themselves from view, when a severe winter is to follow. *

This theme occurs in many animal weather sayings. The tortoise hibernates deep into the ground through *present* cold weather conditions.

INSECTS

ANT

Ants withdraw into their nests and busy themselves with their eggs before a storm. ***

If ants are more than ordinarily active, or if they remove their eggs from small hills, it will surely rain. ***

The world of the ant is similar to the bee. A very highly developed social order and purpose has formulated. Before the reader tries to infer ants as invokers of sun or rain let us quickly crush this hope by saying that there is little evidence to justify such a thought. Having stated this one still has to marvel at their advanced senses and discipline. The saws are true in that worker ants frequently change the position of their eggs or larvae around in the nest chambers according to change in temperature and humidity of *present* conditions.

Ants sometimes get down fifteen inches from the surface before very hot weather. **

If ants their walls do frequent build,
Rain will from the clouds be spilled. **

When ants are situated in low ground, their migration may be taken as an indication of approaching heavy rain. **

In the beginning of July the ants are enlarging and building up their piles, an early and cold winter will follow. *

An open ant hole indicates clear weather, a closed one, an approaching storm. *

With their unique language of odours, especially with regard to food smell and alarm scents, the observations in the sayings are probably correct but only regarding ant activity.

Expect stormy weather when ants travel in lines, and fair weather when they scatter. ***

Another marvellous countryman's observation is of ant movement. In 1933 T.C.Schneirla found with use of a mirror that a homing ant's path is partly guided by the direction of the sun. It seems that the ant also compensates for gravity. Cloudy conditions would presumably see the ant following a meandering course.

HONEY BEE

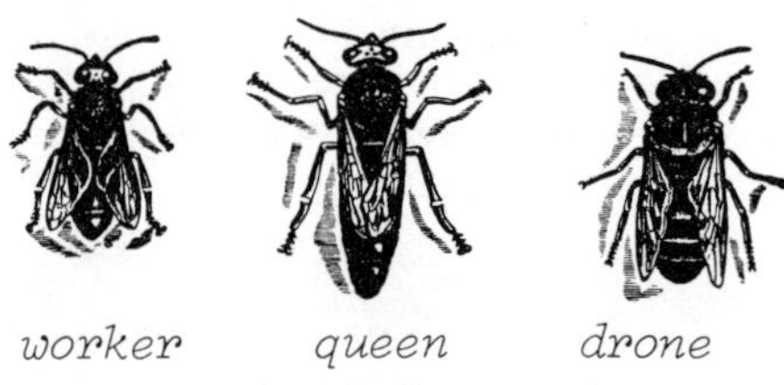

worker *queen* *drone*

Bees early at work will not go on all day.

Honey bees have possibly the most highly developed social laws and senses in the insect world. The worker bee (the one who performs the gathering and storing of flower nectar and pollen) is always more active in warm sunny but calm or light breezy days. It hates wet stormy or cold weather. So, as the saw suggests, an early warm sunny start will allow flowers to open allowing the worker bee to go about his task. His labour rate is so fast, an early ending becomes apparent by late afternoon.

Bees will not swarm
Before a near storm. *****

When the bees crowd out their hive,
The weather makes it good to be alive. **

When the bees crowd into their hive again
It is a sign of thunder and of rain. **

The first saying is absolutely true. The first swarm with the old queen takes place in quiet placid sunny weather. Swarms *do* occur in rain showers and storms but only with very young queens. The second and third saws may apply to these differing swarms.

When bees to distance wing their flight,
Days are warm and skies are bright; ****
But when their flight ends near their home,
Stormy weather is sure to come. ****

If bees stay at home,
Rain will soon come; ****
If they fly away,
Fine will be the day. ****

A bee was never caught
in a shower. ***

Foraging of nectar and pollen by the worker bee is perfect over long distances in quiet sunny weather. Rain or showers have a hostile effect on them by drastically cutting down their search radius. Infact they possess a biological clock which gives them an instant indication of the sun's position even on partly cloudy days. Their social contact is so advanced that a worker returning from a new nectar source will perform the "bee dance" in the hive by waggling its body into a rough figure of eight. The angle of the diagonal combined with the sun's position instantly communicates the distance and direction of the nectar to the other bees.

Whenever the bees get about in
February, I have always noticed
that we are certain to get wind
and rain next day. **

When warm February weather occurs, worker bees become restless. Whether the settled conditions continue or not is unrelated to the bees.

A swarm of bees in May is worth
a load of hay, *****
A swarm of bees in June is worth
a silver spoon, ****
A swarm of bees in July is not
worth a fly. ***

Refer to the May chapter for the meaning of this saw.

Beetle

The clock beetle, which flies
about in the summer evenings
in a circular direction, with
a loud, buzzing noise, is
said to foretell a fine day. ***

If the clock beetle flies in a
circle and buzzes, it is a
sign of fine weather. ***

A certain long-bodied beetle
is called in Bedfordshire the
"rain beetle", on account of
always appearing before rain. ***

Bedfordshire provides this adage. Apparently the Rain Beetle is any of several black hairy beetles that belong to the genus *Pleocoma,* closely related to the Scarab Beetle.

When little black insects appear
on the snow, expect a thaw. ***

Presumably the start of a mild spell is the cause for a sudden appearance of black insects.

BUTTERFLY

The early appearance of
butterflies is said to
indicate fine weather. ***

Abundance of butterflies of course means a previous excellent breeding season when all conditions were perfect. Also butterflies are chiefly seen in warm sunny weather.

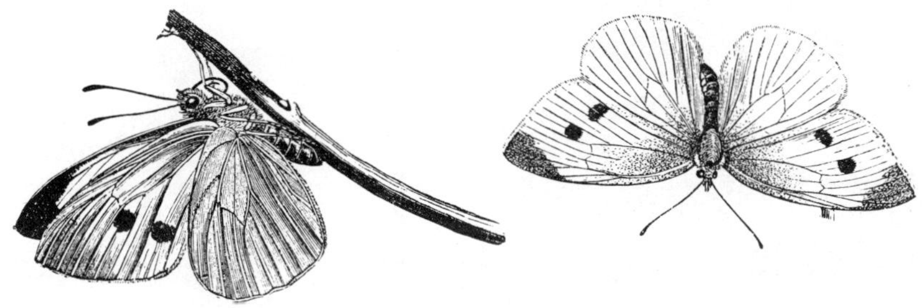

When the white butterfly flies
from the south-west, expect rain.

A South-Westerly is notorious for rain and changeable weather. The insertion of the White Butterfly in the adage just specifies the time of year - summer.

CRICKET

Before rain the beetles and
crickets are more troublesome
than usual. **

When crickets chirp unusually,
wet is expected. **

Classical response to forthcoming rain - all false.

FIREFLY

Fireflies in great numbers
indicate fair weather. **

This saying has the usual theme where excess numbers of insects indicate good weather - all incorrect.

FLEA

When fleas do very many grow
Then twill surely rain or snow. **

When eager bites the thirsty
flea
Clouds and rain you sure shall
see. *

The second saw is like the first fly maxim. No reliability can be placed here.

FLY

If flies' stings are more
troublesome than usual,
change approaches. **

FLY

When harvest flies hum,
Warm weather to come. **

The fly sayings are all related to *actual* weather conditions. They are separated into their specific groups.

House flies coming into the house
in great numbers indicate rain. **

If flies in the spring or
summer grow busier or blinder
than at other times, or are
seen to shroud themselves in
warm places, expect either
hail, cold storms of rain,
or much wet weather. **

The usual activity theme.

A fly on your nose, you slap, and
and it goes;
If it comes back again, it will
bring a good rain. *

If flies cling much to the
ceilings, or disappear,
rain may be expected. *

Silly but likeable saws.

If in autumn the flies repair
unto their winter quarters,
it presages frosty mornings,
cold storms, and the approach
of winter. Storms or small
flies swarming together and
sporting in the sunbeams give
omen of fair weather. **

The fly becomes a sensational weather prophet.

GLOW WORM

When the glow-worm lights her lamp,
The air is always damp. **

If glow-worms shine much, it will rain. **

When they shine more brightly than usual, they indicate rain within forty-eight hours, more especially when they remain luminous a short time after midnight. **

No forecast of rain applies here. The wingless female glow-worm *(Lampyris noctiluca)*, which is a beetle, emits small areas of intermittent green light on her thorax and abdomen. The larvae also transmit this nightime luminescence. The glow is only connected with mating.

GNAT

If little flies or gnats be seen to hover together about the beams of the sun before it set, and fly together, making, as it were, the form of a pillar, it is a sure token of fair weather. **

If gnats play up and down, it is a sign of heat, but if in the shade, it presages mild showers. If they collect in the evening before sunset, and form a vortex or column, fine weather will follow; while if they sting much, it is held to be an unfailing indication of rain. **

If gnats fly in compact bodies in the beams of the setting sun, expect fine weather. **

Hundreds of male gnats or midges forming a pillar or mass above the ground on a summer's evening usually occurs in September. They are waiting for a female easily recognised by her flight tone of 300 beats per second which they receive on an antenna. Although the mass flight takes place on a warm evening the maxim's meaning is of a sexual not a forecasting nature.

Many gnats in spring indicate
that the autumn will be warm. ****

Abundant gnats in spring indicate a warm season. Warm or very warm springs were tested for similar autumns resulting in a low figure of 49 percent. 55/112 (49)

Gnats in October are a sign of
long fair weather. **

Gnats in October are a sign of unusual warm weather which may or may not last.

If gnats fly in large numbers,
the weather will be fine. **

If gnats bite sharper than usual,
expect rain. **

Familiar themes covered by most insect weather lore.

HORNET

Hornets building nests high
before warm summers, and low
before cold and early winters. *

Akin to rook weather lore with similar conclusions.

SNAIL

When black snails cross your
path,
Black cloud much moisture hath. *

Black snails indicate black
clouds with much moisture. *

Because most slugs and snails like moist areas it probably represents the main reason for their pseudo reputation as rain prophets.

SPIDER

Spiders work hard and spin their webs a little before wind, as if desiring to anticipate it, for they cannot spin when the wind begins to blow. *

Before rain or wind spiders fix their frame-lines unusually short. If they make them very long, the weather will usually be fine for fourteen days. *

If spiders break off and remove their webs, the weather will be wet. *

If spiders make new webs,
and ants build near hills,
the weather will be clear. *

When the spider cleans its web, fair weather is indicated. *

If spiders in spinning their webs make the terminating filaments long, we may, in proportion to their length, expect rain. *

When spiders' webs in air do fly,

SPIDER

The spell will soon be very dry. **

If spiders undo their webs, tempests follow. *

If the garden spiders break and destroy their webs and creep away, expect continued rain. *

The majority of spider weather lore are concerned with its web. All kinds of future weather has been attributed to this creature. Unfortunately no such prophetic power exists. Like so many instances in animal saws they react to *present* weather conditions. Of the several hundred kinds of spiders in this country no two spin their web in the same way.

Spiders' webs scattered thickly over a field covered with dew glistening in the morning sun indicate rain. ***

When you see a gossamer flying,
Be sure the air is drying. ***

The gossamer or fine thread found on calm autumn mornings in dewy fields is also dealt with in the November chapter. Gossamer is initiated by hundreds of tiny baby spiders just out of the cocoon. On a quiet warm autumn evening they stand on the ends of plants and grass and pour out a stream of silk which is gently caught by any breeze leaving the fields covered in fine gossamer. Such fine mornings may or may not last.

If the spiders are indolent, rain generally soon follows. Their activity during rain is a certain proof of its short duration. If they mend their webs between six and seven pm, it is the sign of a serene night. *

If the spider works during rain, it is an indication that the weather will soon be clear. *

Spider

Spiders, when they are seen crawling on the walls more than usually, indicate that rain will probably ensue. This prognostic seldom fails, particularly in winter. ***

Spiders do spin webs in slight rain but avoid activity in heavier precipitation or strong winds. Again victims of prevailing weather conditions.

When, after a long drought, you observe in hedges some very densely-woven webs, funnel-shaped, there will be a change of weather within three days. **

Whichever species of spider spin this type of web they would not have any pre-knowledge of future weather.

Spiders bring an easterly wind.

This maxim from Whitstable, Kent, is intriguing in its strangeness. One cannot possibly think how the easterly wind becomes apparent with a spider's appearance. Even in early November when baby spiders emerge the normal weather pattern is unsettled and mobile. (See November chapter.)

If spiders fall from their webs or from the walls, it signifyeth rain. *

Presumably sudden increase in wind would be the cause for falling spiders.

Wasp

When wasps build their nests high on the banks of a stream you may expect a wet summer; but if near the level of the water, a dry summer is said to be indicated. *

Wasp

Wasps building nests in exposed places indicate a dry season. *

These two maxims follow the usual run of mill activities in animal and insect weather - both being false.

Woodlice

If wood lice run about in great numbers, expect rain. **

This theme can be found in many insect weather adages.

Cicada Lava

It is easy to foretell what sort of summer it will be by the position in which the lava of Cicada (Aphrophora Spumaria) is found to lie in the froth or cuckoo spit in which it is enveloped. If the insect lie with its head upwards, it infallibly denotes a dry summer; if downward, a wet one. *

This beautiful piece of country weather lore seems a shame to discredit. One almost feels one wants to forget the scientific and statistical evidence and believe in such a delightfully written tale. But the position of the larva depends on the weather conditions *at the time*.

MOON

Weather lore related to the moon is both varied and fascinating, except for lunar haloes and colourings (refer to solar and lunar and sky colours chapters), there is no truth in them. Apart from the moon causing a very small measurable tidal movement of the Earth's atmosphere and sea tides (which has negligible effect on the weather), no other meteorological consequence is detectable. One wise sage obviously know this when he originated the famous true weather saw below.

The moon and the weather
May change together,
But change of the moon
Does not change the weather.
If we'd no moon at all,
And that may seem strange,
We still should have weather
That's subject to change. ******

Parhelia, or mock suns, and
paraselenae, or mock moons,
very seldon occur, but are
generally followed by fair
weather. ***

Moon

If two or three moons appear at a time, it presages great wind and rain and unseasonable weather for a long time to follow. ****

The two or three moons refer to the paraselenae or "mock moons". They are moon images very similar to "mock suns" or parahelia. These weak mock moons are seen on either side of the moon at the same elevation (a single one occurs on one side). They are caused by refraction or bending of moonlight as it hits ice crystals (hexagonal) in high Cirrus clouds (see cloud chapter). Mock moons are poorly coloured and very rare because of their weak light intensity. They are therefore mostly seen at time of full moon. The suggestion of observing them 2 to 3 days after full moon in the above saw therefore seems strange.

Moonlit nights have the hardest frosts. ***

Clear moon
Frost soon. ****

Moonlit nights (the few days around full moon) are only visible with little or no cloud, which of course is perfect for the lowest temperatures which frequently produce frosts in the winter half year. The saying is untrue in summer.

The moon appearing larger at sunset, and not dim, but luminous, portends fair weather for several days. ***

This is a Bacon maxim. The appearance of a clear moon, whatever phase it has reached, again means the sky is clear or partly cloudy at that time. Sometimes these dry conditions can last a few hours or for days. A cloudy moon would have similar results. The significance of the clear moon at sunset is clever as it is the time of day when unstable cloud disperses inland. The saying has little else to offer.

If the full moon rises red, expect wind. ****

Moon

If the full moon rises pale,
expect rain. ****

If the moon appears a reddish-
brown through the haze, the
weather will stay fair. ****

Moon colour saws are similar to those in the Sun chapter.

A fog and a small moon
Bring an easterly wind soon. *

A Cornish saw not unlike a saying in the South wind chapter where "a southerly wind" is substituted here by "a small moon". The poor results there (29 percent) equally apply here.

If the moon changes with the
wind in the east, the weather
during that moon will be foul. *

Moon changes strictly apply to the four phases or quarters (first quarter, full moon, last quarter and new moon), each change lasting about 7 days. But most people remember just the new and full moon. These were tested with an Easterly wind over the period 1959-71 with the weather during the following week where at least 5 days had to be wet. 7/69 (10)

Five changes of the moon in one
calendar month indicate cooler
weather. ***

A lunar cycle is 28 days so some calendar months can include 5 lunar phases. These, for some magical reason, are supposed to bring cooler weather. 38 percent such cases were true. 11/29 (38)

If the lunar period has
continued rainy throughout,
good weather will follow for
several days, followed by
another period of rain, and
vice versa. *

Moon

If the moon be fair throughout and rain at the close, the fair weather will probably return on the fourth or fifth day. *

If the moon is rainy throughout, it will be clear at the change, and perhaps the rain will return a few days later. *

In general a rainy period suggests a mobile weather pattern which can either continue or experience a temporary or complete change. The moon takes no part in these natural weather sequencies.

When the moon runs low, expect warm weather. *

The moon's low orbit has no influence on the weather.

When the moon runs high, expect cool or cold weather. *

A dry moon is far north and soon seen. *

The farther the moon is to the south, the greater the drought, the further west the greater the flood, and the farther north-west, the greater the cold. *

If the new moon is far north, it will be cold for two weeks; but if far south, it will be warm. *

New moon far in the north, in summer, cool weather, in winter, cold. *

New moon far in the south indicates dry weather for a month. *

MOON

The various orbital positions of the moon in relation to an observer on the Earth bears no relationship with weather.

If the moon is seen between the scud and broken clouds during a gale, it is expected to cuff away the bad weather. **

"Scud" refers to fast-moving clouds, "cuff away" means to strike away. But regardless how colloquial the saying is, there is no moon/weather relationship.

Sowe peason and beans in the wane of the moon,
Who soweth them sooner, he soweth too soon. *

This is one of the famous "waxing and waning" pieces of moon farming lore. Of course waxing is the increasing of the moon (new to full) and waning the decreasing (full to new) in the moon's illumination. Waxing was always thought to bring cold weather, so sowing peas and beans would traditionally be a pointless task.

The weather that comes in with the moon will stay like it for a month. *

Hopeless results. 0/161 (0)

When the moon is visible in the daytime, the days are relatively cool.

Visible lunar orbits in the daytime only suggest clear or partly cloudy skies.

Frost occurring in the dark side of the moon kills fruit buds and blossoms, but frost in the light of the moon will not. *

Moon

Another famous old superstition that frost occurring in the old and new moon is more severe than under a full moon. The latter is supposed to have magical "warming" powers from its extreme moonlight. Nice but fictional.

If the moon appears with the points of the crescent turned up, the month will be dry. If the points are turned down, it will be wet. *

A new moon with sharp horns threatens windy weather. *

If one horn of the moon is sharp and pointed, the other being more blunt, it rather indicates wind; but if both are so, it denotes rain. *

Sharp horns do threaten windy weather. *

People speak of the new moon lying on her back or being ill-made as a prognostic of wet weather. *

New moon on its back indicates wind; standing on its point indicates rain in summer and snow in winter. *

The bonnie moon is on her back;
Mend your shoes and sort your thack. *

If the moon is on its back in the third quarter, it is a sign of rain.

When the moon lies on her back,
Then the south-west wind will crack; *
When she rises up and nods,
Then north-easters dry the sods. *

Moon

When the new moon lies on her
back,
She sucks the wet into her lap. *

When the moon's horns are sharp
and well defined, expect rain
the following day, or, in
winter, frost. *

The third maxim comes from the ancient pen of Bacon and 10th hails from Ellesmere in Shropshire. Variations of these famous new moon saws are concerned with the rare occurrence of its up-or-down turned points and sharp or blunt '"horns". The major myth childishly relates that rain is held in reserve in the upturned points for wet weather to come. Conversely the down-turned hold no water so dry weather will follow. This explanation is contradicted in the first saw. Again all these maxims are untrue.

If a snow storm begins when the
moon is young, it will cease at
moonrise. *

At the time of the new or full
moon when the present weather
continues stormy and wet turning
to clear and dry; one forecasts
the fine weather to remain for
the following quarter. If it
lasts it usually continues until
the next full or new moon. If
it lasts this long it will be
probably fine for a total of
four or five weeks. *

As many days from the first new
moon, so many times will it
thaw during winter. *

Really one has to wonder at the inventiveness of these sayings.

If mist in the new moon,
rain in the old; ***
If mist in the old moon,
rain in the new. ***

Auld moon mist
Ne'er died of thirst. ***

The first four days of the new moon and last four days of the old were tested. At least two days from each period had to have its appropriate forecast weather. Again all contained unsatisfactory results.

Mists in new moon rain in old	17/38	(45)
.. .. old .. .. .. new	12/30	(40)

When the new moon comes in at midnight, or within thirty minutes before or after, the following month will be fine. **

A novel maxim with a low rating. 3/10 (30)

When the change of the moon occurs in the morning, expect rain. ****

Moon changing in morning indicates warm weather; ** *in the evening, cold weather.* **

The change of moon was more likely to be a full or new moon. Morning was defined as 0001-1200 local time and evening 1700-2230 with warm or cold weather to follow within two days. One can see that poor results emerge.

Morning moon then rain	71/137	(52)
Morning moon then warm weather	35/137	(25)
Evening .. .. cold ..	14/67	(21)

A Friday's moon
Is a month too soon. *

A Sussex saying meaning a Friday's full moon is the worst weekday it could happen for severe weather. "A month too soon" means too premature.

A Saturday moon,
If it comes once in seven years,
comes once too soon.

Moon

A Saturday full moon is a bad one not wanting to be seen during a 7-year period.

If the moon on a Saturday be
new or full,
There always was rain, and
there always wull. ****

A Worcestershire maxim which was tested for new or full moons and rain within two days. For some reason the results are good, in fact the best of the whole moon chapter. Compare these figures with the weekday chapter. 29/48 (60)

Saturday's change and Sunday's
full
Never brought good and never
brought wull. *

A Saturday's change and a
Sunday's full moon
Once in seven years is once
too soon. *

A Saturday's change and a
Sunday's full
Comes too soon whenever it wull. *

Norfolk originated the first adage and Dorset the third. The general flow is "Saturday change and Sunday's full" and does *not* refer to a Saturday moon "change". It is a weather change from bad to good continuing into Sunday with clear weather when the full moon can be observed. Of the 23 Sunday full moons from 1959-71, 15 were visible, but no major change occurred on the previous Saturday, so a test was not run.

If the moon changes on a Sunday,
there will be a flood before the
month is out. **

A Worcestershire saw with new and full moon changes.
12/41 (29)

Moon

The nearer to twelve in the
afternoon, the drier the moon ***
The nearer to twelve in the
forenoon, the wetter the moon. ***

A Herefordshire maxim. The full moon is the one tested with a dry moon occurring 1200-1800 local time and a wet moon 0600-1200. Only average results emerge.

Wet 0600-1200 local time	19/43	(44)
Dry 1200-1800	15/31	(48)

A hundred hours after the new
moon regulates the weather
for the month. **

An unusual Huntingdonshire saw. Around 4 days after a new moon the weather (combination of rainfall and temperature categories) was tested against similar conditions for the following month but low ratings evolved. 35/146 (24)

The first and second never mind,
The third regard not much;
But as the fourth and fifth you
find,
The rest will be as such. *

Another Huntingdonshire saying following the usual fictional mould.

If the new moon is not visible
before the fourth day, the air
will be unsettled for the whole
month. ***

Bacon penned this one. A shrewd observation that 4 days of unsettled weather usually continues for some time but not usually for a month. The new moon's appearance is immaterial.

To see the old moon in the arms
of the new one is reckoned a
sign of fine weather, and so is ***
the turning up of the horns of
the new moon. *

Moon

To see the old moon in the arms of the new one is a sign of bad weather to come. **

The first comes from Suffolk. Both are famous sayings and are opposed in meaning. "To see the old moon in the arms of the new" calls for a very clear atmosphere usually of polar origin. The forecast of fine weather (45 percent) and wet (30 percent) was still an unsatisfactory result. 9/20 (45)
6/20 (30)

Two full moons in a calendar month bring on a flood. *

A Bedfordshire maxim implying torrential rain. 0/6 (0)

The new moon grows fat on clouds. ***

A beautiful saw meaning that as a moon gets fuller it eats cloud - hence all full moons have clear skies. However only on 43 percent of occasions this happened. 46/106 (43)

The weather is generally clearer at the full than at other ages of the moon; but in winter the frost then is sometimes more intense. ***

A Bacon adage with the full moon clear on 43 percent (see previous saw) of occasions and 38 percent under a new moon.
New moon clear 38/100 (38)

Near full moon, a misty sunrise Bodes fair weather and cloudless skies. ***

Similar sayings in the weekday and fog/mist chapters explain this adage. The appearance of a full moon is superfluous.

The full moon brings fine weather. ***

Moon

Tested on the weather remaining fine for at least three days after the full moon. 54/158 (34)

If the moon is distinct, neither too sharp in outline nor, on the other hand, "watery" and blurred, the weather will stay fair for the time being. **

This is not altogether correct. A clear moon, whatever its phase, really denotes clear polar air which is frequently showery by day.

STARS

The obscuring of the smaller stars in a clear night is a sign of rain. ****

When the stars begin to huddle,
The earth will soon become a puddle. ****

These two adages are similar. For the stars to "huddle" or be in a confused mass, *Cirrus* cloud is present. The night sky then contains areas of dim stars and clear ones not affected by the *Cirrus*. The saws are true and the percentage figures given in the Cirrus/Cloud Chapter for rain to follow *Cirrus* within one, two or three days apply here.

Excessive twinkling of the stars indicates heavy dews, rain, and snow, and stormy weather in the near future. ***

When the stars flicker in a dark background, rain or snow follows soon. ****

When the sky seems very full of stars expect rain, or, in winter, frost. ****

Excessive star twinkling refers to excellent visibility which means an airstream with a polar origin is imminent. These airstreams are usually blowing in a N.W. to N.E. direction. Any of the weather forecast in the saws could occur but an emphasis on cold temperatures must be an obvious choice.

A star dogging the moon foretells bad weather. *

If a big star is dogging the moon, wild weather may be expected. *

Stars

One star ahead of the moon,
towing her, and another astern,
using her, is a sure sign of a
storm. *

The third maxim comes from Lancashire. There is absolutely no truth here.

Moon in a circle indicates storm, *****
and number of stars in the circle
indicates the number of days
before a storm.

The first part is explained in the Moon/Sun Halo Chapter, but the remainder is complete rubbish.

Comets are said to bring bad
weather. *

If many meteors in summer,
expect thunder. **

After an unusual fall of
meteors, dry weather is
expected. ***

A meteor was always regarded as a "shooting star". When appearing in numbers they are known as "meteor showers". Of course they are fragments of solid material entering the Earth's atmosphere at tremendous speeds with blazing trails. There are about 14 periods when these showers reach a maximum frequency. They are 3-4 January, 21 April, 4-6 and 4-23 May, 1-16 June, 26 June-5 July, 28 July, 5-14 Aug, 10 and 20-23 Oct, 3-10 and 16-17 Nov, 12-13 and 22 Dec. The average weather pattern (to be found at the beginning of each month in the Month's Chapter) *after* these dates produced 6 wet, 6 dry and 2 average weather periods. So little reliability can be placed in these maxims.

When the water looks black, the
Cornwall folk say the thunder
planet is about and a storm is
coming. *

It rains by planets. *

Stars

Cornwall provides the first saying. The thunder planet remains a mystery.

When the Great Bear is on this side of the North Pole, the summer is dry; if he gets on the other side, the summer is wet, especially if he be then in conjunction with Venus and Jupiter. *

Another astronomical-cum-weather adage with hardly any truth.

WIND

Before the middle of the 19th century, when weather charts and the understanding of depression movement evolved, the most useful and regularly used weather lore was related to surface wind direction. Each quadrant, whether south-west or east, had its own individual weather being of paramount importance to the practical lives of farmers, shepherds and all countryfolk.

Wind roaring in chimney, rain to come. ****

A brisk wind generally precedes rain. ****

It is often true that gales or a gradual increase in wind strength often precede rain.

The whispering grove tells of a storm to come. ****

This is mainly associated with showers where gusts of wind and cold downdraughts often occur ahead of a heavy shower or thunderstorm.

Wind storms usually subside about sunset, but if they do not, they will go on for another day. *****

The smaller and lighter winds generally rise in the morning and fall at sunset. *****

These two are wonderful pieces of weather observation. In a gentle airstream the wind will normally increase after sunrise and dramatically decrease around sunset as long as the day is not overcast and air temperature is allowed to rise and fall normally. As the sun rises the temperature profile in the first few hundred feet above the ground (lapse rate) changes becoming steeper and therefore unstable. This allows the air to become turbulent with the nett result of strengthening the wind. After the maximum day temperature is reached (around 2-3 pm) it begins to decrease. Its greatest fall is just after sunset, allowing a sudden decrease in the wind speed. If the day has persistent low-cloud cover keeping air temperature steady, or if a strengthening airstream occurs caused by the passage of a depression or trough, wind strength will not follow the normal day and night time pattern. Therefore a strong wind at night often remains another day.

When after a rough and stormy day there is a lull at the going down of the sun, old men say: 'Us shall have better weather now, for the wind's gone to sleep with the sun.' ****

The above saying is from Devon.

A storm will go three miles out of its way to come by Habberley to Churton. ***

There'll be some rain, for the wind has got to Habberley Hole. ****

The first of these Shropshire weather saws relates to the effect of topography on weather. Churton or Church Pulverbatch (Shropshire) lies two miles east of Habberley village which is situated amongst steep hills up to 1,500 feet above sea level. More important is the narrow gorge lying between the villages. This 'funnels' or magnifies the strength of a westerly wind or storm. This is very similar to a wide flowing river increasing its current on entering a narrow channel. The second adage applies to Shrewsbury town lying about 9 miles north-east of Habberly Hole (a long deep ravine). Shrewsbury would receive a wet south-westerly, strengthened by the 'funnelling effect' of Habberly Hole.

We shall have rain, for the wind is in Bodjham Hole. ****

WIND

Sure to rain, the wind's in
Flammer's Hole. ****

Bodjham Hole near Ashford Vale in East Kent and Flammer's Hole on the Chilterns above Dunstable, Bedfordshire, continue the topographical story.

If rain falls before the wind
commences, the wind will last
longer than the rain. But if
the wind blows first, and is
afterwards laid by rain, it
does not often rise again, and
if it does, it is followed by
fresh rain. ****

This old maxim, mentioned by Bacon, looks long and complicated, but is full of sense and observation.

Always a calm before a storm. ***

After a storm comes a calm. ***

The top phrase is a most famous saying equally applied to weather and human behaviour. Unfortunately, if taken literally, it is not always true. Obviously wind speed will increase and decrease but the only cases for a calm before a storm and vice-versa occur with heavy showers and passages of quiet ridges of high pressure and vigorous depressions.

When the wind backs and the
weather glass falls,
Then be on your guard against
gales and squalls. ***

Another half-true weather saw. When depressions or troughs cross the British Isles, the wind usually backs (a change from one direction to another in anticlockwise fashion - such as north to west. Veering has the opposite meaning.) before their arrival bringing rain with gales. Backing occurs around sunset with a pressure fall on most days but is not connected with ensuing rain.

WIND

The wind is said to go "withershins", or contrary to the course of the sun.

Winds that change against the sun
Are always sure to backward run. ****

When the wind veers against the sun,
Trust it not, for back 'twill run. ****

The veering of the wind with the sun prognosticates drier or better weather; the backing of the wind against the sun, indicates rain, or more wind, or both together. ****

A veering wind, fair weather. ****
A backing wind, foul weather. ****

"Withershins" or "widdershins' mean a backing in the wind from west to east against the apparent course of the sun in these northern latitudes. It is always a good rule that when a strong wind backs rain is sure to follow.

It is a sign of continued fine weather when the wind changes during the day so as to follow the sun. **

This seems correct at first glance but it is rare for the wind to veer from east to west during daylight.

If the wind follows the sun's course, expect fair weather. ****

This is subtly different from the previous saying beginning with poor weather and ending with settled conditions.

Wind

In the northern hemisphere a person with his back to the wind has lower pressure on his left hand side than on his right - the converse is true in the southern hemisphere. *****

A man called Buys Ballot of Utrecht originated this correct law in 1857. Imagine a depression or low, i.e. a circle of winds blowing in an anticlockwise direction (in the northern hemisphere). Now if the centre was situated in the Midlands, southern England would experience a westerly wind - so with one's back to it, the left-hand side would point north towards the lower pressure (the depression centre).

A sudden storm lasts not three hours. ****

The sharper the blast
The sooner 'tis past. ****

Sudden storms or winds usually pass with a quick passage, but if wind increases gradually, it generally lasts longer.

Winds changing from foul to fair during the night are not permanent. ***

A blustering night can lead to a fair day. ***

The effect of nightime is unimportant in these two saws. Foul to fair changes can equally be permanent or temporary. The controlling factors of the true meaning lie elsewhere.

The wind never blows steadily, whether it be a winter's storm or a mild summer's breeze, but always in what the old wind-millers used to call plervets. *****

The wind trace shows a continual reading. It is typical of

a breeze with the characteristic high and low gust range. The speed is never steady, but fluctuates within a few knots in as many seconds. The direction reacts similarly but is even more sensitive, often ranging over 60 degrees in one second.

Wind east or west
Is a sign of a blast; ****
Wind north or south
Is a sign of drought. ***

North wind cold,
East wind dry
South wind warm and often wet,
West wind generally rainy. ****

The south wind always brings
wet weather,
The north wind wet and cold
together;
The west wind always brings us
rain,
The east wind blows it back
again. ****

North winds send hail, south
winds bring rain,
East winds we bewail, west
winds blow amain;
North-east is too cold, south-
west not too warm,
North-west is too bold, south-
west does no harm.
The north is a noyer to grass
of all suites,
The east is destroyer to herb
and all fruits;
The south, with his showers,
refresheth the corn,
The west to all flowers may not
be foreborne.
The west, as a father, all
goodness doth bring;
The east, a forbearer, no
manner of thing;

WIND

The south, as unkind, draweth
sickness too near;
The north, as a friend,
maketh all again clear. ****

Easy-to-remember rhymes for the countryman, providing the basic weather characteristics for different wind directions. Bacon penned the second saying and the third originates in Plymouth.

No weather is ill
If the wind be still. ***

In calm situations rain is rare, but frost and fog are common. It all depends on the type of weather the countryman or farmer requires.

All winds bring rain. **

Every wind has its weather. *****

The last saying is a just reminder that every airstream possesses its own weather. A regular wind direction has subtle differences in cloud cover, precipitation and visibility.

The wind that will blow out a
candle will help to kindle a
fire.

A little wind kindles, much
puts out the fire.

A light gentle wind is needed to blow out a candle and to constantly generate flames in a fire. A strong and erratic wind will extinguish any blaze.

When the wind goes down hill it
will be a duck's frost afore
morning. ***

Wind

Wind that "goes down hill" occurs on clear evenings and nights. It is a cold dry breeze, known as a katabatic wind and possesses denser air than its surroundings and often blows down the slope of a valley sometimes causing frost hollows. It is also known as the "drainage wind" and "mountain breeze". It certainly foretells cool conditions in summer and winter frosts.

It's an ill wind that blows
nobody good.

Although bad weather and a wretched wind cause havoc with most people, there are always some that benefit.

Sudden gusts never come in a
clear sky, but only when it is
cloudy and with rain. *

This is incorrect. On a hot day with light breezes of say 8 knots, sudden gusts of 12 to 18 knots frequently blow. They are helped by the instability caused by uneven distribution of high temperatures across fields, woods and hills.

Unsteadiness of wind shows
changing weather. *

This is untrue. Wind, by its nature, constantly changes in speed and direction, which can be applied to a dry, wet or changeable weather type.

A frequent change of wind, with
agitation in the clouds, denotes
a storm.

The maxim is too vague. With so many different cloud types and consequent weather the saying needs to be clearer and more specific.

North Wind

North Wind

The north wind is cold in autumn, winter and spring; sometimes intensely cold in southern districts. Snow and sleet are common in winter with late-spring and early-autumn snow in northern districts on high ground. Also northerlies are connected with late-spring frosts. The onset of a north-type airstream is often accompanied by high winds.

A northern air
Brings weather fair. ***

Mostly true, although wintry showers, especially over the Pennines and north-facing hills, can be a nasty feature.

The north wind, if it should
rise by night (which is unusual),
hardly ever lasts beyond three
days. ***

Bacon wrote this saying. It is hinting that the northerly wind, by freshening at night, is strictly connected with a polar depression moving from Arctic regions into the North sea. In some cases the northerly, as a permanent feature, continues beyond three days.

The north wind is best for
sowing of seeds. ****

The best conditions required for sowing winter and spring cereal seed are a dryish topsoil; certainly not wet or too moist. A cool dry northerly provides the ideal conditions. However I am sure the farm-labourer hand-scattering the seed would have wished for warmer working weather.

All bad things come out of the
north. A bleak, bad wind, and a
biting frost, and a scolding wife
come out of the north. ****

This is more typical of the north wind in the winter half-year.

North Wind

A north wind is a broom for the Channel. ****

The English Channel is referred to in this Cornish weather saw which must mean that as a cold northerly burst sweeps across the water it brings dry clear conditions.

Whenever the wind first blows
from the north, after having
been for some days in another
direction, a fine day or two
will be almost sure to follow. ***

Not always true - the northerly can possess rain or snow.

The north wind doth blow,
And we shall have snow. ***

This saying is only true when applied to the period from about October to April, otherwise rain showers are the usual precipitation.

In a north wind it seldom thunders. ****

If the northerly wind has a well-established airstream, then thunder is rare. Any wind direction can occur in the vicinity of a thunderstorm.

Cream makes most freely with a north wind. *****

Until the middle of the 19th century cream was raised by leaving cow milk in shallow pans for a day or two. The lighter cream, or fattier part of the milk, mainly rose to the top. A fall in temperature speeded up the process. So in a cold northerly cream would certainly make "most freely". In fact icy water was introduced in the 1870's to further accelerate cream raising.

North Wind

If there be within four, five or six days two or three changes of wind from the north, through east without much rain and wind, and thence again through the west to the north with rain or wind, expect continual showery weather. ****

These complicated sets of wind changes seem to indicate minor wind disturbances finally followed by a very cold showery blast from the polar regions.

If the north-west or north wind blows with rain or snow during three or four days in the winter, and then the wind passes to the south through the west, expect continued rain. *****

Another true maxim. The destruction of a three or four-day northerly is frequently caused by the eastward movement of a depression across the United Kingdom. This would back the wind from north to south through west bringing rain.

But the north wind often both rises and falls without any change in the weather. ****

Bacon observed this characteristic in the northerly wind which can be applied at times to any direction, especially during the daytime.

Northerly winds bring showers rather than continuous rains or snow. *****

Perfectly correct - a very cold unstable airstream produces showers instead of general continuous rain.

North-East Wind

North-East Wind

The north-east wind is cold or very cold often with snow or sleet in winter and hail showers or rain and drizzle in summer.

The wind from the north-east
Neither good for man or beast. ****

North-east is bad for man and
beast. ****

This direction, especially with rain or sleet, has a biting damp cold that seems to penetrate everything in its path.

If the wind is north-east three
days without rain,
Eight days will pass before
south wind again. ******

This is one of the famous 26 weather rules of the Shepherd of Banbury (Oxfordshire), first printed in 1744. He was a most observant shepherd who was familiar with the persistence of north-easterlies. A test produced an excellent result of 81 percent.
13/16 (81)

North-east wind brings a long
storm. *****

If the wind is from the
north-east, its storm will
be a hard one. *****

A well-established north-easterly wind produces very good results when lasting for two days or more. The figures are not so good for the sequence to last at least three or four days respectively with 44 and 28 percent. Long-term north-easterlies are a feature of the permanent Scandinavian anticyclone; short-term ones are related to fast-moving depressions rushing east up the English Channel or across Northern France into the Continent.
91/137 (66)
60/137 (44)
39/137 (28)

East Wind

In summer, if the wind holds off a day or more in the north-east, a severe storm is coming. **

Poor results of 21 percent occur for a severe storm to follow summer north-easterlies. 9/43 (21)

East Wind

The east wind is cold in autumn, winter and spring, sometimes intensely cold in southern and exposed areas elsewhere. Occasionally snow occurs in the south and snow or sleet showers in east and north-east England but fine weather can happen in the north-west. Also it is warm in summer, sometimes thundery but fairly dry except in the east and south.

When the wind is in the east,
It is neither good for man or beast. ****

A right easterly wind
Is very unkind. ****

The coldest and most biting weather arises in an east or north-east wind.

A dry east wind raises the spring. ****

This Cornish saying is hinting that dry clear easterlies in early spring, mainly through their sunshine and soil drying properties, will bring on the season.

When the rain is from the east,
It is for four-and-twenty hours at least. *****

Rain in an easterly is more frequent in the warmer months of April to September. The remaining year usually experiences sleet or snow. Very good results occur. 53/79 (67)

East Wind

Wet weather with an east wind continues longer than with a west, and generally lasts a whole day. *****

Bacon came up with a winner with this maxim. The summers of 1861-1971 with wet cyclonic westerlies lasted on average 2.7 days; wet easterlies 3.5 days.

An easterly wind's rain
Makes fools fain. ****

A cold easterly rain is raw and of little use to any countryman, and would certainly make a fool fain or glad.

If an east wind blows against a dark, heavy sky from the north-west, the wind decreasing in force as the clouds approach, expect thunder and lightning. ****

This refers to summertime when thunderstorms are sometimes associated with warm easterlies.

The east and north winds, when they have once begun, are more continuous; the south and west winds are more variable. ***

Annually the two persistant wind quadrants are west and east with average lengths of 3.6 and 2.4 days. The north and south quadrants experience a temporary nature with means of 1.8 and 1.9 days.

The eastern winds make our fresh waters much clearer than the west. ***

This is very similar to the Cornish saying in the north wind section. Inland fresh water areas receive the benefit of fresh clear cold easterlies.

The eastern wind is drier, more biting and deadly, and if blowing much in the spring, injureth fruits by breeding worms. ***

There are many occasions when an easterly is moist with wintry precipitation.

There are a hundred days of easterly wind in the first half of the year. *

This West Country saying is totally false. When an easterly is tested as the predominant daily wind, disastrous results follow. The best year was 1963 with 43 days from January to May. 0/111 (0)

An east wind is a 'lazy wind', that is, it won't blow round you, but it blows straight through you. ****

The "lazy wind" also applies to the north and north-east wind. Often the strength and direction of an easterly wind remain fairly constant during the night and day, hence the straight character of the wind.

An east wind, like an old man, lies down in the sun. *

This is untrue; the strength is fairly constant. It is opposite in character to the north-west wind which decreases around sunset.

SOUTH WIND

The south airstream is warm and thundery in spring and summer and mild in autumn. In winter it is mild or cold depending whether it has maritime or continental origin.

SOUTH WIND

The weather usually clears at noon when a southerly wind is blowing. **

A most unsatisfactory rule. The time of day makes little difference in determining when wet weather changes to dry. If by weather fog is included then on spring and autumn mornings the time of day is important. Usually these fogs will clear before or around midday.

If the wind continues any considerable time in the south, it is an infallible sign of rain. ****

When the leaves curl with the wind from the south, it indicates rain. ****

The definition of "any considerable time" was taken as three days or more with rain to follow within one. The result of 53 percent is only fair - similar results can be applied for a dry day to follow. Not all southerlies are eroded by depressions or summer thunderstorms producing rain. Often the Continental anticyclone will persist leaving a dry south airstream for a number of days. 26/49 (53)

A southerly wind with a fog
Brings an east wind in snog. **

An out (southerly) wind and a fog
Bring an east wind home snug. **

These Cornish sayings include the dialect words "snog" and "snug" which mean with certainty. A test looked into southerlies remaining for two days or more followed by an easterly within seven. Poor results occurred. 29/99 (29)

A southerly wind and a cloudy sky
Proclaim it a hunting morning. *****

South Wind

The fox-hunting season used to occur from November to April. Also related is the hunter's moon, which is the next full moon after the harvest moon (nearest full moon to the autumn equinox around 21st September). Now the strongest fox scent for hounds occurs in mild, moist conditions, so a cloudy south wind would provide such a morning.

When the south wind either
rises or falls, there is
generally a change of weather,
from fair to cloudy, or from
hot to cold, or vice versa. ***

This old Bacon fable is partly true. It is similar in character and result to the second saw in this section.

The south wind, when gentle,
is not a great collector of
clouds; but it is often clear,
especially if it be of short
continuance. But if it lasts or *****
becomes violent, it makes the
sky become cloudy and brings on
rain, which comes on rather
when the wind ceases or begins
to die away, than when it
commences or is at its height. *****

The southern wind
Doth play the trumpet to his
purposes,
And by his hollow whistling in
the leaves
Foretells a tempest and a
blustering day. *****

The first Bacon and second Shakespeare (from *Henry IV*) sayings vary in literal style but possess the same meaning. The first part was tested with southerly winds lasting less than four dry days which produced an outstanding 79 percent result. Part two was defined as a southerly lasting three days or more and rain within one. Again the results were very good.

South Wind

30/38 (79)
80/111 (72)

The south wind warms the aged. *****

When the wind is in the south
It blows the bait in the fishes' mouth. *****

The southerly wind is mostly warm or mild, hence the good 70 percent result. The meaning of the second saw probably refers to the gradual heating of fresh water rivers, especially in a continual southerly. This warmer water stimulates fish to become more active and hungry. 166/237 (70)

If, when the south wind is blowing, any piece of glued furniture makes a noise, it indicates a change to the north. **

Furniture will "creak" or "make a noise" with warm temperatures and high humidity which is typical of a southerly. The test gave poor results confining itself to any change to northerly within four days. 14/85 (16)

When the wind's in the south,
The rain's in its mouth. *****

Another very true adage with 70 percent correct results. All southerlies were tested when lasting for at least one day followed by rain within 24 hours. 165/235 (70)

A southerly wind with showers of rain
Will bring the wind from the west again. **

Poor figures are achieved (25 percent correct) with showers and a southerly wind veering to the west within two days.
21/85 (25)

SOUTH WIND

Fair weather for a week, with a southern wind, is like to produce a great drought, if there has been much rain out of the south before. The wind usually ****
turns from north to south, with a quiet wind without rain, but ****
returns to the north, with a strong wind and rain; the ****
strongest winds are when it turns from south to north-by-west. *****
Also when the north wind first clears the air (which is usually once a week) look out for squalls.

This is the famous Shepherd of Banbury's 17th saying. The first section produced only a few number of occasions - too small to record. The second part concerned with a northerly breaking down into a light southerly is frequently correct especially when high pressure cells form or drift across Central England into Europe. When tested a return of 59 percent was recorded. Wind returning to the north with rain within two days gave 53 percent. The more impressive 64 percent was valid for the notable strength of the northerly occurring when a deep depression travels eastward slowing down as it enters the North Sea.

13/22 (59)
31/58 (53)
37/58 (64)

If the wind in daytime shifts from north to south-west or south, rain is pretty sure to follow, if, on the other hand, ******
it shifts from south to south-west or north, the weather will probably clear up. ***

A Devon saying covering the general rule relating wet and dry weather to be expected after a backing or veering of wind - in this case north to south-west and south-west to North. The daytime is not really significant, the weather change is effective throughout the 24 hours. The tests included cases where wet or drier conditions occurred within two days of wind change. A remarkable 100 percent resulted in the backing and rain figures.

34/34 (100)
27/58 (47)

The north wind is best for sowing seed, the south for grafting.

A cool northerly leaves topsoil dry enough for seed sowing. The southerly may be warm for grafting or farm labouring, but it is often humid leading to unpleasant sweaty conditions.

The south wind, during the winter months, will bring mild, cloudy weather, with drizzle. *****

Another correct adage tested from January to February 1861-1971 for wet weather and mild conditions. 65/89 (73)

SOUTH-WEST WIND

The south-west wind is mild, humid with prolonged rain. This changeable airstream is the prevailing wind over England closely followed by the east or north-east direction.

A south-west blow on ye,
And bluster ye all over. ****

Taken from Shakespeare's *Tempest*, he conjures up two of the characteristics of a south-westerly - its strength and mildness.

Three south-westers, then one heavy rain. *

Ambiguous weather lore - does it mean three consecutive or separate south-westerly days? The latter was researched showing poor results. Heavy rain can occur under any south-west airstream - a gradual accumulation of separate south-westerlies resulting in heavy rain is a myth. 9/66 (14)

In fall and winter, if the wind holds a day or more in the south-west, a severe storm is coming. **

A severe storm was tested to fall within two days after the south-westerly was established. Poor results.

45/214 (21)

When the wind shifts around to the south and south-west, expect warm weather. ******

Predictable statement with expected excellent results of 92 percent. The exception occurs with a depression centred over Northern Britain in the spring and winter. Then the south-westerly has polar oceanic origin. 61/66 (92)

When after a stiff breeze there ensues a dead calm and drizzling rain, with a fall in the barometer, expect a gale from the south-west. ***

This only occurs when a stiff north or north-west blast is replaced by a ridge of high pressure ahead of a depression in the Atlantic. The wind will become calm after the northerly with clear conditions. Sometimes drizzle falling in the ridge well ahead of the depression from a warm front can be experienced. As the depression moves east it brings south-westerly gales and falling pressure, so the saying's weather sequence is fulfilled. It is more often incorrect when a south-west airstream occurs following the passage of a cold front. A wave can form on the front bringing drizzle and falling pressure but is often followed by a veer to north-west winds.

If the wind is from the north-west or south-west, the storm will be short. If from the south-west a warm one. ***

The length of rain storms in a south-westerly can last from a few to many hours. The north-west airstream is usually renouned for short-lived showers.

West Wind

The west wind is generally unsettled with changeable weather, usually with most rain falling in North, North-West and South-West England. It is cool in summer and mild in winter with frequent gales.

When the wind is in the west,
The weather is always best. ****

The wind in the west
Suits everyone best. ****

When wind is west
Health is best. ***

The changeable westerly has such a varied menu it pleases nearly everyone.

When the rain comes from the west,
it will be not more than a few
hours before the weather improves,
and becomes brighter, but showers
are likely to follow. ****

This is perfectly true. A trough with rain in a westerly airstream lasts around four hours bringing cooler showery type weather in its wake.

The west wind is a gentleman,
and goes to bed. *****

The westerly, like the north-westerly, is drastically reduced in strength under clear skies around dusk and hence "goes to bed".

Wind west, rain's next. *****

A western wind carrieth water
in his hand. *****

Both maxims are very true, especially the first one from Devon. Strong westerlies are associated with mobile Atlantic depressions and showery troughs. Lighter westerlies can belong to this hybrid and are also connected with settled dry weather from high pressure centres over France and Biscay.

NORTH-WEST WIND

The north-west wind has cool, changeable weather, particularly in North and East England, sometimes accompanied with fresh or gale force winds.

Do business with men when the
wind is in the north-west. *****

When the wind is in the
north-west,
The weather will be at
its best. ****

North-west is far the best. ****

The first is a lovely Yorkshire saying meaning that its cool fine weather sometimes occurring in a north-westerly can improve temper. A man in good spirits is always easier to do business with.

In summer, if the wind changes
to the north-west, expect
cooler weather.

This is just a statement of fact. A north-west airstream brings cool temperatures the year round.

An honest man and a north-west
wind generally go to sleep
together. *****

North-West Wind

Another lovely country adage beautifully phrased. The north-west wind, in a clear evening, will abate in strength quite dramatically around sunset. The reason is the rapid drop in temperature and change of vertical temperature profile or lapse rate.

A nor'wester is not long in
debt to a sou'wester. ****

The set of four figures give the general picture for south-westerlies to follow north-westerlies. To occur within one or two days 47 and 57 percent chances arose. Better figures of 66 and 71 percent followed when applied to the wind backing within 3 and 4 days.

111/236 (47)
134/236 (57)
155/236 (66)
167/236 (71)

North-west wind brings a short
storm. ***

If the wind is from the
north-west or south-west,
the storm will be short. ***
If from the north-west a
cold one.

Showers are usually short and gusty but prolonged rain and winds can occur especially in warm sector conditions.

If in unsettled weather the wind
veers from south-west to west
or north-west at sunset, expect
finer weather for a day or two. ****

This is usually true. It implies that a veering wind, often associated with cold fronts and troughs, brings short settled periods. Sometimes the time of day is important - if the veer to north-west occurs in the morning, showers could form as temperatures rose. If the veer happens at sunset then low temperatures would allow a clear night. Also a situation can present itself with a cold front wave forming returning wet weather for a few hours after a temporary veer from south-west to north-west.

A north-westerly gale
Brings showers of hail. ***

With the rain from the
north-west, expect showers
of hail. ***

Hail showers can occur in a north-west airstream but it's the colder more unstable northerly where they often originate.

RAIN

Some rain, some rest;
Fine weather isn't always
the best.

To a farmer fine weather is welcome but a long sequence of slight rain then sun and so on is more appreciated.

No one so surely pays his debt
As wet to dry and dry to wet. *

Be it dry or be it wet
The weather'll always
pay its debt. *

Wiltshire provides the first saw. Many countrymen believe that there is a true balance between wet and dry weather. For example that a summer drought will be followed by an autumn deluge and vice-versa. A test was carried out over the period 1727-1971 where monthly wet and dry totals were totalled over each calendar year. The author thought a 12-month period would be long enough to test the theory of equal dry and wet spells. So when equal annual monthly totals occurred a correct mark was allotted. Unfortunately mother nature does not work in these mysterious ways hence the very low rating of 11 percent.

27/245 (11)

Rain, rain pouring
Sets the bulls a-roaring. *

This Suffolk saying contains poor observation - bulls roar for many different reasons. (See cow/bull section of the Animal chapter.)

Rain from the east,
Two days at least. *****

Rain from the east,
Will last three days at least. ***

Similar adages and test figures can be found in the Wind chapter under the easterly section.

Rain from the south prevents the drought;
But rain from the west is always best.

Rain with south or south-west thunder brings squalls on successive days. *

If it rains at midnight with a southerly wind, it will generally last about twelve hours. ****

Again other saws akin to the previous ones which can be compared with those in the various direction sections of the Wind chapter are interesting weather lore.

The faster the rain, the quicker the holdup.

Rain

This maxim hails from Norfolk stating the obvious that heavy rain will fill dykes or flood ground quickly and consequently hold up many jobs on the land.

Rain long foretold, long last;
Short notice, soon past. ****

Small showers last long, but
sudden storms are short. ****

If it rains well
it will shine well. ***

The second adage appears in Shakespeare's *Richard II*. All three are very true. Sudden rain or showers frequently pass through under an hour but the gradual expectation of slight rain continues much longer.

Rain at seven, fine at eleven, ****
Rain at eight, not fine till eight. **

Next follows one of the most famous of all English weather lore. Of course seven is included to rhyme with eleven. The reader must remember that rain does not fall conveniently at any *special* time, it is not geared to any clock, it falls at any moment of the 24-hour day. Test figures over 317 days in 1978-79 (in mainly spring, summer and autumn to avoid winter sleet and snow in Oxfordshire) showed that rain occurred least at 0300 local time with 30 occasions (9.8 percent) and most at 0700 with 47 occasions (15.3 percent) - so little hourly variation. The test also showed that by measuring the duration of rain, drizzle and showers the average length of rainfall was 2.5 hours. Rain at 0700 and fine before 1100 produced a good result of 57 percent - remember that frontal rain could cease say at 0930 followed by immediate showers. The *prolonged* rain period from 0800 till 1800 would therefore seem unlikely and in fact produces only 13 percent. 27/47 (57)
5/40 (13)

Rain before seven
Lift before eleven. *****

Rain

Fine before seven
Fine before eleven. *****

These maxims are the ones most people remember. Notice there is a subtle difference between these and the previous saws. It's rain *before* 0700 and fine before 1100 that's tested here. A better result of 69 percent is achieved. 27/39 (69)

If rain begins at early morning
light,
Twill end ere day at noon is
bright. ******

Rain was investigated to begin around dawn. "Ere" means before so a dry 1200 (noon) was searched for. The final figure was excellent with 87 percent, but remember only March to August with sunrises varying from 0400 to 0700 were checked. The winter figures would shorten the time period between sunrise and noon and presumably offer a lower percentage.

40/46 (87)

For a morning rain leave not
your journey. ***

Testing was limited to any rain from sunrise to 1200 followed by no rain 1200 to sunset. Not a very encouraging result. The figures vary so much between this saw and the previous one because often a shower or occasional slight rain would occur during the afternoon even though there was a dry noon.

37/87 (43)

If it rains before daylight it
will hold up before eight
o'clock. If it rains about ****
noon it will continue throughout
the afternoon. If it rains *
before nine p.m. it will rain
the next day. *****

If the rain ceases after mid-day
it will rain the next day. If ****
the rain ceases before mid-day
it will be clear next day. ***

If it rains before five p.m.
it will rain throughout the

night. If it rains between ***
eight o'clock and nine o'clock
in the morning it will continue
until mid-day if it has not **
ceased by then it will carry on
until the evening. ***

This long and specific piece of weather lore was tested for eight of its prophesies. The middle section concerned with wind directions was left (these are dealt with in the Wind chapter). The eight results varied from 14 to 76 percent depending on the time involved with each rain prognostication.

Rain before daylight will cease before 0800	23/38	(61)
" " noon " continue throughout afternoon (till 1700)	6/43	(14)
" after 2100 clearing overnight will rain again next day	68/89	(76)
" ceases after 1200 then rain " "	24/39	(62)
" " before " " clear " "	9/26	(35)
" before 1700 then rain throughout night	14/36	(39)
" " 0800-0900 then rain till 1200	14/52	(27)
" " " " " " " evening	5/14	(36)

Night rains
Makes drowned fens. ****

This East Anglian maxim is possibly hinting that no evaporation occurs at night so more rain affects the earth.

Rain a short time before
sunrise will be followed at
least by a fine afternoon; ****
but rain soon after sunrise
generally by a wet day. **

The first part of this adage was tested by noting rain during the hour before sunrise followed by a fine afternoon (1200-1700 hour). Only a 54 percent correct result emerged. Rain during the hour after sunrise with a wet afternoon produced only 28 percent.

20/37 (54)
11/39 (28)

A hasty shower of rain falling
when the wind has raged some
hours, soon allays it. *

There seems to be no logic here.

Marry the rain to the wind,
and you have a calm. **

In certain frontal systems, especially cold fronts, this maxim rings true. Equally there are occasions when it does not occur.

A small rain may allay a
great storm.

To use the verb 'may' renders any saw as useless.

If it rains when the sun shines,
it will rain the next day. *****

If it rains when the sun is
shining, the devil is beating
his grandmother. He is
laughing, and she is crying.

Sunshine and shower,
rain again tomorrow. *****

If it rains when the sun shines,
it will surely rain the next day
about the same hour. **

A sunshiny shower
Never lasts half-an-hour. ****

Sunshiny rain
Will soon go again. ****

The fourth saw hails from Suffolk, fifth Bedfordshire and sixth Devon. All are true. Showers are brief periods of rain, hail or snow caused chiefly by convective cumulus or cumulonimbus clouds and by definition are scattered. Therefore sunny intervals often occur between them. A showery airstream can last or indicate an unsettled weather pattern and the 66 percent result for rain the next day is a good figure. The Suffolk saying only emerged with 28 percent. 66/101 (66)
28/101 (28)

Rain

After rain comes sunshine. ***

If this saw literally means rain and not showers then it is not necessarily true.

There is usually fair weather
before a settled course of rain. ***

Again this is correct in some synoptic situations but not in others.

Wet continues if the ground
dries up too soon. ****

For a wet surface to quickly dry it presumably experiences a strong drying wind (of low humidity) or strong sunshine. Both are more often associated with short dry settled spells.

Who soweth in rain,
he shall reap it with tears.

Who soweth in rain
Hath weed to his pain;
But worse shall he speed
That soweth ill seed.

Good old fashioned farming lore.

Although it rains,
throw not away thy watering pot. ****

The weather is so changeable in England, what seems like a wet period soon becomes a dry spell.

When the rain causes bubbles to
rise in water it falls upon, the
shower will last long. ***

This Essex maxim is intriguing. For rain to cause water bubbles on rivers and lakes presumably it has to possess a fast downward velocity which only occurs in moderate or heavy rain or showers. As in previous saws in this chapter a sudden heavy rain soon passes over which tends to contradict this Essex saw.

Rain

It is raining heavens high.

It is raining heavens hard.

Yorkshire and Norfolk provide the first and second sayings. "Heaven" in this context is the region of the atmosphere where clouds are situated. The expression "the heavens opened" meaning a cloudburst or downpour is very similar and probably has the same meaning as the two above.

If the rain comes down slanting,
It will be everlasting. ***

"Slanting rain" is caused by strong low-level winds which can be associated with rain lasting for short or long periods.

In wet weather it rains
without half trying. ****

More subtle than it appears. In a long rainy spell or season the wet weather seems to painfully continue as if without asking. In meteorology once a long dry or wet sequence has become established its *persistence* is hard to break.

If it raineth when it doth flow,
Then take your ox and go to
plough.
But if it raineth when it doth
ebb,
Unyoke your oxen and go to bed. **

If it rains with the flow,
thee can go out to snow;
If it rains with the ebb,
thee can go back to bed. **

These two saws come from the Severn Estuary. Unfortunately there is no scientific or meteorological reason why tidal changes should affect the weather in a major way. The saws contain little truth. But the ebbing and flowing of the sea will always be believed by people to influence the weather - it is so deep rooted.

RAIN

A poor man's rain
cometh at night.

Presumably a rich man grows affluent with a perfect growing combination of daytime rain and sun, whereas a poor man collects only half of this at night.

It never rains but it pours. ***

A very famous phrase more connected today with the human experience of finding that events, usually misfortunes, have an uncanny way of suddenly all coming together around the same time. Weatherwise it only occurs with well-established depressions, active fronts or heavy showers.

A sharp shower of rain
following a period of
light, but continuous,
rain or drizzle is a
sign that the weather
will soon improve. ****

Showers and sunshine, the two
in their turn,
Bring certain good weather
for which we do yearn. ****
But showers and sunshine, then
gloom overhead,
Will bring on more rain
for some hours, it is said. ****

Two sharp country observations of rain, shower and sunny interval sequences that are absolutely correct. The first saw seems to apply to the passage of a cold front or one with a warm sector. The clearance behind the cold front has usually clearer weather sometimes with showers. The last part of the second maxim possibly indicates an extensive shower or trough of showers indicating prolonged rain.

Small rain can lay a great dust. *****

If very light, short showers
come during dry weather, they
are said to "harden the drought" *****
and indicate no change.

RAIN

In a way these two arc like the recent saw connected with drought or wet weather. A prolonged dry spell, especially inland in the summers of 1975 and 1976, builds up its own dryness factor on the ground with foliage and soil. Any attempt to rain or shower is checked or partially "dried out" through this reason.

CLOUDS

People tend to have difficulty in distinguishing all the different types of cloud. Before the days of official cloud classification, English cloud weather lore often used terms such as "mackerel sky" and "curly wisps" to describe the shape and construction of a particular cloud. Infact the sayings contain a wealth of beautiful descriptive prose as well as prophecy.

To understand clouds two items are important; the type and height of base. The type depends on whether the cloud is in a layer or heap. Height of cloud base determines into which of the three major cloud levels it belongs. When all put together the following list makes up the official cloud classification:

High cloud	16,500 - 40,000 ft	*Cirrus (Ci)* *Cirrocumulus (Cc)* *Cirrostratus (Cs)*
Medium cloud	6,500 - 23,000 ft	*Altocumulus (Ac)* *Altostratus (As)* *Nimbostratus (Ns)*
Low cloud	Surface - 6,500 ft	*Stratocumulus (Sc)* *Stratus (St)* *Cumulus (Cu)* *Cumulonimbus (Cb)*

CIRRUS

The high level or *Cirrus (Ci)* clouds consist of ice crystals and very low temperatures. *Cirrus* (from the Latin meaning a lock of hair, tuft of horsehair or bird's tuft) is often fibrous and white. Depending on its shape one can foretell much in future weather.

After a long run of clear
weather the appearance of
light streaks of cirrus cloud
at a great elevation is often
the first sign of a change.

****

Clouds

The longer the dry weather has lasted the less is rain likely to follow the cloudiness of the cirrus. *****

These two saws are opposite in meaning, but as can be seen in the results the general trend is that this type of *Cirrus* presages rain - a 50 percent chance within one day and a 71 percent chance within two.

If cirrus clouds dissolve and appear to vanish it is an indication of fine weather. ****

Cirrus of a long, straight, feathery kind, with soft edges and outlines, or with soft, delicate colours at sunrise or sunset, is a sign of fine weather. ****

Curly wisps and brown-backed pieces are not a bad sign. ****

Three maxims indicating good weather to follow. This is not really true as to remain fine for one day results give a 50 percent chance and for two dry days only 29 percent.

Trace in the sky the painter's brush,
Then winds around you soon will rush. ***

The cloud called 'goat's hair' or the 'grey mare's tail' forbodes wind. ***

The second adage mentions the famous phrases "goat's hair" and "gray mare's tail".

If woolly fleeces strew the heavenly way,
Be sure no rain disturbs the summer day. ****

This one hints of possible rain the same day.

Thin *Cirrus* then rain within one day	114/228	(50)
" " " " " two days	163/228	(71)
" " " " " three "	206/228	(90)
Thin *Cirrus* then dry for one day	114/228	(50)
" " " " " two days	65/228	(29)
" " " " " three days	22/228	(10)

Slightly undulating lines of cirrus occur in fine weather; but anything like a deeply indented outline precedes heavy rain or wind. ******

When the cirrus clouds appear at lower elevations than usual, and with a denser character, expect a storm from the opposite quarter to the clouds. ***

The last part of the initial saying describes dense *Cirrus* cloud with solid outline. Often these are the blown-off anvil tops from *Cumulonimbus (Cb)* cloud tops - hence the surety of violent showers in the forecast. The test provided an excellent 100 percent result. 22/22 (100)

When looking in a westerly or easterly direction, if the centre of the bank of cirro-velum is to the right of the point from which the edge, or the cirro-fillum outside the edge, is moving, the probability of bad weather is not nearly so great as if the centre was to the left of this point. But looking in a northerly or southerly direction if the centre lies to the right of the direction of motion of the bank, the ensuing weather will be worse than if it lies to the left. ****

If the upper current of clouds

comes from the north-west in the morning, a fine day will ensue. *

If clouds drive up high from the south, expect a thaw. ****

High upper clouds, crossing the sun, moon, or stars in a direction different from that of the lower clouds, or the wind when felt below, foretell a change of wind towards their direction. **

This long and complicated piece of Victorian prose comes from the Rev. Clement Ley. If an observer faces south and sees the *Cirrus* bank moving from the west (then the centre of the cloud will be to the right of the cloud's motion) poor weather will ensue. Basically the clergyman is just viewing the wind direction at *Cirrus* levels, in this case S.S.W. to N.N.W.

Feathery clouds, like palm branches or the fleur-de-lys, denote immediate or coming showers. ****

When the tails are turned downwards, fair weather or slight showers often follow. **

Cirrus clouds announce an easterly wind. ** *If their undersurface is level, and their streaks pointing upwards, they indicate rain;* ***** *if downwards, wind and dry weather.* *****

When the streamers point upward, the clouds are falling, and rain is at hand; when streamers point downward, the clouds are ascending, and drought is at hand. *****

A large formation of murky white cirrus may merely indicate a backing of wind to an easterly quarter. **

This type of *Cirrus*, especially in the form where the streaks point upward, strongly denote wind and rain. The upward streamers (ice crystals which have grown and fall out of the main *Cirrus* cloud) denote winds increasing with height (shear) through the cloud layer. Often this cloud progressively invades the sky and is the classic forerunner of rain and overcast conditions. The downward streamers denote fine and settled weather. The easterly wind in the third and fifth maxims is to be expected.

Dense *Cirrus* then rain within one day	376/607	(62)
" " " " " two days	516/607	(85)
" " " " " three days	565/607	(93)
Dense *Cirrus* then dry for one day	231/607	(38)
" " " " " two days	91/607	(15)
" " " " " three days	42/607	(7)

The barred or ribbed cirrus is considered, as good a danger signal as that given by a falling barometer. *****

The barred or ribbed *Cirrus (Cirrus vertebratus)* is a definite indicator of rain.

If the cirrus clouds appear to windward and change to cirrostratus, it is a sign of rain. ******

When cirrus merges into cirrostratus, and when cumulus increases towards evening and becomes lower, expect wet weather. ******

The cirrocumulus, when accompanied by cirrostratus, is a sure indication of a coming storm. ******

All three sayings are excellent observations of bad weather. In fact rain within 24 hours yields a test result of 81 percent and the average time interval between the first appearance of the cloud and the first rain is 6.9 hours.

Ci and *Cs* clouds then rain within one day	13/16	(81)
" " " " " " " two days	14/16	(87)

Cirrus moving from north or north-east with high barometer is a sign of settled weather in summer, and of temporary fine weather in winter; with low barometer, it is a sign of marked improvements in the weather. *****

Cirrus moving from east (a rare occurrence) is a sign of fine weather in winter, but of unsettled weather in summer. *****

Cirrus moving from the south-east (which rarely occurs in a low or unsteady barometer) is a sign of improving weather in winter, and in summer frequently indicates coming thunderstorms. *****

Cirrus moving from the south generally indicates unsettled weather, especially in summer. *****

Cirrus moving from the south-west indicates unsettled, and sometimes stormy, weather in winter. In summer it often precedes thunderstorms; but with a high barometric pressure and a high temperature it frequently has no disturbing influence, and is then usually replaced by cirro-macula (cirrocumulus). *****

Clouds

If cirrus comes from the west it is commonly in summer a symptom of fair weather, but is less so in winter. *****

When cirrus comes from the north-west, when not tending to the form cirro-filum (thread-like cirrus), it is an indication of temporary fine weather, especially in summer. *****

A V-point north in cirrus commonly indicates improving weather over and to the south, but distant atmospheric disturbances in the north and north-west. *****

A V-point north-east in cirrus, expect temporarily settled weather, especially with high barometer. *****

A V-point east in cirrus, expect settled weather in winter; in summer, with high temperatures, it sometimes indicates disturbances, which will be felt most to the south-west of the place of observation. *****

A V-point south-east in cirrus, fine weather in winter, except when occurring immediately after heavy rain, when it is commonly followed by squalls. In summer it is almost invariably followed by thunder, with damp and sultry weather. *****

A V-point south in cirrus with a fairly low barometer, after a fall of rain, indicates *showery weather in summer, and rough, squally weather in winter, with south-west or west winds, especially if the cloud velocity is great. With a high barometer, it indicates in summer thunderstorms from the south-west, but in winter may be taken as a sign of favourable weather.* *****

A V-point south-west in cirrus, moderately fine weather. *****

A V-point west in cirrus, fine weather in the warm months. The weather to the south and south-east of the observer is then normally dry and warm but to the extreme north-west unsettled. In winter it is a symptom of unsettled weather. *****

A V-point north-west in cirrus is bad; when it occurs just after a rise in the barometer, it indicates a sudden fall, with wind and rain. *****

A V-point between west-north-west and north-west, especially with rapid cloud movement, is always followed by unsettled weather. *****

These closely observed rules of V-point cirrus are the sole work of the Rev. Clement Ley mentioned earlier in the chapter. In practice they describe the movement of cirrus cloud or the wind direction at these levels. The associated weather is true.

CIRROCUMULUS

Cirrocumulus (Cc) cloud is easily recognised by its regular pattern of fish scales. It often occurs with other types of *Cirrus* cloud and can be the sign of bad or good weather to come. The famous "Mackerel sky" of course refers to the mackerel's back resembling the dappled small white fleecy clouds of *Cc*. Sometimes very high *Altocumulus (Ac)* can be included as a mackerel sky. All 10 saws refer to the unsettled changeable weather to follow. Rain occurred within 24 hours 69 percent of the time.

Mackerel sky then rain within one day	70/102	(69)
" " " " " two days	85/102	(83)
" " " " " three days	95/102	(93)

Cirrocumulus is commonly called 'mackerel sky'.

Mackerel sky and mares' tails
Make lofty ships carry low sails. *****

A mackerel sky denotes fair weather for that day, but rain a day or two later. *****

Mackerel sky, mackerel sky,
Never long wet and never long dry. *****

Mackerel clouds in sky
Expect more wet than dry. *****

A mackerel sky
Is as much for wet as tis for dry. *****

Mackerel scales
Furl your sails. *****

A mackerel sky,
Not twenty-four hours dry. *****

Mackerel sky
Rain is nigh. *****

Clouds

If clouds look as if scratched
by a hen,
Get ready to reef your topsails
then. *****

Hen's scarts and filly tails.
Make lofty ships carry low sails. *****

These two maxims mention "hen's scarts" or scratchings - a descriptive phrase referring to *Cc* cloud. Infact the same as a mackerel sky. The forecast is emphasized here for wind.

Cottony shreds, rounded and
clear in outline, indicate
dangerous disturbances. *****

Small floating clouds over a
bank of clouds, sign of rain. *****

If in the north-west before
daylight ends there appear a
company of small black clouds
like flocks of sheep, it is a
sure and certain of rain. *****

Small white clouds like a flock
of sheep, and red in colour,
wind follows. *****

If the sky, from being clear,
becomes quickly fretted or
spotted all over with bunches
of clouds, rain will soon
follow. *****

Small white clouds, like a flock
of sheep, driving north-west,
indicate continued fine weather. **

Further country descriptions of the *Cc* cloud. The last adage differs in that it forecasts fine weather.

A curdly sky
Will not leave the earth long
dry. *****

Curdled cirrus cloud often
indicates the approach of
bad weather. *****

A curdly sky
Will not be twenty-four hours
dry. *****

"Curdly" is a rough interpretation of *Cc* with rain to ensue.

Cirro-macula (speckle-cloud)
nearly always occurs in warm
weather, when the atmosphere
at the earth's surface has but
little lateral motion. **

A sky dappled with light clouds
of the cirrocumulus form in the
early morning generally leads to
a fine and warm day. **

Before thunder, cirrocumulus
clouds often appear in very
dense and compact masses, in
close contact. ***

A blue and white sky
Never four-and-twenty
hours dry. *****

The first sayings hail from the Victorian vicar, the Rev. Clement Ley, calling *Cc* a speckled cloud. Northamptonshire provides the last maxim which can just about be passed off as *Cc*.

CIRROSTRATUS

In unsettled weather sheet
cirrus (cirrostratus) precedes
more wind or rain. *****

When a plain sheet of the wane
cloud is spread over a large
surface at evening tide, or
when the sky gradually thickens
with this cloud, a fall of

steady rain is usually the consequence. *****

If long lines of cirrostratus extend along the horizon, and are slightly contracted in their centre, expect heavy rain the following day. ***

The waved cirrostratus indicates heat and thunder. ***

A high sheet of cloud spreading across the whole sky, and casting a general gloom over the countryside, presages rain and wind. *****

If the sky looks washed with a milky white,
The rain is near though not yet in sight. *****

Cirrostratus (Cs) or sheet *Cirrus* nearly always covers the whole sky and is of a white milky colour. The sun can still be observed often with the famous 22° halo (see Halo chapter). *Cs* cloud is nearly always associated with jet streams (an upper core of maximum winds) and warm fronts. As a warm front approaches *Cs* is normally followed by *Altostratus (As)* then rain and lower cloud. Rain followed within 24 hours on 67 percent of occasions. Also 6.1 hours was the mean time interval between the first *Cs* and first rain. The last saw refers to *Cirrostratus undulatus* or undulating or wave *Cs* occurring where there are strong upper waves near jet streams.

Cirrostratus then rain within	1 day	62/93	(67)
" " " "	2 days	93/93	(100)

ALTOCUMULUS LENTICULARIS

Altocumulus lenticularis (Ac len) (alto means height or upper air, cumulus means heap and lenticularis shaped like a lens or lentil) appears in the form of long cigar-shaped clouds at medium levels.

When the ark is out,
North and south,
In the rain's mouth. ****

Clouds

When the ark is out,
Rain is about. ****

A long stripe of cloud, sometimes called a salmon, sometimes a Noah's ark, when it stretches east and west, is a sign of a storm; but when north and south, ***
of fine weather. ***

This cloud is called in the Yorkshire Dales 'Noaship', and the old Danes called it 'Nolskeppet'.

The fish (hake) shaped cloud, if pointing east and west, indicates rain; if north and ***
south, more fine weather. ***

North and south, the sign of drought; ***
East and west, the sign of blast. ***

The fourth saw comes from Yorkshire and fifth Bedfordshire. The "ark", "Noah's ark", "salmon", "Noaship", "Nolskeppit" and "fish-shaped" from the saws *all* refer to the shape of *Ac len* cloud. When positioned north to south fine weather is forecast, when east to west rain. This almond-shaped cloud is directly connected with mountain lee-waves. For example when a westerly upper wind blows across the Welsh mountains waves on the lee-side occur. Sometimes clouds form in their wave crests at right angles to the westerly. So a north to south "Noah's ark" indicates medium level westerly winds which often bring rain. The test for all orientated *Ac len* gave a 55 percent chance of rain within one day after the cloud was sighted.

Ac len then rain within one day	31/56	(55)
" " " " " two days	33/56	(59)
" " " " " three days	38/56	(68)

Altocumulus

Long parallel bands of clouds in the direction of the winds indicate steady high winds to come. ***

The ordinary *Altocumulus* which is often seen offers a high 68 percent chance of rain within 24 hours.

Altocumulus then rain within	one day	257/376	(68)
" " " "	two days	311/376	(83)
" " " "	three days	348/376	(93)

CUMULUS

Cumulus (Cu) clouds are of course those cottony heap clouds varying from small "fair weather" *cumulus* to huge towering *Cumulonimbus (Cb)* clouds producing heavy sometimes thundery showers. Therefore two important distinctions are made. The first is obvious - the deeper the cloud the more showery its nature. The second is that the colder the cloud (a lower freezing level) the higher the risk of showers.

Cumulus clouds are called
rain balls in Lancashire.

A round-topped cloud, with
flattened base,

Carries rainfall in its face. **

The rounded clouds called
'water-waggons' which fly
alone in the lower currents
of wind forbode rain. **

The first saw comes from Lancashire. The three suggest that *all cumulus* clouds produce rain or more correctly showers which of course are confined to the larger deeper ones. Records kept in Oxfordshire show that only 31 percent of *cumulus* cloud provided showers within 6 hours. 197/634 (31)

When clouds appear like
rocks and towers,
The earth's refreshed by
frequent showers. ***

When mountains and cliffs in the
clouds appear,
Some sun and violent showers are
near. ****

Towering *cumulus* or *cumulonimbus* clouds should be a safe bet for showers. It came as a shock to find that only 45 percent of occasions provided showers within 6 hours. On reflection a shower falls over a relatively small area and often many regions remain dry. Even so a better result was hoped for.
106/233 (45)

Clouds like globes at sunrise
announce clear, sharp weather. ***

When the cumulus clouds are
smaller at sunset than they
were at noon, expect fair
weather. ***

Global cloud possibly denotes morning *cumulus* which usually accompanies clear sharp weather or an unstable cool airstream. The second adage follows the normal daily sequence of *cumulus* as it disperses around sunset - as air temperature falls inland the thermal activity to maintain the cloud is lost.

Clouds

The formation of cumulus clouds to leeward during a strong wind indicates the approach of a calm with rain. ***

When cumulus clouds become heaped up to leeward during a strong wind at sunset, thunder may be expected during the night. ***

The first saying is difficult to understand. It may relate a windy showery airstream which is quickly stabilizing or losing its ability to produce *cumulus*. This often happens in the evening but sometimes occurs when a ridge of high pressure precedes a warm front. Here earlier gales would quickly be followed by frontal rain and calm. The second adage presents no solution.

Stratus

Stratus (St) cloud (meaning to extend, spread or flatten out or cover with a layer) is a low sheet of cloud with a base ranging from the surface to about 1,500ft. It is very important to distinguish between two types of *stratus*. The first is associated with dry weather and more often forms at night and during the morning. It is grey and can be a complete sheet or broken. Normally in spring, summer and autumn it begins in the early morning as a sheet. As the temperature rises the cloud will thin and lift often with sun's outline visible. Finally it will "burn off" or disperse but can form into *cumulus* cloud. The second type is connected with stormy wet weather being a *ragged* dark cloud sheet.

Stratus clouds have always been regarded as the harbingers of fine weather, and there are a few fine days in the year when the morning breaks out through a disappearing stratus cloud. ***

Stratus is *not* always a forerunner of fine weather as explained in the previous paragraph. Tests over a year (1979) in Oxfordshire showed that with any amount of *stratus* and a base 1,000ft or less was followed by rain within 6 hours on 59 per-cent of all occasions. 541/918 (59)

Clouds

Misty clouds, forming or hanging on heights, show wind and rain coming, if they remain, increase, or descend. ***** *If they rise or disperse, the weather will improve.* *****

Clouds upon hills, if rising, do not bring rain; ***** *if falling, rain follows.* *****

The first saw has the best description of the two *stratus* types and their subsequent weather.

If mists rise to the hilltops and there stay, expect rain shortly. *****

When it gangs up i'fops,
It'll fa' down i' drops. *****

When the clouds are upon the hills,
They'll come down by the mills. *****

The second maxim hails from Northern England where "it gangs up i' fops means the cloud covers the hills. Hampshire provides the last saying where the second line refers to heavy rain which will fill springs and streams to run watermills. Test results give a high 68 percent rating for *stratus* covering hills followed by rain within 6 hours. 465/679 (68)

When the Pendle's Head is free from clouds, the people thereabout expect a halcyon day, and those on the banks of the Can in Westmorland can tell what weather to look for from the voice of its falls. ****

When Firle Hill and Long Man has a cap,
We at Aston gets a drap. *****

Clouds

When Wolsonbury has a cap,
Hurstpierpoint will have a drap. *****

If Bever hath a cap,
Your churls of the vale look
to that. *****

When Ladie Lift.
Puts on her shift,
She feares a downright raine; *****
But when she doffs it, you will
finde
The rain is o'er, and still the
winde,
And Phoebus shine againe. *****

If Riving Pike do wear a hood,
Be sure the day will ne'er be
good. *****

If Roseberry Topping wears a
cap,
Let Cleveland then beware of
a rap. *****

When Roseberry Topping wears a
hat,
Morden Carre will suffer for
that. *****

When Eston Nabbe puts on a
cloake,
As Roseberry a cappe,
Then all the folks on
Cleveland's clay
Ken there will be a clappe. **

When Bredon Hill puts on his
hat,
Ye men of the Vale, beware
of that. *****

When Hoar Down has a hat,
Let Kenton beware of a skat. *****

Old Mother Goring got her cap on
We shall have some wet. *****

When Fairlie Down puts on his
cap,
Romney Marsh will have its sap. *****

These thirteen weather adages maintain the hill stratus theme with emphasis to a particular local hill or mountain often referring to it as being covered by a cap, hat, shift or hood of low cloud *(stratus)*. The first saw refers to Westmorland; Sussex claims the second and third; Leicestershire the fourth; Herefordshire the fifth where Ladie Lift refers to a clump of trees near Weobley; Lancashire the sixth; Yorkshire seventh, eighth and ninth; Worcestershire the tenth. A "skat" in the eleventh is a shower; Sussex claims the twelfth referring to Chanctonbury Ring, a tree clump on the South Downs on the Goring estate; finally Kent originates the thirteenth. The test results of the previous paragraph apply here.

Helm Cloud

A cloud, called the 'helm cloud',
or 'helm bar', hovering about the
hilltops for a day or two, is
said to presage wind and rain. ****

The "Helm bar" is a nearly stationary slender roll of whirling cloud which rests along or just above the Crossfell Range in Westmoreland and Cumberland, especially east of the river Eden. It appears and forms in a strong cold North-East wind (the Helm wind) most frequently in late winter and spring. It is an example of a mountain lee-wave and appears above a point ½ to 3½ miles from the foot of the fell.

THUNDERSTORMS AND CUMULONIMBUS CLOUDS

Thunderstorms and hail are associated with the vigorous Cumulonimbus (Cb) cloud - a very deep vertical cumulus cloud often with an anvil-looking cirrus top. Terrific up and down currents control the cloud's life cycle. They occur in cool unstable polar Westerlies and in warm moist summer polar South-Westerlies. Sometimes Altocumulus Castellanus (Ac Cas) cloud can be responsible for thunderstorms. They are the medium-level deep convective cloud often with bases as high as 6,000 feet. Remember lightning is a discharge of static electricity which can be *seen*. Forked lightning is seen as an irregular fork, sheet lightning is a mass glow of light. Thunder is the sound *heard* produced by the violent expansion of the air along the path of the lightning flash. Since light (lightning) travels faster than sound (thunder) one can judge the distance of the lightning from the observer by counting the number of seconds between the flash and the thunder and dividing by five. This gives the distance in miles. Using this method one can plot the path of such a storm. Thunderstorms continue throughout the year but are most active from May to September with a summer peak in July.

Usually three conditions are required for a Cb or thunder cloud to form. Firstly a very deep vertical unstable layer with the cloud beginning as a cottony cumulus cloud vigorously growing into a hugh Cb with tops 25,000-40,000ft (6-8 miles deep). Secondly plenty of water vapour is needed at the surface to supply the rapid cloud growth. Finally a trigger action is required to set off the convection, often in England by high afternoon maximum air temperatures (insolation). Trigger action from sea and windward coasts is also available with constant high sea-surface temperatures. One of the favourite situations for thunderstorms are stationary depressions and troughs sometimes helped by the lifting action of mountains.

The thunderstorm of the season
will come from the same quarter
as the first one. **

This fanciful idea that all thunderstorm clouds in one season move from one general quarter is intriguing but false.

Thunderstorms

First thunder in winter or
spring indicates rain and
very cold weather. *

Thunder and lightning early in
winter or late in fall indicate
warm weather. *****

Lightning brings heat. *****

The air useth to be extreme hot
before thunders. *****

One saw indicates cold weather and two others warmth after a thunderstorm. They produce poor results but the forecast of warm weather hits the jackpot with 80 percent. Of course this is to be expected as the majority of thunderstorms are associated with moist mild unstable airstreams. Bacon's saw is last.

1st thunder in winter/spring then wet/very cold	2/16	(13)
" thunder in early winter/late autumn then warm	8/10	(80)

Winter thunder,
The old folk death, to young
folks plunder. ***

Presumably this means winter thunderstorms bring on humid heat which used to kill off old people but suited others.

The first thunder of the year
awakes
All the frogs and all the snakes.

A poetic way of saying the first year's thunder (occurring any month January to April) *can* coincide with end of winter hibernation of the frog (February/March) or snake (April).

When it thunders in the morning,
it will rain before night. *****

Thunder in the morning denotes
winds; at noon, showers. *****

Morning thunders signify winds;

noon thunders, rain; roaring thunders, rough wind; crackling thunders, wind and rain. ****

Thunder in ye morning signifies wynde, about noon rayne, in ye evening great tempest. ****

If there be thunder in the evening, there will be much rain and showery weather. ****

Bacon originated the second saw. Thunder or lightning or both occurring at any time of the day (except nightime) signify heavy showers of rain (sometimes hail) with strong gusts.

If in a clear and starry night it lighten to the south-east, it foretelleth great store of wind and rain to come in from those parts. ****

If there be sheet lightning and a clear sky in spring, summer and autumn evenings, expect heavy rains. *****

The distant thunder speaks of coming rain. *****

If on fairly clear nights lightning is seen, especially to the S.E., it tells of heavy showers to come. The S.E. lightning denotes thundery activity in the English Channel or relevant coasts often denoting storms to arrive later.

Forked lightning at night,
The next day clear and bright. **

Lightning without thunder after a clear day, there will be a continuance of fair weather. **

Opposite in meaning to previous maxims and basically incorrect. Only on very few occasions does the weather continue fine.

If it sinks from the north
It will double its wrath.
If it sinks from the south,
It will open its mouth.
If it sinks from the west,
It is never at rest.
If it sinks from the east,
It will leave us in peace. ****

If the lightning is in the colder quarters of the heaven, in the north and north-east, hailstones will follow; but if in the warmer, as the south and west, there will be showers with a sultry temperature. ****

Lightning under north star will bring rain in three days. *

Lightning in north will be followed by rain in twenty-four hours. ****

Lightning in north in summer is a sign of heat. ***

When it lightens only from the north-west, look for rain the next day. ****

Thunder from the south or south-east indicates foul weather; from the north or north-west, fair weather. ****

If from the south or the west it lightens, expect both wind and rain from these points. ***

Lightning signifies the approach of wind and rain from the quarter where it lightens; ***
but if it lightens in different parts of the sky, there will be severe and dreadful storms. ****

Thunder from the south or south-east indicates long storms; from the north or north-west, short storms. ****

These adages, with the first from Kent and second from Bacon's vigorous quill, are examples of very good observation and excellent forecasts. The main point to remember about thunderstorms is that they move or are steered by the wind at medium levels. For a Cb around 10,000-18,000ft. The surface wind in the vicinity of the thunderstorm would be under a barrage of violent up and down draughts causing it to experience *any* direction and speed. For example a Cb cloud can bodily move from the south to the north with east or west surface gusty winds.

Abundance depends on sour milk. ***

Every so often one comes across some vague weather saw which can be easily scoffed at and at first glance regarded as useless. This one intrigued the author. After a number of inquiries the true meaning appeared. (Never regard old country weather lore as ridiculous - they often hide subtle meanings.) This saw relates that thunderstorms aid crops. The increase in atmospheric electricity is supposed to oxidize the ammonia of the air forming nitric acid. In turn this affects milk - hence the "sour milk". Tests were conducted 1947-66 with very few cases.

Hay	3/6	(50)
Wheat	1/6	(17)

When it thunders, the thief becomes honest.

If anyone has been very close to a lightning flash with its instant thunder, its terrific frightening explosive sound and suddenness, one will never forget it. Indeed it's enough to make a thief honest.

Thunderstorms go round and round the valley and cannot escape. **

A quaint maxim hailing from the Thames Valley around Oxford. The saying isn't true as the valley is shallow (only deep mountainous valleys affect the tracking and life cycle of thunderstorms). If one is slow moving it means the medium-level steering speed is light. Often in these situations more than one thunderstorm joins together giving the impression that they remain in one area for a long time.

Some claim thunder is "God moving His furniture about."

An old country way of explaining why it thunders.

When a house-leek grows on the roof of a house, that house will never be struck by lightning. *

Many wild flowers and plants have this non-lightning strike property. The house-leek is one of them. (Refer to the flower chapter for similar saws.)

It never thunders but it rains. ****

After much thunder, much rain. ****

Thunderstorms and heavy rain showers go together. One may hear thunder in the distance and escape rain, but this is the exception.

The sound of bells is supposed to dissipate thunder and lightning. *

Although this looks like an intriguing maxim with a deep meaning, the author cannot see one.

HAIL

Hail is always associated with showers and Cumulonimbus (Cb) cloud and nearly always with thunderstorms. The latter occur all through the year but are most frequent from May to September peaking in England in July. If a large hailstone is cut the inside is similar to an onion with alternating layers of clear and opaque ice. In its early stages of development the hailstone gets caught up in vicious undraughts transfering it to the top of the Cb cloud where the temperatures are very low. Here the hailstone acquires a layer of opaque ice or rime. In its turbulent up and down journey it accumulates its multilayers finally descending to the ground.

Hail brings frost in the tail. ***

A hailstorm by day denotes
a frost at night. ***

Because hail is an ice phenomenon clearly the two saws associate it with cold weather and night frost. This is nearly always true in winter when hail is scarce. Summer hail is rarely followed by ground frost although often occurs with a cool airstream.

If hail appears after a long
course of rain, it is a sign
that the weather will improve
very soon indeed, but showers
will follow if the wind is
westerly, and the stronger
the wind the sharper the
showers - which may be of hail. *****

This is a correct observation of the passage of a vigorous cold front, trough or line squall. The change from continuous rain to hail is caused by the transfer from stable cloudy weather to squally showers and partly cloudy weather. In *this particular* case it is true that the stronger the westerly wind the heavier the shower.

RAINBOW

The old Norsemen called the rainbow "the Bridge of the Gods".

When a rainbow is formed in an approaching cloud, expect a shower; but when in receding cloud, fine weather. *****

When a rainbow appears in the wind's eye, rain is sure to follow. *****

If a rainbow appears in fair weather, foul will follow;
But if a rainbow appears in foul weather, fair weather will follow. *****

The rainbow, after a long drought, is the precursor of a decided change to wet weather; and it happens also that a perfect bow, after an unsettled time, is a precursor of fair weather. *****

Rainbow to windward, foul falls the day;
Rainbow to leeward, damp runs away. *****

Before discussing the merits of the five saws it is best to state a few basic facts about a rainbow. There are sometimes more than one or the primary rainbow - they are the secondary and supernumary bows. Remember a rainbow can only appear to an observer when the sun is behind him and is illuminating raindrops *ahead* of him. The rainbow is made up of red, orange, yellow, green, blue, indigo and violet - easily remembered by the abbreviation ROYGBIV. The sun's rays of white light are refracted and reflected in the raindrop to produce the rainbow with the red on the outside. Also nearly all of the rainbows are connected with *showery* weather where short sunny showers provide the two vital basics for rainbow production. It becomes apparent, for example, that in the morning with the sun in the SE a rainbow would form to the NW of an observer. If this is into wind then it is certain a shower is almost imminent. The reverse also applies.

A dog in the morning,
Sailor, take warning,
A dog in the night,
Is the sailor's delight. *****

A rainbow in the morn,
Put your hook in the corn;
A rainbow in the eve,
Put your hook in the sheave. *****

If there be a rainbow in the eve,
It will rain and leave;
But if there be a rainbow in
the morrow,
It will neither lend or borrow. *****

A rainbow in the morning
Is the shepherd's warning;
A rainbow at night
Is the shepherd's delight. *****

If the rainbow comes at night,
The rain is gone quite. *****

The rainbow in the marnin'
Gives the shepherd a warnin'
The car' his gurt cwoat on his
back;
The rainbow at night is the
shepherd's delight;
For then no gurt cwoat will
he lack. *****

A rainbow at night
Fair weather in sight.
A rainbow at morn,
Fair weather all gorn. *****

The second adage hails from Cornwall, fifth from Suffolk and Wiltshire provides the sixth. A "dog" is a rainbow. Once the sun's elevation reaches above 42°, rainbows cannot normally form. So the main or primary rainbow occurs more frequent in winter than summer and is observed more often in the morning and late afternoon/evening time. It is impossible to see one in the middle of a summer's day. Based on the principle that most of our weather travels west to east, a morning rainbow seen in the west would signify showers and cloud to follow and an evening rainbow in the east clearer weather. Although no tests were carried out the result expected would be about 70 percent. Similar figures can be compared in the Rain Chapter.

When a perfect rainbow shows only two principle colours, which are generally red and yellow, expect fair weather for several days. ****

If the blue should predominate, the air is clearing. *****

If the green be large and bright in the rainbow, it is a sign of continued rain. If red be the strongest colour, there will be rain and wind together. After much wet weather the rainbow indicates a clearing up. If the bow disappears all at once, there will follow serene and settled weather. *****

When the rainbow is broad, with the primatic colours very distinct, and green or blue predominating, expect much rain the succeeding night. If the red colour is conspicuous and the last to disappear, expect both rain and wind. ****

If the rainbow forms and disappears suddenly, the prismatic colours being but slightly discernable, expect fair weather next day. *****

RAINBOW

The general rule about rainbow colours is that the larger the raindrop (in a thunderstorm or heavy shower) the more vivid and beautiful the rainbow colours. A decrease in drop size produces a general fading of the colours. In fact in fog where the water droplets are so small, a rare fogbow is always white.

Whenever you observe the rainbow
to be broken in two or three
places, or perhaps only half of
it visible, expect rainy weather
for two or three days. ****

When the rainbow does not
reach down to the water,
clear weather will follow. **

These two maxims contradict each other. It would seem that a partial rainbow occurs in very windy and showery conditions leaving little time for the sun's rays to form the rainbow. It is therefore thought the first adage is the truest.

A bow low down on the mountains
is a bad sign for the crop. If
seen at a great distance,
it indicates fair weather. ***

Very small rainbows can only occur near the horizon extending from the ground to the cloud base.

Seven rainbows, eight days rain. **

Just playing with numbers occurs here. Of course 7 rainbows would indicate an extremely showery if not thundery airstream.

A rainbow in spring indicates
fair weather for twenty-four
hours. *

This is totally incorrect.

The bow in the morning, rain
will follow; if at noon, heavy

rain; if at night, fair weather. *****
The appearance of double or
triple bows indicates fair for
the present, but heavy rain soon. ****

A double rainbow contains the primary and secondary bows where the latter lies outside with reversed colour notation. A second rainbow does not indicate clearing weather, if anything the opposite.

WILD FLOWERS AND PLANTS

I find plant and flower weather lore one of the most pleasing chapters in this book. It must be the combination of the beautiful shapes and colours of the flowers with the mysteries of weather. Many plants are sensitive to humidity and sunlight changes and of course countrymen believe that in this lies the answer in forecasting weather. Flowers tend to close more when humidity increases, then the favourite forecast is rain but often moist air can naturally occur in dry periods in the evening and in mist and fog.

Most flowers close at night but some remain open. This can occur when overnight temperatures are high and humidity low, which also means a good breeze or cloud cover is present. This is often true when changeable weather is imminent.

Wood Anemone

The yellow wood anemone and the wind flower close their petals and droop before rain. ***

The wood anemone never opens its petals but when the wind blows, whence its name.

The Wood Anemone is nicknamed the Wind Flower (which blooms from March to June) because its flowers nod and shake in the wind. Indeed the petals are very sensitive to disturbance. Certainly any strong increase of wind is always a sound forecast of rain to come, whether it be the downdraught of an oncoming shower or the first signs of a depression. It is interesting to note that its other nicknames are *Windflower* in Devon, Somerset, Hants, Glos, Bucks, N'thants, Warwicks and Cheshire; *Fairie's Windflower* in Dorset and *Wind Plant* in Lincs.

Bladder Campion

This is known as *Thunderbolt* in Kent and blooms from June to September.

WHITE CAMPION

The flower is out between May and June and locally called *Thunderbolt* in Rutland and *Thunderflower* in Cumberland.

CHICKWEED

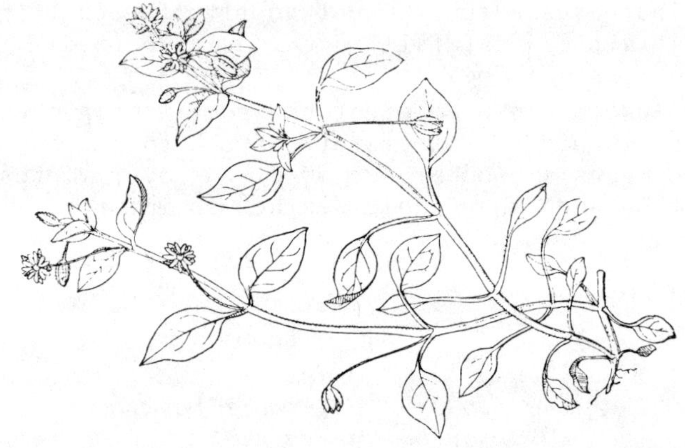

Chickweed expands its leaves boldly and fully when fine weather is to follow; but if it should shut up, then the traveller is to put on his great coat. **

The half opening of the flowers of the chickweed is a sign that the wet will not last long. **

Much early work in observing flowers and weather scientifically was done by Norman L. Silvester during the period 1917 to 1923 in London and Yorkshire. He observed flowers within 200 yards of his Stevenson screen (a purpose-built latticed enclosure for housing thermometers and other meteorological instruments) mainly in spring, summer and autumn. The common Chickweed flower, which is open all the year round, responds to temperature and humidity. Once above a soil temperature of 50^0 Fahrenheit (10^0 Centigrade) *and* air temperature over 51^0F

(10.6^{0}C) the flower answers to humidity, closing at 81 percent. Poor results of 22 percent occurred for rain to follow within 6 hours after the Chickweed flower closed.

26/120 (22)

CINQUEFOIL

Expect rain if the flower of the cinquefoil expands. **

This is a North Riding of Yorkshire weather saw.

CLOVER

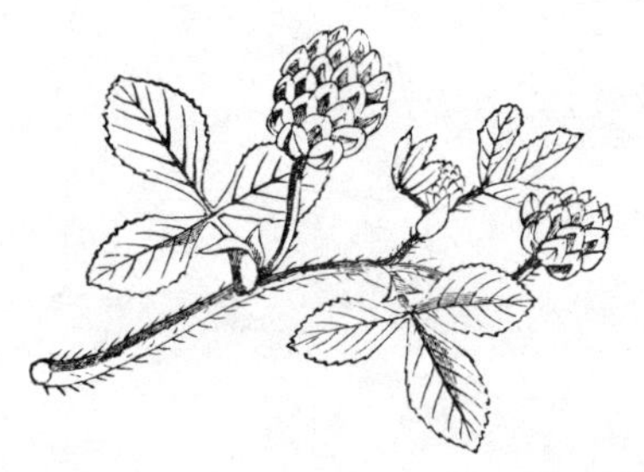

Clover contracts its leaves at the approach of a storm. *

Clover grass is rough to the touch when stormy weather is at hand. *

Expect rain if the stalks of clover stand upright. *

The third saying is from the North Riding of Yorkshire. Temperature and humidity do not seem to be controlling factors over clover movement. Silvester found the overriding reason for leaf closure was wind. On a 42-feet mast he found that in the daytime a wind gust of less than 20 m.p.h. left the leaf open; over 20 m.p.h. it nearly closed, shutting on reaching gale force (gusts of 49 m.p.h. or more). Poor figures evolved from a test of 11 percent success rate giving rain within 6 hours

after the clover leaf closes. Also it was established that an increase in wind did not occur under similar circumstances.
1/9 (11)

CONVOLVULUS

The convolvulus folds up its petals at the approach of rain. **

This trumpet-shaped twining plant, flowering from July to September, is another sensitive type.

COWSLIP

The cowslip stalks being short are said to foreshow a dry summer. *

This beautiful flower, blooming from April to May, will have short stalks due to poor weather conditions of the *previous* seasons.

DAISY

DANDELION

Although no weather lore can be found about the movement of the common daisy's flower (blooming from January to October) or leaves, humidity and temperature cause it to close its flower. Silvester found it opened only when the ground temperature ranged from 52°F (11.1°C) to 58°F (14.4°C) *with* relative humidity 64 to 82 percent. Once the last figure was reached the flower closed. The poor results relate to rain expected within 6 hours after the flower closed. 31/92 (34)

OX-EYE OR MOON DAISY

The great white ox eye closes before rain. **

Another plant known as *Thunder Daisy* in Devon and Somerset which responds to humidity change. It flowers from June to August.

DANDELION

When the down of the dandelion contracts, it is a sign of rain. *

If the down flyeth off colt's foot, dandelion, and thistles, when there is no wind, it is a sign of rain. **

The dandelions close their blossoms before a storm. **

When the dandelion blooms early in spring, there will be a short season. When they bloom later expect a dry summer. * ***

Silvester found that above 51°F (10.6°C) the golden Dandelion (which flowers March to June) always remained open. Below 46°F (7.8°C) they were completely closed. He further found that wind and humidity had no effect. The myth about the down or Dandelion "clock" of white fruits taking off before rain has no foundation. The flower is one of the first to bloom in March. The last weather maxim means that an early spring (very warm March) brings an overall cold or short-spring season and a cold March followed by a warm April or May portends a dry summer.

A test of these last two statements proved negative.

8/105 (8)
12/29 (41)

FERN

It was anciently supposed that the burning of fern drew down the rain. **

Another variation of the above saying occurred in 1636 when Charles I was due to visit Staffordshire. His Lord Chamberlain, Lord Pembroke, wrote to the county's High sheriff asking him not to burn ferns in case they should invoke rain for the expected royal party. The real connection lies deep in the mists of time. However, in very rare cases, the heat from forest fires in the ascending flames and smoke can cause a deep cumulus cloud to grow producing a rain shower.

GENTIAN

The gentian closes up both flowers and leaves before rain. **

WHITLOW GRASS AND LADY'S BEDSTRAW

We may look for wet weather if the leaves of the whitlow grass droop, and if ladies bedstraw becomes inflated and gives off a strong odour. **

Whitlow grass leaves drop because of increasing humidity, usually at its highest at night. Lady's Bedstraw provides a delightful illustration, when, in the evening or when the air is damp, its myrial flowers smell of honey and dry with a scent of hay.

AFRICAN MARIGOLD

If the African marigold do not open its petals by seven in the

morning, it will rain or
thunder that day. It also
closes before a storm. **

This means that in normal weather conditions the plant will open its petals by 7 a.m. If not then mist or cloudy conditions prevail which may lead to rain.

CAPE MARIGOLD

If the small Cape marigold
should open at six or seven in
the morning, and not close till
four in the afternoon, we may
reckon on settled weather. ***

The saw means that on a sunny day, the forecast of dry weather is a good bet.

MARSH AND COMMON MARIGOLD

The marsh marigold blows when
the cuckoo sings. *

The marigold that goes to bed
with the sun,
And with him rises, weeping. ***

Stillingfleet in Yorkshire's East Riding provides the first saw which proves difficult in producing a sensible meaning. The last saying is from Shakespeare's pen.

MISTLETOE

Mistletoe hanging in a room
affords protection against
lightning. *

This parasitic plant growing on trees, like many others, has thunderstorm protection properties originating in ancient folklore.

HOUSE LEEK

Country people grew a house leek on their cottage roof to keep lightening away. *

Houseleek with its pink flowers growing on walls and roofs is nicknamed the *Thunder Plant* in Somerset. The myth that it protected one from lightning originates from the Romans who called it *Jupiter's Plant*. One of the Roman god's emblems was lightning.

SCARLET PIMPERNEL

When the pink-eyed pimpernel (ploughman's weather glass) closes in the daytime, it is a sign of rain. **

Pimpernel, pimpernel, tell me true
Whether the weather be fine or no; ****** **
No heart can think, no tongue can tell,
The virtues of the pimpernel.

Now, look! Our weather glass is spread,
The pimpernel, whose flower
Closes its leaves of spotted red
Against a rainy hour. **

Our pimpernel, whose brilliant flower
Closes against the approaching shower,
Warning the swain to sheltering bower
From humid air secure. **

If the red pimpernel has its

Scarlet Pimpernel

flowers fully opened first thing in the morning, no matter what the barometer may indicate, it will be a sign to say that there will be no rain that day, and harvesting may proceed without fear. ******
On the other hand, if the petals are still closed in the morning, then rain is on its way. **

This is the most famous weather flower of all. It is better known as the Ploughman's Weather Glass. Its scarlet flowers bloom from May to September and are sensitive to temperature and air dampness change, often closing in wet and humid weather. Silvester found that the flowers stayed open for 8 to 9 hours even on the shortest lit day (normal time of opening $4\frac{1}{4}$ hours after sunrise and closing $1\frac{1}{3}$ hours before sunset). They never opened at night in all of his 247 observations. The controlling factor was relative humidity reaching a critical value of 80 percent when the scarlet gem was only partially open. By taking Silvester's data, average daylight and the Pimpernel's daily blooming time the following results evolved. With the flower closed in the daytime rain followed within 6 hours on only 17 percent of occasions. However an excellent figure of 81 percent was scored for dry weather to occur 6 hours after the flower opened.

Some of the countryman's weather nicknames for the flower make fascinating reading. *Change-of-the-Weather*, *Grandfather's Weatherglass* and *Old Man's Weatherglass* are all found in Somerset; *Ploughman's Weatherglass* in Wilts and Beds; *Poor Man's Weatherglass* in Somerset, Hants, N'thants, Warwicks, Cheshire and Cumb; *Shepherd's Calendar* in Devon; *Shepherd's Dial* in Middlesex; *Shepherd's Glass* in Norfolk and Rutland; *Shepherd's Warning* in Somerset and Lincs; *Shepherd's Weatherglass* in Devon, Somerset, Wilts, N'thants, Notts, Lincs, Yorks; *Weather Flower* in Dorset; *Weatherglass* in West Wilts, Bucks and Leics and *Weather-Teller* in Somerset.

24/139 (17)
87/108 (81)

Pitcher Plant

Expect rain if the flower of the pitcher plant turns upside down. **

Another saying from Yorkshire's North Riding telling of

the unique weather change to this unusual plant.

WATER PLANTAIN

This plant which flowers from May to August is locally called *Great Thunderbolt* and *Umbrellas* in Somerset. The latter because of its wide leaves growing near the ground resembling open parasols.

PONDWEED

Pondweed sinks before rain. **

Pondweed is a special aquatic herb growing in still water and is not a general term for any number of water weeds. Presumably the maxim means that any freshening of wind (often a forerunner of rain) will disturb still water and agitate the Pondweed.

POPPY

English children believe that poppies should not be picked for fear of a thunderstorm and placing along the timbers under the roof warded off lightning. *

Another flower blooming June to August which if placed in the house, especially in the roof timbers, repelled lightning. Many country children were too scared to pick the poppy in case a thunderstorm erupted. It seems curious that most large red flowers have some relationship with thunder or lightning, perhaps because the red colour traditionally has always been a sign of danger. The Poppy is also known as *Lightnings* in Northumbs; *Thunderball* in Warwicks; *Thunderbolt* in Devon, West England, Shropshire and Cheshire and *Thunder Flower* in Wilts.

RAGGED ROBIN

Called in Yorkshire the *Thunder-Flower*, it blooms from May to June.

Purple Sandwort

Purple sandwort expands its
beautiful pink flowers only
when the sun shines, but closes ***
them before the coming shower. **

Another plant sensitive to weather changes.

Burnet Saxifrage

The burnet saxifrage indicates
by half-opening its flowers
that the rain is soon to cease. **

The Burnet Saxifrage probably reacts in humidity changes.

Seaweed

A piece of kelp or sea-weed
hung up will become damp
previous to rain. ***

At last we have the old favourite - the saying that every weatherman has his leg pulled about. Like the pine or conifer cones the seaweed reacts to humidity change. Many hours of high humidity moistens the kelp which can be caused by wet fogs (100 percent humidities), moist airstreams with no rain or occasionally in cases ahead of rain. The seaweed like many other sensitive plants is not a precursor of rain or sun but a crude instrument recording actual present weather conditions.

Sorrel

A species of wood sorrel
contracts its leaves at the
approach of rain. **

Expect rain if the flowers of
the sorrel close.

Another sensitive plant, flowering from April to May, reacting to humidity differences presenting itself as a natural hygrometer. The second saying hails from Yorkshire's North Riding.

GERMANDER SPEEDWELL

The germander speedwell closes
its blue petals before rain, **
and opens them again when it
has ceased. **

This sensitive flower is interestingly referred to as the *Strike-Fire* in N'thants.

STAR OF BETHLEHEM

The so called Star of Bethlehem
has a star flower recalling the
Nativity Star. They shut early
in the day and always in dull
weather. ***

The Star of Bethlehem, so-called because the flower resembles the Nativity Star, normally closes around midday as can be seen from the following county nicknames. It is known as *Betty-go-to-Bed-at-Noon, Jack-go-to-Bed-at-Noon* and *Eleven O'clock Lady* in Somerset; *Noon-Peeders* in Wilts; *One O'clock* in Devon; *Twelve O'clocks* in Cornwall, Somerset, Dorset and Oxon and *Wake at Noon* in Wilts and the Isle-of-Wight.

GREATER STITCHWORT

The picking of the greater
stitchwort provokes thunder. *

The picking of the flower which blooms April to June is said to provoke thunder. In Dorset it is known as the *Thunderbolt* and *Thunder-Flower* in Cumberland.

TEASEL

Teasel or Fuller's thistle hung
up will open for fine weather,
and close for wet. ***

Cut'em in June, they'll come
again soon;
Cut'em in July, they may die;
Cut'em in August, die they
must.

Another sensitive humidity plant similar to the famous pine cones and seaweed, i.e. to open and shut on demand. The second Shropshire saying is perfectly true - an example of true nature observation.

SOW THISTLE

The non-closing of the flower
heads of the sow thistle warns
us that it will rain next day, **
whilst the closing of them
denotes fine weather. ***

This Bacon saying proclaims another sensitive hygrometer; this time affecting the plant's stalk.

TREFOIL

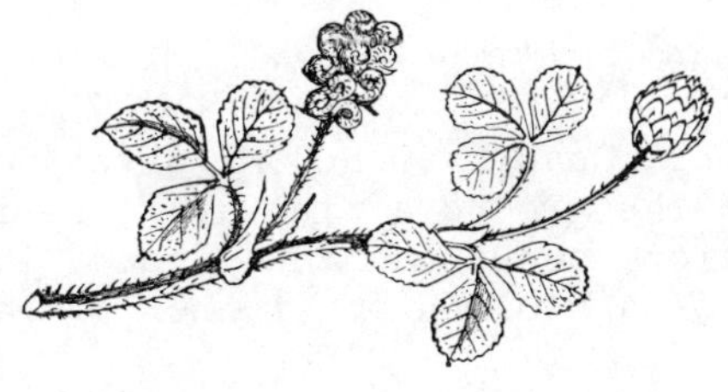

The stalk of trefoil swells
before rain. *

RED VALERIAN

In Devon and Hants referred to as the *Scarlet Lightning*.

TREES

Trees snapping and cracking in
autumn indicate dry weather.

An observation of the obvious rather than a forecast. A long dry spell in autumn will often dry the land and plants, especially trees.

When dry leaves rattle on the
trees, expect snow. **

Poetic turn of phrase, not always true.

When the leaves show their
undersides,
Be very sure that rain betides. ***

This is one of the more famous of tree weather lore. It seems that there can be two possible meanings to this saw; a period of damp air which softens leaf stalks and when strong winds manoeuvre the leaves. Both are supposed to be forerunners of rain.

Dead branches falling in calm
weather indicates rain. ***

A subtle meaning. Dead branches are often caused by disease. When they fall to the ground a wind aloft is indicated eventhough calm conditions occur near the ground. This often is the first indication of a blow, a forerunner of rain.

Short boughs, short vintage. ****

Weather saw related to English wines.

Plenty of berries indicate a
severe winter. **

Ash and Oak

This theme occurs throughout the chapter.

Ash

Avoid an ash,
It courts a flash. ***

An ash tree, like the oak, is prone to lightning strike.

Ash and Oak

When the oak comes out before
the ash, there will be fine
weather in harvest; but when **
the ash comes out before the
oak, the harvest will be wet. **

The series of saws to follow are related to the ash and oak. Luckily the author discovered records kept in Marsham in Norfolk of the first oak and ash leafing of the year from 1736 to 1935 by the Margery family. Of the 122 years actually observed 83 saw the oak leaf before the ash, 35 times the reverse and 4 when both leafed on the same day.

The first adage from the Midlands comes off poorly. The two results were tested for an August and September harvest. Averaged Norfolk data showed the oak to leaf on 24 April and ash 29th.

Oak	before	ash	= fine weather	in		August	harvest	23/83	(28)
"	"	"	= "	"	"	Sept	"	22/83	(26)
Ash	"	oak	= wet	"	"	August	"	9/34	(26)
"	"	"	= "	"	"	Sept	"	12/34	(35)

When the ash is out before the
oak,
Then we may expect a choke; **
When the oak is out before the
ash,
Then we may expect a splash. **

When buds the oak before the ash,
You'll only have a summer splash. **

The ash before the oak
Choke, choke, choke; **

The oak before the ash,
Splash, splash, splash. **

The first saw hails from Shropshire. "Choke" refers to a drought and "splash" a rainy, though not a torrential, period. Since both trees average leafing in late April, May was tested for a dry or wet month. The results are disappointing.

Ash before oak then a choke	9/34	(26)
Oak " ash " " splash	25/83	(30)

If buds the ash before the oak,
You'll surely have a summer soak; **
But if behind the oak the ash is,
You'll only have a few light splashes. ***

This saying is completely opposite to the normal oak and ash theme, and refers to flowering of the trees not their leafing. Note we have the first reference to "soak" or torrential wet periods.

If the ash is out before the oak,
You may expect a thorough soak; **
If the oak is out before the ash,
You'll hardly get a single splash. ***

Here we have the usual phrasing of the legendary weather maxim. But poor results become evident.

Ash before oak then a soak (wet May)	11/34	(32)
Oak " ash " " splash (dry May)	30/83	(36)

Oak, smoke. **
Ash, squash. **

This brief Kentish saying recalls "smoke" as a hot summer and "squash" as a wet one. Poor results emerge.

Hot summer	14/83	(17)
Wet "	10/34	(29)

The oak before the ash,
Prepare your summer sash; **
The ash before the oak,
Prepare your summer cloak. **

Dorset provides this adage. A "sash" either refers to a scarf worn over the waist or around the collar or a window sash which would have to be freed in hot sticky summer weather. The test and results in the next maxim equally apply here.

If the oak is out before
the ash,
Twill be a summer of wet
and splash; ***
But if the ash is before
the oak,
Twill be a summer of fire
and smoke. **

This Hampshire variation of the popular theme also gains poor results.

Wet summer	33/83	(40)
Dry "	10/34	(29)

BEECH

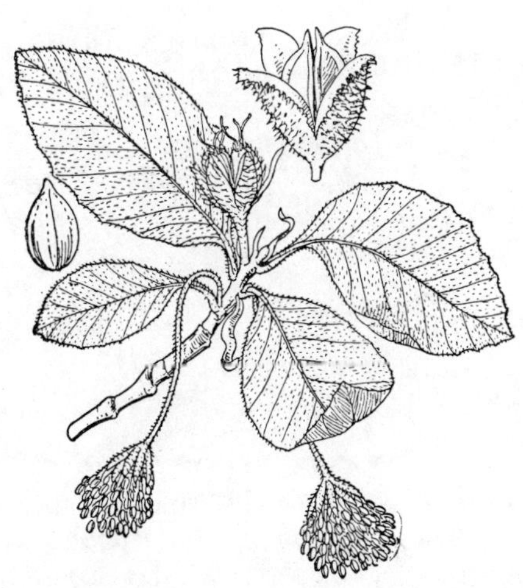

When the beech mast thrives well
and oak trees hang full, a hard
winter will follow, with much
snow. ***

Another "plenty of nuts, severe winter" type theme.

When beech nuts are plentiful,
expect a mild winter. ***

No records are available for plentiful beech nut years but the author thought that testing for early beech leafing years would be a reasonable substitute. Norfolk data for 1736-1926 were used. Records of 49 years of earliest leafing of the beech were judged to fall before its average date of 19 April. Poor results emerged.

Mild winter	21/49	(43)
Hard "	17/49	(35)

BROOM

If the broom be full of flower,
it signyfieth plenty. **

The broom having plenty of
blossoms is a sign of a
fruitful year of corn. **

The broom's yellow flower begins to bloom in May and June. Prolific growth is related to previous good weather seasons.

DOGROSE AND WHITETHORN

If many whitethorn blossoms
or dog-roses are seen, expect
a severe winter. **

DOGWOOD

When the blooms of the dog
wood tree are full, expect a
cold winter; when the blooms **
are light, expect a warm winter. **

Excessive or deficient blooms again are only the result of previous good or bad growing seasons.

ELDER

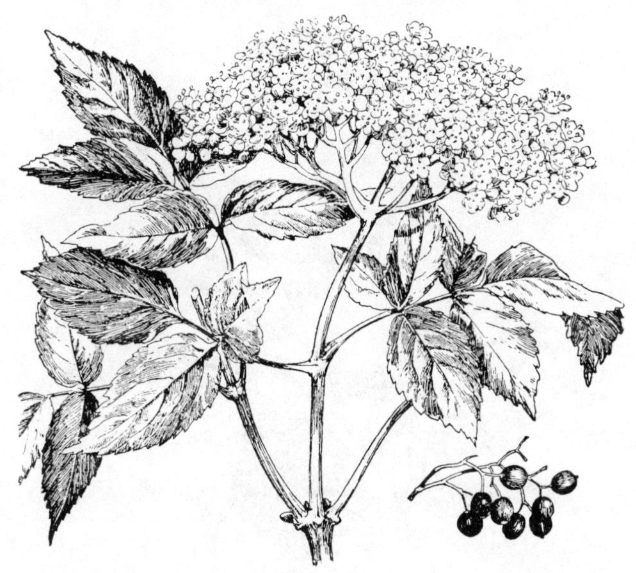

You may shear your sheep
When the elder blossoms peep.

Dangerous weather-cum-farming lore. Frosts can still occur after the elder tree blossoms.

ELM

When the elmen leaf is as
big as a mouse's ear,
Then to sow barley never fear. *
When the elmen leaf is as
big as an ox's eye,
Then says I, "Hie, boys! hie!" ***

When elm leaves are as big as
a shilling,

Plant kidney beans, if to plant-em you're willing; **
When the elm leaves are as big as a penny,
You must plant kidney beans, if you mean to have any. ***

The second saw comes from Worcestershire. If early leafing of the elm is accepted as a year when large leaves emerge then the tests are valid. The opposite applies to a small leaf or "mouse's ear". Early leafing occurs before 31 March and late leafing after 12 April. All poor results.

Late leaf = good barley harvest	1/8	(13)
Early " = poor " "	8/18	(44)

Hawthorn, May or Whitethorn

It is always cold when the hawthorn blossom. **

This is not always true. Hawthorn mainly blossoms in May into June. The most frequent cold snap during this period is in the first two weeks of May when northerlies are dominant. The test provides terrible results. 8/28 (29)

When the hawthorn has too many haws
We shall have many snaws. **

Usual balance maxim. Country folk believe nature provides abundant haws as food for the hungry birds in a forthcoming severe winter. Of course it is a measurement of previous good weather growing seasons.

The leaves of the may tree
bear up, so that the underside
may be seen before a storm. ***

Refer to the beginning of the chapter for the meaning here.

HOLLY

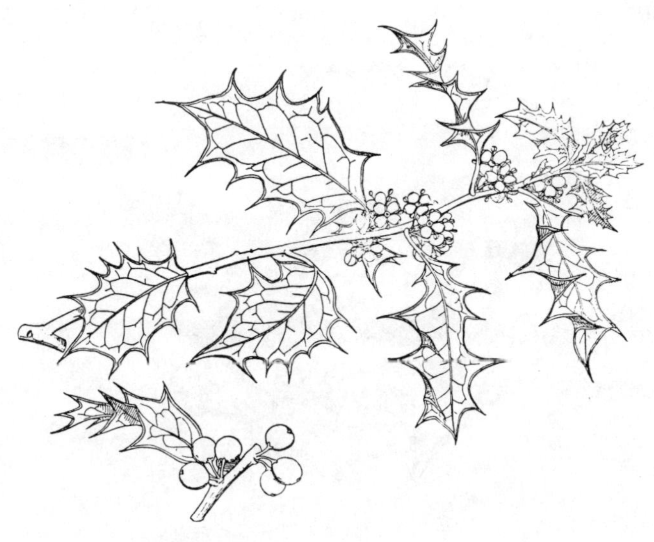

Grow holly alongside your house
as it is considered to be a
protection against thunder and
lightening. *

This adage is like the saw in the plant chapter connected with the houseleek. There may be some connection in that most of these thunder plants have *red* or *pink* flowers/berries which in itself is a sign of danger.

MULBERRY

When the mulberry hath shown green leaf, there will be no more frost. ***

Gloucestershire provides this saying.

OAK

There is no doubt that the old oak tree was connected with Thor the god of thunder. The oak is struck more by lightning than any other tree.

You must look for grass on the top of an oak tree.

This adage means that grass only really grows quickly after the oak begins to leaf.

If the oak bears much mast, it foreshows a long and hard winter. **

Another "many berries, hard winter" type maxim which is all explained in similar saws in the September chapter.

When the oak puts on his gosling gray,

'Tis time to sow barley,
night or day.

The reasons for the underside of leaves to show can be seen at the beginning of the chapter.

Pine

Pine cones hung up in the house
will close themselves against
wet and cold weather, and open
against hot and dry times. ***

A very famous saw which nowadays is used in conversation as a mocking phrase. There is no doubt that cones, pine in particular, close in high humidity and open with dry low humidities in the air. Unfortunately it is only a natural instrument for measuring *actual* conditions as they are, not the weather to come.

Rowan

Many rains, many rowans, ***
Many rowans, many yauns. ****

"Yauns" are light or poor crops. The rowan (mountain ash) probably refers to its berries in the saw. There seems to be a lot of common sense in the harmful and abundance effect of wet springs and summers.

Sloe or Blackthorn

When the sloe tree is white
as a sheet,
Sow your barley, whether it
be dry or wet.

The sloe tree or blackthorn when in full white flower bloom has always been regarded as a time for sowing of barley.

Sycamore

Before rain the leaves of the
lime, sycamore, plane, and
poplar trees show a great deal
more of their undersurfaces
when trembling in the wind. ***

GARDEN AND FARM PRODUCE

Plant the bean when the moon is light;
Plant potatoes when the moon is dark.

If apples bloom in March,
In vain for'um you'll sarch; ****
If apples bloom in April,
Well then they'll be plentiful; ****
If apples bloom in May,
You may eat'um night and day. ****

Onion's skin very thin,
Mild winter coming in; **
Onion's skin thick and tough,
Coming winter cold and rough. **

The first and second are old-style land and fruit farming maxims. The onion weather lore applies to *previous* good or bad seasons.

There gay chrysanthemums repose,
And when stern tempests lower,
Their silken fringes softly close
Against the shower. **

Poetic treatment of actual conditions.

Under the furze is hunger and cold,
Under the broom is silver and gold.

Possibly meaning the type of soil these two shrubs are found on. Furze prefers waste ground.

The tulip and several of the

compound yellow flowers close
before rain. **

For a comprehensive survey of closing and opening flowers before rain plough through the Wild Plant chapter.

The sudden growth of mushrooms
presageth rain. 

If toadstools spring up in the
night in dry weather, they
indicate rain. ****

At last two true sayings. Sudden growth of toadstools, especially mushrooms, is caused by very warm *and* humid weather conditions by day *and* night. This is virtually always a forerunner of rain from late July through to early October.

I find it will be a dear year;
the blade of the corn grow
withersones (contrary to sun's
course), and when it grows
sonegatis about (with the
course of the sun), it will be
a good cheap year. *

Another nonsense adage.

Indian corn fodder dry and crisp
indicates fair weather; but damp
and limp, rain. It is very
sensitive to hygrometric changes. ***

Ears of Indian corn are said to be covered with thicker and stronger husks before hard winters. **

A double husk on maize indicates a severe winter. **

An old farming maxim.

A beard of wild oats, with its adhering capsule, fixed on a stem, serves the purpose of a hygrometer, twisting itself more or less, according to the moisture of the air.

Abundant wheat crops never follow a mild winter. *

This saw is literally incorrect. In fact 16 "abundant wheat crops" followed 41 mild winters.

SUN, SUNRISE AND SUNSET

Red Sunset

This chapter contains some of the most beautiful weather lore of all. With the different colour hues of the cloud and sky in a setting or rising sun one cannot help but feel a romantic flavour entering the sayings. When the saws refer to a red *sky* at night or morning, clear and cloudy skies are both included. The setting or rising sun offers a longer distance for its own white light to travel to an observer. Now sunlight or white light is composed of seven basic colours (rainbow colours) red, orange, yellow, green, blue, indigo and violet (easily remembered by their initials ROYGBIV). Each colour component has its own wavelength with the red possessing the longest. Since the violet end of the sun's spectrum has the smallest wavelength, any dust particles in the lower atmosphere similar in size will scatter the violet colour . This will leave a mixture of the remaining six colours to be received by an observer. As larger atmospheric particles appear so other colours are scattered. So a red/orange light is seen when the remainder are deflected. When bigger particle sizes arrive beyond the red wavelength so much scattering occurs that the nett light received on the surface of the Earth is a dim white illumination. So the general theory is that the Earth's lower atmosphere between the setting or rising sun and an observer appears red due to scattering by dust particles or dry air. As most of England's weather systems traverse from west to east a red sunrise is indicating dry weather present or past (in the east), so rain should be expected soon. Conversely a red sunset hints of dry weather to come from the west.

Smoke or dust haze reflects sunlight diffusely producing a white sky - the thicker the haze the whiter the sky. So blueness of sky is a direct measure of the content, or lack, of atmospheric particles. Cloud colouring, say a red cloudy sunset, is the result of the red sun illuminating the underside of the cloud often with grey/white tops illuminated by the scattered blue of the sky.

Red sky at night,
Shepherd's delight; *****
Red sky in morning,
Shepherd's warning. *****

Sunset

Sky red in the morning
Is a sailor's sure warning; *****
Sky red at night
Is the sailor's delight. *****

The skie being red at evening,
Foreshewes a faire and cleare
morning; *****
But if the morning riseth red,
Of wind and raine we shall be
sped. *****

A red sky in the morning
Is the shepherd's warning; *****
Though a red haze at night
Is the shepherd's delight. *****

The red sun setting with distinct outlines, and with or without a red sky, is a sure sign of a fine day to follow, and the redness is caused by the dry dust in the air. *****

Red west at sunset, not extending up to the sky, and having no thick banks of black cloud, will be followed by a fine day. *****

Red clouds at sunrise foretell wind; at sunset, a fine day for the morrow. *****

Narrow, horizontal, red clouds after sunset in the west indicate rain before thirty-six hours. *****

Nobody is quite sure when the verse form was derived of "Red sky at night, shepherd's delight". It probably was influenced by the Shepherd of Banbury's adage "If the sun rise red and fiery - wind and rain", which dates at least back to the early 18th century and almost certainly way before. Of course the red sky can be found in the Old Testament of the Bible and throughout different literatures of the world. The test figures are the records of Spenser Russell who in London from October 1918 to September 1924 observed sunrise and sunset colours. He graded them into three main groups ; 1. reds or yellows, 2. predominance of red over yellow or vice-versa and 3. combination of both colours neither one being dominant. For a red sunset and a dry day to follow within 24 hours the tests produced an excellent 69 percent result. 111/161 (69)

If the sun in red should set,
The next day surely will be wet; **
If the sun should set in grey,
The next will be a rainy day.

The first part of this saw is the only one found to be in "opposition" to the famous red sky at night theme. It yielded only 31 percent correct results. 50/161 (31)

If the sun set with a very red
eastern sky, expect wind; if
red to the south-east, expect
rain. *****

The red eastern sky may be the purple or pink glow which occurs over the whole sky after sunset known as the First Purple Light. It could also be redness affecting the appearance of a steely-blue segment in the eastern sky at sunset which is the Earth's shadow thrown by the sun into the atmosphere. No observations are available.

YELLOW SUNSET

The weary sun hath made a
golden set,
And by the bright track of the
fiery car
Gives token of a goodly day
tomorrow. ****

Clouds before sunset of an
amber or a gold colour, and
with gilt fringes, after the
sun has sunk lower, foretell
fine weather. ****

This Shakespeare quote means a dry day to follow a yellow sunset. Unfortunately only 49 percent were true.
281/579 (49)

SUNSET

When the sun sets with a golden yellow colour, with disc ill defined, and rays extending four or six degrees, a strong wind and much vapour exist at a considerable elevation, and rain usually occurs within twenty-four hours. ****

A bright yellow sky at sunset presages wind; a pale yellow, wet. ****

When the sun rises or sets of a golden yellow colour, with the disc ill defined, and rays extending four or six degrees, and strong winds and much vapour exists at a considerable elevation, and rain usually occurs within twenty-four hours, which will continue for some time if there are any opposing currents, whether direct or lateral. ****

Brassy-coloured clouds in the west at sunset indicate wind. ****

A yellow sunset to produce rain within 24 hours also gave unsatisfactory figures. The special conditions set out in the third saw relate to the upper air jet streams or upper levels of strong winds (often in excess of 100kt) which are almost always associated with mobile stormy weather systems.

298/579 (51)

OTHER SUNSETS

After sunset if the western sky has a whitish yellow extending to a great height then there will probably be rain during the night or next day. **** *After sunset if the western sky is gaudy or has unusual hues with hard definite outlined clouds then rain is foretold with probable wind.* *** *Before sunset if the sun is diffuse and brilliant white*

and the sky bright blue near
the zenith then one forecasts
fine weather. ****

The second part fails miserably with only 33 percent. Its final part is very interesting. A bright blue sky and white sun at setting hints at very clean and clear air. 109/335 (33)

When the sun sets bright and
clear
An easterly wind you need not
fear. **

One would have thought that a clear sunset (usually associated with west, north-west or north airstreams) could easily turn to an east wind. Certainly with the same frequency as any other airstream experienced at sunset.

When the air is hazy, so that
the solar light fades gradually,
and looks wet, rain will almost
certainly follow. *****

If the sun goes pale to bed,
Twill rain tomorrow, it is said. *****

When the sun appears of a light
pale colour, or goes down into
a bank of clouds, it indicates
the approach of a continuance
of bad weather. *****

When the sun sets in a bank
A westerly wind ye shall not
lack. ***

A sunset and a cloud so black,
A westerly wind ye shall not
lack. ***

Thy sun sets weeping in the
lowly west,
Witnessing storms to come, woe
and unrest. *****

Sunrise

The fifth adage comes from Yorkshire and sixth from Shakespeare's quill. The general rule is that any pale or grey sunset or sunrise denotes a moist atmosphere (dry air holding dust particles turns sunsets red, orange etc) and is a classic example for rain to occur within 24 hours. The sixth saying shows a watery sun which is the appearance of altostratus (As) cloud (a medium-level cloud sheet - see cloud chapter) which foreruns a warm front. Here rain can be expected within 1-3 hours.

Red Sunrise

If at sunrise small reddish-looking clouds are seen low on the horizon, it must not always be considered to indicate rain. The probability of rain under these circumstances will depend on the character of the clouds and their height above the horizon. It has frequently been observed that if they extend ten degrees, rain will follow before sunset; if twenty or thirty degrees, rain will follow before two or three p.m.; but if still higher and near the zenith, rain will fall within three hours. *****

When the sun at rising assumes a reddish colour, and shortly afterwards numerous small clouds collect, the whole day will soon become overcast, and rain may be expected in the course of a few hours. *****

If red the sun begin his race,
Be sure the rain will fall apace. *****

Red clouds in the east, rain the next day. *****

The first saying was introduced by a Mr C L Prince during the 19th century. His accurate observations proving that the higher the red cloud (cirrus cloud over 30° above the eastern horizon) the nearer the rain and red low cloud rain within 24 hours. The principle involved is that red cloud between an observer and sunrise indicates dry air, which on the usual west to east weather pattern of changeable types indicates rain from the west. In fact within 24 hours rain occurred on 68 percent of occasions - a very good result indeed. 218/319 (68)

In the winter season, a red sky at sunrise foreshows steady rain on the same day. ***** *The same sky in summer betokens occasional violent showers, wind in both cases generally accompanying.* *****

To distinguish between winter and summer red sunrises is misleading. Excellent figures of 67 (winter) and 70 percent (summer) emerged for rain to fall within 24 hours. More red sunsets occurred in winter. 143/212 (67)
75/107 (70)

GREY SUNRISE

A grey sky in the morning presages fine weather. ***

Dark clouds in the west at sunrise indicate rain on that day. ****

Similar in context to previous maxims but no figures are available for testing.

GAUDY SUNRISE

A gaudy morning bodes a wet afternoon. **

Poor results evolve for a wet afternoon after a gaudy sunrise. 51/230 (22)

GENERAL SUNRISE

The morning sun never lasts the day. ***

This is only true when the atmosphere is very clear and clean with visibility 30km or more. This indicates a polar air-stream which is often unstable. So cumulus clouds form during the morning changing into showers in the afternoon obliterating the sun. Conversely a long settled spell often with haze (certainly in summer) sees little cloud formation.

SUNRISE AND SUNSET

Rose tints at sunset and grey
dawn, a fine day to follow. *****

Evening red and morning grey,
Two sure signs of one fine day. *****

The evening red and the morning grey
Are the tokens of a bonny day. *****

An evening grey and a morning
red
Make the shepherd hang his head. *****

If the evening is red and the
morning grey,
It is the sign of a bonnie day; *****
If the evening's grey and the
morning red,
The lamb and the ewe will go
wet to bed. *****

Evening red and morning grey
Help the traveller on his way; *****
Evening grey and morning red
Bring down rain upon his head. *****

The fifth saying hails from just over the border into Scotland at Yarrow. All saws are in agreement and are an advanced extension of the basic "red sky at night and morning" theme by adding a grey dawn or evening. The results would be excellent and in the same high range as the red sunrise and sunset.

SUN

A red sun has water in his eye. *****

Sun

A red sun only indicates rain when it rises.

When solar rays are visible in the air, they indicate vapour and rain to follow, and the sun is said to be "drawing water". ***

These solar rays are called crepuscular (twilight) rays which include three types. The saw here applies to sunbeams that penetrate a low cloud sheet and appear luminous because of water or dust particles in the air. The phenomenon is known as the "sun drawing water" or "Jacob's ladder" (see Genesis).

If rays precede the sunrise, it is a sign both of wind and rain. ****

A high dawn indicates wind. ****
A low dawn indicates fair weather. ****

The first maxim is taken from Bacon's pen. An interesting set of rules. A "high dawn" is when first daylight is seen over a bank of clouds and a "low dawn" occurs when streaks of light first appear on or near the horizon. Very sound and factual saws but no data were available to test them.

If the sun appears concave at its rising, the day will be windy or showery; windy if the sun be only slightly concave, and showery if the concavity is deep. ***

Another Bacon saying which looks fascinating. Certain cloud types plus the sun's atmospheric refraction at sunrise can cause odd overall shapes of the golden orb.

Storms are said to decrease at the rising or setting of the sun or moon. ****

If storms mean heavy showers then they do decrease or die-out *inland* after dusk. Any other interpretation is false.

Make hay while the sun shines. ****

Hay should only be made when a few dry days are guaranteed. To make hay when the sun shines continuously would be better phraseology. Sunny intervals can indicate rain showers.

If the sun's shining pale with
a watery eye,
Be sure the soaking ere
nightfall is nigh. *****

Similar to the maxim containing a "weeping" sun in the sun-set section.

HALO

Moon and Solar Halo

If there be a ring or halo around the sun in bad weather, expect fine weather soon. ***

A bright circle round the sun denotes a storm and cooler weather. ****

A white ring round the sun towards sunset portends a slight gale that same night; but if the ring be dark or tawny, there will be a high wind the next day. ****

If the sun or moon outshines the 'brugh' (or halo), bad weather will not come. ****

The circle of the moon never filled a pond; the circle of the sun wets a shepherd. *****

HALO

The third saw comes from Bacon's quill. Two sun haloes can be observed when looking at Cirrus (Ci) or Cirrostratus (Cs) cloud. They are the common 22° halo and the rarer 46° halo. They are coloured red on the inside with a white outer edge. Haloes are formed by the sunlight rays being deflected or *refracted* through thousands of randomly placed hexagonal *ice crystal* prisms in high cirrus clouds. These 60° and 90° edged ice crystals refract sunlight to produce the 22° and 46° halo. It is believed that sun haloes forecast rain. An investigation by Mr. J.P. Brain in Bristol from 1 January 1969 to 2 March 1971 came up with some very interesting results.

It has often been thought that sun haloes in Ci or Cs cloud are most frequently connected with warm fronts, i.e. the cirrus cloud lies well ahead of the surface warm front giving ample warning (usually 3-12 hours) of forthcoming rain. Brain's observations confirm this by showing that 30 out of 40 (75 percent) true haloes (including coronae) were associated with warm fronts, 6 with cold fronts and 4 on occlusions. Unfortunately he combined *all* halo phenomena (including mock suns/moons and sun pillars) to give one result in forecasting rain instead of separating them. However it must be inferred that a very high percentage (probably 70-80 percent) would be true for rain to follow a sun halo or moon corona within 48 hours. Brain's final figures are given at the end of this chapter.

MOON CORONA

If the moon rises haloed round,
Soon you'll tread on deluged
ground. ****

The moon with a circle brings
water in her beak. ****

Double or treble rings round
the moon foreshadow rough and
severe storms, and much more
so if the circles are not
pure and entire, but spotted
and broken. ****

A circle or halo round the moon
signifies rain rather than wind,
unless the moon stand erect
within the ring, when both are
portended. ****

Corona

If the moon show a silver
shield,
Be not afraid to reap your
field; ****
But if she rises haloed round,
Soon we are to tread on deluged
ground. ****

Bacon originated the third and fourth maxims. The moon ring is called a corona and strictly is not a halo. It is formed by moonlight being bent or *diffracted* by *water droplets* in Altocumulus (Ac) cloud. Sometimes it can be perceived in Stratocumulus (Sc) cloud. (Refer to the cloud chapter for information on these types.) A corona is a very small ring centred around the moon possessing a blue colour on the inside and red on the outer. Sometimes two coronae can be seen side by side. It is also true that coronae can occur around the sun.

The bigger the ring, the nearer
the wet. *

Near ring far rain, *
Far ring near rain. *

Far burr near rain. *

When the wheel is far, the
storm is n'ar; *
When the wheel is near, the
storm is far. *

The word "burr" occurring in the third adage means a moon corona. A "far burr" is therefore the largest ring. These four saws follow the popular theme "the bigger the ring the nearer the rain". Unfortunately it is completely false. The corona is largest with small cloud water droplets and smallest with big droplets. So a large ring means the Ac or Sc cloud is well-broken and dispersing - a sign of dry weather. A better saying would be "the bigger the ring the further the rain" or "far ring far rain".

The open side of the halo tells
the quarter from which the wind
or rain may be expected. *

Circles round the moon always
foretell wind from the side
where they break, and a
remarkable brilliancy in any
part of the circle denotes wind
from that quarter. *

The last saw again somes from Lord Bacon. On the face of it both maxims look promising. On close inspection a gap in the cloud (where the corona is broken) only signifies that there is broken cloud. No truth occurs here.

Mock Sun

Dog before,
You'll have no more; ***
Dog behind,
Soon you'll find. ***

Most of the mock moon (paraselene) and sun (parhelion) saws are dealt with in the moon chapter but this one was kept aside for its individual charm. A "dog" is a sun dog or mock sun. The words "before" and "behind" probably refer to the mock sun occurring before the sun starts to rise too high and sets too low in the sky. Mock suns only exist when the sun is at a low elevation (usually below 20°) and can be observed at the intersection of the 22° halo and the sun's horizontal line. They can appear as one or two bright spots.

Eclipse weather is a popular
term in the south of England
for the weather following an
eclipse of the sun or moon,
and it is vulgarly esteemed and
not to be depended upon by
the husbandman. *

A common-sense attitude appears in this adage which is lacking in the majority of the sayings.

A dim or pale moon indicates
rain; a red moon indicates wind. ****

Pale moon doth rain,
Red moon doth blow, ****

Moon Colour

White moon doth neither rain
or snow. ***

When the moon is darkest near the
horizon, expect rain. ***

The different moon colours tend to follow the same explanation in the sunrise/sunset chapter.

In the decay of the moon
A cloudy morning bodes a
fair afternoon. ***

When the moon rises red and
appears large, with clouds,
expect rain in twelve hours. ****

These are more specific than the previous set of maxims. A red moonrise, which can occur during the day or night, begins in the eastern sky. As with the red sunrise the reasons and results will be the same, so the saws are true.

Results apply to all solar and lunar halo phenomena.

Frontal rain to follow within	6 hours	9/80	(11)
" " " " "	12 "	20/80	(25)
" " " " "	24 "	36/80	(45)
" " " " "	36 "	43/80	(54)
" " " " "	48 "	45/80	(56)

SKY AND AIR

The farther the sight,
the nearer the rain. ******

When the distant hills are more
than usually distinct, rain
approaches. *****

When the Lizard is clear,
Rain is near. *****

Is Lundy high?
It will be dry.
Is Lundy low?
There will be snow.
Is Lundy plain?
There will be rain. *****

When the Isle of Wight is seen
from Brighton or Worthing,
expect rain soon. *****

The third and fourth maxims hail from Cornwall, the latter from Boscastle on the north coast. Lundy is a rocky island 50 km or 34 miles due north in the Bristol Channel. The last saw tells us that the high point of the Isle of Wight is about 50 miles from Brighton and Worthing. Excellent visibility of 30 km or more is always associated with an airstream with a polar origin. This cold clear air is often unstable or showery, hence the wet flavour in the saws. The excellent test results (made in Oxon in 1980) show that rain or showers follow visibility of 30 km or more within 24 hours on 77 percent of occasions.

30km or more then rain/showers	in 24 hours	366/476	(77)
" " " " rain	" " "	150/476	(32)
" " " " showers	" " "	216/476	(45)

When the landscape looks clear,
having your back towards the
sun, expect fine weather; but
when it looks clear with your
face towards the sun, expect
showery, unsettled weather. *****

This means that a clear landscape with a hazy sun ("back to the sun") is associated with settled weather but a completely clear atmosphere relates to showery polar air.

This section refer to a cloudless sky.

A very clear sky without clouds
is not to be trusted, unless
the barometer is high. *****

If the mountains are clear in
the morning, there'll be
fountains by evening. *****

These maxims are similar to those at the beginning of the Air Section.

If the sky is of a deep, clear
blue or a sea-green colour near
the horizon, rain will follow
in showers. *****

If the sky in rainy weather is
tinged with sea-green, the rain
will increase; if with deep blue,
it will be showery. *****

A dark, gloomy blue sky is windy,
but a light, bright blue sky
indicates fine weather. When
the sky is of a sickly-looking,
greenish hue, wind or rain may
be expected. ****

A deep blue sky means no dust particles are present (the airstream has polar origins), in fact the air molecules scatter the sunlight to produce a blue sky. Sea green skies are often a forerunner of showers or heavier rain in already wet conditions. The results in the Air section readily apply here.

When as much blue is seen in the

sky as will make a Dutchman's jacket (or a sailor's breeches), the weather will be clear. ****

If taken literally the saw would only be half true. In showery weather blue patches of sky are often seen. This famous saw should strictly be applied to the passage of a cold front or trough where wet cloudy conditions are normally followed by partly cloudy weather as the trend passes to a drier airstream.

If there be a dark grey sky with a south wind, expect frost. **

The dark grey sky (cloudless) is an indication of thick haze or mist. A southerly wind provides the clue that an anti-cyclone would be centred roughly over the Continent. The saw would be true in winter but wildly out from late spring to early autumn.

If the sky should fall we should be able to catch larks. *

A quaint pleasant saying. Larks fly high in the sky, so if the sky fell one would catch them. In practice it may refer to when torrential rain and turbulence occur grounding any lark.

From a cloudless sky a bolt may break. *

A phrase similar to a "bolt from the blue" meaning a complete surprise. Lightning which is associated with Cb clouds and is obviously the meaning of bolt rarely seems to occur in cloudless skies.

The Carle sky
Keeps not the head dry. ****

A "Carle sky" is an abbreviation for a "Carlisle sky". It refers to a stormy looking yellow sky over Carlisle in Cumberland looking from the area around Dumfries and Gretna (i.e. to the S.E.). A yellow sky is nearly always a forerunner of rain. Similarly an angry red sky is an indicator of excess water vapour in the sky and a "gentle rose" sky means dust particles.

SOUND

There are basically three good reasons why sound waves travel fast and far through air. First high air temperature; second increase of wind vertically with height; and finally a low-level temperature inversion often occurring at night.

A good hearing day is a sign
of wet. ****

A sound in air presaged
approaching rain,
And beasts to covert scud
across the plain. ****

The ringing of bells is heard
at a greater distance before
rain; but before wind it is
heard more unequally, the
sound coming and going, as
we hear it when the wind is
blowing perceptily. ****

Sound travelling far and wide,
A stormy day will betide. ****

Bacon penned the third saying. These saws are mainly true. With wind increasing with height (often the conditions before rain and gales) sound waves travel long distances and if the temperature is high will move fast (velocity of sound is proportional to the square root of temperature degrees Absolute). Once strong winds arrive the turbulent atmosphere limits sound travel.

A murmuring or a roaring noise,
sometimes heard several miles
inland during a calm, in the
direction from which the wind is
about to spring up, and is
known as calling of the sea. ****

When the sea is heard to make
a raking noise on the beach in
the bay to the west of Saint
Leonard's, the fishermen say they
"hear the Bulverhythe Bells",
and this is held to be a sure
sign of bad weather from the
westward. In winter, during
frost, it is an indication of
approaching thaw. ***

The second adage hails from St Leonard's near Margate, Sussex. These two have been lumped together as sea examples of sound travel. The previous explanations apply here.

When Pons-an-Dane calls to
Lariggan River,
There will be fine weather;
But when Lariggan calls to
Pons-an-Dane
There will be rain. ****

The mountain and river in this true Cornish saw incorporate sound and geographical siting to forecast rain and fine weather.

In the collieries of Dysart, and
in some others, it is thought by
the miners that before a storm
of wind a sound not unlike that
of a bagpipe or the buzzing of
the bee comes from the mines,
and that previous to a fall of
rain the sound is more subdued. *****

This Welsh maxim from Dysart, Wales, has been included to show the dual role of atmospheric pressure and sound travel. Most old coal mines, in conditions when large pressure falls occur ahead of a depression, experience gas and air escaping from their underground crevasses. The falling atmospheric pressure forces them out. In fact the old miners said the released gases sounded like the buzzing of bees.

Sounds are heard with unusual
clearness before a storm. The

railway whistle, for instance,
seems remarkably shrill. ****

It will be a good day, we can
hear the trains. ****

The famous sound of the train whistle or its wheels racing over the track or line is frequently true for bad weather to come especially when the noises are heard over long distances. The reasons as explained before are mainly wind increasing with height and high temperatures. But sometimes at night the story can be different. In dry settled weather (often at night) low-level temperature inversions occur. For example the surface may record 7°C and as ones travels upward to say 200-300ft above the ground it could rise to 15°C. Now travelling sound waves will be bent or reflected by this temperature inversion and together with effect of warmer temperature aloft will be able to send the waves over a number of miles. But as the reader can see these conditions are favourable for dry settled weather, so here the two adages are false.

SNOW

Snow cherisheth the ground and anything sown in it. ***

Corn is comfortable under snow as an old man is under his fur coat. ***

An eight day mantle of snow is like a mother to the earth, but if it lasts longer it is like a mother-in-law. ****

A foot deep of rain,
Will kill hay and grain;
But three feet of snow,
Will make them grow mo. ***

A foot deep of rain
Will kill hay and grain;

Snow

But three feet of snow
Will make them come mo. ***

Three feet of snow will make
the hay and corn come more. ***

Snow is the poor farmer's muck.

Bacon originated the first saying and the fourth hails from the West Country. A good depth of snow covering the country-side acts as insulation for ground seed and growth against hard air frost and biting cold winds. The soil temperature under these conditions should maintain a level around 0°C. However eventually, as hinted in the third maxim, persistent frosty days will harden the snow lowering the soil temperature and harming virgin vegetation. The fifth saw comes from Devon.

In winter, during a frost,
if it begins to snow, the
temperature of the air generally
rises to thirty-two degrees
Fahrenheit (or near it), and
continues there whilst the snow ****
falls, after which, if the
weather clear up, expect severe
cold. ***

Snow in England usually falls under two separate conditions. Any showers or general falls of snow from the NW, N, NE or E direction are frequently associated with persistent cold weather. Snow from the W, SW, S or SE more often than not instigates a thaw. When tested the first part of the maxim provided quite good results (62 percent correct). Unfortunately the last section yielded a poor figure (46 percent) from records kept in Oxfordshire over winters from January 1971 to February 1980.

69/111 (62)
51/111 (46)

If the snowflake increases in
size, a thaw will follow. *****

When the snow falls dry, it
means to lie;
But flakes light and soft
bring rain oft. *****

Snow

These observations are perfectly true. Snow falling as minute ice crystals and dry occurs with air temperaturés well below $0^{o}C$ but as the snowflakes become larger the temperature rises nearer to $0^{o}C$. In these latter conditions a thaw often occurs, whether short or long, showing the saws to be true.

If the first snow sticks to the
trees, it foretells a bountiful
harvest. *

I'm afraid this type of weather saying is ridiculous. One certain type of snowstorm cannot possibly rule the year's harvest.

A heavy fall of snow indicates
a good year for crops, and a
light fall the reverse. **

The poor results for barley, hay and wheat can be seen in a similar saying in the Season's chapter.

Snow coming two or three days
after new moon will remain on
the ground some time, but that
falling after new moon will
soon go off. *

As many days old as the moon
is at the first snow, there
will be as many snows before
crop-planting time. *

Further foolish moon and snow maxims.

The number of days the last
snow remains on the ground
indicates the number of snow
storms which will occur during
the following winter. *

A number of these type of saws occur in the Monthly and Season's chapters - all of no avail.

Snow

If the snow that falls during the winter is dry, and is blown about by the wind, a dry summer ***
will follow. Very damp snow indicates rain in the spring. ***

These balance themes - dry winter snows bring a dry summer and wet winter snows a wet spring - when tested were no good.

Dry winter snows = dry summer	20/53	(38)
Wet " " = wet spring	13/34	(38)

When in the ditch the snow doth lie,
Tis waiting for more by-and-by. ***

If snow hangs about (along ditches and hedgerows), then it is waiting for more. ***

Unfortunately this well-known saying is not entirely true as the test figures show.

Further snow after 1 day	70/140	(50)
" " " 2 days	34/140	(24)
" " " 3 days	13/140	(9)
" " " 4 days	6/140	(4)

When the snow falls in the mud, it remains all winter. **

This infers that snow falling in November, December or January on mud will be followed by a severe snowy winter. There is no way of forecasting a severe winter. The author has spent many fruitless hours trying to find the magic formula to forecast such a winter. Previous winter cycles over 300 years; wet, dry, cold or warm previous seasons and months and even sunspot cycles have all been tried but in vain. In this saw a mild wet October, November or December singly or collectively were tested but results were useless.

Walk fast in snow,
In frost walk slow,
And still as you go,
Tread on your toe.

Snow

When frost and snow are
both together,
Sit by the fire and spare
shoe leather.

Snow that lies flattens
the ground.

Obvious meanings to snow and frost situations showing how dangerous it can be to the mortal foot.

FROST

A hoar-frost,
Third day crost,
The fourth lost. ******

A white frost never lasts more
than three days. ******

The records were taken in Oxfordshire from October 1968 to December 1973 of ground frost, that is grass temperature falling below $0^{o}C$. Hoar or white frosts are ice crystals deposited on surfaces by the air being cooled (usually at night). They are mainly composed of frozen dew droplets and ice formed from water vapour below $0^{o}C$. The two sayings are very famous ones with the second hailing from Lancashire. The results are excellent with an 88 percent rating, which states that any ground frost will last for 3 successive nights and no more. As one would expect there are single and many continued night frosts but the peak is for three. 204/233 (88)

If hoar-frost come in mornings
twain,
The third day surely will have
rain. ***

This saying, although not lacking in sense, has only average results. Frost is often associated with settled anticyclones of the autumn, winter and spring. They can either persist or be of a mobile nature. 102/227 (45)

Three frosts in succession
are a sign of rain. ***

Light or white frosts are
always followed by wet weather,
either the same day or three ****
days later. ****

Three white frosts and
then a storm. ****

Take this a stage further and more disappointing results become apparent.

1 day of frost then rain	75/132	(57)
3 days	108/216	(50)

Hoar-frost indicates rain. *****

As a general statement hoar frost is a good indicator of rain to come. 156/233 (67)

Rain is sure to follow after
frost that melts before the
sun rises. ****

When the frost gets into the
air, it will rain. ****

This is the situation when a hoar frost on the ground encounters increasing wind or cloud and becomes a *black frost*. The latter is not black ice which is a modern term for glazed ice or rain freezing on a road surface to form a layer of ice. Black is used not as the colour of the road or ice but as a danger term for pedestrians and motorists. Now a *black frost* is an invisible frost although the temperature is below 0°C and the air too dry or turbulent. *Black frost* so termed to distinguish it from white or hoar frost. For testing purposes a surface wind of 13kt or more and temperature less than 0°C was regarded as a *black frost*. Results of 64 percent showed that when "the frost gets into air" rain is a good bet.
18/28 (64)

Three rimy frosts,
and then it rains. ****

Here we have a slightly different type of frost. Rime or rimy frost, not to be confused with a hoar frost, is caused when supercooled water droplets from fog/mist come in contact with solid objects with temperature less than 0°C. A rough white ice crystal deposit is left which in windy areas accumulate on the windward side of an object looking like fingers or horizontal stalagmites. The saying however should still have about the same amount of success as the ice/rain adages.

Frost

Hoar frost and gipsies never stay nine days in a place. ******

One of the author's favourite maxims, mainly for its flowery phrase and most excellent result. Virtually all successive nights of frost last less than 9 days. 231/233 (99)

Bearded frost, forerunner of snow. ****

This type of frost frequently occurs when very low temperatures persist and the thickening deposits of hoar frost resemble matted hair or a beard. Any precipitation to follow would then be of snow or sleet.

A single white frost is almost a sure sign of a fine day. In seventy-three cases, fifty-nine times fine days succeeded, and ****
fourteen times rain. But if ***
the white frosts continue several mornings, then rain generally follows. ***

Mr E. J. Lowe in the Victorian era confidently thought that a fine day would occur 59 out of 73 times (81 percent) after a single frosty morning and therefore 14 times (19 percent) would see rain to follow. The author's exhaustive results showed 57 and 43 percent respectively. A quick glance at the results of rain following days of frost can be seen below.

Number of successive days of frost followed by rain.	Result	
1 day	75/132	(57)
2 days	102/227	(45)
3 days	108/216	(50)
4 days	34/73	(47)
5 days	26/48	(54)
6 days	13/27	(48)
7 days	9/17	(53)
7 and 8 days	7/18	(39)

If the first frost occurs late, the following winter will be

mild, but weather variable. **
If the first frost occurs early,
it indicates a severe winter. ****

Early frosts are usually
followed by a long and
hard winter. ****

An old weather favourite. The test covers 1877-1964 and showed little in the final analysis. The first air frosts of the autumn/winter ranged from 29 September to 17 December. The early frosts were reckoned to occur before 21 Oct and late ones after 15 November.

first air frost early then severe winter 14/28 (50)
.. .. .. late .. mild .. 7/27 (26)

The first and last frosts are
the worst.

The first winter frost will damage late crops and late spring frosts young budding growth.

Black frost indicates dry,
cold weather. ****

Black frost is followed by dry weather on 53 percent of occasions. 39/74 (53)

A black frost is a long frost. ****

Black frost, long frost; ****
Hoar-frost - three days and
then rain. ****

A good result is obtained when at least two days of black frost occur. 45/74 (61)

Frosts end in foul weather. *****

A slight difference from the previous sayings as all frosts are included in the figures. 188/289 (65)

Frost

Frost suddenly following heavy
rain seldom lasts long. ***

For frost to be short lived after heavy rain one would expect a mobile weather pattern to exist. Unfortunately this is not always the case. Heavy showers and moderate rain belts can initiate a long quiet period of frosty dry weather.

It is observed, that so far as
the frost penetrates the earth
in winter, so far will the heat
in summer. *

Another variation of the balance maxim where a severe winter (being a rough measure of deep earth frost penetration) is compensated by a warm hot summer.

Severe winter followed by hot summer	6/52	(12)
Cold .. .. .. warm ..	9/56	(16)

Quick thaw, long frost. ****

One of the oldest pieces of English weather lore coming from the Anglo-Saxon period. In winter a persistent cold spell can be influenced by a short mild interlude but is often only a temporary feature.

When the corn is over the crow's
back the frost is over. ***

A Cheshire saw meaning that the frost season ends around April or May when winter corn is about 9 to 12 inches high (average height of a mature crow) and late spring is reached. The exception is after a mild wet winter when the corn can grow quickly and catch March/April frosts.

A frost hurts not the weeds.

Presumably weeds are hardy enough to withstand frost - of course fruit blossoms are affected.

Frost

Walk slow in frost.

The obvious reason is probably the main one, but these sayings have a knack of providing hidden subtle meanings.

Heavy frosts are generally
followed by fine clear weather. *****

Heavy frost is taken as meaning the excessive crystal deposits of the hoar frost. This is helped by low temperatures, an indication of a well-established cold spell. The very good results (67 percent) prove this point. 93/138 (67)

MIST, FOG AND DEW

Mist and fog are composed of water droplets. Fog is internationally agreed to occur when visibility is less than 1,000 metres (1,100 yards) with relative humidity about 100 percent. Mist often occurs with visibilities 1,000-4,000 metres and contains smaller water droplets. Humidities tend to range from 90 to 100 percent. Haze is another matter made up of smoke and dust particles.

In summer-time, when the sun at rising is obscured by a mist which disperses about three hours afterwards, expect hot and calm weather for two or three days. *****

A white mist in the evening, over a meadow with a river, will be drawn up by the sun next morning, and the day will be bright. **** *Five or six fogs successfully drawn up portend rain.* *

When the fog falls, fair weather follows; ****** *when it rises, rain ensues.* *

Fogs are a sign of change. ***

The first set of test figures offer a 56 percent chance of an evening mist continuing into the morning (from second saw). There are 88, 75 and 61 percent chances of having 1, 2 and 3 dry sunny days respectively after a misty morning in summer. So the first maxim receives excellent results. The summer results were virtually identical with other seasons' figures.

1 dry day after a misty summer's morning	= 151/171	(88)
2 " days " " " " "	= 129/171	(75)
3 " " " " " " "	= 104/171	(61)
4 " " " " " " "	= 89/171	(52)
5 " " " " " " "	= 70/171	(41)
6 " " " " " " "	= 55/171	(32)

Mist, Fog and Dew

To achieve five or six successive fogs is fairly rare but in the 45 cases found rain took a long time to appear - rain appeared within 3 days with only a 47 percent chance. So the last part of the second saw is false.

5 or 6 successive fogs then rain within	1 day	7/45	(16)
" " " " " " " "	2 days	16/45	(36)
" " " " " " " "	3 "	21/45	(47)

If mist rises in low ground and soon vanish, expect fair weather. ******

Thin, white, fleecy, broken mist, slowly ascending the sides of a hill or of a mountain whose top is uncovered, predicts a fair day. ******

These two are similar to the previous adages and are true.

If there is a damp fog or mist, accompanied by wind, expect rain. *****

An originally dry fog that is becoming gradually damper indicates rain, and probably wind. *****

When wind and dampening fog occur the likely cause is the approach of a front or a moist airstream (say a S.W.l'y) - the classic forerunners of rain.

Light fog passing under the sun from the south to the north in the morning indicates rain in twenty-four or forty-eight hours. ***
*****

A southerly flow to advect the fog occurs here. The results are very good giving a 70 percent chance of rain within 2 days.

A S.l'y wind with fog then rain within	1 day	47/103	(46)
" " " " " " " "	2 days	72/103	(70)

Mist, Fog and Dew

When the fog goes up the mountain, you may go hunting; when it comes down the mountain you may go fishing. In the former case it will be fair, in the latter it will rain. *****

When the mist is from the hill,
Then good weather it doth spill. *****
When the mist is from the sea,
Then good weather it will be. ***

In many cases fog and very low cloud often go together. The comments and test results for stratus in the Cloud chapter equally apply here. Mist from the sea can either be associated with warm moist air and rain (often in S.W.l'ys) or summer sea fog (for example sea fret or haar in an Easterly along the NE English coast) with warmth and sun just inland.

Heavy fog in winter, when it hangs below trees, is followed by rain. *

Heavy or dense winter fogs below trees point to wind strength above tree level. Sometimes this limited vertical extent of fog indicates rain but tests do not bear this out.

Winter fog then rain within	1 day	14/132	(11)
" " " " "	2 days	34/132	(26)
" " " " "	3 "	49/132	(37)
" " " " "	4 "	63/132	(48)
" " " " "	5 "	74/132	(56)
" " " " "	6 "	84/132	(64)
" " " " "	7 '	93/132	(70)

A fog cannot be dispelled with a fan. *****

During a thick town fog a breath of air on the face, followed by a slight swirling, is generally the first sign of a clearance. *****

True country observation. Fog and mist patches form with *no* wind - a gentle breeze is needed to "mix" or develop a widespread fog. So a "fan" would only help to maintain it. Strong winds lift or disperse fog.

MIST, FOG AND DEW

A curious phenomenon is
observable in the neighbourhood
of Cocking, west Sussex. From
the leafy recesses of the
hangers of beech on the
escarpments of the downs, there
rises in unsettled weather a
mist which rolls among the trees
like the smoke out of a chimney.
This exhalation is called
'foxes-brewings', whatever
that may mean, and if it tends
westwards towards Cocking,
rain follows speedily.
Hence the local proverb:
When foxes-brewings go to Cocking,
Foxes-brewings come back dropping. *****

This unusual but quaint saying was taken from Lower's "History of Sussex". The village of Cocking lies immediately north under the steep escarpment of the West Sussex South Downs. Beech trees surmount these hills and when a moist S. or S.E. airstream appears (usually ahead of a warm front), low cloud will be seen to cover the heights and gradually put Cocking into fog. Rain nearly always follows such a phenomenon.

Black mist indicates coming rain.

Black mist is a rare phrase meaning low cloud. It refers to wet frontal cloud having a dark ragged appearance opposite to the white mists of summer and autumn in dry weather.

Three foggy nights in a week;
then expect foggy days as well. *****

It is unusual that the saw does not imply three successive foggy nights. Three random foggy nights in a week is fairly strong evidence for a quiet prolonged period; three in succession would be almost a certainty.

DEW

Dew is water vapour condensing in small drops on cool surfaces such as grass. Perfect conditions for dew formation are a calm wind, clear skies and moist air. It therefore follows that these conditions also serve dry weather periods. Dewless nights are connected with wind and cloud often leading to rain. Dew-ponds are an interesting spin off. They are artificially constructed ponds high up on chalk downs with watertight bottoms of clay or mud. The idea was that during long droughts overnight dew collected in the dew-ponds helping to water the sheep. In fact there were once such people as professional dew-pond makers. In reality the dew-ponds do retain water longer than ponds at lower-levels but only because more rainfall occurs the higher one is situated above sea-level. Dew does aid the dew-pond water level but only to a small extent. In very long droughts dew-ponds become dry.

The dews of the evening
industriously shun;
They're the tears of the
sky for the loss of the sun.

A poetic introduction to the evening dew.

With dew before midnight,
The next day will sure be
bright. ******

Dew in the night
Next day will be bright. ******

Dew is an indication of fine
weather; so is fog. ******

When the dew is on the grass,
Rain will never come to pass. *****

The test shows that there is an 88 percent chance of a fine day after a dewy night and 54 percent for 4 fine days.

Night dew then fine for	1 day	296/336	(88)
" " " " "	2 days	251/336	(75)
" " " " "	3 "	212/336	(63)
" " " " "	4 "	180/336	(54)
" " " " "	5 "	151/336	(45)
" " " " "	6 "	127/336	(38)
" " " " "	7 "	100/336	(30)

Dew

If there is a profuse dew in summer, it is about seven to one that the weather will be fine. ******

A 7/1 or 86 percent chance of fine weather to follow a profuse summer is perfectly correct. In fact it yielded 88 percent.
226/258 (88)

If there is a heavy dew, it indicates fair weather; ****** *no dew, it indicates rain.* *****

Heavy dews in hot weather,
Foretell fine weather; ******
No dew after sun,
Hot weather on the run. *****

If on clear summer nights there is no dew, expect rain the next day. *****

If nights three dewless there be,
Twill rain you're sure to see. *****

When there is no dew at such times as usually there is, it foreshoweth rain. *****

Dewless nights occur for a number of reasons. Too much wind; cloud cover; dry (low humidity) airstream or combinations of these reasons. The theme was not tested but the chances of rain must be high.

SHEPHERD OF BANBURY'S WEATHER RULES

One of the first books entirely about weather lore was called *Shepherd of Banbury's Rules to Judge the Changes of the Weather*, published in 1744 and written by John Claridge (shepherd) who may have been this Banbury (Oxfordshire) shepherd. There are 26 rules which contain small to large saws and stupid to accurate ones. The complete set is laid out although certain ones are repeated throughout the book (refer to index for the appropriate pages).

Rule 1

If the Sun rise red and fiery
Expect wind and rain. *****

If red the sun begins his race,
Be sure that rain will fall
apace. *****

Rule 2

If cloudy and it soon decreases
Certain for fair weather. ****

A red evening and a grey
morning
Sets the pilgrims awalking. *****

Rule 3

If clouds are small and round,
like a dappley grey, with a
north wind, expect fair weather
for two or three days. ***

If woolly fleeces spread the
heavenly way
Be sure no rain disturbs the
summer day. ****

Rule 4

If there are large clouds,

like rocks, expect great showers. ***

Rule 5

If small clouds increase, expect much rain. ***

Rule 6

If large clouds decrease, expect fair weather. ***

Rule 7

If mists rise in low ground and soon vanish, expect fair weather. *****

Rule 8

If mists rise to the hill tops, expect rain in a day or two. *****

Rule 9

A general mist before the sun rises, near the full moon, expect fair weather. ***

Rule 10

If there are mists in the new moon, expect rain in the old. *

Rule 11

If mists in the old moon expect rain in the new. *

Rule 12

Observe that in eight years time there is as much south-west wind as north-east, and consequently as many wet years as dry. *** **

Rule 13

When the wind turns to north-east and it continues two days without rain, and does not turn south the third day nor rain the third day, it is likely to continue north-east for eight or nine days, or fair; and then to come to the south again. ******

Rule 14

If it turn out again out of the south to the north-east with rain, and continues in the north-east two days without rain, and neither turns south nor rains the third day, it is like to continue north-east for two or three months. The wind will finish these turns in three weeks. ***

Rule 15

After a northerly wind for the most part two months or more, and then coming south, there are usually three or four fair days at first, and then, on the fourth or fifth day, comes rain, or else the wind turns north again, and continues dry. ***

Rule 16

If the wind returns to the south within a day or two without rain, and turn northward with rain, and return to the south in one or two days, as before, two or three times together after this sort, then it is like to be in the south or south-west two or three months together, as it was in the north before. The wind will finish these turns in a fortnight. ***

Rule 17

*Fair weather for a week, with a
Southern wind, is like to produce
a great Drought, if there has
been much rain out of the South
before. The wind usually turns* ****
*from North to South, with a quiet
wind without rain, but returns* ****
*to the North, with a strong wind
and rain; the strongest winds* ****
*are when it turns from South to
North by West. When the North* *****
*wind first clears the air (which
is usually once a week) look out
for Squalls.*

Rule 18

In summer or harvest, when the wind has been south two or three days, and it grows very hot, and you see clouds rise with great white tops like towers, as if one were upon the top of another and joined together with black on the nether side, there will be thunder and rain suddenly. *****

Rule 19

If two such clouds arise, one on either hand, it is time to make haste to shelter.

Rule 20

If you see a cloud rise against the wind or side wind, when that cloud comes up to you, the wind will blow the same way that the cloud came; and the same rule holds of a clear place, when all the sky is equally thick, except one clear edge.

SHEPHERD OF BANBURY

Rule 21	*Sudden rains never last long: but when the air grows thick, by degrees, and the sun, moon, and the stars shine dimmer and dimmer, then it is like to rain six hours usually.*	***** *****
Rule 22	*If it begins to rain from the south, with a high wind for two or three hours, and the wind falls, but the rain continues, it is likely to rain twelve hours or more, and does usually rain till a strong north wind clears the air. These long rains seldom hold above twelve hours, or happen above once a year.*	****
Rule 23	*If it begins to rain an hour or two before sunrising, it is like to be fair before noon, and so continue that day, but if the rain begins an hour or two after sun rising, it is like to rain all that day, except the rainbow be seen before it rains.*	**** ***
	A rainbow in the morning, *Is the shepherd's warning;* *A rainbow at night,* *Is the shepherd's delight.*	***** *****
Rule 24	*If the last eighteen days of February and ten days in March be for the most part rainy, then the spring and summer quarters are like to be so to; and I never knew a great drought but it ended in that season.*	***

Rule 25 — *If the latter end of October and beginning of November be for the most part warm and rainy, then January and February are like to be frosty and cold, except after a very dry summer.* **

Rule 26 — *If October and November be snow and frost, then January and February are like to be open and mild.* *

BIBLIOGRAPHY

Brain, J.P. (1972). Halo Phenomena - An Investigation. *Weather*, vol 27, pp 409-410.

Brazell, J.H. (1968). London Weather.

A Century of Agricultural Statistics of Great Britain, 1866-1966. (1968). H.M.S.O.

Claridge, John. (1744). Shepherd of Banbury's Rules to Judge the Changes of the Weather.

Davis, N.E. (1969). Diurnal Variation of Thunder at Heathrow Airport, London. *Meteorological Magazine*, vol 24, pp 166-172.

Davis, N.E. (1972). Classified Central England Temperatures and England and Wales Rainfall. *Met. Mag.*, vol 101, pp 205-217.

Folklore Guide to the Weather. No 1 in Handy Guide Series.

Inwards, Richard. (1898). Weather Lore.

Jackson, M.C. (1977). A Classificatio- of the Snowiness of 100 Winters - A Tribute to the Late L.C.W. Bonacina. *Weather*, vol 32, pp 91-97.

Lamb, H.H. (1972). British Isles Weather Types and a Register of the Daily Sequence of Circulation Patterns, 1861-1971. *Geophysical Memoirs no 116*.

Lower, M.A. (1870). A Compendious History of Sussex.

Margery, I.D. (1926). Marsham Phenological Record (Norfolk 1736-1925). *Quarterly Jnl of Royal Met. Soc.*, vol 52, pp 30-37.

Merryweather, Dr George. (1851). A Tempest Prognosticator.

Mirrlees, S.T.A. (1929). St Swithun's Day. *Met. Mag.*, vol 64, p 143.

Nicholson, G. (1969). Wet Thursdays. *Weather*, March 1969.

Russell, Spencer C. (1926). "A Red Sky at Night ---." *Met. Mag.*, vol 61, pp 15-17.

Silvester, Norman L. (1926). Notes on the Behaviour of Certain Plants in Relation to the Weather. *Quarterly Jnl of Royal Met. Soc.*, vol 52, pp 15-23.

The Standard Cyclopedia of Modern Agriculture and Rural Economy. (c1909). Editor Sir R.P. Wright.

DATA SOURCES

BARLEY records of cwt/acre cover 1885-1966 for England and Wales were taken from *A Century of Agricultural Statistics of Great Britain*. The figures were statistically weighted for 1941-66 and finally all were divided into three equal classes to give bad, average or good yields.

CATTLE survey by the author in Yorkshire during the summer of 1980 studying the standing and sitting habits in relation to sun, rain and wind.

CLOUD data covered all types (from high Cirrus to low Stratus) and their relation with forthcoming rain during 1979 in Oxon.

DAILY WEATHER of Great Britain bring different airstream directions with anticyclone or cyclonic connections. Each airstreams having its own temperature, rainfall and weather properties. Nearly 37,000 reports were used in Lamb's figures for 1861-1971. So the weather proverbs relating to St David's Day (1 March) or the 40-rain days of St Swithun (15 July- 23 Aug) could be easily tested.

DEATH numbers per 1,000 of the population in Oxford from 1871-1911 were used for Jan-March with no weighting. Final data were equally grouped into three giving a high, average and low death rate.

FLOWER records of Silvester were used. They were made in London and Yorkshire from 1917-23 (spring to autumn). The author introduced the average monthly daylight duration (sunrise to sunset) from March to November to acquire the final figures.

Air and ground FROST figures come from Oxon from Oct 1968 - Dec 1973. Also the year's first ground frost (usually in autumn) appears in Brazell's 1841-1964 data.

All sun and moon HALO records come from Brain's collection for Bristol from 1 Jan 1969 to 2 March 1971.

HAY figures are from the same source as BARLEY ones covering 1885-1966. No weighting was necessary.

MILK data covers 1941-62 using two weighting periods 1941-51 and 1951-62. The same source as the Barley records apply. Final figures were divided equally into three classes.

MOON phase dates were taken for the U.K. from 1959-71.

PIG records again were the same source as those in the Barley section covering 1866-1966. 1916-20 and 1941-52 were ignored (due to poor production during the two world wars and their post-war recovery). 1866-1915, 1921-40 and 1953-66were weighted with final numbers, as usual, divided equally into three.

POTATO data as the Barley source covering 1884-1966. Weighting introduced for 1959-66. Final division by three occurred.

RAINFALL figures came from Davis' England and Wales monthly and seasonal collection of 1727-1971. No weighting needed and were divided into three equal classes, wet, average and dry. HOURLY RAINFALL for testing adages like "rain at seven, fine before eleven" were confined to Oxon in the non-winter period of 1978-9. WEEKDAY RAINFALL figures came from Nicholson's Teddington records of Oct 1953 - Sept 1968.

SHEEP data are the same as in the Cattle section.

SNOW records of daily significance were taken from Oxon in the winters Jan 1971 - Feb 1980. Longer-scale data came from Jackson's list of Bonacina's work covering the period 1875-1975 of snow in the U.K.

SUNSET/SUNRISE colour figures are used in Russell's London record from Oct 1918 - Sept 1924.

TEMPERATURE values from Davis' Central England collection covered 1698-1971. Here monthly and seasonal temperatures were divided into 5 equal classes (quintiles) of very cold, cold, average, warm and very warm.

TREE records were taken from the Margery Collection of 1736-1925.

Good VISIBILITY data was obtained from Oxon during 1980.

WHEAT records from the Barley source covering 1885-1966. The period 1948-66 was weighted with final figures equally divided into three to give good, average or poor wheat yields.

INDEX